LOVE & LIES

"I wish to believe you want me to do this."

His arms suddenly went around her, pulling her close. His lips settled over hers before Christine had time to react. They were warm, like the heat rising from his half-naked torso. And firm. And insistent. The piece of paper clutched in her hand floated to the floor as she raised her fists to ward him off. But instead of pounding at his flesh, her palms slid up his smooth chest and rested there, feeling the strong beat of his heart.

He slanted his mouth over hers and delved deeper, caressing her with his tongue until she responded. Responded as if she'd been kissed a hundred times by this man, her husband, a stranger. The last thought helped her regain her sense. She pulled away from him and backed toward the door.

"Believe what you wish, but know for certain I never want you to touch me again."

The heat was back in his eyes. He smiled slightly. "I only know one thing for certain, Christine. You may or may not be a thief, but from what your lips just told me, you certainly are a liar."

Other *Leisure* books by Ronda Thompson:
IN TROUBLE'S ARMS
PRICKLY PEAR
COUGAR'S WOMAN

RAVE REVIEWS FOR
SCANDALOUS!

"Ronda Thompson is one of those authors that you should have on your author's list. . . . *Scandalous* is a wonderfully wry Regency . . . that makes you want to come back for more."
—*Romance Communications*

"Ronda Thompson is not to be missed. An innovative writer, she is not afraid to take chances. *Scandalous* is a juicy Regency which will have you smiling over the foibles and fancies of the period. Wonderful as usual."
—*Affaire de Coeur*

"*Scandalous* is a fast-paced romp readers will find difficult to put down until the last page is read. Strong characters provide high quality entertainment, while the chemistry between Christine and Gavin sizzles."
—*Under the Covers Book Reviews*

"Turn up the air-conditioning! Tantalizing repartee and sizzling sexual tension mark Ronda Thompson's *Scandalous* a book for anyone's keeper shelf. A MUST read."
—Dia Hunter, author of *The Gentle Season*

Scandalous

Ronda Thompson

LEISURE BOOKS NEW YORK CITY

A LEISURE BOOK®

December 2000

Published by

Dorchester Publishing Co., Inc.
276 Fifth Avenue
New York, NY 10001

Copyright © 2000 by Ronda Thompson

ISBN 0-8439-4805-1

Printed in the United States of America.

Visit us on the web at www.dorchesterpub.com.

To my mom and dad, Sam and Yvonne Widener, whose love and support has nurtured me through the years, whose kindness helps me strive to be a better person, and whose generous spirits fill me with more than aspirations to write, but with the need to give of myself the way they have given to me.
I love you.

ACKNOWLEDGMENTS

A special thank-you to DeWanna Pace and Charlotte Goebel for taking time from their hectic schedules to help a fellow author and friend. To a great group of ladies on my Leisure loop who answered those niggling questions research took too long to uncover on my own. To Kurt Bose for his continued support of me, for ordering the research books I need, and turning my novels face-out on the shelf. And to Nan Doporto, Teri Dohmen and April Redmon for taking on my fat manuscript in order to give me early reviews. I appreciate all of you.

Prologue

The day had turned dark to Christine, even though the sun shone above. A promise made in a moment of weakness had caught up with her. Her pledge to a dying man. A vow she could not keep. She paced a small hill over-looking the poor parish below, her thoughts in turmoil. She would *not* marry him. She simply could not. Her duty lay elsewhere.

She had committed herself to the teaching of children. To the poor, the sick, the destitute. How could she forsake them all to marry a nobleman? A member of the very class whose pompous attitudes and selfish natures made a mockery of her own beliefs? A class of society known to turn a blind eye to the suffering around them, more concerned with their coiffures and their fine clothes.

"I cannot," she said. "It would go against all that I believe in. All that I am."

The vicar, who'd come to fetch her, sighed wearily. "Did you not promise the old marquis on his deathbed,

Christine? Did you not swear before God you would honor his wishes?"

Christine bowed her head submissively, although her blood still churned with outrage. "I did promise," she admitted. "How could I refuse him? The marquis has been generous to the parish over the years and kind to me. I loved him like a father, could not have loved him more even if he has done this dreadful thing to me."

The man smiled. "Dear Christine, do you know how many would trade places with you? With the swipe of a pen, you will go from being a penniless orphan to a grand lady. You should thank God for your good fortune."

Falling to her knees, Christine clasped her hands together, as if in prayer. "It is God's work I want to do. The parish is the only home I have ever known. The only home I want to know. Forcing me into a society I detest, one that will detest me in return, is the worst punishment."

Black robes flapping in the wind, the vicar assisted her to her feet. "We all have our trials. Your calling has changed. Come and meet Gavin Norfork. Sign the marriage agreement."

Her knees started to shake. "I need more time," she pleaded. "What is the man's hurry?"

A frown shaped the vicar's lips. "He is leaving immediately to travel abroad. Norfork wants the matter quickly and quietly resolved. Patience does not appear to be a virtue with him."

"Does he have any virtues?" she asked. "His father never spoke of him until he called me to his deathbed. Why has the son never come to visit the parish? Greenhaven is not far."

"From what I gather, there was no love lost between father and son. The young marquis does not care for the country estate. He had not visited his father in years."

Nothing said concerning Gavin Norfork gave Christine comfort. "Who could not have loved the old marquis? He

16

was the kindest of men, and so generous to the church."

"He was not always kind and generous," the vicar informed her. "Sometimes it only takes one kind heart to turn a cold and bitter man into a warm and giving one. Remember these words, Christine. You may have need of them in the future."

The future. It looked dark indeed. What would become of the children she taught? And if the old marquis had not wanted her to become a teacher for those less fortunate, why had he sent the best tutors to train her? His dying request made no sense. Nor did a nobleman marrying a girl of her breeding. Christine had no station. No last name.

Her parentage was questionable, to say the least. From what she'd been told, her mother, probably a harlot, had stumbled into the parish church dressed in rags. Far into labor, the woman had delivered Christine, named her, and promptly died. A small white cross in the church cemetery and a silver brush with the initials C. B. were all Christine had ever known of her mother. Of her father, she knew nothing.

"Maybe he hasn't come to sign the marriage agreement at all," she reasoned. Hope sprang to life inside her. "Perhaps he's only come to apologize for refusing me. That would make more sense. I am an orphan. A commoner. I would only be an embarrassment—"

Taking her arm, the vicar said, "You may be all of those things, Christine, but you are also a beautiful young woman. If Norfork has reservations about the marriage, seeing you will most likely staunch them."

She pulled away, outraged again. "I want no man to desire me for my face alone. I want no man to desire me at all!"

An expression of pity settled over the man's craggy features. "Then your beauty will become a cross to bear, child. Come now, we've kept the man waiting too long.

Having already witnessed his lack of patience, I fear he may well grow weary of the wait and leave."

That was the miracle Christine prayed for as the vicar steered her down the hill. She'd been thinking with her heart instead of her head when she'd promised to marry the old marquis's heir. The son would have to be daft were he to sign the marriage agreement. With his title, he could marry a woman of position. He could marry a woman who actually cared about his wealth and his property.

Christine only cared about the poor people of the parish. And her service to God, which she supposed was an attempt to make amends for her sorry entry into the world. She'd grown comfortable with her lot in life over the years, her peaceful if poor existence. One promise to a dying man had compromised everything.

As they neared the church, Christine's desperation grew. What if the vicar was right, and the mere sight of her caused Norfork to commit the most grievous of errors? Christine hadn't given much thought to her looks, although the poor men of the parish and their sons seemed to stare overlong at her.

She knew little about men, and nothing about this man she had promised to marry. If he truly could be taken with outer appearance, perhaps she should attempt to alter hers before they met. Supposing the vicar would not permit another delay, Christine didn't see how she could accomplish such a feat. Not until the answer was almost upon her.

They moved through a portion of the parish where the livestock were kept. It had rained earlier that morning. A big mud puddle where the pigs wallowed lay directly ahead. Christine viewed it as her only option. She marched straight for the puddle. Purposely ignoring the vicar's shout of warning, she pretended to slip, falling headlong into the mud.

"Good heavens, Christine. Are you all right?"

The man's waxen complexion caused her a moment of guilt. Christine had never done anything so deceitful. God would surely understand given her circumstances, she reasoned.

After wiping mud from her eyes, she made a pretense of attempting to rise. She fell back into the mud, coating herself a second time for good measure.

"I seem to have twisted my ankle," she said.

Her companion reached for her, noted her filthy state, and quickly withdrew the offer.

"If you could find me a stick to lean upon," she suggested.

The vicar hurried to do her bidding. He retrieved a crooked, if sturdy, stick from the ground, extending it toward her. Christine grasped the handle and made a good show of carefully rising from the mud. She limped from the puddle, her back bent in a way that made her spine appear as crooked as her crutch.

She'd only hobbled a few feet when she dared a glance toward the church. A figure in black stood in the shadows. A tall man who paced back and forth, so she could see nothing of his features. Christine bowed her head again, shuffling along at a pace meant to try the patience of a saint.

"Hurry, child," the vicar urged. "At this wretched speed, we will never reach the church."

A smile threatened her mud-caked lips. If the kindly vicar was already vexed with her, how much more annoyed must Gavin Norfork be? Recalling the gait of a three-legged dog that once roamed the parish, she tried to hurry, mimicking the dog's pathetic attempts to run. She imagined she resembled a lame hunchback. Another glance toward the church found the shadows empty.

Moments later, the thundering sound of a horse's hooves filled the silence. Christine's head snapped toward the road. A white stallion appeared, his rider a man dressed in black. A coach loaded with luggage followed at breakneck speed. Christine crumpled to the ground.

"He's gone," she whispered, relief spreading through her. "My prayers have been answered."

Hurrying past her, the vicar disappeared inside the church. Christine bowed her head, tears of joy making muddy streaks down her face. She wouldn't be taken from her home. She wouldn't be forced to become any man's wife, whether he be a commoner or a nobleman.

Slowly, she lumbered to her feet. She threw the stick aside and swatted at the flies attracted by the slime coating her clothes. Her skin began to itch. Despite her discomfort, she wanted to twirl with wild abandonment—wanted to skip like a child. She did both. Twirling one minute, then skipping in a circle.

A subtle clearing of a throat halted her. She glanced around to find the vicar watching her, his frown of disapproval proof he'd discovered her deception.

"I have never known you to practice deceit, Christine."

Her behavior brought the shame she deserved. "Forgive me," she whispered. "And may God have mercy upon my soul."

His features softened. "I'm afraid He has not, child. Gavin Norfork signed the marriage agreement before he left. And knowing you are a person of conscience, you will also sign. A coach is waiting to take you to Greenhaven."

Christine's heart felt as if it dropped to her knees. "Is he mad? Why would he do anything so foolish?"

Shrugging, the vicar answered, "Perhaps he, too, made a promise to his father. Although knowing what I do of him, it surprises me he would honor his word."

Her stomach twisted. "You know more of him than you've led me to believe. I have never known you to practice deceit, either."

A guilty flush spread over the vicar's face. "Gossip is

the devil's handmaiden. I did not wish to dissuade you from keeping your promise. This is a grand opportunity for you, Christine. One you deserve."

Tears filled her eyes again, but this time, they were not tears of happiness. "What have I done to deserve this? To be taken from my home, from those I care for, from you?"

Regardless of her filthy person, he touched her shoulder as if to offer comfort. "It is your destiny, Christine. It is not for me or you to argue. Will you sign the contract?"

She would, only because she had promised, had sworn before God. "Tell me what you know of Gavin Norfork. I deserve the truth."

"I fear it will not make signing the agreement easier," he warned. "His reputation is not good. He is said to be a man totally unafraid of compromising his soul to eternal damnation. A man who enjoys card playing and liquor. A man well known for his skill with a pistol and sword, but better known for his talent at winning the ladies."

A drunkard and a womanizer? Christine sighed. "I promised to marry him. I never promised to remain married."

"An annulment is not easily granted," the vicar commented. "Nearly impossible for a woman to obtain."

"And what of a man?"

He stroked his chin thoughtfully. "I have heard of special cases," he admitted. "If Norfork wanted to use your lack of blue blood as cause, he might secure an annulment from Parliament, or if he thought you had shamed him."

"Shamed him in what way?"

The man's face reddened. For a moment, she thought he would not elaborate. Then he said, "If you were to publicly flaunt yourself before other men. Cause speculation that you were having adulterous affairs. But I know you would never do such," he quickly added. "Neither your faith nor your conscience would allow it."

Not in truth, she silently agreed. But if she couldn't

Ronda Thompson

convince Norfork to annul the marriage for practical purposes, would a pretense of brazenness be a sin? If deception were used as a tool to further her service to others, would it be wrong?

She had much to consider, and since the man had already deserted her, time to decide how to dissolve a distasteful marriage. Reluctantly, she moved toward the church to sign the agreement.

Chapter One

Gavin Norfork, Marquis of Greenhaven, hated these affairs. They offered nothing more than an excuse to exchange gossip. A place for London's elite to search for prospective spouses for their children, or new lovers for themselves. Under normal circumstances, he wouldn't waste his evening on a social ball. Tonight, however, he had reason to attend. Some nasty business that needed to be brought to an end.

His gaze strayed past tables loaded with sweetmeats and all manner of food, beyond the musicians, who had already drawn dancers onto the floor, and settled upon a small group of men he actually counted as friends. Young noblemen who wouldn't be here either, were they not still under the influence of their mothers.

Grabbing a glass of champagne as a servant passed, Gavin made his way toward the group. He frowned upon noting their strange behavior. All were craning their necks as if trying to see over the crowd.

"Who is she?" Gavin heard Chester Thorton ask as he joined the group.

"She, who?" he countered.

"Bloody well time you made an appearance, Norfork," Chester scolded. "Fashionably late is one thing. Strolling in long after the gray heads have nodded off in their seats is another. What, or I should probably ask who, detained you? A mistress? Or perhaps a friend's wife?"

Gavin took a sip from his glass. "Thorton, you know I am not the sort who'd go behind a friend's back and seduce his wife. Luckily, I have few friends."

Chester laughed. "Luckier still, what few you have are still unmarried." He turned his gaze in the direction his companions stared. "Only a handful of us have managed to escape the last four seasons of beautiful debutantes and remain single. This season, I fear I may fall victim."

His admission lifted one of Gavin's dark brows. "I assume the lady under discussion as I joined you is responsible for your change of heart? Well, where is she?"

"Along the back wall." Chester nodded. "The delicious creature surrounded by men. I haven't been successful in learning with whom she arrived, and no one seems to know her name. She is a mystery."

"No woman is a mystery for long," Gavin replied in a dry tone. He slowly surveyed the room in search of the affair's hostess. Although Adrianna Shipley, the Duchess of Montrose, did not face him, he recognized the length of her back displayed by a daring low-cut gown. She currently conversed with an old dowager.

The poor dowager's heart would surely give out were she to know the affair's polite hostess had the manners of a she-cat in bed. Clawing and biting. The duchess had the instincts of an alley cat, as well. Never sleeping in one place for long. He supposed she sensed his appraisal of her, for she turned her head in his direction. Once she spied him, her dark eyes narrowed dangerously. Had she, in fact, been a cat, Gavin suspected she would have raised her back and hissed.

He met her heated stare with cool detachment. Adrianna had become too possessive to suit him. Her husband, the duke, being too old to perform his husbandly duties, turned a blind eye to her infidelities. And Adrianna had many affairs. Gavin had thought when she'd blatantly invited him into her bed two months prior, it would be a short liaison.

But Adrianna refused to become bored with him. She treated him more like a wife treated a husband, demanding to know his every move. He'd decided it was well past time to end the affair. And tonight he would.

"I believe the girl is too fast to be virtuous, Chester," James Dumont said, breaking into Gavin's thoughts. "Just look at her. Fluttering those long lashes and giggling behind her fan at no doubt every stupid witticism Thomas Wentworth has to say. Not only him, but by God, all of them. She's flirting outrageously with every man within ten feet of her."

Chester sighed. "You're right, James. I suppose I'll have to take her as my mistress."

James cocked a brow. "Mark my words. A sweet piece such as her is already some man's mistress. Besides, keeping her would cost you your family's fortune."

"Right again," Chester agreed. "She's too expensive for me. Say, Gavin, she doesn't by chance belong to you, does she?"

In the process of watching Adrianna make a slow, stalking approach, Gavin glanced at Chester. "What?"

"The vision against the far wall. Is she one of your mistresses?"

Gavin hadn't bothered to strain his eyesight in order to see the woman. Too many men surrounded her to bother. "I am currently without a mistress," he answered. "And were I to employ one, she would not embarrass me by attending this social event, nor would she allow herself to be pawed and slobbered over like a common tavern whore."

"Now, see here," Chester blustered. "You don't have to insult the girl. Not one of her many admirers have managed to coax her onto the dance floor."

"I doubt if the lady came here to dance," Gavin mumbled distractedly. "Perhaps she has been jilted and is searching for a new provider."

"If she were to pick and chose among the gentlemen present, my money would be on you, old boy," James said. He rubbed his hands together as he often did when anticipating a wager. "I'll wager twenty pounds Gavin can make her his before the night's end."

Chester scoffed at the bet. "If he wished, Gavin could make the old dowager herself his before the night's end."

Gavin winced at the thought. "Gentlemen, it is not polite to wager on the reputation of a woman, or on mine for that matter. I have no interest in greedy little girls." Noting that Adrianna was nearly upon him, he added, "I have enough problems with greedy grown women."

"Gavin," Adrianna growled. "So nice of you to attend this evening."

He took the hand she offered, wondering why she seemed out of sorts with him. Did she suspect the true intent of his visit tonight? "You look lovely, Adrianna." He glanced around. "And have managed to gather most of titled society into your nest. But there is one bird among us who has young Chester and James ready to quit bachelorhood. Perhaps you could arrange an introduction for them? She—"

"No need to point her out," Adrianna interrupted, her gaze leveled upon him. "The bird has been making a spectacle of herself since she arrived."

And now Gavin knew why the duchess was out of sorts.

She was not the center of attention. Adrianna wasn't accustomed to playing second to anyone.

"Will you give them both an introduction?"

Her painted lips tightened. "Why, Gavin, you are in a much better position to introduce them than I am. I'm not nearly as acquainted with her as you are. In fact, I had forgotten about her existence entirely."

When Adrianna glared at Gavin, he arched a brow. "You seem to suffer the delusion I am acquainted with the lady." To make certain he wasn't, Gavin humbled himself to stare over the heads of those dancing and try in earnest to see the mystery woman.

Had she been an inch shorter, catching a glimpse of her would have been impossible. He wasn't prepared for the jolt of pure attraction that traveled through him. She was indeed a vision. Although younger than he preferred his women, she had the kind of beauty that would age well. Her skin looked like the finest porcelain; her upswept curls were a golden halo that framed the face of an angel.

An angel? Innocent? The thought struck him as absurd. Innocence did not exist among the London ton, only scheming beauties with the intention of snaring a rich husband, and scheming men who planned to seduce them.

"I have not had the pleasure." With difficulty, Gavin removed his gaze from the mystery woman. "Who is she?"

The duchess stomped her foot, then blushed upon realizing her show of temper had received attention. "I am not amused by your attempt at feigned ignorance, Gavin. You could have warned me she was in London. My mouth probably dropped to the floor when she introduced herself."

"Why would I warn you about her?" Chester, James, and the whole party listened to the discussion, and if Adrianna refused to be discreet, dammit, he wouldn't, either. "I told you, I am not acquainted with the lady."

27

Adrianna summoned a fake smile, an expression he felt resulted from the curious stares directed toward their small party. "That's odd," she bit out. "Especially since she introduced herself as the Marchioness of Greenhaven. Your wife."

When Adrianna wheeled away, Gavin didn't outwardly respond, although his blood pumped through his veins at an alarming rate.

"Your wife?" Chester echoed, shocked. "I'd forgotten you had a wife. All of London's forgotten you married some penniless girl at your father's dying request. Heavens, that was two years ago. Where has she been all this time?"

"Greenhaven," Gavin answered, distracted with trying to get another glance at the beauty without seeming obvious.

He recalled the day he'd signed the marriage agreement, recalled the pathetic, filthy creature who'd hobbled toward the church. He'd thought at the time that his father had found a way to torture him even in death, and had vowed to ignore the woman from that day forward. He had also ignored the letters he received from her requesting an audience, fearful the hag might wish to consummate the marriage.

"That"—he nodded toward the woman—"is not who I married."

"An imposter?" James Dumont lifted a brow. "But why would she claim to be your wife if she is not?"

"Perhaps she wishes to capture his attention," Chester suggested. "If she is searching for a provider, she may well of heard of our friend's wealth, not to mention his reputation of pleasing the ladies."

"If she wants to capture my interest, she's going about it all wrong," Gavin grumbled. A young man had taken hold of the woman's arm, and although his actions appeared innocent. Gavin knew his hand had brushed the

28

side of her breast. "I don't care to handle merchandise that's obviously been handled by too many."

Whatever the woman's intentions, he was not amused by her claiming to be his wife among a roomful of his peers. She would make them both the object of gossip. Although Gavin was no stranger to scandal, the awful things said about him were for the most part true. A subtle tap on the shoulder drew his attention from the group.

"One of your staff from Greenhaven is in the hall," a servant informed him. "He wishes a word with you and insists it is of the utmost importance."

The hairs on the back of Gavin's neck prickled. He started to excuse himself, then realized there was no need. His young friends were too busy ogling the woman claiming his title to notice the interruption. Once in the entry hall, Gavin spotted a young man wearing Greenhaven livery.

"Be you Gavin Norfork, the Marquis of Greenhaven?" the man asked.

"Who else would I be?" Gavin snapped.

The man bowed his head respectfully, then blurted out, "She's gone! We thought she went to the parish, as she often does, but then she didn't come home. For three days she didn't return. I went to fetch her, but the vicar said she hadn't been there."

"She, who?" Gavin asked for the second time that night.

"Why, your wife, My Lord Marquis."

"My wife?" he repeated. A thought occurred to him. "Then you have seen her? Could easily identify my wife?"

His servant regarded him in odd fashion. "Oh, aye, Your Lordship." He grinned. "She's an angel, that one."

The hairs on the back of Gavin's neck prickled again. He ushered the servant from the hall. Careful to be discreet, he took him up a set of stairs that led to the upper bedchambers. Stairs he knew all too well. A balcony lined

29

the second floor, one that allowed him to look down upon the ballroom below. Gavin stationed the man behind a thick pillar.

"Do you see my wife among the guests below?"

The man gawked and stretched his neck, searching the dancers below. Much to Gavin's embarrassment he pointed, proclaiming loudly, "There she is!"

Gavin snatched the man's hand. "I am trying not to call attention to us," he explained. "Now, with a subtle nod, indicate the woman's position."

Regaining a smidgen of dignity, the servant obeyed. Gavin followed his nod to the angel with porcelain skin and the golden curls atop her head. The same woman on the dance floor below being held indecently close by Thomas Wentworth.

"You are certain?" he demanded.

"Oh, aye, Your Lordship," the man responded. He eyed Gavin curiously. "Begging your pardon, but I thought you had met your wife when you both signed the marriage agreement."

His gaze trained on the woman below, on the expanse of her creamy shoulders and the generous display of bosom his position above afforded him, Gavin said, "I did not meet her. I saw her . . . or I thought I did."

"Well, the minute we all got a look at the new mistress, we knew why you had agreed to marry the girl," the servant said.

Greenhaven's staff had no idea why he'd agreed to the marriage, why he would have agreed to it regardless of his wife's appearance. What the devil was going on? Had she purposely misled him? And if so, why? He'd made a poor orphan into a grand lady. A commoner into a woman of wealth. What of life could she possibly want if not that? Gavin intended find out.

"You are dismissed," he said to the servant. "Return to Greenhaven. I will see to my wife."

"As you wish, Your Lordship."

The servant shuffled away, leaving Gavin alone with his confusion. Confusion that turned to anger the longer he watched the spectacle taking place below. People were watching his wife and Wentworth, whispering behind their hands. What manner of whore had he married? One who caused him public embarrassment. A woman who flirted and allowed herself to be pawed by every man in the room. He would put a stop to her shaming him.

Gavin descended the staircase and made his way back to his friends. The short journey did not diminish his anger, nor had his wife ceased dancing with the fop Wentworth. Gavin had no idea if she felt his heated stare boring into her, or if she purposely turned her head to look at him when the couple swept past, but her eyes locked with his.

The pure violet of them sent a jolt through his body. The smile on her lips suddenly waned and bright spots of pink settled in her cheeks. His wife should be embarrassed, Gavin thought. At least she had the sense to appear unnerved by his presence. But then, did she know his identity? He didn't believe she'd been close enough at the parish to see his features, if indeed the pitiful creature he'd mistaken for his intended had been this woman.

Once his mother died, the old marquis had stripped the estate of all likenesses not only of her, but of her son as well. Someone had pointed him out, Gavin reasoned. His wife, blast, what was her name? He tried to recall, but could not.

When young Wentworth leaned down to whisper in her ear, probably a bold compliment, or worse, an indecent proposal, Gavin nearly growled. He bit back the response and did something more out of character instead.

Shocked and curious faces swam past as he approached the couple twirling around the dance floor. To Wentworth's good fortune, he spotted Gavin before he made a total fool of himself. The young man's eyes widened, the color drained from his face, and he ceased the dance in midstep.

Wentworth's haste to disentangle himself from his dance partner did not go unnoticed by Gavin, nor, he imagined, by a single soul at the gathering. The young idiot bolted, deserting the woman. Those damnable bright spots of color rose in her porcelain cheeks again. Her violet eyes darted from left to right, then settled upon the reason she had been abandoned.

Gavin thought she looked like a doe who'd glanced up to find herself face-to-face with an arrow. Without a word, he took her cold fingers in his, placed a hand on her slim waist, and twirled her into the flow of dancers—dancers stepping all over each other in an effort to watch them.

Although she'd played the brazen with Wentworth, his wife felt stiff in his arms. She kept her soft curves at a proper distance, her eyes downcast. Her demure behavior irritated him sorely.

"What is your name?" he snapped.

The long, sooty lashes resting against her cheeks lifted. He tried not to suck in his breath when she turned her gaze upon him. At so close a range, the jolt he'd earlier experienced seemed minor in comparison.

"Perhaps no one has instructed you on the proper way to introduce yourself to a lady," she said. "I find your mannerisms barbaric and humiliating. If you would be so kind, I wish to end this dance. Please escort me from the floor."

Refusing to release the hand she tried to wrest from his, he countered, "Etiquette does not seem a subject you've been well schooled in either, m'lady. There are several wagers being placed as to whose mistress you are soon to become. Since I am the man most likely to win such a wager, I would appreciate a name to put with that fetching face of yours."

He received the pleasure of watching the pink completely vanish from her cheeks. Not as subtly as before, she tried to free herself. "My husband shall hear of this," she hissed through her perfect little teeth. "I am positive he will call you out, insensitive, arrogant, womanizing beast that he is," she added angrily. "You have no idea whom you have just insulted!"

And his wife obviously had no idea with whom she danced. He smiled. The knowledge pleased him. "That is why I asked your name."

"Marchioness of Greenhaven. His Lordship Gavin Norfork's wife," she provided with an arrogant lift of her brow.

By her expression, Gavin knew she expected a response. He shrugged. "I do not wish to discuss your husband, and I would prefer your given name. It would seem odd to call you by your formal title while we . . . well, while the two of us are being intimate together. Too many words to whisper passionately."

The color he'd stolen from her cheeks returned with a vengeance. She shoved him away, then slapped him soundly in front of God and worse, the whole social set of London.

"I will grant a dead man his last request," she huffed. "My given name is Christine. And now, ungallant sir, I would have your name, so that my husband can find you and properly chastise your rude behavior."

In a mocking gesture, Gavin bowed. "There is no need to inform your husband of my actions. He's witnessed the whole sordid affair."

A slim hand lifted to her throat. Her gaze darted around the room. "Surely you are mistaken. I understand he rarely honors an invitation to any event in which he cannot either gamble the night away, or otherwise occupy himself with sinful indulgences."

Gavin enjoyed her sudden nervousness. And he saw no

point in lying to her. "The hostess of this particular gala and your husband have been having a discreet affair for the past two months. You see, my lady, no one knows your husband's weakness for sin more than I."

Her mouth with its tantalizing fuller lower lip trembled somewhat. "A-and why is that?"

"The most logical explanation that comes to mind is that *I* am the Marquis of Greenhaven, Gavin Norfork. Your husband and the man you have shamed this night. Perhaps I should have sent someone to teach you—"

Before he finished the lecture, his wife did the first proper thing she'd done during the entire evening. She fainted dead away.

Chapter Two

That smell. What was that horrid smell? Christine's eyes stung. Her throat constricted. She coughed, sat straight up, and came face-to-face with the handsome rogue she had earlier wanted desperately to escape. The same man whose very nearness made her blush, made her heart pound and her knees go weak. The same man who claimed to be her husband.

The marquis's gaze did not waver as he removed the smelling salts from beneath her nose. Nor did he look away from her or speak. Christine felt trapped. Mesmerized much like a bird snared by the hypnotic stare of a snake. And what eyes he had. Not light brown, not chocolate, but black. Black as sin. Inky as a pen well. His brows, lashes, and hair were the same color of midnight.

His cheekbones were high, his nose straight and a perfect fit for the rest of his face. And she found no fault with his mouth. His lips were neither too full nor too thin. Again, simply perfect. His features could well have been carved by a master, she admitted, sculpted from marble.

35

But his soul, what lay within the confines of such perfection, she knew to be foul.

Christine tried to drag air into her lungs, but her gown fit too tightly. Tiny dots began to blur her vision. She saw his darkness spread, saw it seep from him slowly. His fingers at the laces of her gown abruptly halted her descent.

"W-What do you think you're doing?" she gasped.

"Loosening the laces. I'm not surprised you fainted. The way you've molded yourself into this gown."

"You will kindly stop this instant!" Christine started to swat his hands away, only to discover they had covered a considerable distance. It was all too true, the gossip she'd heard from servants, the gossip she'd read in the *Times*. Her husband was a womanizer. The skill with which he unlaced the front of her gown attested to as much.

"There, that's better."

True, she could breathe again, but her gown fell away at the neck and, God forgive her for wearing such an indecent garment, he must be able to see clear to her waist. Protectively, her arms crept up. He smiled.

"A little late for a show of modesty, isn't it? Wentworth and those other slobbering fops were ogling your generous display far longer than you've allowed *me*. Seems odd, considering I'm your husband."

"Odder yet that you recall your married status," she countered, annoyed that she allowed anger to flavor her voice. This sudden attack of jealousy was not part of her plan. Christine was on a mission. One that had prompted her to intrude upon a society ball in hopes of starting unappealing rumors about Gavin Norfork's wife. Never had she counted on meeting him at the function.

"Yes, I do have trouble recalling my marital status," he agreed. "I may be all that you earlier accused me of, but I am not a hypocrite. Were you the muddied hag I saw limping toward the church the day I signed the marriage agreement?"

She felt a blush creep into her cheeks. "I took a nasty spill into a mud puddle," she explained. "And I hurt my ankle, for your information. That is the reason I was limping."

"Was it?" His brow lifted. "But then, you had no reason to deceive me," he answered himself. "What are you doing in London, Christine? And without a proper chaperon?"

For two years she'd bided her time at Greenhaven, waiting for the lord of the manner to return. Waiting for at least a response to her requests for an audience with him.

"I grew tired of waiting," she answered. "And as for arriving improperly escorted, I am a married woman. Doesn't that entitle me to flit around the countryside on a whim if I choose? To behave as improperly as my husband? I haven't received a great deal of instruction as to what my role as your wife entails. However, judging by the *Times* and the gossip I've heard exchanged amongst the servants, I am behaving very much like a titled lady. Much as you behave like a titled gentleman."

To her satisfaction, the lazy smile he wore slid from his lips. "Have you come for wifely instruction, then?"

His voice was a low, husky sound that raised the gooseflesh on her arms. His question might have been taken as an innocent inquiry had his dark eyes not lowered to her exposed bosom. It suddenly dawned upon her that they were no longer at the gathering. No longer surrounded by people. They were in a bedchamber. Alone.

"Where am I?" she demanded.

"In my town home. Luckily, it isn't far from the duke and duchess's apartments. You haven't answered my question. Why are you here?"

She supposed bluntness wasn't a bad attribute. "I've

come to ask for an annulment. I don't wish to be your wife."

In response, he laughed. "I believe it's also a little late to express your displeasure over a marriage you agreed to two years ago."

"A marriage I agreed to only at the request of your late father. A marriage in name only," she stressed, then lowered her gaze, cursing the heat that settled in her cheeks again.

"If that's all you want, it won't take long to correct my oversight. We can see to the matter immediately."

From beneath her lashes, Christine watched him remove his necktie. How causal he appeared at the prospect of consummation, and how arrogant! Did he think she would simply allow him liberties? That she was a strumpet? Then Christine mentally cursed herself. Perhaps she'd had no need to shame him quite so quickly or so thoroughly.

She had reasoned causing a scandal would help sway him toward an annulment, if for some reason he proved hesitant to dissolve the marriage. Christine had wanted him to see right away she had none of the qualities a gentleman might expect from a wife. Nothing he would want.

"I'm not here in hopes our marriage would be c-consummated," she stuttered, uncomfortably aware not only of him, but of the soft mattress on which she rested, the tall posts of the bed, the masculine scent of the room. "I told you why I'm here. I want an annulment."

True to form in the art of removing clothing, he'd already stripped away his coat. Christine swallowed loudly. Lord, he was tall. His shoulders strained against his shirt. A shirt that was covering what appeared to be a broad chest that tapered into a trim waist. His legs were long and muscular beneath the snug fit of his trousers. With a degree of difficulty, she returned her gaze to his, noting the draw of his brows above the straight line of his nose.

"Surely you're not serious," he said. "An annulment is out of the question. For people of my class, anyway. I'm afraid we're stuck with one another. An arrangement that doesn't suit me, either. Perhaps we should make the best of it."

Again, his gaze raked her meaningfully. His insulting familiarity was beginning to wear on Christine's nerves. He stared at her as if he knew what she looked like without her clothes—as if he had the right to know! The enormity of her situation struck her with force. He did have the right. And by confronting him, she had reminded him of that fact.

"I don't love you," she said evenly.

He never hesitated while pulling his shirt from his breeches. "Love? What the bloody hell does that have to do with us? No one marries for love. Love is a word to soften lust, or greed, or convenience. Love is for fools and poets. Love is for the poor, because they have nothing else."

Cynical? She hadn't attached that unattractive trait to him. Nor had she anticipated the way her blood would heat as he tugged impatiently at the buttons on his shirt. Glimpses of hard flesh enticed her. She knew the proper thing to do would be to avert her gaze. To run! And she did scramble to the far side of the bed when he finished his task, his shirt gaping open to reveal a finely muscled chest sprinkled with dark hair. Her knees almost buckled when she stood. Her gown fell from her shoulders.

"My God, you're beautiful."

His words floated across the space separating them, falling like a caress upon her skin. Christine shivered, aware of her bare shoulders, aware of his bare chest, aware of the danger, but helpless to flee. Light sprang to life in his dark eyes, filling them with heat. She wanted to move, to speak, to avoid whatever seemed to be happening between them.

This was not part of her plan, these feelings he so effortlessly solicited from her. Strange emotions she had never felt for a man, and certainly shouldn't feel for this one, coursed through her. His touch didn't startle her into sanity, but lulled her deeper into a trance. His fingers brushed the stray curls from her neck. Almost like the feather-light kiss of a butterfly's wings.

His hands were less gentle upon her shoulders. He pulled her roughly against him, one hand clasping the back of her head, his fingers tangled in her hair.

The smoldering heat in his eyes flared, then slowly, his face lowered to hers. He hesitated a heartbeat from her lips, time enough for Christine to fully understand his intentions . . . what she was about to allow him to steal from her. Her future, her pledge to the poor.

"No," she whispered, pushing hard against his chest. She struggled, stepped on the long hem of her gown, and almost displayed the whole of her bosom in the process. Her feet tangled up, Christine tripped, falling backward onto the bed.

Frantically, she clutched the gown's low bodice to her breasts, moaning softly when her unruly mass of curls began to fall down her neck and, thankfully, over her shoulders. Her breath sounded ragged in the silence. "No," she warned again when he took a step toward her.

He halted, his dark stare leveled on her. "No?" he repeated, as if the word were foreign to him. "By neither my choice or yours our lives have been bound together. It is within my rights to take you."

"It is not right!" Christine shot back at him.

"Because you don't love me, nor I you?" he demanded.

"Because my heart belongs to another!"

His gaze widened slightly. "Oh, I see. You want an annulment so you can marry another?"

40

His assumption was not incorrect. Perhaps only somewhat misunderstood. She would become a servant of the Lord, she supposed, married in a sense to God. Christine debated whether to tell him the truth, then quickly rejected the idea. Norfork wasn't a religious man, or he wouldn't carry on the way he did. Even the vicar had said her husband had no concern for his own soul. Why would he care about hers?

"Yes," she answered, worried that the lie formed so easily on her tongue. "Now do you understand why I must insist upon an annulment?"

He nodded, his expression back to boredom. "Being married can be an inconvenience. Granting you an annulment would be more of one. My father's will clearly states that if I allow you one, or seek one myself, Greenhaven and its lands must be forfeited to charity. To the poor, the orphans, the churches. He had a very warped sense of humor, the marquis," he added bitterly.

Now she understood why he had married her. Why he would have married her had she been the muddied hag he'd once thought her to be. She felt embarrassed he'd been forced into the marriage. Again, she had to wonder over the old marquis's insistence she wed his son. For that matter, his low-handedness in forcing his only heir to marry a girl of her station, or rather, her lack of station.

Suddenly the reason dawned upon her. The wise old marquis had found a way to leave those less fortunate his wealth without having his son challenge his actions. He'd known she would not want to be married to a rake like his son, had counted upon her to see the marriage ended, and his wealth distributed where he truly thought it belonged. This way, he would not publicly shun his son, but merely manage to see his will done through her.

"How generous of him," Christine said. If she could convince Gavin to release her, she would truly have the

41

freedom to follow her calling, and a fortune to aid the church.

"Well, I am not so generous," he drawled. "I like my title and my lands. I'm sorry, Christine. There will be no annulment. Tell me, does your lover know you're in the habit of allowing young fops like Wentworth to touch your breasts and whisper naughty suggestions in your ear?"

Christine hoped her mouth did not drop open. She'd thought the young man's hand had brushed her there by accident. "Are you concerned on his behalf?" she asked. "I find it difficult to believe you can be sympathetic to anyone's feelings save your own. Otherwise, you would have thought of the way you've shamed me and used more discretion yourself. Therefore, I intend to embarrass you as much as I find being your wife an embarrassment."

"An eye for an eye, is that it?"

"Call it what you will."

"I call it very foolish."

His sudden appearance beside her upon the bed took Christine by surprise. He moved quick as a cat, and every bit as graceful. Before she could react, he'd pinned her down, his tall frame pressing her into the soft mattress.

"I'm not overly fond of threats, and usually react unbecomingly to them. Go home. And do try not to get yourself with child. I will, at some later date, be forced to produce an heir. Until then, enjoy yourself, but do it far from London."

"Are you giving me permission to be an adulteress?" she asked.

Gavin frowned. "I suppose having permission doesn't make it nearly so exciting. Perhaps you can keep my condescending attitude to yourself, so at least he, whoever the fortunate man is, continues to feel as if he's getting away with something. Although I'm not by nature jealous,

I am curious as to what he is getting away with. I don't think a little sample is too much to ask."

Christine wasn't certain what he meant to do until his mouth fastened upon hers. She tensed in outrage, started to turn her head away, then found the attempt foiled as his hands captured her face. She knew her strength was no match for his, but suspected her will was the stronger.

She would allow the touch of his lips against hers, suffer it for the sake of her cause, but he would receive no response from her. A lie. The feel of his tongue tracing the shape of her mouth shocked her so that she gasped, further stunned when the offending thing found its way between her parted lips.

He wielded the weapon boldly, thrusting and parrying until she became breathless . . . until the very flames of hell must have engulfed her. Heat tore a path up her legs, and in its wake, a tingling sensation that spread throughout her body.

This is sin, she thought. He is sin in the flesh. The deepest, darkest core of it. And she, Christine, with no last name until he had given her one, was truly her mother's daughter. A weakness for the flesh must be her birthright.

Stop! Her mind screamed the warning, and as if he'd heard her, he ended the kiss. Could she breathe normally, she might have sighed in relief. Instead, she sucked what air she could back into her lungs sharply. His mouth abandoned the torture on her lips, but it did not cease its attack. Down her neck it traveled, his teeth nipping lightly at the skin on her shoulders, then lower . . .

"Don't." Her fingers curled in his thick hair, reveling for the slightest second in the soft silky feel of it, before he lifted his head to look at her. "Please," she whispered pleadingly.

"Please do, or please don't?" he asked softly.

"Please release me."

For an alarming moment, he didn't respond. Then he rolled away and stood. The cool air against her flushed skin made her shiver.

"Cover yourself." He handed her his coat. "Then, dear wife, I suggest you get the hell out of here before . . ."

She scrambled to a sitting position, clutching his coat against her breasts. He seemed to have difficulty looking at her. Had he known the sinful feelings he stirred in her? Was he repulsed? So much so that he might reconsider her request for annulment?

"Before?" she prompted.

He smiled, but only slightly. "Before you make a liar out of me. I won't admit to being jealous, but I am, at the moment, very envious of your lover. Go home before you tempt me to find out *everything* he's been getting away with."

Chapter Three

"We're going back? But I've just unpacked everythin', m'lady. We've only been in London for three days. You mean to tell me it was that easy?"

Christine couldn't meet the young maid's stare. This was one morning she welcomed the unruly mass hanging down around her face. Her lips were slightly swollen, her spirits deflated. After last night, she simply could not stay. Her husband was a dangerous man.

"He said he won't grant me an annulment, Tillie. What is to be gained by staying?"

"Surely you didn't think one night of shaming him would do the trick? You've got to keep at it until he can stand no more. You've got to give him no choice."

Having finally met the Marquis of Greenhaven, His Lordship, Gavin Norfork, Christine had difficulty envisioning her husband admitting defeat in any area. What she had little trouble recalling, unfortunately, were his eyes, the tall, muscular shape of him, his kiss. She was no match for him. How could she be, an innocent country lass raised in a quiet parish?

"I made a mockery of flirting. Those men." She shivered. "They stood so close, brushed against me indecently. I didn't know what to say, what to do. It was horrible."

"Of course it was," the young maid crooned. "I'm sorry, Your Ladyship. I don't know much about flirting as an art. It's a pity there isn't someone who can teach you. A grand lady well schooled in such matters."

"Yes, a pity," Christine mumbled, reaching for her chocolate and a copy of the *Times*. "I made a fool of myself, Tillie. I don't belong here."

"Beggin' you pardon, but I thought that was the reason you came." Tillie moved to a large trunk and opened the lid. "Have you given up on your belief you were meant to serve the needy? Have you decided so quickly your calling was false?"

The sinful feelings Christine had experienced in her husband's arms had left her deliberating that question long into the night. Morning found her grappling for explanations. A test, she decided. Gavin Norfork had been thrown into her life to test her faith, her dedication to her calling.

"What should I do with this?" Tillie asked.

Christine glanced up to see Tillie holding a dark coat toward her. Heat rose in Christine's cheeks. He'd insisted she wear the garment, and had ordered her delivered to the hotel in his carriage. "Has he accompanied you to London?" he'd asked casually before the servant arrived to escort her downstairs.

At first, Christine hadn't understood. The look he'd turned on her hadn't appeared as casual as his question. Then she'd realized what he'd asked. He'd thought she had a lover, and hadn't known she served a spiritual being. "He is with me always," she'd answered in parting.

"Have a hotel servant send it to the marquis's town home," she now instructed.

"My, but he's broad at the shoulders. And by the length of his coat, tall, too. Is he as handsome as I've 'eard, Your Ladyship?"

Heavens, yes, he was handsome. Indecently so. "He is not without a certain appeal," Christine answered. "Tillie, please do not address me formally. You know to do so annoys me."

"But, Your Ladyship, we're not in the country now. What if someone were to hear me call you by your given name? Allow me to play the maid in truth, for it's an injustice you've done me. Never ordering me about or even allowing me to help you dress until last eve when you couldn't figure the gown's workings. This is my calling, don't you see?"

At Tillie's impassioned plea, Christine couldn't help but laugh. "Oh, all right, then. I order you to sit beside me and have a cup of chocolate while I read the *Times*. I want to see if there was mention made of my embarrassing debut into London society last night."

"There is," Tillie assured her, draping the coat over the back of Christine's chair before settling herself. "It's right there on the society page."

Christine cast her a dark look. "I should have never taught you to read."

"And it was a blessed gift you gave me," Tillie replied dutifully.

Christine was suddenly distracted by a haunting scent. One she recognized from the previous night. "Why don't you simply tell me what you read," she suggested, rising to remove herself from the coat draped across her chair.

"I can't say it just the way they did. Would you like me to read it to you?"

"If you don't mind, please."

Tillie frowned. "It would have sounded more like an order if you hadn't said please."

"Just read it!" When the young maid's eyes widened,

47

Christine hurried to the table. "Forgive me, Tillie. I didn't mean to snap at you. I don't know what's wrong with me." She slumped into her chair, shoving her heavy hair from her face. "I have this horrible headache and—"

"What's wrong with your mouth?"

Her hand automatically flew to her lips. "What?"

"Your lips look funny." Tillie stretched her neck as if that would help her see around Christine's hand. "All puffy, and your cheeks, they're red and irritated like something scratchy has rubbed—" The maid abruptly ceased her observations. Her eyes widened.

Christine shot out of her chair. She stood with her back to Tillie, shame coursing through her body. A traitorous body. Tillie knew. The maid knew why her lips were swollen, and her cheeks were stinging with both embarrassment and the irritation Gavin's whiskers had caused against her sensitive skin. She sighed, wishing God had not led her down the wicked path to London.

"Read, Tillie . . . please."

"Perhaps the most interesting information gleaned from the many social events that took place in London last evening was the arrival of a beautiful woman at the home of the Duke and Duchess of Montrose's gala. An angel whose behavior, we are told, was less than angelic. An angel who claimed to be none other than His Lordship, Gavin Norfork's wife. Yes, he is married, although most of us have forgotten, most especially the fairer gender of our dear London. Imagine the duchess's surprise upon learning her identity.

"Now that we are reminded of Norfork's status, let us also remember this young woman is one he married two years ago in accordance with his deceased father's wishes. A girl, we understand, who is an orphan raised in a parish near the marquis's country estate. Perhaps that explains the young woman's indiscreet flirtations with

*several young men present at the gala. One of whom ran
from the dance floor in fear for his life when Norfork
approached the couple during a dance.*

*"The woman fainted shortly afterward, carried from
the gala by none other than the man she claims is her
husband. What happened next is surely a subject being
discussed much over scones this morning. Who is this
mysterious beauty? The marquis's wife in truth? Or a
slighted mistress out to publicly embarrass him? Many a
man would like an answer to that question. In all likelihood, many a woman, too."*

Gavin buttered his scone meticulously in the silence
that followed.

"Well?" Chester Thorton asked, putting the paper
down.

"I expected worse."

"I'm not referring to the article," Chester said, clearly
irritated. "Is she truly your wife? And what happened after
you carried her from the gala?"

"Yes, she is my wife, and I pitched her into a gutter,"
Gavin answered dryly, then glanced up at the two men
seated at his table. "What do you think happened? I
brought her here."

Chester Thorton smiled smugly across the table at
James Dumont. His gaze strayed to the stairway leading
upstairs.

"She is not in my bed, if that was the wager," Gavin
remarked, returning to the task of buttering his scone.

"What do you mean she isn't here?" Chester demanded,
reaching toward a fruit bowl to snatch a handful of plump
strawberries. "A delicious tidbit like her, your wife in the
bargain, and she isn't upstairs in your bed? Where the
bloody hell is she then?"

In another man's bed. The thought annoyed Gavin
more than he cared to admit. It was a thought that had
plagued him throughout the night. A thought that caused

him to toss and turn. A thought that had made him damned mad by morning. Still, he displayed none of his inner turmoil, taking a bite of the scone, then replacing it on his plate.

"I imagine she's on her way back to the country, where I ordered her to return. I'm considering sending someone to teach her how to properly conduct herself in titled society before allowing her to venture too far from the country again. Shall we meet at Brook's tonight for a game of cards?"

An expression of disbelief crossed Chester's features. "That's it? Your wife appears in London for one night, a woman who, although she could use instruction as you've stated, is only the most gorgeous creature I have ever laid eyes on, and you just send her home?"

"What did you expect I'd do, Chester? Flaunt her before my past mistresses? Pretend I have suddenly developed a taste for married life, which I promise you I have not. She doesn't belong in London. Not yet, anyway."

"I think what His Lordship is trying to say is that he isn't ready to settle down," James Dumont explained to the flustered Chester. "He's certainly not ready for the responsibility of a wife, and what a burden that one will be. Although, now that she's made a rather embarrassing launch into society, I'm not certain the country is the best place for her, either."

"And why would that be?" Gavin asked, reaching across the table to grab a handful of strawberries himself. He was in no mood to discuss his wife. In all truth, he wasn't in the mood to entertain the two young nobles sitting at his table.

"Well," James began hesitantly. "Now that she's been seen, that is to say, with her there and everyone knowing that you're here . . ."

"She isn't safe," Chester said finally catching the gist. "Wentworth or, for that matter, any young pup who took a notion could simply pay her a call. Say their carriage lost a wheel, use all manner of excuses to entertain the marquis's wife in his absence. And the ladies—I suspect their curiosity is running rampant. It wouldn't be in the least improper to pay a visit—"

"Enough!" Gavin slammed his hand down on the table, smashing a few berries into pulp in the process. His head had begun to throb. A scandalous vision entered his mind. His lovely wife, her hair spilling over her shoulders, her tempting mouth swollen from a man's passionate kisses, stumbling down the stairs of his country estate to greet a foyer full of curious guests.

Then her lover would appear. Half naked, his breeches hastily donned, standing at the top of the stairs so that those below had little doubt as to what their unannounced visit had interrupted. Damn her! She wouldn't humiliate him in this fashion.

His voice depicted none of the anger building within him when Gavin said, "If you gentlemen will excuse me, I have business to attend to. Feel free to finish your breakfast, then kindly see yourselves out."

Neither James nor Chester spoke a word as he rose, snatched up his coat, and left them sitting openmouthed at his formal dinning table.

"What the devil's gotten into him?" Chester asked.

James smiled while lifting a strawberry to his mouth. "Not the devil. His wife. I'll wager you fifty pounds our friend will shortly be on his way to her hotel for a word with her."

"Hotel?" Chester echoed. His gaze narrowed. "You knew she wasn't here when you tempted me to wager on whether or not we'd find her in his bed this morn. Bad form, James. I have half a mind not to wager with you as to His Lordship's destination, however, I imagine he's off to smooth things over with the duchess."

"I'll take the bet," James said. "Even were he to arrive

51

at Adrianna's home to smooth things over, he will learn that she's out paying a visit herself this morning. On my way over, I saw her coach pull up at the very hotel Gavin had his wife escorted to last night. Who do you suppose she's visiting?"

Chester had just popped several small berries into his mouth, and nearly choked. "The duchess would not create yet another scandal by paying her a visit. Surely you are mistaken."

"Fifty pounds says I am not. Gavin will shortly find himself in an awkward situation if he is in fact calling upon his wife. Imagine his face when he discovers she is entertaining another guest. His lover."

"Oh, to be a fly on the wall," Chester sighed. He promptly straightened in his chair and regarded James reproachfully. "I think you forget, dear fellow, who we are discussing. Our friend is not an ordinary man. Gavin will dismiss his beautiful wife without further incident. I say he won't visit her at the hotel. He avoids love as if it were an affliction."

"The bet is a hundred pounds, friend," James said. "Do you accept the wager that Gavin will pay his wife another visit?"

Chester grinned. "A hundred pounds and fifty more."

"Done."

The smile on Chester's mouth waned. "You agreed much too quickly." His gaze narrowed again. "What do you know that I don't?"

Sitting back in his chair, James lifted a strawberry and studied it. "I believe Gavin has finally met a woman who can shake that damnable control of his. And I know, as do you, that His Lordship suffers more than an aversion to love. He also suffers one to strawberries. And I saw him pop a few in his mouth just minutes ago."

His friend groaned. "What a silly gift we chose to bring him. I'd forgotten His Lordship does not eat fruit.

52

And his wife has bedazzled him, all right. His thoughts are so full of her he must have forgotten, as well. The woman may cost me my father's fortune after all." Chester buried his head in his hands, cursing before he pulled away to study his sticky hands. "Exactly what happens to Gavin when he eats strawberries?"

James sobered. "I'm not sure."

Both men sat silently for a time.

"Fifty pounds says he breaks out in hives," James finally said.

"I'll refrain from filling your pockets with more of my funds than I already have," Chester growled. "What a bad morning our friend may have. Forced to be in the same room with both his wife and his current lover, with God only knows what horrible affliction waiting to strike him down. Poor man."

"Yes, we should feel sorry for him."

Their eyes met across the table. James was the first to laugh.

"So sorry not to have sent a note around asking for an appointment, Your Ladyship. You obviously retired late last eve and meant to sleep in this morning."

Christine counted Adrianna Shipley's admitted *faux pas* much less rude than the first—having the nerve to visit her lover's wife. She'd been shocked to see the woman standing in the hallway after Tillie answered a soft rap at her door.

Shocked and annoyed at her disappointment upon learning the intruder's identity. Whom had she expected? Certainly not the devil come to inform her he'd had a change of heart, or to at least reclaim his fine coat.

"May I offer you a cup of chocolate?" Christine asked, determined to mask the strange resentment she felt toward the beautiful duchess. So what if the woman had been intimate with her husband? So what if Christine felt very much the destitute orphan standing in her nightclothes before a grand lady?

Self-conscious, Christine pulled the flimsy neck of her robe together and lifted her chin, waiting for the duchess to answer.

"Let us not exchange pleasantries," the woman said, then strolled to the open wardrobe where, to Christine's embarrassment, very few gowns hung. "It would appear as if you aren't planning an extended visit, which would show you have a measure of intelligence. Perhaps you've only come to demand a higher allowance, or to gain permission to redecorate Greenhaven. Surely you're not in London in hopes of gaining your husband's affections?"

Her daring surprised Christine. She'd assumed titled ladies conducted themselves in a more refined manner. The way the woman studied her from head to toe, without the least amount of subtlety, further unnerved her.

"I don't believe my reasons for visiting London are any of your concern." She made an attempt to regard the duchess with the same snooty expression leveled upon her. "Now, if you'll excuse me, I have private matters to attend."

The woman's gaze strayed to the trunk Tillie had opened earlier. "He sent you packing, didn't he?" The duchess raised a jeweled hand when Christine opened her mouth. "No need to deny the truth. I know Gavin *very* well. He isn't the type to be strapped with a wife, most especially an orphan who is nothing but an embarrassment to him. It doesn't surprise me that he's become bored with you after only one night. Don't take it personally, my dear. It would take a more worldly woman than you to hold his attention for long."

"A woman such as yourself?" Christine asked, schooling her features into a cool mask of indifference, although her knees had started to shake beneath her nightgown.

Color darkened the woman's cheeks, but not enough to

count as a blush. "That, my dear, was an improper question. One my refined upbringing will not allow me to answer."

The younger of the two shrugged. "No need. His Lordship told me you were lovers." She purposely stressed the word "were." "If you are not here to admit as much to me, why did you come?" To her satisfaction, the duchess's face darkened. An angry red color crept up her neck and coated her pale skin.

"Out of duty," the duchess snapped. "My duty to inform you that I will not tolerate your presence in London any more than will your husband. You see, quite frankly, I'm not finished with him. Your unwanted appearance in London has turned all heads in his direction, and if my husband is an indulgent one, he does demand discretion."

Tillie's eyes, Christine noted, had grown quite huge. The maid stood next to the door with her hand against her heart, her face as white as the starched apron she wore. Had Tillie known her duties in truth, she would have found something to occupy herself within the adjoining servants' quarters. Christine was greatly embarrassed by Adrianna's bluntness. Much more for Tillie than herself. Country life was boring for the young maid, she supposed.

Tillie wasn't accustomed to brazen admissions of adultery. Nor, for that matter, was Christine. Regardless, she tilted her chin and walked regally toward the door, where Tillie stood gape-jawed.

"So sorry to have inconvenienced you and my husband, your grace," Christine said, "But you see, I have no intention of leaving. I'm not finished with him, either. And having settled that, I'll ask you to leave."

Christine opened the door wide, waiting for the duchess to huff from the room. She waited . . . and waited. It took her a moment to realize the duchess wasn't staring at her with a shocked expression, but directly into the hallway.

Curious, Christine poked her head around the open

door. She nearly screamed. Gavin stood there, his eyes riveted upon Adrianna, his hands clawing at his necktie.

"Your grace," he said simply, inclining his head somewhat before he entered, uninvited.

Without so much as a hello to Christine, he walked across the room to the bureau mirror, still struggling with his tie. He sighed loudly upon loosening the article, then flung it from him and set to pulling his lawn shirt from his breeches. Suddenly, he seemed to recall Adrianna's presence. His eyes met hers in the mirror.

"I believe you were on your way out."

Chapter Four

Color suffused the woman's pale cheeks. If Christine hadn't been rendered dull-witted with shock, she might have smiled smugly at the woman's dismissal. As it was, she simply stood at the door, a mindless statue, frozen in place by her husband's audacity.

"I'd like a word with my wife," he explained when the duchess remained. "A private chat."

Adrianna found her voice, although it emerged from her throat in a croaked whisper. "Is that what they're calling it these days?" The duchess lowered her gaze to his hands, which had paused in the process of removing his shirt. "A word? A chat?" Her dark eyes narrowed on him. "I thought we were to have a *word* with each other last night!"

"I was detained."

Accompanying the emotionless explanation was a glance toward Christine. She didn't care for his implication, nor did she care to witness a lovers' spat between her husband and his current mistress.

"I'd like the both of you to leave," Christine said. "Go before—"

"Your lover returns?"

The annoyance in his tone was unmistakable, although his gaze remained cool. She looked at the duchess. The woman lifted a brow.

"That would certainly add embarrassment to an already uncomfortable situation," Christine said softly. "Especially were my lover to return before yours departs."

He smiled—she supposed in acknowledgment of her daring—or perhaps he found humor in such a predicament. Christine didn't feel in the least proud of herself. Why couldn't she seem to control her wicked tongue in her husband's company? Why couldn't she control the racing of her heart, the trembling in her legs?

"You may want to use the servants' stairwell, your grace," he said to Adrianna, reaching beneath his shirt to scratch his stomach. "I received more than one curious glance when I walked to the desk and inquired as to which room my wife occupied. I can only assume the lobby is now crowded with patrons waiting to see how long I'll stay. I trust you will be as discreet upon leaving the hotel as I know you were upon entering."

"I'd already used the servants' stairwell," she remarked. "I had my footman inquire about the orphan's location, then drive me around back so that my visit would remain secret. You are good, Gavin, but not good enough to risk my husband's fortune over. He's old. I am rather hoping to have the both of you someday."

"Until then." He nodded, a mockingly polite gesture.

"Yes, until then," she agreed, then walked to the door where Tillie still stood, stunned.

"The door, you idiot," Adrianna growled under her breath.

Christine tensed over her rudeness. The girl hurried to do Adrianna's bidding, and the parting glance the duchess cast in Christine's direction sent foreboding shivers up her spine. If evil had a face, in that instant, it belonged to Adrianna Shipley.

"Maid, fetch a basin of cold water and some cloths for washing."

Her husband's instructions brought Christine from her dazed state. She glanced at Gavin. He no longer stood before the bureau, but sat upon the bed. Without an ounce of modesty, he removed his shirt. Tillie and Christine's gasps merged in the now-silent bedchamber.

"Be quick about it, girl," he commanded. "I have need of my wife's services."

Services? Christine felt the morning's events crowding in on her. Being called on by her husband's mistress was really too much for a girl accustomed to country life. Now, having a half-naked man perched on her bed, while plainly announcing his foul intentions in front of poor Tillie, snapped what little control she maintained.

"Stay, Tillie," she ordered. To her husband, Christine said, "I asked you to leave. Who do you think you are? Barging into my suite, ordering my servants and me about?"

"I am your husband," he answered in the same impatient tone. "My funds paid for this room. My funds pay for your maid. She is not your servant, but mine—a fact she may have well forgotten."

Tillie crumbled beneath his dark glare. When the maid rushed into the servants' quarters and threw home the bolt, Christine wished she herself stood on the other side of a sturdy wall as well. Thoughtfully, she regarded the door leading into the hallway.

"If you're truly bent on scandal, go ahead," he said, "What interesting reading the *Times* will have for their next edition."

Christine felt tempted. Sorely tempted. Instead, she squared her shoulders and forced herself to look at Gavin.

Fear was an expected reaction; the subtler responses unfolding within her were not. He was handsome. Sinfully so. His dark complexion contrasted sharply against the whiteness of the sheets. His skin looked . . . splotched, red and angry-looking. Only then did she notice his scratching.

"What foulness have you brought into my bed?"

"Nothing you can catch," he assured her, scratching like a man possessed. "Strawberries and I have never gotten along well. Cool cloths will soothe the discomfort."

"Oh." Christine suddenly realized why he'd made the peculiar request of Tillie. For a moment, she had thought Gavin had implied his wife could use a good scrubbing before . . . before he required her services. "I'll fetch the water."

She was grateful for something to busy herself with, something other than being forced to bed her husband. Christine crossed the room and rapped softly upon the servant's door.

"Tillie, it's me," she called. "Open up, please."

A second passed, and then another. "Tillie," she tried again. "I need the water and the cloths His Lordship requested. Please unbolt the door."

When the maid refused to answer, Christine stole a nervous glance toward her husband. He stood before the bureau again, frowning. He'd taken to scratching himself with her fine silver brush.

"Please?" he echoed, the red blotches on his chest spreading up his neck. "What have you done to the servants who attend my country estate? Forced your bad manners upon them?"

As Gavin stormed toward her, Christine flung herself in front of the door. "You've frightened her is all. And if you had the manners to visit your country estate in the past ten years, you'd know your servants. They are simple folk. Unaccustomed to harsh commands!"

He drew up short, his face darkening, if that were possible. "A true lady does not so gallantly defend those of a station below her. You have much to learn, Christine."

Defiantly, she lifted her chin. He towered above her. Blotched and miserable as he appeared, he smelled heavenly. "Who better to teach me hypocrisy than a man whose mistress, mere moments ago, I was forced to entertain."

He smiled, and still managed to nearly steal her breath away. Gavin placed a hand on either side of her head, blocking possible escape. "You sound jealous."

Was she jealous? Insulted, Christine quickly assured herself. Appalled by his wickedness. "I care not what you do, Your Lordship, or whom you do it with. An annulment is all I ask."

"And you might as well set your sights on the throne of England."

Their eyes locked. "If I wanted the throne, I would find a way to get it," she assured him.

"I, too, have a reputation for getting what I want," he countered.

Christine slipped beneath his arm. "A reputation that has preceded you. Sit on the bed and I will attend you."

Without waiting for a response, Christine went to her trunk and removed several fine handkerchiefs. The pitcher and basin in her room had been used to rinse her face earlier, but it would have to do. She felt more in control when she did something ordinary, such as tend the sick, and she desperately needed control at the moment.

It surprised her when he obeyed. The sight of him trying to scratch his back with her brush had her hurrying toward the bed.

"That is not your possession," she informed him, removing the brush from his fingers. "This belonged to my mother, or some poor soul she stole it from," she added, having long ago concluded that a woman dressed in rags would not own anything so fine.

When Gavin groaned and tried to reach behind him in an effort to scratch, Christine took pity upon him. His nails were short and square, not at all suitable for so menial a task. She removed his hand and replaced it with her own, using her longer tapered nails to offer him relief.

He sighed. His muscles bunched and rolled beneath her fingers. Christine found his back fascinating. Strong and smooth. But he'd obviously made the same mistake of eating strawberries not long ago, for she saw fading scratches from his previous error. She stared closer at his shoulder. What appeared to be the slight imprint of teeth marks stood out clearly against his dark skin.

Strange, she thought. Had he gotten himself into a fight in which his opponent had had the bad manners to bite? No telling. Having heard of his bad reputation, she assumed he'd gotten into a brawl with dockside riffraff. The sailors were said to have few scruples when it came to fisticuffs.

"You should take more care with whom you tangle," she commented. "And in the company you keep."

He turned his head to the side, his brow furrowed in puzzlement.

"The teeth marks," she explained. "They have not yet faded. Only someone of low character would stoop to biting in a scrap."

She thought he smiled for a moment. "You are correct, m'lady. I should take more care with whom I . . . tangle."

His back muscles flexed beneath her fingers, reminding Christine of the task at hand. She resumed her scratching, but had difficulty remaining unmoved by the sight of so much exposed flesh. Was it a sin, she wondered, to look upon a man of foul character and find him beautiful? Certainly it was weak-minded, since she herself had condemned the idea that any man should desire her for her face and form alone.

"Harder," he commanded quietly.

As she obeyed him, Christine noticed the door to the small servants' quarters open a crack. She hoped Tillie had regained her senses and would bring fresh water and cloths so Christine wouldn't have to use her fine handkerchiefs.

"Oh, God, yes," Gavin groaned beneath the onslaught of her nails.

Although the long red streaks her nails left against his skin were proof she should cease and soothe him with cool cloths, she humored him a bit longer. Christine willed Tillie to emerge from her hiding place.

"Harder," Gavin ordered, his voice raw and husky. "Faster."

The servants' door slammed shut again. Christine silently scolded Tillie for a lack of backbone, and ceased her scratching. "Any more, Your Lordship, and I will draw blood." She crawled from the bed, moving to the washbasin. With regret, she dipped her fine handkerchief into the water. Christine had allowed herself few luxuries since becoming a marchioness.

The generous allowance sent to her monthly by her husband's retainer, she gladly gave to the poor. It surprised her to learn the old marquis had not provided for the parish upon his death. Of course, with her new insight into the terms of his will, she realized the old man had expected her to do so. And far more grandly than she'd been able to do during the past two years.

But how could she fulfill such expectations of her? How could she when her husband stood to lose as much as she stood to gain? Christine supposed her choices were few, and perhaps shaming him to the point where he must demand the marriage dissolved was the wisest one. The next obstacle presented itself. She was an innocent and knew nothing about creating scandal.

With a sigh, she took the wet cloth to Gavin's broad back. Soon, she became totally engrossed in her ministrations, not even realizing she'd moved from behind him to kneel before him, running her cool handkerchief over his chest. She followed the rash up his neck, and over the shape of his mouth.

When his lips parted slightly, her gaze shot up to his eyes. The only time she'd seen such heat in a man's gaze was when the fever had him. In her experienced opinion, Gavin Norfork suffered from no such affliction.

He reached out and traced her own lips with his fingers, then ran them down the side of her face. "Did I do that to your delicate skin?"

Christine jerked away from him, flustered by the effect his touch had on her. She rose, marching with purpose toward the door. After throwing it wide, she said, "Please leave."

He made no move to oblige her. "I want to meet your lover. See what manner of man he is. Close the door."

Anger and embarrassment merged inside her. He'd have a long wait, and she wasn't of a mind to entertain him, or to obey him. "I asked you to leave politely," she said. "But since you refuse, I have no choice."

His smug smile took what had only been a fleeting thought, and turned it into a plan of action. Christine closed the door, walked to where his discarded clothing lay, then scooped it up. She returned to the entrance, opened the door, stepped outside, and tossed his clothing over the banister.

It was satisfying to watch his fine linen shirt float down into the crowd. Humorous until she noted the heads start turning upward. Realizing she wore only her nightclothes, she tried to step back. She came up flush against a warm body.

"Since you seem foolishly bent on scandal . . ." His breath tickled her ear. "We might as well give them something to talk about."

The moist heat of his mouth found her neck. Christine gasped, then wheeled around. He picked her up in his arms, instigating loud catcalls from below. Gavin carried her back into the room, using his booted foot to slam the door closed behind them.

He moved to the bed and dropped her as if she were only so much baggage. Christine scrambled to the far side of the bed. "I asked you to leave," she reminded.

"I don't care to be ordered about." He walked to the chair where the coat that had earlier been such a distraction lay draped. With a sigh, he lifted the garment and shrugged into it. "You will pack your belongings and return to Greenhaven immediately."

"I don't care to be ordered about either," she said, rather amazed by her own bravery. When he turned a look upon her that she suspected had sent many a brave man scrambling, she swallowed the lump forming in her throat. "I will not leave until you grant me an annulment."

In three long strides he stood beside the bed. "I will never grant you an annulment, Christine. Do as you've been told."

She supposed he expected her to back down then, to submissively do as he demanded. It was what a proper wife would do . . . which was why she asked, "And what if I refuse?"

The red had not completely faded from his face, and what little remained darkened a shade. "You cannot refuse me. Not in this or any other matter. I am your husband."

"In name only," she protested, then cursed her tongue for bringing up their lack of intimacy together.

"There you go complaining again," he grumbled. "I could have you dragged back to Greenhaven. Locked in a room. Guarded so that even your lover could not call upon you."

Would he? Christine wondered. She hadn't known her husband more than a few hours, but she sensed he was not the type of man to misuse a woman. A rake to be sure, but one who obviously had some principles; otherwise he might have already consummated the marriage without her consent. The only way to know what he would or would not do was to call his bluff.

"Then order it done," she said. "For that is the only way I will return to Greenhaven. And the only way you will keep me there."

Her husband stared at her in the oddest fashion. As if he couldn't believe she had given him an ultimatum. "Don't think I won't," he warned, then started to pace before the bed. Back and forth he walked, his expression growing darker by the minute.

Christine thought she might have pushed too far, assumed too much about a man who was, after all, a perfect stranger. She couldn't stay locked in a room. Guarded like a criminal. Her continued service to the parish and the church had been her only joy during the past two years. And perhaps she should have left well enough alone.

She hadn't lived a bad life as a marchioness. The staff at Greenhaven were simple country folk like herself. She'd been able to visit the parish whenever she wished, to go about her life, the only true burden being the knowledge she had a husband, even if he wouldn't show himself.

Who could say if he'd have ever presented himself to her? Perhaps he would have come hobbling home when they were both old and gray, she well past her childbearing years. Had she made a mistake by confronting him? By demanding an annulment? Now he had a name and a face to put with the wife he had chosen to ignore. A name and a face that made her a person.

Although it was tempting to give in and scurry back to Greenhaven, the terms of the will of the late marquis would not allow her. She'd been given a true mission in life.

"Will you send your henchmen to have me dragged away and locked up then?" she asked.

His pacing came to an abrupt halt. He regarded her in a cool fashion. "No. But neither will I allow you to stay in this hotel and shame me with the comings and goings of your lover. Finish packing. If you want to remain in London, you will do so under my roof."

Imprisonment at Greenhaven suddenly didn't sound so horrible to Christine. Never had she considered that her husband would demand she reside with him. She with him? Under the same small roof? Forced into constant contact with one another? She shuddered, but from exactly what reaction, she couldn't say.

What evil magic might he work on her under the protection of his own roof? What foul plans for seduction might he concoct? She would be at his mercy. The mercy of his dark eyes and his sensuous mouth. Doomed surely if he took the notion to see their marriage consummated.

Besides being appalling to her, consummating the marriage would greatly compromise the chances of it being annulled. She must remain chaste at all cost. And she had no doubt that unless he forced himself upon her, she would. Small town house or not, perhaps she would have very little contact with her husband. Or so she prayed.

Chapter Five

It was not so small a roof. For three days Christine had been a prisoner, not at Greenhaven, but at His Lordship's stylish London home. Three days in which she'd been subjected to the stuffy attentions of Gavin's head manservant, a Mr. Graves, and denied the unappealing company of her husband.

He obviously did not have any dark plans for her. For the man couldn't work his evil magic upon her if he refused to come home! Restless, Christine paced the spacious confines of her room, disturbed by her thoughts, and the slight irritation she felt over being abandoned.

"You'll wear out the fine carpets if you keep that up, m'lady," Tillie said from her comfortable position upon a delicate chaise longue. "Come sit with me and we'll read the paper together."

Christine cast the maid a dark glance. Tillie's hands had been too idle for the past three days. The stuffy head servant refused to allow the girl to touch anything in the house, and like herself, Tillie had become a pampered prisoner. Only, unlike herself, Tillie seemed to enjoy her imprisonment.

"You've already said there has been no mention of me since the first article," Christine said. "It's as if all of London has already forgotten about me. Not to mention my husband's short memory," she added irritably.

Tillie raised a suspicious brow. "Are you vexed by His Lordship's absence from your bed?"

Heat immediately suffused Christine's cheeks. "Of course not, Tillie. I am vexed by the absence of further discussion concerning an annulment. How could you ask me such an indecent question?"

Perhaps too comfortable in Christine's company as well, the maid shrugged. "His Lordship has a temper, and he's a rake to be sure, but he's a handsome devil. Ye might be a saint to those poor souls of the parish, but ye're still a woman. Human like the rest of us."

There was as good a reason as any to explain Christine's disturbing contemplation as to whom her husband had been sharing a bed with for the past three nights. To her knowledge, he'd spent no time in his own. And what difference should it make to her where he slept as long as it wasn't with her?

"It's this blasted idleness," she said, resuming her pacing. "I'm not used to lounging the days away. I need something to do."

The maid sighed. "Well, I'm quite enjoying myself, m'lady." Her gaze swept the room. "Have you ever seen so many fine things all gathered under one roof? Puts that dreary Greenhaven to shame, it does."

Christine could not argue. Greenhaven, huge as it was, did seem shabby in comparison. A rather dark, brooding place with little warmth. Still, much grander than anything she had known. Up until her arrival at the town home, anyway.

What a country bumpkin she must have seemed to the

servants when she first entered the parlor downstairs. The night she'd found herself in Gavin's bed, she'd paid scant attention to her surroundings, only wishing to escape in all haste. While her pitiful luggage had been unloaded, she had stood in the huge parlor downstairs.

The room could only be described as cluttered. But it was littered in such a fascinating way. There were not one, but three desks, all sporting such interesting knick-knacks. There was scarcely a place on the wall not filled with fine paintings. The room's decor was almost more than a person could stand to look at, because there was so much to see.

"You've given me an idea," she now said thoughtfully. "There are many fine things in His Lordship's home. Things that will fetch a high price once my marriage is annulled and all my husband's worldly possessions become the property of the poor."

" 'E's not going to let that happen," Tillie reminded her. "I told you right enough when I said there was no point now in staying, not after you told me the terms of the old marquis's will. No amount of shaming him will make him part with his fortune."

Christine feared the maid was correct. She could not, however, give up so easily. Not when it was obviously God's will she pursue an annulment.

"We will see," she said, then marched to a desk and withdrew sheets of paper along with charcoal drawing sticks. "Since Mr. Graves cannot bring himself to come upstairs unless summoned, I say we begin an inventory."

Tillie's eyes lit with mischief. "You mean we're going through the house and writing down all that's in it?"

"Exactly." Christine handed the maid a sheet of paper and a charcoal pencil. "You begin in here. I will start with the other bedchambers. I don't want His Lordship finding a way to end the marriage and keep his wealth in the bargain."

Rising, the maid replied, "The only way I see he could do that, was if something were to 'appen to you, m'lady."

A strange feeling came over Christine. A coldness settled around her, as if someone had walked over her grave. "Yes, I suppose if I were to meet with an unfortunate accident . . ." She let her voice trail off, then immediately shook off the dark thought. "Let us begin."

Thankful for something to do at last, Christine left the room. In the hallway, some of her enthusiasm faded. What if she ran into the stuffy Mr. Graves? He'd already indicated he didn't care for her roaming the house. He was quick to bring meals to her room and even quicker to quit her company. The servant obviously did not approve of her, and more obviously, did not consider her his mistress.

She'd received the same reception when she'd first arrived at Greenhaven. The servants all knew who she was, or more damning in their eyes, who she wasn't. Married to their employer she might have been, but to the working class, she was no better than they, and some thought not as good. She'd cried for the better part of a week, alone in a big room without warmth.

Then she'd gone on about her life, walking the distance to the parish when none of the coachmen were of a mind to drive her. In time, she'd befriended the servants, even worked alongside them. Soon, the staff at Greenhaven were coming to her for advice about running the house, and after a while, they became the family she'd never had. With resolve, Christine vowed to befriend the stuffy Mr. Graves before her stay in London ended. And it would not end until she'd achieved her objective.

Morning melted away as she and Tillie made their inventory list. Had Christine not been elated by the number of items recorded that would fetch a high price at auction, she would have been livid over His Lordship's total disregard for spending. With him living alone in the house and no one to appreciate the luxuries each room housed, it made her twice as angry.

"All done upstairs but the one room," Tillie said, joining her in the hallway.

Christine eyed "the one room" with trepidation. It was His Lordship's bedchamber. Dare she enter that dark den of iniquity where she'd experienced her first taste of sin? She had no doubt the room was unoccupied, that it had been so for the past three days. Still, she made no move to enter where common sense said she should not.

"I don't blame you for being afraid to go in there, m'lady," Tillie whispered. "Although, being the master suite, it should hold more treasures than all of the other rooms combined. But fearing His Lordship as you do, well—"

"I do not fear him," Christine snapped. And it wasn't exactly a lie. She feared her own traitorous reactions to his kisses. And she worried that she could not bend him to her will. And yes, maybe she was a little frightened of him, but she would have to get past her fears in order to see her obligation fulfilled. In short, she refused to compromise her calling because of her own weaknesses.

"It must be an accurate inventory," she said, proud her voice didn't tremble, prouder still that her knees weren't shaking when she walked to the door and placed her hand on the knob. "Will you accompany me?"

When Tillie didn't respond, Christine glanced toward the maid. She'd disappeared. The door to her own suite closed softly. Tillie was at least honest. She made no pretenses about bravery when none existed.

"But I must be brave," Christine said aloud. "If not for myself, for all the poor souls whose future rests in my hands." Bolstered by her own words, Christine turned the knob and slipped inside.

The drapes were drawn. Her eyes had trouble adjusting to the darkness. She stood very still, waiting to gain her bearings. Although she remained stationary, his scent found her. A musky, male fragrance that quickened the already racing beat of her heart. Christine closed her eyes and leaned lightly against the door. She fought the remembered feel of his strong body pressing her down into the soft mattress, the warm touch of his lips against hers.

Willing the disturbing memories away, she opened her eyes again and scanned the room. Slowly, she distinguished the outline of the furniture. Still, there was not enough light to make her inventory. Christine considered fumbling her way across the room to open the drapes. Then the fading embers in the fireplace drew her gaze. With little effort, she imagined she could bring the flames back to life.

After she stacked more wood in the grate and fanned the flames, a cozy glow filled the dark bedchamber. Satisfied the fire would not go out, she straightened. A silver locket twinkled from atop the mantel. Christine ran her fingers over the ornate design, picked it up, and opened the locket. Although the light wasn't strong, she made out the portrait of a beautiful woman.

"My mother."

She jumped, nearly dropping the delicate locket. Her head jerked in the direction of the voice. It took her a moment to locate him. Her husband lay sprawled across his massive bed, staring at her. Firelight played against the dark hue of his skin. The sheets were draped low over his hips, leaving little doubt he wore nothing beneath them.

"I thought you came in here to rob me . . . but perhaps not."

Realizing she stared, she lifted her gaze abruptly. Her cheeks stung with embarrassment. How shameful to gawk at him so, to gape and find pleasure in his surface beauty.

"I am not a thief, Your Lordship." Christine replaced the locket. She clutched her paper tighter. "I am doing an inventory. I thought this room was unoccupied."

He shifted, obviously unconcerned that the sheet draping his hips slipped lower. "An inventory? For what purpose?"

Christine found it difficult to converse with a man about to expose himself. She seemed to be holding her breath, waiting for him to display more than a decent woman should care to view.

"Perhaps we should discuss this at a more appropriate meeting." She turned toward the door. Salvation loomed before her one moment. Then her exit became blocked the next. She gasped at his lack of modesty, knowing full well he stood before her naked.

"Have you no shame?" she ground out, keeping her gaze locked on his face.

For a moment, confusion clouded his dark eyes. He glanced down, and it took all of Christine's willpower not to do the same.

"I suppose not," he replied, his tone as casual as if he were fully clothed. "You are no innocent, Christine. I don't imagine I have anything your lover doesn't have." He smiled. "Maybe more of it." Then he frowned. "Or less."

She would not discuss the male anatomy with him. Certainly, she knew there were differences between men and women, but even though she often tended the sick, she had remained somewhat sheltered regarding the matter.

"I don't care to make comparisons, your lordship," she said. "Now, if you will excuse me . . ."

"You have permission to call me Gavin," he offered, but did not move from her path. "Under the circumstances, addressing me otherwise seems ridiculous."

The whole situation was ridiculous, and grating sorely upon Christine's nerves. She'd been a virtual prisoner in her own room for the past three days. Now she found herself a prisoner in her husband's lair.

And her current circumstances were much more dangerous. If he took a sudden notion to consummate their marriage, the battle was half over. All he need do was rip her modest morning gown from her body and ravish her. No one would come to her aid. Not his servants, and to be sure, not the frightened Tillie.

Her screams would fall upon deaf ears as the master of the house subdued her, forced his disgustingly skilled kisses upon her, and did Lord knows what else. Christine's knees suddenly felt weak, the room, with its cozy fire blazing in the hearth, much too warm. She swayed, steadied by the same strong hands she'd a moment ago imagined defiling her.

"Are you going to faint again?" he asked. His dark brows furrowed. "For an admitted adulteress, you have a prudishness about you, Christine." His gaze roamed her face. "And an innocence. An irresistible innocence."

The room grew hotter. Christine refused to succumb to the vapors, however, for he was right. Virtue was a blessing in a bride, and she intended to show nothing of the sort. If innocence held any appeal for him, she would pretend as if she possessed none. Of course, how to convince him of that eluded her for the moment . . . but only for a brief moment.

The soft glow of the fire reflected in his eyes, and she had to admit he was indecently handsome. That she felt in jeopardy of succumbing to his charms, when they were all clearly physical ones, greatly upset her. She refused to be that shallow, or to give him the satisfaction of flustering her.

Summoning her courage, she allowed her gaze to slide down his body in what she hoped appeared to be a casual manner. She tried not to swallow loudly at the sight of his broad chest. Nor to marvel at how smooth and warm his skin looked in the firelight. Lower her gaze traveled, impressed by the rock-hard flatness of his stomach. His hips did not flare slightly as did hers, but seemed merely an extension of sleek, muscled flesh.

Christine supposed that to fully convince him she lacked morals, she must force herself to continue her survey. Distasteful as she found the task, she willed her gaze lower. Her sharp intake of breath startled even her. Face burning, her gaze shot back up to his face.

"I take it, by the roundness of your eyes, more seems to be the case rather than less," he said.

Beads of moisture popped out on her forehead. The earlier weakness in her knees spread to her entire body. She could not faint. And since he still blocked the door, she could not run, which was the stronger of the two inclinations. That left her only one option. To act unimpressed by what she'd just seen.

She shrugged. "More or less makes no difference to me, Your Lordship."

He laughed, his teeth flashing white against the dark contrast of his skin. "A dishonest claim of most unfortunate women who find themselves stuck with the latter. Are you curious as to what you've been missing?"

His dark eyes glittered with an elusive promise she could not grasp. The warmth from his body spread to hers, and she found herself staring at his mouth. Was this the seduction she feared? The dark magic he would work upon her?

Oh, aye, she mentally answered herself, using Tillie's infectious Cockney accent. "I must go," she whispered, noting the panicked edge to her own voice.

In response, he leaned back against the door. "But you haven't finished your inventory."

"I have seen quite enough," she countered before considering her words. "I-I mean, it can wait."

"Not too long, I think." He shrugged away from the door. "You haven't told me why you're taking inventory of my home."

She could breathe again. The door stood clear, but Christine suppressed a desire to scamper from his lair like a frightened rabbit.

"I would think it obvious. I need a full accounting of what will shortly belong to me, or I should say, the poor souls who will benefit from our annulment."

"I have told you more than once, there will be no annulment, Christine."

Gone was the seductive warmth from his voice. She stole a glance at him, relieved to find he'd donned a pair of trousers. In the process of searching for a shirt, he paused to look at her.

"And I don't believe for one moment a poor orphan girl would give up a nice fat allowance just to marry a man of her choice. Probably a poor one at that. What are your real plans? A hefty bribe to convince a member of Parliament to glance the other way while you and your lover strip my estates of all valuables before they are put on the auction block?"

What a horrible opinion he had of her, which infuriated Christine. The man did not know her at all. She marched toward him, hands clenched at her sides.

"How dare you pass judgment upon me! Because you are callous, calculating, and obviously eaten up with greed, you expect all others to be as unprincipled as you are!"

He smiled. "Now who is making assumptions, dear wife?"

She loathed his mocking endearment. "I have not developed my opinion of you without cause. I have read of your scandalous behavior. I have seen with my own eyes how you've squandered your father's wealth on trinkets and expensive chamber pots. I have had the misfortune of meeting your latest mistress!"

He lifted a discarded shirt from the floor, studied the garment, then threw it back down. "What is your point?"

His casual attitude further angered her. "You know nothing of me, have not taken the time to learn who I am or what is important to me, yet you have concluded I am nothing more than a thief."

Gavin stared at her for a moment, then closed the space between them. "I have not encountered an orphan in all of London who was not intent upon picking my pocket. Why should I believe you are any different? I have not met one person in my life whose very existence did not revolve around their own selfish needs and wants. Why should I believe you are any different?"

He gently brushed a stray lock of hair from her cheek. "Tell me you are more than only a beautiful woman out for her own selfish gain. Tell me you possess the courage of a saint and, the rarest of qualities, a truly selfless nature. Tell me that, and I will give you my heart here and now."

Good Lord, she didn't want his heart. And she didn't welcome the squeezing sensation in her chest at the sincerity reflected in his eyes. He wanted to believe, in her, or perhaps merely in someone or something. How had he become so cynical about his own society? Worse than any seduction of her body, he had reached deep inside her and tugged at the strings of her own heart, using perhaps her greatest gift, that of compassion, to disarm her.

In the silence that ticked past, she realized that what he asked of her was the simplest of confessions. For it would be true, and giving it would damn her cause forever. She could not be that rarest of jewels he sought, that one selfless soul who might change his opinion of a whole race.

For she was selfish, selfish to serve, to ease the plight of those less fortunate, and the man before her had to be sacrificed for the good of all.

"I cannot tell you what you want to hear," she said. "Believe of me what you wish."

Until she saw it flicker and die, she hadn't realized his gaze reflected a tiny ray of hope. In its place, boredom and cynicism returned. And perhaps a little relief that the world as he knew it had not changed. That he would not be forced to change, as well.

"Then I wish to believe you want me to do this."

Gavin's arms suddenly went round her, pulling her close. His lips settled over hers before Christine had time to react. They were warm, like the heat rising from his half-naked torso. And firm. And insistent. The piece of paper clutched in her hand floated to the floor as she raised her fists to ward him off. But instead of pounding at his flesh, her palms slid up his smooth chest and rested there, feeling the strong beat of his heart.

He slanted his mouth over hers and delved deeper, caressing her with his tongue until she responded. Responded as if she'd been kissed a hundred times by this man, her husband, a stranger. The last thought helped her regain her senses. Christine pulled away from him and backed toward the door.

"I said believe what you wish, but know for certain I never want you to touch me again."

The heat was back in his eyes. He smiled slightly. "I only know one thing for certain, Christine. You may or may not be a thief, but from what you lips just told me, you are certainly a liar."

Chapter Six

Gavin tried to concentrate on his shipping receipts. Thoughts of Christine plagued his mind. She was odd. That was the only solid conclusion about her he had settled upon. His wife had flirted outrageously with other men the night he first saw her at the duke and duchess's gala. She had admitted to having a lover, and yet, when he'd kissed her, he'd sworn her lips were innocent.

And her clothing. By God, he gave her enough of an allowance to outfit herself in more than modest apparel. Frugal? Could he have actually found a woman not set on filling her wardrobe with more frills than she could possibly ever wear?

"Your mind is not on your work, cousin. You've been staring at the same receipt for more than an hour."

He glanced across the room to where his cousin, William Hamstead, sat. "Have I?" he remarked casually, then tried harder to decipher the invoice.

William laughed. "When are you going to tell me about her?"

Gavin shrugged. "I assume you refer to my wife, and there is little to tell."

A chair scraped as William rose from behind his desk. "If you are not talking, others are. It's been rumored you've locked her in a room and refuse to let her out. It has even been suggested you've turned your pretty wife into a love slave. Chained her to the bed and—"

"Oh, enough." Gavin slammed the receipt down. "She is perfectly free to do whatever she chooses. As long as she is properly chaperoned," he added.

His cousin snorted. "By one of those thugs you have posted outside of the house? Your attitude toward the woman is, well, embarrassing to say the least. What next? Will you demand she wear a chastity belt when she ventures outside?"

Lifting a brow, Gavin considered the possibility for a moment before snatching the same receipt again. "There is nothing wrong with ensuring my wife has protection while I'm away from home."

William walked to Gavin's desk. "Protection from whom? And if you are so worried about her, why have you been spending your nights in this cramped office? I'd think if you wanted her spied upon, you'd save the family from further embarrassment and do the job yourself."

Gavin ran a hand through his hair, replaced the receipt and stood, stretching his stiff muscles. "I have a business to run. A life to lead. I don't have time to follow my wife around making sure she doesn't shame me at every turn. Besides, I imagine she'll grow weary of her stay in London shortly and return to Greenhaven."

"I don't see why you didn't simply have her dragged back to the estate if that is where you want her to be," William said. "Instead, you allow her to take up residence in your home, then spend your nights sleeping in a chair in your office. Why don't you simply go home well after

81

the clubs have closed if you don't wish to spend time with her?"

"I tried that once," Gavin admitted, recalling all too well the feel of Christine in his arms, the sweetness of her lips, and the hunger her response stirred in him. "The house no longer seems like my own." He walked from behind his desk to stand at a small window overlooking the docks. "I can smell her from down the hall. A hauntingly sweet fragrance that is hers alone."

Silence followed. Then William said, "Good God, man, you act as if you're smitten with her." He joined him next to the window. "Worse than smitten, I think you're bloody afraid of her."

Gavin automatically straightened, his stance defensive. "Don't be ridiculous, William. Why would I be afraid of any woman?"

His cousin eyed him curiously. "Perhaps because your wife is not just any woman. Is she as beautiful as they say?"

Gavin swept past him, returning to his desk to shuffle the stacks of receipts awaiting his attention. "I've known many beautiful women."

William would not be put off. He rejoined Gavin at his desk. "Then, she is." He paused as if searching for the right words. "She suits you well in the bedchamber?"

The question surprised Gavin. His cousin did not share his dark reputation. William did not drink, did not gamble, and as far as Gavin knew, did not involve himself with women.

"I wouldn't know," Gavin mumbled, pretending an interest in an old invoice he'd settled months before.

"Ahhh," William drawled. "And therein lies the problem. What cannot be had is always the most desired prize." He frowned. "You must be slipping, cousin."

To be pitied by William did not improve Gavin's foul mood. "I have not paid the matter much attention," he said casually. "And besides, she has a lover."

William's dark brows shot up. "Then the two of you are well matched. I should think the situation would suit you well. If your wife is pleasantly occupied, it gives you leave to carry on in the manner to which you are accustomed."

"Right," Gavin agreed. "But there is a problem." He slumped down into his chair. Rarely did he find a need to confide in anyone, or to unburden himself of his troubles, but William was his cousin, and therefore, a man he trusted without question. Whatever he told him would not go beyond the office.

"She wants an annulment," Gavin said flatly.

William appeared momentarily shocked by his admission. He slid into a chair on the opposite side of Gavin's desk. He sat there for a moment before his eyes brightened.

"Well, that's perfect then, isn't it? You didn't want to be strapped with a wife, and now she's given you a way out. I've never understood why your father forced you to marry a woman so obviously unsuitable in the first place."

Although William did not travel in the same circles as Gavin, being the poorer relation on his mother's side, he had managed to become as snobbish as his wealthier cousin. "Because he hated me," he answered. "The marriage was one of his sick ideas of a joke. A way to taunt me even in death."

Fussing with his neck tie, William said, "I certainly never knew him, being on the wrong side of the family. If not for your good graces, my mother and I would have been reduced to beggars after your mother's death."

"You did not miss anything by not knowing him," Gavin offered dryly.

William leaned forward in his chair. "And what is the problem concerning an annulment?"

"The will," Gavin sighed. "The late marquis's will

states that not only did I have to marry the girl, but if the marriage were to be dissolved, I must forfeit the portion of the estates and wealth left to me to charity."

His cousin's eyes widened. "Give up Greenhaven? That's preposterous." William took a moment to digest the information, then his gaze slid slyly to Gavin. "And what of your wife? Did your late father leave stipulations for her in the will if the marriage were to be dissolved?"

Gavin shook his head. "I'm sure the bastard didn't give a damn what happened to her in case of an annulment."

"But then, he would have known you would never give up your title and property," William pointed out. "He had no need to feel concern over your wife's future."

"I suppose," Gavin agreed.

Rubbing his chin thoughtfully, William said, "So you cannot dissolve the marriage." He shrugged. "I guess you must make the most of it. Let her have her lover and go on with your life. I don't see the problem."

"*She* is the problem," Gavin explained. "Christine must have figured out a way to get her hands on some of the money, or she wouldn't want an annulment. I'm positive she thinks to set herself and her secret lover up comfortably. Otherwise, I can't see why she'd want an annulment."

"Maybe she's daft enough to honestly love the man," William offered. "Perhaps that is enough for her."

Gavin considered his cousin's explanation for a full five seconds. "Don't be daft yourself, William. No one throws away a fortune for the sole sake of love. Christine may be an orphan, her beauty extraordinary, and her background less than appealing, but she is not an idiot."

William frowned. "I have never heard a woman complimented in quite that fashion before, cousin." He steepled his fingers over the bridge of his nose. "So, in short, your new wife is a greedy opportunist out to steal your fortune and see herself comfortably settled with the man of her choice."

Rising to return to the window, Gavin said, "So it would seem. Yet . . ."

"Yet?" William prompted.

Gavin had no idea why he felt a need to defend Christine, for the need confused him as much as the woman. "Yet she does not seem greedy. You've sent her the generous allowance I advocated over these past two years, haven't you?"

"Of course I have, Your Lordship," William blustered. "I have taken on the responsibility of Greenhaven by your command, and if you believe I'm not running the estate admirably—"

"I did not say that," Gavin interrupted, turning to his cousin. "I am thankful to let you run an estate I feel no attachment to, but Christine dresses in a manner that leads me to believe she is still poor. Odd that she doesn't flaunt her new status with expensive clothing."

"I'd say her sense in the matter is a great asset in a wife," William commented. "Maybe she isn't greedy. Perhaps her lover is the one spurring her to steal your fortune."

Gavin's dark mood grew darker. "Greedy and a coward. Not once has he tried to contact Christine during the past week."

William sighed. "Then the man is obviously no idiot, either. Your abilities with a sword and pistol are not well-kept secrets, cousin. Nor would any fool try to approach her with your henchmen stationed all around the house. If you truly want to discover who her lover is, give her enough rope to hang herself."

It wasn't a bad idea. If Gavin could discover the man's identity, and either run him off or pay him off, she would have no reason to want an annulment. Christine would return to the country, and he could return to his former style of life.

"What do you suggest?"

Raising his hands, William said, "I want no part of plotting your personal life . . . but perhaps a shopping outing to begin with. You did say she needed proper attire befitting her station. If you intend on giving her free rein, you don't want her roaming London dressed like a beggar."

"A shopping outing is innocent enough," Gavin agreed. "But she should have a chaperon."

"You could use a bit of air," William hinted. "Why not take her yourself?"

Gavin considered the suggestion for a moment, then quickly dismissed it. "I cannot take her. Her lover would not approach while she's in my company. No, I need someone I can trust, someone who would be considered a proper escort in society's eyes, yet a person her lover would not find threatening."

"Hmm," William mumbled. "I can't think of anyone who meets your criteria."

A smile broke out on Gavin's lips. "I can."

"Are they still out there, m'lady?"

Christine turned from the window. "I'm afraid they are, Tillie." She took up her pacing, which had very nearly worn a place in the carpet. "If Gavin is trying to break me, he is going about it quite admirably. I cannot stand this room or this house a minute longer!"

"It's fresh air and activity you be needing," Tillie informed her, settled back against the settee, popping iced cakes into her mouth as if there were no tomorrow.

"I know that," Christine snapped. "But I can't very well go out with those ruffians guarding the house."

The maid shrugged. "Then sit with me and have one of these delicious cakes. It will help pass the time."

"Eating has become too much of a pastime with you, Tillie," Christine said. "You're straining the buttons on your gown."

Iced cake poised halfway to her mouth, Tillie lowered her gaze to the waistline of her gown. She immediately replaced the cake on the tray. "But there's not much fun to be had but to make that sourpuss Mr. Graves run up and down the stairs with requests for more food."

Christine couldn't help but smile. Tillie had developed a fondness for aggravating the stuffy head servant. "We are not here to have fun," Christine reminded her. "And it is past time to put my plan into motion. If I must walk around the city with my husband's henchmen on my heels, so be it. Grab your bonnet and a light wrap, Tillie. We're going out. Gavin will not have his way with me any longer."

"Gavin, is it now?" Tillie lifted a brow.

"It is his name," Christine said defensively, flustered that she had referred to him in so personal a manner.

Tillie rolled off the settee. "Aye, it is, but I've never heard it said in such a soft, breathless kind of voice. Which 'way' were you referring to, m'lady?"

Heat crept into Christine's cheeks. She should have chosen her words more wisely. "I meant he will no longer hold me prisoner in this room," she explained. "Now, be quick, Tillie, before I lose my nerve."

"Mind that's not all you lose in this house," Tillie called to her as she moved toward the adjoining room.

The maid's warning held little weight with Christine. She certainly was in no danger of losing anything precious under His Lordship's roof. Except her freedom. So what if she'd foolishly responded to his kiss the other morning? She was only human. Not a saint, after all. And she hadn't been lying in the least when she'd told him she never wanted him to touch her again.

If she wanted to borrow that kind of trouble, she might

as well travel to some remote island and throw herself into a volcano. The comparison—Gavin's kisses, and flames licking at her body—suddenly disturbed her.

"The flames of eternal damnation," she muttered, then walked to her bureau mirror. Christine wasn't one to waste time with fancy coiffures. Her hair hung loose around her shoulders. She pulled it back with a ribbon, frowning at the inevitable curls that escaped to frame her face.

"A bonnet will help," she told her reflection. A moment later, she realized there was little help to be had concerning her morning gown. She had stitched the gown herself, using what she considered practical material. She looked like a street vendor. Not at all like a grand lady bent on creating a scandal.

"I'll wear a cape," she decided, but knew the only capes she owned were of the same practical quality as her gowns. She was tempted to fetch the indecent gown she'd worn to the gala from the wardrobe, but realized wearing it in broad daylight would be more of an embarrassment than setting out on the town dressed like a beggar.

"All ready, m'lady," Tillie chirped, entering the bedchamber. She drew up short. "What's that miserable face you're wearing?"

Christine blinked back tears. "Look at me, Tillie. If I go out dressed this way, it is me who will be the laughingstock, not His Lordship."

"Then we will shop. You mustn't think of it as a waste, but as a means to an end. If you're going to shame His Lordship by having one scandalous affair after another, you must look your best."

Good heavens, how horrible her plans sounded when spewed from the mouth of another. "I don't really intend to have scandalous affairs, Tillie. Only to seem as if I am."

The maid shrugged. "Makes no difference. You still

have to display your charms to their best advantage. There are many beautiful women in London during the season. To be noticed, you must outshine them all."

Christine walked to the bed and collapsed. She buried her face in her hands. "Impossible," she whispered. "I need a small miracle. A guardian angel to intervene on my pitiful behalf."

A soft rap sounded at the door. Christine glanced up abruptly, her and Tillie's gazes locking. When Mr. Graves asked permission to enter, she sighed, disappointed her prayers had not be answered. The servant had probably come to fetch their dishes from mid-morning tea.

After the servant entered, it surprised her when he said, "You have a caller downstairs."

"Me?" Christine asked. She knew it was a silly question when Mr. Graves rolled his gaze heavenward.

"Mr. William Hamstead," he provided. "His Lordship's cousin."

"A relative?" she asked. "Here to see me?"

"That is what I said," Mr. Graves answered stiffly. "Would you like me to ask him to wait while you make yourself presentable?"

Glancing down at herself, Christine said, "I'm afraid this is as presentable as I get, Mr. Graves."

She couldn't swear to it, but she thought the servant's lips almost turned up in a smile. "I will see Mr. Hamstead settled in the main parlor. It is proper to make an unexpected caller wait for a short while," he added.

"Oh," Christine responded. She had intended to follow the head servant downstairs. "Thank you, Mr. Graves, for calling the matter to my attention."

He bowed, and for the first time, she did not think it a mocking gesture. Mr. Graves gathered the remains of earlier tea, frowning at Tillie over the amount of iced cakes missing from the silver tray. Just to annoy the man, Christine imagined, the maid snatched another cake and popped it into her mouth. To Christine's surprise, and no doubt Tillie's as well, Mr. Graves merely smiled at the maid before he quit the room.

"What's gotten into him?" Tillie asked, her mouth full.

"I can't be certain, but it seems as if our stuffy Mr. Graves has softened toward us."

"Toward you maybe," Tillie snorted. "I can't have him being all polite to me. What's the fun in that?"

"We have both been idle for too long," Christine said. "And you have become too fond of annoying poor Mr. Graves. Help me pass the time while we foolishly make my caller wait."

"I could pin that wild hair of yours up," Tillie offered. "It might detract from the commonness of your gown."

At times, Christine questioned her insistence that the servants at Greenhaven look upon her as their equal. Tillie could be blunt to a fault. "I suppose it would be something to do," Christine said with a sigh. "Although having a fancy coiffeur will probably only call more attention to the commonness of my clothing."

She walked to the chair Tillie pulled up before the bureau mirror and seated herself. "His Lordship's cousin will take one look at me and find me pitiful. An embarrassment to the family."

Another curious glance from Tillie had Christine wondering why being an embarrassment to Gavin would bother her in the least. She'd come to London with the plan to embarrass him, shame him.

"Leave it, Tillie," she instructed. "I'm going downstairs."

"But Mr. Graves said it wasn't proper not to make the gentleman wait, m'lady," the maid reminded her.

Christine smiled sweetly. "I don't intend on being proper, remember?"

Chapter Seven

Despite her decision to give her appearance little consideration, Christine unconsciously smoothed the wrinkles from her gown as she entered the main parlor. The man stood staring out of a window, his back to her. He was tall like his cousin, with dark brown hair. Although he was about the same height as Gavin, William Hamstead's build appeared noticeably thinner.

His manner of dress did not mark him as a nobleman, but as a businessman. She suddenly realized why his name sounded familiar. He signed the drafts sent to her at Greenhaven. Christine squared her shoulders and walked toward him.

"Mr. Hamstead?"

He turned, a slightly annoyed expression marring his plain features. As his hazel gaze met hers, the wrinkles in his forehead disappeared. The tight line of his lips softened, parting when he sucked in his breath sharply. Christine wanted to run back upstairs.

"Oh, dear, you *are* beautiful," he whispered; and she

thought he sounded somewhat distressed by the discovery. He straightened. "Forgive my unguarded response. I've just made a total ass of myself."

Christine smiled. "You have not," she assured him. "You have complimented me when I deserve little praise." She glanced down at her gown. "I am quite unpresentable."

"I'm afraid yours is the rarest of beauty," he said, and again, he sounded less than pleased. "That which could not even be hidden beneath a burlap bag."

Supposing he had in fact, flattered her, she said, "You are too kind."

William Hamstead's gaze narrowed for a moment. "And humble in the bargain." He reached out and lifted her chin. "Does my cousin realize what a rare find has landed in his lap? I think not."

Hamstead's form of strange flattery made Christine nervous. She pulled away from him and walked to a cluttered desk, fondling a trinket resting there. "If I failed to see a resemblance between you and my husband at first glance, I see it now."

"You mustn't misinterpret my intentions." William approached her. "Forgive my forwardness. Unlike my cousin, I'm not practiced at complimenting beautiful women. I fear I've made you uncomfortable, when all I desire is for us to be friends."

When she met his gaze, sincerity shone in his eyes. Christine relaxed. "We should begin again." She held out her hand. "I am Christine . . . Norfork."

William took her hand. "I am William Hamstead. Your husband's cousin . . . and now your cousin, as well."

The man's willingness to readily accept her into the family further warmed Christine toward William. "I'm pleased to make your acquaintance, sir."

"No more pleased than I am to make yours, Your Ladyship."

She frowned. "If we're going to be cousins, you must call me Christine."

"Then you must call me William," he countered.

Her frown became a smile. "It is agreed."

They stood there, awkward to have just become cousins and friends. Finally, Christine asked, "To what do I owe the pleasure of your visit, William?"

"I have come to escort you on a shopping expedition."

When his gaze lowered to her gown, she felt embarrassed all over again. Why hadn't she thought to purchase more suitable clothing before venturing to London? Because she hadn't planned on staying long, she answered herself. And because her allowance was much better spent on those in need.

"My husband sent you," Christine predicted. "I am an embarrassment to him."

William looked away from her, which was answer enough. She straightened her shoulders.

"I have never been one to covet fancy trappings, and I care not if I am an displeasing to my husband. You may return to your cousin and tell him I said so."

A gleam of something close to admiration entered William's eyes. "There is spirit in you to match your beauty. As I've already said, Gavin is a very lucky man. A pity he is unaware of the fact."

"You mustn't tell him," she whispered.

William smiled. "Rest assured, dear cousin, my lips are sealed. Unspoiled, however, is not a word usually associated with the women who move in Gavin's circle. If you are determined to mask your admirable traits, you must act as flighty and frivolous as the rest of the flock."

She tilted her head to one side. "I don't imagine it would please His Lordship if I spent a great deal of his money on a feminine whim to empty every shop in London."

"No, I don't imagine it would."

Christine's spirits lifted. She had been given an opportunity to put her plans into motion. "We will shop," she announced. "I shall fetch my wrap . . . and my maid. Tillie is not suitably outfitted, either. Not for a servant befitting her station."

William walked over and pulled the bell cord. Mr. Graves appeared immediately. "We shall need a coach and a driver," he ordered.

Staring haughtily down at the man, Mr. Graves asked, "Open-air or closed, sir?"

Her husband's cousin eyed Christine's simple gown again. "Closed," he decided.

Gavin paced the main parlor, cursing the room's stylishly cluttered interior. He could scarcely walk without bumping into a desk, a settee, or yet another desk. What had he been thinking when he allowed William Morris to decorate the entire house? He'd been thinking better someone else be bothered with the nonsense than himself.

The cost had been staggering, but Gavin was determined that his home would display a degree of taste and warmth. Unlike the cold, sparsely furnished rooms at Greenhaven, his childhood home. The country estate had not always been a lifeless, dreary place.

Before his mother's death, he recalled laughter and warmth there. Bright colors and expensive furnishings. At the age of five, his world had come crashing down around him.

His mother had died in a carriage accident. She had been killed while trying to escape with her lover. Even at so tender an age, Gavin had not been spared the sordid details by the late marquis. Nor had the man failed to mention that the heartless whore had not loved her son enough to take him with her.

Then the lowest blow. Gavin had learned he wasn't who he believed himself to be. Not the adored only son of a titled gentleman, but the bastard child of his mother's lover. A groomsman, no less.

His mother had destroyed both of their lives to satisfy her own selfish needs. The sins of the flesh. She would have willingly traded a life of luxury for one of misery, and all for the sake of the passion she found in a commoner's arms. Gavin walked to a desk and poured himself a snifter of brandy.

After his mother's death, the marquis had disposed of all in the house she had purchased. The warmth had fled with her passing, and all that remained was the emptiness of a home destroyed, and a man turned bitter by his wife's betrayal.

Lifting the snifter to his lips, Gavin threw back his head and downed the contents, hoping it would chase the chill of his memories away. The late marquis would not add further shame to his name by disinheriting Gavin.

On the contrary, in everyone else's eyes he'd remained the doting father. But Gavin's life had become a living hell. The marquis never forgave his mother, never forgave *him*, and the terms of the will had not really surprised him.

By demanding he marry an orphan, a common girl, the old man had found a way to constantly remind Gavin of his true heritage, of what he deserved in life rather than what he'd been given. Gavin had learned to wear snobbery well, as if by pretending his blood was bluer than most, he might someday come to believe it.

He held tight to his social standing, because he could not bear to have it taken from him. Could not stand to be what the man who'd bitterly raised him and claimed his as his own had told him he was often enough. Nothing. Not even worthy of a common father's love.

"The kitchen staff wishes to know if they may serve supper, Your Lordship?"

He turned. Mr. Graves stood in the doorway. It was

growing late. Where in the hell was his wife? He'd decided after his cousin's departure that he would not spend another night in his cramped office. Afraid of Christine? It had been a ridiculous accusation. And it made more sense, if he wanted her to scurry back to the country where she belonged, for Gavin to force his unwanted presence onto her as often as possible.

He would not be charming, or entertaining. She would soon grow bored and take her leave. Mr. Graves cleared his throat softly, as if to remind him of the question.

"Tell them to begin," Gavin answered. He met his head servant in the doorway and handed him his empty glass. "I will not wait supper on my wife."

"Very good, Your Lordship," Mr. Graves responded, walking into the hallway with his employer.

Both men were moving toward the dining room when the front door burst open. Christine stumbled inside, holding several hat boxes, her sweet laughter filling the house. William followed her, his arms loaded down with boxes.

Gavin's gaze widened when Christine's maid entered, her arms stacked with boxes, only to be followed by James Dumont and Chester Thorton, both straining with more boxes.

Good God, had she bought out every shop in London? The sight of so many purchases did not annoy him nearly as much as the pretty flush on Christine's cheeks, the dancing lights in her eyes. She seldom laughed in his company.

What really galled him was the fact that not one person in the cheerful party had even noticed him standing in the hall. William, James, and Chester were all staring at Christine as if she were the first and only woman in the world.

Mr. Graves cleared his throat again. And not as subtly as he had a moment earlier. All faces swung toward them. Gavin hadn't realized how much he enjoyed Christine's smile until he saw it fade from her lips. The pretty flush in her cheeks disappeared.

"Gavin, old boy," Chester blustered. "We weren't expecting to see you."

Gavin purposely lifted a dark brow. "This is my home, is it not?"

James, always the braver of the two, stepped forward, awkwardly trying to juggle his armload. "It has been rumored of late you spend very little time here. Since Chester and I have not had the pleasure of playing cards with you, we assumed you had become otherwise distracted."

By a woman, Gavin mentally added, completing the thought. It almost embarrassed him to realize he hadn't given another woman a thought since Christine had intruded upon his life.

"Place the boxes on the floor. Mr. Graves, send someone to take them upstairs," he instructed.

The servant responded more quickly than the rest of the group. "Shall I set more places for supper, Your Lordship?"

Gavin ran a cool glance over James, Chester, and his cousin. "I'm sure they all have more pressing pursuits."

Wisely receiving their cue to depart, the three men placed their burdens on the floor. Mr. Graves hurried off to do as instructed. William, Gavin noted, appeared rather smug.

Whatever his cousin had to relate in the way of suspicious activity during the shopping trip would have to wait until the morrow. Chester tried to slink through the open front door in his usual spineless manner, but James grabbed his friend's coat.

"Chester and I have learned some most distressing news." He wet his lips, a telltale sign that he was not as brave as he pretended. "It seems your enchanting wife has never seen an opera. We've invited her to be our guest next Thursday evening. Of course, with you along as well," he quickly added.

"Of course," Gavin drawled. "But as you know, James, I have private seats at the opera. If Christine wishes to go, I will accompany her. Perhaps we will see you there."

James cocked his head. He quickly bowed to Christine before beating a hasty retreat, Chester's coat still clutched in his hands.

William stood alone. "Will there be anything else, Your Lordship?"

Gavin walked forward to place a hearty slap upon William's shoulder. "Cousin, you only address me formally when you're nervous. I trust today's outing went well?"

William's gaze slid toward the many packages stacked on the floor. "Very well, indeed," he answered quietly.

"You may tell me all about it at the office tomorrow. I'll see you bright and early." He gave William's shoulder a squeeze and steered him toward the door.

"William." Christine's soft voice halted them. She stepped forward and offered his cousin her hand. "Thank you for a wonderful afternoon."

His cousin stared at her hand for a moment, glanced defiantly at Gavin, then took it. "Thank you, Christine." He turned to Gavin. "Your wife is a breath of fresh air."

"Breathe somewhere else," Gavin countered softly. "Good night, cousin."

He'd barely gotten William out and closed the door when he heard the shuffle of feet. He turned to see Christine's shy maid reach the landing at the top of the stairs and disappear. She must have taken them two at a time. Christine was slower, and had only made it a few steps.

"Where are you going, m'lady?" Gavin asked.

She turned to face him. "I have had a long day, Your Lordship. I'm tired and wish to retire to my room."

Gavin glanced at the boxes. "Surely, with all the shopping you have accomplished, you are famished as well."

He moved to the stairs and held out his arm. "Join me for supper."

It was not a question, or a mere request, Christine realized. It was an order. She didn't care to be ordered about by Gavin Norfork, or to be frightened by him.

"I will not be cowed as easily as your friends. I was appalled by your rude behavior toward them and must question which of us is in most need of lessons concerning manners."

A set-down was obviously the last thing he expected from her. It did her racing heart good to see the cocky twist to his lips become a straight line of aggravation.

"A married woman does not traipse all over London in the company of unmarried men."

"William is unmarried," she quipped, lifting her chin even higher. "I believe it was by your instruction that he accompanied me."

"My cousin is related to you by marriage, which is perfectly acceptable."

"Well, your treatment of me during the past week is not!"

She hadn't meant to raise her voice. Christine vowed when next she saw her husband, he would find her cold and unresponsive. A contradiction to the woman he'd kissed indecently in his bedchamber the morning she'd ventured into his lair.

"Posting ruffians outside the house was embarrassing, to the both of us, I would think," she said more calmly.

"True," he surprised her by admitting. "Give me your word you will not shame me by inviting your lover into my home, and I will give you mine I will not embarrass you in that fashion again."

His wasn't much of a condition. No loss at all, really. She had no lover to sneak into her room. Still, it irked her to surrender anything to him. "Only if you will give me yours you will not entertain women beneath this roof."

"Not ever?" he asked incredulously.

Ignoring a slight sting of jealousy, and choosing instead to label it as indignation, she answered, "Not as long as I am in residence here."

The length of time he gave the matter thought also irritated her. Finally, he shrugged. "Agreed."

There seemed nothing else to say to one another. Christine started to turn away, but his hand settled upon her arm. She felt the warmth of his fingers through the thin sleeve of her newly purchased gown.

"Will you dine with me?"

His eyes were so devilishly black. But not cold. Even when his voice could chill her to the bone, the heat in his gaze remained.

"Perhaps another time," she said. "I am not hungry."

Slowly, his fingers slid from her arm. He smiled. "Then I shall dine alone. But once I've finished, I would like to see the purchases you made today."

Shame flooded her. She had spent a small fortune in the space of one afternoon. And she had done so deliberately, and maliciously, for the sake of revenge. She might lie to herself and say she'd done so to further her plans, to make herself undesirable as a wife, but she'd done it to even the score. To punish Gavin for kissing her, for posting guards around the house, for refusing to bend to her will.

"The boxes are there." She indicated the pile of packages. "You are welcome to go through them."

His smile broadened. "You don't understand. I want to see you in your new things."

A lump formed in her throat. "See me in them?"

His smile melted away. If his eyes refused to reflect coldness, they could reflect hardness. "I want to make certain all of your purchases were necessary, or at the least becoming to you. If not, I will send them back."

Christine swallowed the lump in her throat. "Very well," she said.

He turned toward the dining room. "I shall retire to my room after supper. You may join me there."

His room? If she hadn't been so defiant about dining with him, all she might have been forced to do was sit through a meal with Gavin. But the horrible truth was that she was starving. Now she would have to reenter his room. Be alone with him in so intimate a setting. If there *were* any food in her stomach, she feared she'd lose it.

Chapter Eight

Christine knew Gavin had retired to his room. She heard him banging around clear down the hallway. Her hand shook slightly as she smoothed a stray curl from her temple. Then she pinched her cheeks to add color to her pale face. She shouldn't have refused supper. The shaky, weak feeling stealing over her might be a result of hunger, but more probably, it stemmed from nervousness.

Tillie had laid all her new gowns across the bed. At the moment, Christine wore a bright yellow morning dress made of silk. The high neck and loose sleeves, with delicate lace under the sleeves, suited her well, and the color complemented her complexion, but the dress alone would have cost her half a month's allowance.

It seemed as if Gavin had an account with every shop in London, and William had assured her it was proper for her to charge the purchases to him. She had done so gladly, but now wished she hadn't been so free with her husband's money. William had practically goaded her into spending more than she really thought necessary.

"I'm thinking you'd best join His Lordship before he comes barging in here." Tillie glanced nervously toward the door. "He's made enough racket to wake the dead to let us know he's waiting."

Christine turned from the mirror with a sigh. "Fetch me the cap that goes with this gown, Tillie. And the little silk cape, as well."

The cape wasn't a necessity, but it did complement the dress. She hadn't been warmly greeted when she and William entered the first shop. The clerk had taken one look at her and turned up her nose.

After William explained who she was, and that His Lordship wished her to have a whole new wardrobe, the clerk had thawed considerably. News must have spread, because Christine had been welcomed with open arms into every shop thereafter.

"How do I tell him this isn't even the half of it?" she whispered while Tillie placed the cap on her head. "How do I tell him this is only what fit me or could be altered quickly?"

"You must have evening wear, m'lady," Tillie explained. "Does His Lordship expect ye to wear a morning dress, or a riding habit, to a fancy ball?"

"I don't believe His Lordship planned on me attending any balls," she answered. Tillie settled the cape around her shoulders, and there was nothing left to do but face the consequences of her actions.

Her feet felt leaden as she approached his room. Christine knocked softly on the door, hoping against logic that he wouldn't hear her. When he bade her enter, she took a calming breath, then turned the handle and entered the room.

A fire blazed, adding a cozy glow to the huge room. To her relief, Gavin was not sprawled upon his bed naked, but sat fully clothed in a chair across from the hearth. He had removed his coat, leaving his shirt open at the neck.

In one hand, he held a snifter of brandy. With the other, he motioned her forward.

Dutifully, she went to stand before him. He eyed the gown, not exactly frowning, but not wearing a pleased expression, either.

"Turn around," he instructed.

She felt very self-conscious, parading herself before him, but did as he asked, making a slow turn until she faced him again.

"It will do," was all he said. He took a drink, then lifted a brow when she kept standing there. "You have others to show me, do you not?"

"Y-yes," she stuttered.

"Then be on your way. Judging from the amount of boxes my servants hauled to your room, this will take some time."

Marching from the bedchamber, Christine stomped down the hall to her room. She slammed the door after entering. Tillie jumped.

"Was His Lordship not pleased with your dress?" Tillie ventured.

"It will do," she bit out, moving to the bed to study her purchases. "He barely gave it a once-over."

"Try the riding habit," Tillie suggested. "The dark burgundy velvet sets off your pale skin to perfection."

The maid helped her undress, then dress again. The jaunty slouch hat with a single elegant feather gave Christine an air of sophistication, one she tried to maintain while returning to His Lordship's room.

She did not tremble upon entering the room, nor had she knocked. Head held high, she took up her position before Gavin. Without being asked, she turned slowly, placing her hands on her hips once she faced him again.

"Adequate," he mumbled, taking another sip from his snifter. "Do you ride?"

Christine smiled sweetly at him. "No, Your Lordship. I have never sat a horse."

The evening wore on, draining what little strength Christine had left. Her temper went from a slow boil to a rolling one as outfit after outfit was modeled for her husband, and none of them caused so much as a lift of his brow. Finally, she wore the last purchase, a lovely visiting dress of light gray.

"Although gray is a suitable color for most, it does not become you," Gavin commented. "Still, I guess—"

"It will do," she finished for him. "This is all I brought home," she told him. "I purchased a few things for Tillie, as her wardrobe is unfitting for a maid of her station."

Gavin merely nodded agreement. He didn't act in the least angry. Christine fully intended to displease him, and his unwillingness to oblige her in the matter further angered her.

"I also ordered a few gowns," she said. "Evening wear that had to be special made for me. Quite expensive, I'm afraid."

He shrugged. "I suppose since I told Dumont and Thorton I intend to take you to the opera next Thursday, I must follow through. You'll need something suitable for evening."

She wanted to stamp her foot in frustration. Her spirits sank. Gavin had not acted as if a single purchase she'd made was unnecessary. A thought suddenly occurred to her. A devious thought, but one that would surely receive some sort of reaction from her husband. Gavin had not seen all she'd purchased, after all.

"There is one thing more," she said. "Excuse me while I change."

He showed about as much enthusiasm as if she'd just announced her chamber pot needed to be emptied. His attitude brought more bravery to her spirit than was perhaps wise. Christine left the room, moving with purpose to her own.

"Quick, help me undress, Tillie."

Tillie jumped up from the settee and hurried over. The maid's fingers were swift as she unfastened the buttons down the back of Christine's dress. Quicker still as she pulled the gown down over her shoulders and helped her step from the garment. Christine's bed was still littered with clothing.

"Please hang these clothes in my wardrobe." Christine went to the mirror and removed the pins from her hair. When the unruly curls cascaded over her shoulders and down her back, she ran her fingers through her hair irritably. Setting her jaw, she marched toward the door.

"M'lady?" Tillie asked nervously. "Where are you going?"

"To His Lordship's room."

"B-but you've nothing on but your new underthings," Tillie pointed out.

Christine smiled. "This chemise I'm wearing is the finest silk money can buy. Look at these petticoats. Made from Brussels lace, and these stockings are pure silk. I nearly fainted dead away when I learned the price. The corset is satin, and look at all these silk ribbons. Have you ever seen anything so preposterous? My underthings alone cost more than two morning dresses."

Tillie blinked. "And the point being, m'lady?"

"The point is, why would any woman need to spend a fortune on something no one will see? This is by far the most frivolous purchase I made today, and His Lordship is going to see it!"

"Wait," Tillie warned, but Christine paid the maid no heed. She couldn't wait to see the look on Gavin's face when she told him the cost of her underwear. She couldn't wait to see his complexion darken in anger, or hear him bellow about the money he must fritter away for finery no one would view.

So anxious was she, Christine nearly ran the length of the hall to Gavin's room. She burst through the door and walked to her position before the fire, placing her hands on her hips.

"What do you think of this, Your Lordship?"

In the process of reaching for the brandy decanter, Gavin turned his head to look at her. The decanter toppled over, spilling brandy across his fine mahogany table. He seemed not to notice. Force of habit, Christine guessed, for she scrambled to the floor to mop up the mess.

Only then did she realize she had nothing to soak up the brandy, and that she was kneeling between Gavin's powerful thighs. She glanced up at him, and couldn't call his expression angry, although the sudden heat that flared in his eyes nearly scorched her. His gaze lowered to the neckline of her chemise.

Christine tried to slow her breathing. The tight corset pushed her breasts up to the point where they were nearly exposed above her filmy chemise, and she feared they were dangerously close to spilling out altogether.

Stupid. The word echoed through her head. What had she been thinking to flaunt herself in front of him wearing so little? That the cost alone would blind him to the fact she sat before him nearly naked?

"What new torture is this, Christine?" he asked softly.

She blurted out the first thing that came to mind. "Fifty pounds."

A dark brow lifted, then his gaze settled on her lips. They seemed to part of their own accord, and so did his.

"Have you taken to whoring?"

Christine blinked. Surely she hadn't heard him correctly. "Pardon?" she asked, moistening her lips because they suddenly seemed dry.

Gavin shifted uncomfortably. "Fifty pounds is a lot of

money. But I find myself tempted to pay that much for the sole pleasure of removing what little you're wearing."

Her face grew hot. "Fifty pounds for the underthings," she bit out.

"Agreed." Gavin reached for the silk ribbons tied at the top of her chemise. Christine slapped his hand away.

"You don't understand," she whispered frantically.

He sighed. "You wish to be paid first." Gavin leaned forward and twisted his fingers in her unbound hair. "I must warn you. I can be greedy, too. I intend to get my money's worth."

With frightening clarity, Christine realized that he though she was bartering her flesh, not telling him how much she'd spent on her frilly underclothes. It made her furious that he would think so little of her. That he could believe she would trade her virtue for any price!

"Unhand me this instant," she hissed up at him. "However wealthy and privileged you are, you haven't got enough to buy me. You'll never have enough!"

Rather than release her, he used his hand in her hair to pull her up and closer, his face mere inches from hers.

"What foolish game are you playing, Christine? You flaunt your desirability before me, incite me to lust so raw and uncontrolled I had forgotten what it felt like to really want something badly, or someone. Was this your greedy lover's idea? To whore yourself to put extra money in his pockets? Did you think to go through with it, then decide at the last minute you could not? Why can't you finish what you started? Am I so hideous?"

Her head started to spin. How had her plan to anger him over the price of underwear gone so horribly wrong? He gave her no time to answer. His fingers left her hair, both hands settling upon her shoulders.

Gavin propelled her up to a standing position. Her knees were weak and she swayed, falling against the solid form of his tall frame. Fine as her petticoats were, they could not protect her from the rigid feel of him against her. She lifted startled eyes to his face.

"See where your folly has led? If it was your plan to tempt me beyond sanity, you have been granted your wish." His face lowered to hers. "I must be able to offer something more important to you than your disgust of sharing my bed." His lips brushed hers. "Name it, and it will be yours."

Christine had trouble thinking, The spinning in her head grew worse. Could he not understand she would not sell her body at any price? There was nothing she wanted from him. Except one thing . . . and it would be the only worthy sacrifice for giving him what he wanted. A sacrifice that would benefit many.

"My price is my freedom," she whispered back, amazed that she had found the nerve to put her bargain into words. "The annulment."

The tight line of his jaw became tighter. "That is the only thing I cannot give you, and you know it."

"Then release me," she commanded, amazed at the calmness of her voice when her knees were shaking and her head felt as if it were spinning round and round. "I will give you nothing."

His hands moved from her shoulders to her waist, pulling her closer against him. "You forget one small problem with your plans, wife. It is I who am not honor-bound to purchase your affections. I am your husband. What I want is already mine by right." His lips brushed her neck. Then he sank his teeth softly into her flesh for a moment, soothing the spot with a warm, moist kiss.

The weak feeling in her knees grew worse. Her head felt light. "I do not find you hideous," she said. "In truth, you are as beautiful as a man can be. But what I do find you is much worse than hideous in my eyes. I find you heartless if you would take what is not given willingly."

He flinched as if she'd stabbed him with more than

words. Taking her hand in his, he settled it over his heart. "Can you not feel my heart beating? At this moment, it beats only for you. Yet you would rip it from my chest and throw it at my feet. Which of us, dear wife, is heartless?"

She didn't expect him to release her, and when he did, there was nothing solid to keep her upright. Christine swayed, trying to maintain her balance.

"Go," he said, turning away. "I threatened you out of anger. Whatever I am, hideous or heartless, I am not a man who'd force myself on a woman. Or at least, I don't think I am. Go before you test the strength of my convictions."

Christine was trying to go, to move, but her legs wouldn't work. Darkness began to descend. "I think I'm going to . . ."

"Don't," she heard Gavin warn. But that was all she heard.

Issuing a loud curse, Gavin rushed forward and caught her before she hit the floor. He gathered her up, his gaze automatically fastening upon the ripe mounds of her breasts, practically within sampling range. His gaze strayed toward the bed, the strength of his convictions very much in disagreement with the persistent ache in his loins. With another muttered curse, he moved toward the open doorway.

Christine's slight weight was no burden to him. He carried her easily down the hallway to her own chambers. The door was not open, so he used his booted foot to gain entrance. The maid turned from hanging a gown in the wardrobe. Her eyes widened as he swept into the room. Gavin paid her little heed, moving directly to the bed.

He settled Christine upon the down mattress, then sat beside her, lifting her limp wrist with the intention of rousing her.

"W-what had you done to Chris—Her Ladyship?" Tillie stammered.

Gavin cast the maid a dark glance, noting her hand raised to her throat and the paleness of her pretty features. "Nothing," he answered. "Yet."

The added afterthought surprised even him. It obviously more than befuddled the usually shy maid. She bit her lip, then straightened her spine, venturing a step toward him.

"Ye will not 'arm her over the price of her undergarments, will ye, Your Lordship?"

His brows drew together. "The price of her undergarments?"

"Fifty pounds for such frills may be a lot for some, but not so much very much for you, is it?"

"Fifty pounds was the price of her finery?"

The maid nodded, then began wringing her hands. "She meant to get a rise out you, Your Lordship," she explained.

His mouth twisted sarcastically. "She certainly did."

"Ye had no call to hit her," the maid blurted out, her face flushing, but her stance indicating she meant to defend her mistress should the need arise. "I warned her, but she just went off rushing down the hall to flaunt her purchase in your face. She's not usually like that."

"Like what?" he prompted, curious about exactly what his wife was or wasn't.

The maid opened her mouth, then quickly closed it. Either she'd been about to sing Christine's praises and thought better of it, or she realized her mistress possessed no qualities worth defending.

"I will not harm her," he said. "Seek your own bed."

The hand-wringing grew worse. "I should see to my mistress," she fretted. "I've not yet lit a fire, and the bed's not turned down."

He fixed her with a look that usually received no argument. "I will see to it." When the maid continued to stand there, wringing her hands to the point of distraction,

Gavin sighed. "I did not hit her. She's merely fainted."

"Poor lamb," Tillie gushed. "She said she was starvin'
and neither of us had supper," she complained.

"What is your name again?"

"Tillie," she quickly provided.

"Well, Tillie, why don't you sneak down to the kitchen
and find yourself something to eat. Then I grant you leave
to retire."

Her stomach growled loudly at the mention of food,
but her gaze kept darting between him and her helpless
mistress. Gavin had tried to be polite, but the plump little
maid strained his patience, and he'd been strained enough
for one evening. "Out!" he demanded.

She jumped, then scurried toward the door. Tillie hesitated there, throwing a nervous glance in his direction
before her gaze settled, with pity, upon her mistress. Then,
showing at least a thimble of good sense, she left, closing
the door softly behind her.

Gavin glanced down at Christine. Her hair tumbled
around her shoulders. Long, sooty lashes rested against
the paleness of her porcelain cheeks. She still breathed,
he noted. What, he wondered, while watching the hypnotic rise and fall of her breasts, was he going to do to
her? *With* her, he quickly amended.

Chapter Nine

Sunlight slipped through the part in the heavy drapes of her room, beckoning Christine to open her eyes. Her lashes fluttered; then she stretched, sighing with pleasure over the sinfully delicious feel of silk against her skin.

She lifted her arms overhead, confused for a moment as to why they were bare. Where were the soft cotton sleeves of her nightdress? She groped beneath the covers. What was she doing wearing her fine silk underwear to bed?

Abruptly, Christine sat up. The previous night came rushing back to her. A heated flush spread over her entire body. Gavin thought she'd been whoring herself to him. Her heartbeat slowed when she remembered he had released her—told her to leave. But she couldn't recall leaving his room. She couldn't recall anything after that.

Her gaze darted around. Everything looked in order. Embers winked at her from the fireplace, proof a fire had blazed there during the night. Warily, her gaze drifted to the other side of the bed. She sighed in relief.

Empty, save for her. The covers were clumped around her in disarray, but that was perfectly normal. She never recalled waking to find them otherwise, as she was a fitful sleeper.

Still, how had she come to be in her bed? And where were the corset and fine petticoats she'd been wearing, along with the silk chemise and drawers? She moved her legs. Her silk stockings were missing as well. Before she allowed herself a free rein with her fears, she glanced at the connecting door that led to Tillie's smaller quarters. The maid would know what had happened last night.

"Tillie?" she called weakly, then realized she would have to rise and knock on the door. She started to push the covers aside, but the door flung open as if the maid had been standing there with her ear pressed against the frame.

Tillie rushed into the room, and the fact that her gaze also darted nervously about brought a sick feeling to Christine's stomach. "Tell me you were the one who put me to bed last night," she whispered.

Red flooded Tillie's cheeks. She began wringing her hands. "He ordered me out," she said defensively. "I didn't want to leave ye at his mercy, but him being the master and all, what could I do?"

Christine wasn't nearly so worried about what Tillie could have done, as she was about what her husband had done.

"Did he hurt you, m'lady?" the maid whispered, tears filling her eyes.

To her knowledge, she wasn't hurt anywhere. Her stomach was currently gnawing at her backbone for lack of any other nourishment, but other than being famished, she felt fine.

"No," she answered. "I don't think so."

"He said he wouldn't, but men, ye can't trust them when they're lust-crazed. Or so I've heard," Tillie added.

Lust-crazed? The vision of Gavin's dark eyes filled with heat resurfaced in her memory. That, along with the proof of his arousal she had felt through her petticoat. Now she recalled what happened. She'd become dizzy and had most likely fainted. But what had happened afterward?

"Tillie, did you remove my corset, my petticoats, and my silk stockings?"

The maid blushed again, another answer without words. Christine's stomach rolled. Still, she couldn't believe Gavin would do anything indecent. He'd said he wouldn't take a woman who was unwilling. Of course, he hadn't said he wouldn't take one while she was unconscious.

"If anything improper happened between us, there would be signs of such, wouldn't there?" Christine asked.

"Oh, aye," Tillie assured her. "Me mam, God rest her soul, lived long enough to tell me that. Ye being pure and chaste, there'd be blood on the sheets if ye lost yer virginity."

"Blood?" Christine repeated, horrified by the information. She lifted the covers and looked. There was no blood. A sigh of relief left her lips and she fell back against the pillows. "Nothing must have happened."

Tillie, too, appeared relieved. She scurried over to the bed and sat down. "And there would be other signs as well, you can mark my words on that," she said to her mistress. "A big, strapping man like His Lordship. If he was to have gotten between yer legs, you'd be knowing it this morning."

Renewed embarrassment flooded Christine. She and Tillie, or she and anyone for that matter, had never discussed such delicate and, from the sounds of it, disgusting matters. Tillie had more to offer.

"April, the parlor maid at Greenhaven," she explained unnecessarily. "Ye know she married that poor farmer what lives at the parish last spring?"

Christine nodded. She thought the couple to be very happy with one another.

"Well." Tillie glanced around as if the walls had ears. "About a week into the marriage, I catch her hobbling around the parlor dusting, moving like an old woman. I ask her what's wrong, did she sprain her leg or something, and she flat out tells me that oaf of a husband of hers cannot leave her be at night. She says he's gotten her so sore between the legs she can hardly walk."

It was neither a pleasant nor proper tale to be discussing. Christine shifted uncomfortably against the mattress. Her stomach made a gurgling noise.

"Think about it, m'lady," Tillie said, eyebrows raised. "That scrawny husband of hers ain't nearly so strapping as His Lordship. If poor April can suffer so from a part I suppose is just as scrawny as the rest of him, imagine—"

"Tillie," Christine warned, not wanting to imagine any such thing. "Enough of this vulgar talk. I'm starving. Would you pull the bell rope to summon Mr. Graves?"

At the mention of the head servant, Tillie's eyes danced with mischief. "It'd be quicker for me to go downstairs and tell him myself," she said. A giggle escaped her lips. She covered her mouth, but giggled again.

"What's so amusing?" Christine asked, although her empty stomach didn't want to know what Tillie would probably tell her, asked or not.

"Last night, after His Lordship ordered me from your room, I went downstairs to find a bite because I had no supper, as you know. I caught Mr. Graves in the pantry getting himself a bite as well. He was wearing his nightshirt."

The picture that came to Christine's mind wasn't all that amusing. "And?" she prompted.

"And I saw his bare legs," she whispered.

Her maid was obviously easily entertained, Christine

116

thought. And it did not sit well with her to know that while she'd been upstairs possibly being defiled by her husband, Tillie had been downstairs stuffing her mouth and ogling poor Mr. Graves's legs.

"Were his legs skinny?" Christine asked, trying to find the humor in Tillie's tale.

The maid sobered. She sighed wistfully. "Oh, no, m'lady. 'E's got grand legs."

A peculiar realization suddenly dawned upon Christine. "Tillie, are you soft on Mr. Graves?"

Her cheeks reddened. "I suppose a plain, plump girl like myself could do worse," she admitted.

Christine laughed. She couldn't help it. At Tillie's wounded expression, she quickly said, "But he's much older than you."

The maid lifted her chin. " 'E ain't so old. He just seems old because he's so stuffy. Last night with his hair all messed, I realized he wasn't that old at all. I bet he's not much older than His Lordship."

Mr. Graves's age, or his desirability as a man, was certainly nothing Christine had given much thought to. She did find it odd that Tillie crooned over the head servant, especially given their most recent discussion.

"Oh, I figure he's too refined to do anything vulgar with a woman," Tillie said, as if she'd read her thoughts. "He blushed as red as I did when he caught me looking at his legs. He'd be a safe man to marry. Not like His Lordship."

The two were hardly comparable, Christine had to agree. The stuffy Mr. Graves and her husband. Gavin, dark eyes full of heat and forbidden promises of pleasure. Sleek, powerful body. Face of a saint, soul of the devil. She shivered, both hot and cold at the same time. Tillie pulled the covers up closer around her.

"I'll be back to help you dress after I've had Mr. Graves order us a huge breakfast."

Christine welcomed the reprieve. Tillie could prattle

until her ears hurt. She smiled as the maid fussed with her hair and straightened her clothing before leaving the room. Tillie and Mr. Graves? She couldn't picture them together as a couple.

But then, she recalled the way the stuffy head servant seemed to enjoy his bickering with Tillie. How his eyes sparkled when she ordered him about. Perhaps there was an attraction there, and Christine had missed it because it had been subtle.

Nothing subtle about Gavin. He made no bones about the matter if he desired a woman. Her husband was used to getting whatever he wanted, and with very little effort. A lingering glance, a hint of a smile, and most women probably fell at his feet, or more to his wishes, into his bed. She would not be so easily seduced by a man's outer appearance. However sinfully handsome he might be.

And whatever had she done to make him believe she'd been offering her body to him in lieu of payment? Unpleasant as she found the task, Christine tried to recall when Gavin had gone from being bored by her to being far too attentive. His demeanor changed when he glanced up to find her standing there in her fine underwear. But it wasn't until she'd scrambled to floor to clean up the spilled brandy that all signs of passiveness in him fled.

She'd been kneeling between his legs when she glanced up at him. The fire burning behind her seemed to jump into his eyes. Her thoughts skittered around what had followed. She tried to forget the heat swirling around them, the racing of her heart when his mouth settled upon her neck, then the jolt when he softly sank his teeth into her flesh.

Her face became so hot, she fanned herself. Best to concentrate on what had happened once she'd fainted. Nothing at all came to her for a few minutes; then she did have a fleeting memory. Hands, strong, yet gentle, at the fastenings of her corset, and the relief of being able

118

to breathe normally once it pinched her no more. The soft swishing sound of her petticoats sliding down her hips.

Hotter yet her face grew at the remembered feel of fingers moving down her legs, the cool touch of silk contrasting to the warm one of human contact. Gavin had undressed her, and maybe not as thoroughly as he could have, but his hands had been upon her.

Had he touched her anywhere else? Perhaps looked at her while she lay helpless? She tried to remember, but all she could recall after the stockings were removed was having the covers pulled up around her. She remembered hearing noises. The subtle opening and closing of drawers. Sounds she would have easily identified with Tillie, and not with her husband.

Had he put away her things? Lit the fire that kept her warm throughout the night? Not likely, she decided. Perhaps Tillie had come into the room later, or maybe Mr. Graves. As if merely thinking of the head servant summoned him, Tillie opened the door, to be followed inside by Mr. Graves, carrying a huge tray of food. His sudden appearance surprised her. She thought she'd be suffering for at least an hour while he had the meal prepared.

"They've been keeping it warm," Tillie said, practically rubbing her hands together in anticipation of the meal.

"His Lordship left me strict instructions before he left this morning to see you well fed, Your Ladyship," said Mr. Graves.

It wasn't so much the way he said what he said, but the way he lifted a curious brow before he placed the tray upon a nearby table that had Christine's stomach twisting into knots again.

"Mr. Graves," she mumbled. "Were you in my room late last evening?"

He drew himself up indignantly. "Most certainly not, Your Ladyship."

"Oh," she said flatly. "Of course not."

"Will that be all, Your Ladyship?" he inquired in his clipped voice.

"Yes, thank you."

Christine noted a brief moment of eye contact between the head servant and Tillie before he left the room. The maid's cheeks were flushed.

"Tillie," Christine said, immediately pouncing upon the maid. "Did you enter my room last night and put away my things? Light the fire?"

The maid's brown curls bounced when she shook her head. "I was afraid of what I might see were I to poke my head inside this room."

"Your loyalty is a comfort," she countered dryly. She had trouble imagining Gavin taking on a role as servant. And why had Mr. Graves flashed her that curious look when he'd said His Lordship had ordered her well fed this morning? Of course the order was due to the fact she'd fainted from hunger last night. Wasn't it?

"Oh, my," Tillie breathed. She turned, a silver warming cover in one hand. "There's more for you than food beneath this cover, m'lady."

Curious, Christine tried to see around her. "What is it?"

Tillie scooped up the plate and brought it to the bed. Against a stark white backdrop of fine china rested a perfect red rose, beneath it a note.

Her hand shaking slightly—from hunger, Christine assured herself—she lifted the rose. The petals were velvety soft when she brushed the flower against her cheek, then inhaled its sweet scent.

"What's the note say?" Tillie demanded impatiently.

Christine picked up the note, written on thick crisp stationery. She read the bold script, then fanned her face with the paper.

"What does it say?" Tillie nearly jumped up and down. Her hand falling limply to her side, the note clutched between her fingers, Christine whispered, "It says, 'Forgive me for last night.' "

Tillie's eyes widened a fraction. Neither of them spoke for a moment; then Christine laid the plate, the note, and the rose aside, jerking the covers up to check the sheets again.

"And no one suspicious tried to approach her?"

William rolled his eyes at his cousin. "I've told you, no one but Thorton and Dumont. They spotted us on the last leg home and, I'm certain merely out of curiosity, joined our party."

Gavin frowned, recalling how the two young men had ogled Christine. Of course she was very beautiful. She would be ogled by many men. He had to accept that. Just as he accepted full responsibility for his bad behavior the previous evening.

Christine had wanted more than a bored response from him over the purchases she'd selected, and although he'd thought her fetching in all of her new clothes, he couldn't tell her as much.

Instead, he'd made her angry enough to attempt shocking him with the cost of her fine underclothes. He had been rather startled to glance up and see her standing half naked in front of him. Shock had immediately given way to lust the moment she'd kneeled before him. Her hair had been wild around her shoulders, and the firelight had danced upon her creamy skin.

Then her lips had parted in what he'd only perceived as an invitation. The memory had no less impact on him at the moment. He willed it away, and the tightening it brought to his lower regions.

"What do you think of Christine?" he now asked.

His cousin's expression remained wary, as it had been from the moment Gavin had stepped into his office early that morning. "Do you want an honest answer, or one that

121

will spare me another of your sudden fits of jealousy?"

The question surprised Gavin. "What fits of jealousy?"

William laughed, although it sounded as strained as the conversation. "I thought you would call us all out last night for the simple sin of making Christine laugh. You are behaving most unlike yourself, cousin. Have you already fallen in love with your wife?"

If William's earlier question surprised him, the latter one stupefied him. "Don't be ridiculous. I'm merely worried about my future. I can't have Christine shaming me to the point the whole country will believe me addle-brained were I not to dissolve the marriage. And this lover, I need to find a way to rid both her and me of him."

"You're not planning to kill him, are you?" William asked dryly.

Gavin rose from behind his desk, stretching his cramped muscles. "I would never take a man's life over a woman, my wife or not." He began pacing. "Besides, doing away with Christine's lover would only make her dislike me more than she already does."

William also rose, but instead of pacing beside his cousin, went to a window overlooking the docks. "This is difficult for you, isn't it?"

In midpace, Gavin stopped. He glanced toward his cousin. "What?"

William smiled. "Having a woman dislike you. Quite a change from what you're accustomed to."

A bruised ego was hardly worth consideration with all that was at stake. "What is difficult is having my future hang in the balance. I need to find a way around the late marquis's will. A way to foil Christine's plans."

"Short of murdering her, I don't see one," William offered.

Returning to his desk, Gavin picked up a copy of the *Times*. A small mention of his wife's shopping trip had been included, a sarcastic pun adding that she'd obviously been released from her prison or had managed to escape His Lordship's henchmen. It only added to his foul mood.

He'd been cast in the role of jealous husband, not a role he'd played before. Gavin didn't like it one bit. He'd handled Christine's appearance in London badly.

"Your silence is beginning to worry me," William said. "I was merely jesting, cousin."

Momentarily confused, he glanced at William.

"About murdering your wife," William explained. "An investigation would surely uncover your motive. Title or no, I imagine you'd end up in prison."

Gavin waved away his suspicions. "I was trying to figure out a way to undo the damage I've already done to my reputation, not plotting Christine's demise. I suppose the only thing to do is to let her go and make a fool of me, and act as if I don't particularly care. People will only assume we both have a fondness for variety."

"But what of her lover?" William asked. "What if she truly cares for him and she still demands the annulment?"

"Her lover," he bit out angrily. "Spineless cad. If I wanted a woman, a titled husband wouldn't stop me from pursuing her."

"It hasn't in the past," William agreed. "Rather fitting that you should be on the other side of the fence for a change."

Gavin glanced at his cousin. "You seem to be enjoying my circumstance."

William smiled. "In all honesty, I am. I find it is amusing to see a man of your reputation with the ladies being duped. And by your own wife, no less. I'm sorry, Gavin, but you have to admit there's a certain poetic justice to it all. You were forced to wed a wife beneath you, only to learn she doesn't want to be beneath you, or even married to you. Instead, she prefers her lover, who is, in all likelihood, as common as she."

"I find nothing amusing about that," Gavin said, but a

solution, as ridiculous as it was, had come to him while William reminded him of his situation. "I know what I must do," he said. "How to get rid of Christine's lover and keep my title and my lands."

"Short of seeing they both meet with an unfortunate accident, I'm not following you," William said.

Gavin smiled at him. "It seems Christine has left me no choice but to seduce her."

William's brows shot up. "And what purpose would that serve?"

"My own, of course." Gavin walked to the liquor cabinet, removed a bottle of port, and poured himself and his cousin a drink. "If Christine were to fall in love with me, she would then give up her lover. I hadn't planned on producing an heir so soon, but were she to find herself with child, she would retire to the country where the air is better and social life less taxing on her strength."

"But she would still be your wife," William pointed out, joining him. He took the glass Gavin offered him. "And more fully entrenched in that role by giving you an heir."

Gavin shrugged. "I suppose that can't be helped. There is no way to dissolve the marriage and keep the bequest. A child would give Christine something to occupy herself with, and London is no place to raise children."

"So you've found a way to banish her after all," William said, displaying no admiration over Gavin's decided plan of action.

His cousin took note of his sour expression. "It's the only way to settle the matter." Gavin raised his glass in a toast. "If Christine is besotted with me, she'll abandon not only her lover, but her plans to shame me in society's eyes. It's a simple case of logic and survival."

William did not raise his glass. "You have never failed at anything in your life, cousin. This is one instance when I hope you do."

An odd occurrence happened in that instant. Gavin felt a twinge of guilt. The emotion caught him off guard. "What would you have me do, William? Give her the annulment? Lose my title and Greenhaven for the sake of her and her lover, a cowardly man obviously undeserving of Christine's spirit?"

His cousin lifted a brow over the last question. Gavin refused to retract the compliment given to his wife. She did have spirit. Too much, he feared.

The man sighed. "No, you cannot give up your title or the estate. I suppose you have no choice but to execute your plan, although I wish there was a less drastic way of handling the situation."

Relief that William agreed lifted Gavin's spirits and chased away any guilt associated with his decision. Oddly, he found himself rather anxious to begin. Uncommonly excited by the prospect of seeing his wife again.

"I shall begin immediately," he decided. "I trust you can handle things here for a while?"

William glanced at the invoices and ledgers stacked on both his and Gavin's desks. "A short while, cousin."

Gavin smiled. He supposed he was somewhat cocky in his opinion of himself, but then, he had no reason to be otherwise. "It won't take long, William."

Chapter Ten

Christine couldn't have been more taken aback when Mr. Graves informed her His Lordship had returned home and wanted a word with her. The morning was not yet gone. Except for the one one day, the day she'd snuck into his room to find him still abed, he'd spent little time at home. She preferred his absence, and wondered if his unusual visit had anything to do with the previous evening.

Warmth crept into her cheeks. She felt positive nothing unseemly had occurred between them last night, but still, the man had undressed her and tucked her into bed. That was embarrassment enough. And the note had taken her off guard. She didn't imagine Gavin Norfork often, if ever, apologized for anything. What did he want?

"You'd best go now," Tillie suggested. "Ye've kept him waiting for a time. In my short acquaintance with His Lordship, patience does not appear to be a virtue with him."

It was a fault Christine had discovered about Gavin from the first day she'd seen him waiting in the shadows of the parish church. She supposed Tillie was right, and to stay upstairs in her room might indicate she feared a meeting with him. Christine refused to fear him. She refused to give him the satisfaction.

With a slight nod, she quit Tillie's company and went downstairs. She found Gavin in his study, a book in hand. Lost in the novel, he didn't notice her. Christine took the time to study him. His elegant clothing fit him to perfection, and she liked that he wore dark colors rather than outfitting himself like a peacock. A wisp of midnight hair rested across his forehead, adding to his rakish appearance.

She admired the length of his lashes, felt envious of them, in fact. They were much too long and thick to belong to a man. His gaze lifted, as if he sensed himself being appraised, and his dark eyes locked with hers. Christine was momentarily struck by his handsomeness, so much so that she had trouble forming words in her head. She knew she should say something, but exactly what eluded her.

"You look lovely this morning, Christine."

His compliment only added to her problem. She'd expected a sarcastic remark about her appearance, or about last night. He appeared sincere in the remark, which only increased her befuddlement. Since he seemed to be waiting for a reply, she said the first thing that came to mind.

"What do you want?"

The pleasant smile on his disturbing mouth faltered, but he recovered quickly. "I thought we might spend the afternoon together."

Again, only a blunt response came to mind. "Why?"

Gavin laid his book aside and approached her. That was when she noticed the way he moved. Like a sleek predator stalking its prey. Christine tamped down a natural instinct to retreat, and tried to ignore the strange stirring with each step that brought him closer.

"Do you enjoy reading?" he asked.

She'd been in the study once, thinking to take her inventory before Mr. Graves caught her and ran her out. It was a room she could gladly find herself imprisoned inside. Volumes of fine leather-bound books were stacked on shelves that went all the way to the ceiling.

"Yes," she answered. "I love to read."

"Then you must feel free to visit the study whenever you choose."

His polite attitude had the fine hairs on her arms prickling. "Mr. Graves said you don't want anyone snooping around in your study," she said. "He said you are very protective of your collected works."

Gavin shrugged. "Only protective against those who do not respect the written word or the property of others. Since you plan to see the whole house sold off, I know you would take care of any books you wish to borrow."

There it was, finally. The sarcasm that usually accompanied his every word. He seemed to realize his mistake. "I meant to say, what is mine is also yours."

She smiled at his slip. "Perhaps I will choose something while I'm here. It would be a pleasant way to pass the afternoon."

He blocked her when she thought to step toward the book shelves. "I had hoped we could do something more adventuresome."

God, he smelled good. She took a step back. "What did you have in mind?"

"You said you don't ride, but you've purchased such an attractive riding habit. I have a stable at our disposal, and a gentle mare I think would suit you. I thought we might ride through the park."

The temptation proved great. Christine was not used to being cooped up indoors for long periods of time. She thrived on sunshine and fresh air. She supposed she'd lied when she told him she didn't ride. On occasion, she'd ridden a donkey to the neighboring cottages around the parish. A horse, she imagined, was only a bigger version of a donkey.

"I'll change."

The look of relief on his face almost gave him an innocent boyish appearance. Almost. He was no boy, and certainly no innocent. Perhaps she shouldn't have been so quick to agree.

"The park will be crowded," he warned. "It's a beautiful day and there will be others strolling and riding. Not at all a private outing, if that is your wish."

He knew good and well a private outing would not be to her liking. Very clever, her husband. Still, Christine couldn't see the harm in a short ride. And actually wearing the riding habit would soothe her guilt over the expensive purchase.

"I shall meet you at the stables," she said, turning to leave.

Gavin snatched her hand and pulled her back around. "I behaved badly last night. I jumped to the wrong conclusion when you stormed into my room wearing nothing but your undergarments."

Her cheeks flamed. "I should have never flaunted them, or myself, before you in so brazen a manner. The fault is not all yours to bear."

"Then you forgive me?"

Gooseflesh prickled her skin. This Gavin, the one asking for forgiveness with such sincerity reflected in his dark eyes, unnerved her much more than the other one. The other man, the snobbish rake with hot blood and a cold heart, was rather easy to dislike.

"We shall both forgive and forget the incident," she decided.

His gaze lowered to her breasts, then lifted abruptly. "It will be a challenge. Not the forgiving. But the forgetting."

She'd been watching his white teeth while he spoke, recalling how they sank into her neck for an instant before he kissed the spot. Christine straightened. "I trust you will manage," she said, then pulled her hand from his and left the room.

Once upstairs and changed, she questioned her sanity. She had actually agreed to go off with her husband. And harmless outing or not, Gavin had a way of making even the innocent seem seductive. Perhaps it was just him. He oozed sensuality from every pore. Christine tried not to think about his dark appeal while she set her jaunty tricorn upon her head.

"Ye look lovely in that outfit," Tillie commented. "His Lordship will be proud to have ye by his side today."

Christine frowned at her reflection. She didn't want Gavin to feel proud of her. Of course, in order to attract the attention of other men, she must look her best. And attract them she planned to do. She pinched her cheeks to add color, ran a hand over the skirt of her riding habit, and headed toward the door.

"Try not to pester poor Mr. Graves while I'm away," she said to Tillie in parting.

"Where's the fun in that?" the maid grumbled, but went about straightening the recent damage her mistress had done to the bedchamber.

Once downstairs again, Christine took the back entrance through the kitchen, smiling at the staff as she passed. She walked outside into the bright sunshine. The day proved lovely indeed, lifting her spirits. Inside the stables, Gavin and a young groom waited for her. Her husband ran an appreciative glance over her outfit, then motioned her forward.

"This is Belle," he said, indicating a pretty chestnut mare. "You should become acquainted with her before you climb on her back."

Cautiously, Christine reached forward and ran a gloved

hand over the mare's silky muzzle. The animal stood much taller than a donkey.

"She's so big," she whispered. "I'm not sure—"

"She's also very gentle," Gavin interrupted. "There's no call to be frightened of her."

"I'm not afraid," Christine huffed. "I simply don't know how I shall mount such a huge animal."

"I'll see you seated." Gavin led her around the horse. His hands settled upon her waist. He lifted her as if she weighed nothing, holding her until she fumbled behind her and grabbed the saddle horn.

"You must ride sidesaddle as do all proper ladies," he informed her. "Wrap your leg around the horn."

"Like this?"

"Exactly," he praised. After snatching the reins, he flipped them over the horse's head. "Take the reins, but don't pull up on them."

Christine at least knew about reining. The small donkey she'd ridden around the parish had only had an old blanket thrown over his back, and much to her shame, she'd sat the animal with a leg dangling on either side. She watched Gavin disappear for a moment. Then he walked from a stall leading his magnificent white stallion. The one she'd seen thundering down the road that fateful day when she'd first believed the Lord had delivered her from marriage.

"This is Pegasus," he said.

"Do you know Greek mythology?"

He glanced up. "Do you?"

She felt a spark of excitement. "I find it fascinating."

"So do I," he said. Respect entered his dark gaze, and something more, though she dared not try to identify what. "Almost as fascinating as I find you."

Their eyes remained locked for a moment. Christine quickly glanced away, not at all comfortable with being the object of his admiration. A moment later, she stole a glance at him while he mounted. He did so with his usual confidence and grace. Gavin nudged his horse forward and without having to cue her own animal, the mare followed. A mounted groom set off behind them, keeping at a respectable distance to afford them privacy.

Sunlight glinted off Gavin's dark head, bringing out the shine in his hair. A breeze played with his shoulder-length strands, and Christine found herself wondering how it might feel to run her fingers through his glossy mane.

Her thoughts brought her shame. She tried to concentrate on something else. His shoulders were broad beneath his fine cutaway coat, she noticed. His thighs were powerfully muscled beneath his tight-fitting trousers.

All and all, a man put together nicely. More than adequate, she mentally corrected, recalling his tawny splendor the morning she'd snuck into his room and found him naked. Beyond tempting, she imagined, for women prone to a weakness for the flesh. Which she certainly was not.

Christine snapped her gaze back up to his face, embarrassed to find him looking at her. She tried to think of something to say. "Your boots are nice."

He smiled. "Thank you."

"Well polished," she added lamely.

"I will relay the compliment to Mr. Graves."

Awkward silence.

"Tillie is quite taken with him," Christine blurted out, She wanted to snatch the words back. They smacked of gossip, and she'd never been one to involve herself with such foolishness. Gavin's smile waned. She had the distinct impression he didn't care for flippant conversation, either. But then, that was what she wanted. He should not find her fascinating, or appealing, on any level.

Forcing a girlish giggle from her throat, she added, "My maid found Mr. Graves in the kitchen wearing nothing but his nightshirt. She thinks he has grand legs."

Gavin lifted a brow as if interested, but she saw him

staring off into the distance, and knew he'd become bored with her already. It should have suited her, but she felt somewhat annoyed by his lack of attention.

"Tillie has her sights set on Mr. Graves. She believes he would be a good match for her."

"Mr. Graves is a confirmed bachelor," Gavin remarked. "Your maid had best set her sights somewhere else."

Since the conversation seemed to bore her husband, Christine continued. "I think Mr. Graves is not uninterested in Tillie. Have you noticed the way his eyes light up when the two are in the same room together?"

A frown had settled over Gavin's mouth. "No," he said simply. He turned to look at her. "Are you a romantic, Christine?"

The question took her unawares. Was she? Christine had never thought of herself as one, but then she did enjoy a romantic novel, or a beautifully worded poem. "I'm not certain," she answered.

"Only a romantic would answer in that way. Leaves the door open for possibilities."

"And you do not believe in true love," she stated rather than asked.

"I never have," he admitted. "But then, I've never had a reason to believe . . . up until now."

She hadn't missed the added afterthought. It could be interpreted in two ways. Nothing had changed his mind to this date, or . . . She quickly refused to consider the second choice. Up until he'd met her. There, she'd foolishly considered it after all. Which, she supposed, exposed her for a romantic, and the worst kind. The hopeless kind, for theirs was a relationship truly doomed.

"Tell me about yourself, Christine."

Now he'd begun to unnerve her. He seemed genuinely interested. She shrugged. "There isn't much to tell."

"I'm sure you are fascinating. James and Chester seem to think so, and my cousin William, I'm sure, as well."

"I enjoy your friends," she said with a smile. "And William's company, too, I believe. He is very polite and rather . . . well, unthreatening."

A dark brow lifted. "And it's for the opposite reason that you don't care for mine?"

Her horse stumbled, and Christine's attention momentarily shifted. Once she regained her seating, she studied Gavin from beneath her lashes. He wasn't in the least docile. To either the male or female gender.

"Yes," she answered honestly.

His frown deepened. "Then I must endeavor to become more like my cousin."

An immediate reaction escaped Christine. She laughed, then covered her mouth with a gloved hand.

"Did I say something amusing?"

"I'm sorry, Your Lordship. I fear you and William are nothing alike, nor will you ever be."

The frown he wore softened. "But if it would please you, then I shall still try."

A skitter of pleasure raced through her, quickly followed by a stab of alarm. This new Gavin, she suspected, was much more dangerous than the other one. She'd best keep her defenses up, her head clear, and her heart well guarded.

The park came into view and she breathed a small sigh of relief. Several people strolled about, or rode. The wonderful smells from the vendors' carts made her mouth water.

"Are you hungry?" Gavin asked, and she wondered if her stomach had grumbled.

"I could eat something."

He pulled Pegasus up and dismounted. Approaching her, he lifted his hands to assist her down. Once her feet touched the ground, Gavin motioned the groom forward to take the reins of their horses. He offered Christine his arm. Her fingers wrapped around the strong muscle bulging slightly beneath the sleeve of his coat. They proceeded toward the vending carts. Then reality hit Christine.

This was the first public appearance she would make with her husband. At least the first one where she actually knew his identity. Would anyone pay them any notice? The answer wasn't long in coming. Heads turned in their direction, and the murmurs of soft conversation suddenly intensified, reminding her of the loud buzzing of bees.

Chapter Eleven

The attention made Christine nervous, which she told herself was rather ridiculous given her plan to create a scandal wherever she ventured in London. Of course at Greenhaven, she hadn't exactly thought her intentions through. She'd foolishly ignored the fact that she wasn't at all the type to flirt outrageously with men, or that she knew nothing about the art of being a seductress in general.

A glance at her husband found him collected as usual. She imagined Gavin was accustomed to being gawked at and whispered about. He'd certainly shown a talent for causing scandal in the past. She imagined his gift for doing so stemmed from a total lack of regard for anyone's feelings save his own. If she were to succeed in ridding herself of him, and confiscating his fortune for those less fortunate, she must endeavor to be more like him.

They stopped before a vending cart selling hot pies. Christine eyed the fare hungrily, then felt a moment of guilt when her gaze lifted to the vendor. He was a thin man, not old, but with the eyes of one who had seen too much hardship in life. His pale wife helped him while their small children clung to her skirts. There were four children, all of them wearing rags and with dirt on their faces.

Life was hard for those not born into luxury. Christine had not been one of the chosen, and still, here she was, on the other side of the cart.

"Would you care for a pie?" Gavin asked.

She didn't answer for a moment, staring at the children who were obviously hungry, but whose needs would only be met after the wealthy had been fed.

"Yes," she finally answered. "Two pies."

"Two? For you alone?"

Turning a frosty glance upon Gavin, she amended her answer. "Four then."

He frowned. "Four?"

Christine lifted her chin, refusing to surrender the number. "Can you not afford four pies, Your Lordship?"

His gaze darted around. "That is not the point, Christine. Four pies would go to waste."

She glanced toward the children again. "Not if all four are eaten," she countered.

That a crowd had suddenly gathered around the cart worked to Christine's advantage. Gavin, usually so confident, looked somewhat flustered by her request.

"Four pies for the lady," he said quietly. "And one for me."

The vendor's eyes bugged, then gleamed with satisfaction over a good sale. He quickly produced the pies, then frowned.

"But how will you carry 'em all, Yer Lordship?"

Gavin glanced behind him, obviously searching for the groom.

"Pay the man first," Christine urged him.

He dug into his pocket and produced the correct coin,

his attention returning to the search for the groom.

"We shall need no assistance to carry the one pie," Christine said, causing Gavin's head to swing back around. She took a deep breath. "I fear I am not so hungry as I thought." She purposely trailed a finger along the top of each pie.

"Aye, she's touched 'em," the vendor squeaked. "I can't be selling the pies now."

"Oh, dear." She winced dramatically, although she had removed her glove and knew her hand to be clean. "I suppose you'll have to throw them out . . . or feed them to the children."

The vendor's sunken gaze landed on Gavin. Christine cut her eyes in her husband's direction. His lips were tight, but to his merit, Gavin simply took the one pie and her arm and led her away from the cart. Christine couldn't help but glance over her shoulder, deeply satisfied to see a pie being distributed to each hungry child.

When she turned back, Gavin paused beside a cart selling fresh milk. "Would you care for a cup? Or maybe four?"

Despite his sarcasm, she felt sorely tempted to say the latter. The children could probably do with a cup of fresh milk. She bit her tongue. "One will suffice."

He looked slightly relieved. "Two cups," he requested.

They strolled toward the groom, who held their horses. The young man grabbed a blanket from the saddle of his mount, rushed forward, and quickly placed it on the ground. Gavin managed to handle her cup as well as his, along with the pie, while she settled herself.

He handed Christine her cup, and seated himself without upsetting either his drink or the pie. A smile settled over Christine's lips as she eyed his milk.

"What, m'lady?" he asked.

She nodded toward his cup. "I find it amusing to see you partake of anything that doesn't have a kick to it."

"It is barely past noon. Do you think me a drunkard?"

Her lashes drifted downward. She shooed a fly from her cup. "You seem to have a fondness for brandy."

Gavin lifted her chin. "Not an obsessive one," he told her. "On occasion, it chases the chill from my bones and helps me forget business long enough to sleep."

His fingers were gentle against her skin, warm and pleasing, until he snatched them away, as if he realized the intimacy of his actions.

"Business?" Christine questioned, flustered by their brief contact. "What business are you in, Your Lordship? Other than being inherently wealthy?"

A lopsided grin spread over his lips. "I made my own fortune by the time I was but twenty and one. I joined the Royal Navy, and being the son of an aristocrat, joined as an officer. The spoils of war helped me purchase my first ship. Now I have ten."

"Ten?" Christine couldn't contain her surprise. "But what does a person do with that many ships?"

He laughed, then raised his cup. "I lease them for the purpose of importing and exporting."

"Oh." Christine frowned. "Then you are not reliant upon your late father's inheritance?"

The pleasant expression he wore faded. His gaze drifted to some distant point behind her. "No. I swore long ago never to become reliant upon him, or anyone else, for anything."

Her frown deepened. "Then what you're saying is that you don't need the inheritance?"

Slowly, his gaze returned to her. "What was his is now mine by right. He cheated me enough in life. I won't allow him to do it in death as well."

Although his voice did not reflect anger, she sensed it in him. Like a sore that had been too long ignored. A festering wound deep within him, one that she could neither soothe nor understand. It was if they spoke of two different men when it came to the late marquis.

"A pity you didn't inherit his compassion," she said.

The cup in his hand shook slightly. "Compassion?" he repeated, and this time he did not hide the bitterness in his voice. "He knew nothing of compassion, or of self-sacrifice, or of love. You, poor Christine, were only a pawn to continue the long-standing hate between us. To humiliate me, punish me for—"

She wasn't certain what halted the flow of hateful words spewing forth from him. Whether her feelings of hurt had surfaced on her face, or whether he'd simply realized he'd exposed too much of what he wished to remain hidden from her. Gavin ran a hand through his hair.

"Forgive me," he said. "Believe what you wish of him, but don't expect me to share your sentiments. I knew him far better than you did."

An argument in the late marquis's defense immediately formed upon her tongue. She suppressed it for the sake of keeping peace between them. Gavin had given her a wonderful gift. He would not be financially ruined if he were to lose his father's inheritance. She need not feel guilt on his behalf when she succeeded with her plan to see him relieved of the burden.

Her stomach grumbled. A blush rose in her cheeks. Gavin lifted a brow and handed her the pie.

"Now that the children have been fed, I see that your appetite has returned," he said.

When he glanced toward the vendor's cart, Christine's eyes followed. Although the children now had more on their faces than dirt, they looked content and happy. She smiled.

"You are a mystery, Christine."

The warm lights dancing in his eyes made her uncomfortable. They hinted at admiration, or at least more than a passing interest. Neither of which she desired to inspire in him.

"Shall we share the pie?" she asked.

He reached into his coat pocket and withdrew two silver forks. "Yes. Afterward, if you're still hungry, I'll fetch us another one."

She thought she'd welcome the distraction of eating, but sharing the pie seemed an intimate gesture in itself. Christine found her gaze often upon his mouth, and discovered her husband seemed equally enthralled by hers. Willing her attention elsewhere, she glanced around the park. The Marquis of Greenhaven and his wife were objects of interest, to be certain. Several heads were turned in their direction.

Two gentlemen walked toward them, and she smiled when she recognized them. Gavin groaned.

"Gavin, old boy," James Dumont exclaimed. "What a pleasant surprise."

Any pleasure derived from seeing him, Gavin was quick to surmise, stemmed from the fact that Christine accompanied him. Both James and Chester were grinning like idiots.

"Do join us," his wife suggested.

Gavin stifled another groan. He'd wanted Christine to himself. Had, in fact, been enjoying her company despite their earlier conversation concerning the late marquis. She intrigued him. Her ploy to see the vendor's children well fed, at least for one afternoon, had confused him, and truth be known, caused him guilt. He'd spent most of his life concerned only with his own needs, and preferred to turn a blind eye to the suffering around him.

"Would you care to stroll?" Chester asked Christine, then quickly glanced at Gavin to include him in the invitation.

He and his wife answered at the same time. Two different responses. Christine's cheeks flushed, and she amended her answer the instant Gavin amended his. Their eyes met. She laughed. He couldn't help but laugh with her.

"We will stroll," he announced.

Somehow, within minutes Christine strolled between James and Chester, a hand on each arm, and Gavin followed behind. Their journey had begun with him beside Christine, and his two foppish friends bringing up the rear. He supposed it was good he liked the sound of Christine's laughter, because he heard it often. James and Chester were doing their best to entertain her.

"You are brooding."

Gavin turned his head to encounter Adrianna standing beside him. Without invitation, she slid her hand around his arm. Gavin had made the mistake of lagging behind the group, probably doing exactly as Adrianna accused, brooding over his own poor ability to entertain Christine.

"I don't think it's wise to be seen strolling together in public," he informed her.

"Perhaps not if we were lovers," she countered, using slight pressure to steer him forward. "But we are no longer lovers, correct?"

"Correct," he confirmed, his gaze darting toward the trio ahead of them.

"Good Lord, are you afraid of upsetting her?" Adrianna snarled. "Your lack of proper manners has never been of concern to you before."

"Then I will continue in that vein," he said, turning to look at her. "Our affair is over, and it has nothing to do with my wife. I planned to end it the night Christine made an appearance at your ball, and before I learned her identity."

Adrianna's full lips thinned. "What we had together was good. Can still be good. Meet me tonight, and I will prove our affair is far from over."

Impatiently, Gavin ran a hand through his hair. "You

force me to be blunt, Adrianna. I have no wish to hurt your feelings, but all we shared were a few stolen moments of pleasure. I was not the first lover you have taken since your marriage, and I had no designs to be the last. We were nothing to one another except a pleasant distraction."

He tried to pull away, but Adrianna's nails dug into his arm. "How dare you dismiss me," she hissed. "I decide when the affair has ended. It has always been so. I will not allow you to discard me like a coat you've worn too many times!"

Gavin felt eyes focused upon them. Heard murmurs of conversation around them rise in pitch. He glanced toward Christine and found her staring at him. If her eyes remained cool, her cheeks flamed with embarrassment.

"You are creating a scandal," he said softly. "Your husband may take a mind to send you to the country if you cannot continue to be discreet."

Adrianna glanced about, as if she'd forgotten they were in public view. She loosened her hold on his arm and softened her expression.

"I fear I have fallen in love with you," she whispered.

Her confession did not please him. Gavin suspected Adrianna's obsession with him stemmed simply from the fact that he'd ended the affair before she'd done it herself. There were never any soft moments between them. Hardly any conversation. Just raw and deliberate lovemaking, and nothing more.

"I am not worthy of your love." He moved forward, but still found her attached to his arm. "I cannot accept it, because I cannot return it. Find another plaything, Adrianna. You are a beautiful, desirable woman. You can certainly do better than me."

"You are trying to pacify me," she grumbled. "But I am not so easily distracted, regardless of what you believe. I want you, Gavin, and once you've become bored by your orphan wife, you will realize you want me, too. I shall wait, as I imagine, given your past liaisons with women, it will not take long for you to seek my bed again."

To argue with her would only prolong an already uncomfortable situation. The trio ahead had resumed the stroll, but at such a leisurely pace Gavin would soon be upon them. How did one go about parting company with a past lover in the midst of society without offending the sensibilities of either the lover or one's wife?

"Gavin!"

He looked behind him and found salvation. William hurried toward him. Judging by his winded condition when he reached them, he'd been chasing after Gavin for a while.

"There's a problem," William huffed. "Collins wishes to lease three ships for an upcoming venture."

Gavin lifted a brow. "And what is the problem?"

"He said he'd only deal with you. He wants to trade half his cargo in exchange for payment. He's waiting for you at the office."

Unconsciously, Gavin's gaze strayed ahead of him toward Christine and her companions.

"I can accompany Christine home," William offered, perhaps a little too enthusiastically to Gavin's ears.

Gavin smiled and transferred Adrianna's hand to William's arm. "I shall see Christine home. I ask that you escort the duchess safely to her carriage."

His suggestion received a frown from both parties involved. Gavin gave neither of them time to argue, moving on to catch up with his wife. His reception was understandably chilly, but Christine handled herself well given the circumstances. But then, Gavin reasoned, why would she be angry over his relationship with Adrianna other than the fact that she found it an embarrassment?

"I'm afraid duty calls me to my office," he announced.

Gavin offered Christine his arm. "I shall see you safely home first."

Christine did not accept the arm he offered. "I'm sure Chester and James will see me home, so that you may see to your *duties* with greater haste."

He followed her gaze toward the departing couple. Was that what she thought? That he'd decided to escape for a tryst in his former lover's arms? It was important to Gavin that she not believe he would abandon her company for that of another woman. Important to his cause, he amended.

"Perhaps you would like to see my office?"

Her gaze snapped back to him, widening for a brief moment in surprise. "You would take me there?"

"If you wish."

The slight narrowing of her gaze suggested she still didn't believe his true destination. She smiled sweetly. "I would love to see your office."

"Then please allow me to escort you to the horses."

She took his arm. "Chester, James, you have made for most delightful companions," she said to his friends.

Both fops nearly drooled over the compliment.

"We shall see you Thursday at the opera. Correct?" James asked Gavin.

"Until then," he acknowledged, then led his wife from both besotted fools' company.

The stroll back to the horses felt strained. Gavin could hardly blame Christine for lack of warmth toward him. He didn't suppose it would thaw her any to openly discuss his former relationship with another woman.

He suddenly wondered why he felt so damned guilty about it, when Christine admitted to having a lover herself. And not one she'd recently ended an affair with, either. But then, that had become his plan. To see that she ended the affair. To win her heart away from the undeserving bastard and secure his own inheritance.

"Have I told you today how beautiful you are?" he asked.

She arched a perfect brow. "I don't know, Your Lordship. Have you? Or perhaps you've bestowed the compliment upon another. If you cannot recall what you've told whom, why should I?"

Her answer made him smile. For a poor orphan girl raised in a country parish, Christine could put anyone in his place. He like that about her. Too soon to suit him, they reached the waiting groom.

"Return to the stables," he instructed the lad. "The lady and I will escort ourselves home."

The groom nodded. Gavin helped Christine mount Belle, then climbed upon Pegasus's back. He reined his horse toward his downtown office. Christine followed behind him for a few moments, then urged Belle up beside him, then ahead. He frowned when she nudged the horse into a trot, and then a full gallop.

Admitting his wife sat a horse rather well, considering she'd told him she'd never ridden one before, he kneed Pegasus into a gallop. Gavin gave his stallion more rein and pulled up beside her. Suddenly the stallion reared.

Unprepared, Gavin lost his balance. He hit the ground with a teeth-rattling jar. He was up in an instant, grabbing for Belle's reins. There was no need, he realized, as Christine had already brought the startled mare under control.

"Are you all right?" Christine breathed.

Gavin hadn't taken time to discern the extent, if any, of his injuries. He walked a short distance and snatched the reins of his horse before returning to her side.

"Nothing bruised, I think, but my pride." He ran a hand over Pegasus's muzzle. "What got into you?"

The horse rubbed against him, now docile as a lamb. Gavin glanced around, noting that several people were staring in his direction. Most were snickering behind their hands. Gavin Norfork was known to be an accomplished horseman. Accomplished at whatever he chose to undertake.

"Shall we continue?" he asked Christine.

A hint of a smile formed on her lips. "If you feel up to it, Your Lordship."

His mouth turned up as well. "It seems my horse thought me in need of a lesson in humiliation today."

Still smiling, she let her gaze drift to the stallion. "A very smart beast, to be sure."

Gavin threw back his head and laughed. He mounted his horse and they were off again. They arrived at his office without further incident to find Mr. Collins waiting. The two men conducted business, although Christine proved a distraction for both him and the older gentleman, whose gaze kept straying in her direction.

She was quite beautiful, he admitted. But she also had a sweet, innocent quality about her. One that didn't fit a woman who professed to have a lover, or a woman who meant to viciously see his inheritance stripped from him.

Later, as he rubbed Pegasus down, the incident in the park returned to his memory. He ran a hand over the horse's smooth rump, his fingers finding a slight bump.

"What happened, Pegasus? Bee sting you?"

Gavin drew a lantern close. A slight bruise could be seen beneath the horse's glossy white coat. An insect sting would leave a red bump perhaps, but not a bruise. A small rock hurled at the animal might leave such a bruise.

Children playing, he decided. Unmindful of where the rocks they hurled might land. It suddenly occurred to him that if he hadn't pulled up alongside Christine at the exact moment he had, the rock would have hit her horse instead of his.

Christine, an unskilled rider and a woman delicately boned, might have been seriously hurt had she taken a spill. Possibly maimed, or worse, killed. Gavin put the disturbing thought out of his head. It had been an accident, one that could have ended tragically, but one, thank God, that had not.

Chapter Twelve

Christine stared at her reflection in the mirror, still stunned that the beautiful woman staring back was herself. She sighed, and the image sighed along with her.

"Ye're so lovely," Tillie whispered, tears shimmering in her eyes. "You look like a princess, m'lady."

She smiled fondly at her emotional maid. "This gown would make any woman look grand. His Lordship will most likely keel over dead when he receives the bill."

"Not after he's seen you in the gown," Tillie assured her. "Go downstairs and steal his heart away."

Stealing Gavin's heart was not an option. Although attracting another man's attentions would forward her goals. And perhaps tonight she stood a chance. The gown she wore was finer than anything she'd ever owned. Pure white silk shot through with tiny strands of real gold. It floated around her like a wispy cloud.

Tillie had arranged Christine's hair in an array of attractive curls atop her head. The gown's neckline was a bit low, exposing the soft skin of her shoulders and the rise of her breasts, but the style was decent.

Tonight she would mingle with London society. She would see her first opera, and she would make another attempt to shame her husband. The fact she had not been able to formulate a wise plan for doing so made her nervous. Something would come to her, she told herself.

Surely an opportunity would arise before the night ended. Her thoughts brought her little comfort. Recalling the gala she'd attended the first night she met Gavin, and the pawing of the men surrounding her, Christine shivered.

To fortify herself, she recalled the outing in the park and the humiliation of seeing Gavin with his lover in broad daylight. Even though he hadn't gone to meet the duchess shortly thereafter, as she'd first suspected he meant to, it didn't mean he hadn't visited her on other occasions. Christine had every right to shame him, to flirt with other men and feel no guilt. And so she would.

"Fetch my cape, Tillie," she said. "His Lordship waits, and so does the night."

The maid settled a white satin cape around her shoulders. Christine felt fortunate that the wrap at least allotted her some modesty, if the gown beneath exposed more than she felt comfortable displaying.

"Enjoy yourself, m'lady," Tillie said wistfully.

Her mistress frowned. "I intend to do no such thing," she assured her. "This is but business. A chance to forward my plan."

"Do be careful," Tillie warned, wringing her hands. "It be the devil himself you're dealing with."

Not long ago, Christine would have instantly agreed with Tillie's opinion of Gavin. During the past few days, he'd shown her another side to his character. He'd been attentive but polite each night at dinner. They had even discussed literature and art.

She might have found herself charmed by his company,

had she not known his true nature. And most certainly the meeting in the park with his lover resurfaced in her mind each time she felt any softening toward him. He was up to something. She half feared he meant to seduce her with his gentlemanly conduct of late. His efforts would go wasted, she vowed, casting one last glance in the mirror before she left the room.

Once she reached the top of the stairs, she saw him below, prowling the foyer like a great beast, pacing back and forth, a mark of his impatience. Dressed in formal attire, a dark black that seemed to suit him, he posed a striking picture. She had to admit, he was handsome to a fault. God's compensation, she supposed, for giving him little else in the way of desirable attributes. As if sensing her regard, his gaze traveled up the stairs.

When his dark eyes settled upon her and filled with heat, a warmth that caressed her as physically as if he'd reached out and touched her, she decided Tillie's warning held merit. Gavin was the devil's own, and any and all attributes he possessed surely came from below, rather than above. She forced her feet to move, gliding down the stairs. With each step that brought her closer to him, her heartbeat increased in tempo.

By the time she reached the bottom stair, it pounded loudly in her ears. The snowy ruffled shirt he wore contrasted starkly with his dark hair and skin. The cut of his black coat displayed the broadness of his shoulders to sinful perfection. A diamond stickpin winked at her from his white tie, but failed to compete with the brilliance of his dark eyes.

She didn't realize she'd remained poised on the bottom step, mesmerized, until he reached forward and took her hand. A delicious current raced from her fingertips up her arm. He assisted her down the last step, but continued to stare down at her.

"Your beauty strikes me mute," he said softly. "Even

the greatest poet could not do you justice tonight. You are a feast to the senses. A—"

"It does not appear as if words fail you, Your Lordship," she interrupted dryly, pleased in spite of her earlier vows. "Better give them a rest, and spend them on someone more . . . appreciative."

To her surprise, he smiled. A lopsided grin that increased the fluttering in her stomach. "Christine," he sighed. "It is you who are heartless. For even when I'm at the mercy of your beauty, and cannot control the truth of my words, you cut me off at the knees."

She found it hard to feel too sorry for him. He still wore his mischievous smile. "Shall we go?"

He reached into his pocket. "I-I saw these today and thought you might like them."

A black velvet box was suddenly thrust into her hands. Christine glanced up at Gavin, puzzled. She swore he blushed. "What is it?"

"Open the box and see."

Curious, she did as instructed. An involuntary gasp escaped her. Inside the box rested the most exquisite diamond necklace she had ever seen. Not only a necklace, but ear bobs to match. Her gaze shot up.

"But I can't accept them," she whispered.

His face darkened a shade. "Why not? You're my wife."

"Th-they must have cost a fortune," she stammered, flustered that he would present such a gift to her. "It wouldn't be right—"

"I expect nothing in return," he interrupted, the sarcasm returning to his voice. "Only the pleasure of seeing you wear them tonight."

Christine eyed the jewelry with longing. The diamonds sparkled, winking in the dim light. How easily she might become seduced by the beauty of an object. Forget her humble beginnings and truly imagine herself as a part of Gavin's privileged world.

But she was not of his world, and only a small part of a grander scheme, hard as it was at times to recall her mission. She extended the box toward him.

"The price is too high, Your Lordship, for such a small pleasure."

Gavin refused to accept the box, and instead ran an impatient hand through his hair. "I do not understand you, Christine. You mean to rob me of my inheritance, yet you refuse expensive gifts. You make no sense."

The urge to tell him her true mission nearly overcame her. But of course she couldn't tell him the truth. Gavin cared nothing for the poor or their plight. Compassion was not a weapon to wield with him. She must fight him with the only emotions he understood. Greed and deceit.

"Then, if the jewelry is a gift, the necklace and ear bobs are mine to do with as I choose, correct, Your Lordship?"

"Please call me Gavin," he ground out. "And yes, the baubles are yours to do with as you wish."

They would fetch a pretty price were she to hawk them, Christine decided. Besides what she'd obtained with her husband's money, she owned nothing of great value. Nothing she could turn into quick funds should the need arise.

"Then I accept your gift," she said. "Thank you, Your . . . Gavin," she finished.

He seemed to relax, she supposed because he believed he'd won in a game of wills. "May I put them on you?"

She lifted the box. He removed the necklace and placed the diamonds around her throat. The warmth of his fingers as they brushed the back of her neck caused the same jolt of pleasure to race through her. She tried to ignore the response. Tried also to ignore how closely he stood, the feather-light touch of his breath stirring the loose tendrils of hair framing her face.

Ronda Thompson

"Look at me," he instructed huskily.

Tilting her head back, she met his dark gaze. He slipped a pair of small twinkling diamonds on her ears.

"Even the rarest gem cannot match the sparkle in your eyes."

Pleasure flooded her. She knew she should lower her gaze—break the intimate contact—step away from him. His fingers moved from her ear, sliding along her jawline in a gentle caress before he cupped her chin. His mouth lowered and unconsciously, her lips parted. The sudden dawning that he meant to kiss her, that she had anticipated as much, and actually desired the feel of his mouth moving against hers, brought her to her senses.

Christine drew back. "I thought you expected nothing in return for the gifts."

He jerked away as if she'd slapped him. The light reflected in his gaze flickered, then disappeared. "It was not the cold jewels around your neck, and what I expected to gain by giving them to you that ruled me, but your beauty, and the sweet promise of your lips. Forgive me."

How quickly he went from hot to cold. And how easily he disguised his hurt, for she had seen it in his eyes not a second past. Now they stood awkward with one another. Christine felt a little ashamed she'd accused him of expecting an exchange of favors for the gift, supposing he might have simply been caught up in the moment, as she had been.

"Then you must forgive me as well," she said softly. "I fear I have ruined your evening. The jewels are truly lovely and I thank you for them."

His stiff posture relaxed. "The evening is young," he said. "But the theater will be crowded. We should be on our way."

When he politely offered her his arm, Christine took it. They moved toward the door, where Mr. Graves suddenly appeared, Gavin's cloak and hat in hand.

154

"May I say, Your Ladyship, that you look very beautiful tonight?"

She smiled at the head servant. "Thank you, Mr. Graves."

He bowed stiffly, but smiled at her in return before opening the door. Gavin, she noted, lifted a brow at the servant before accepting his cloak and hat.

Once settled inside Gavin's coach, a fur draped over her lap against the night chill, Christine had trouble keeping her excitement at bay. She loved the arts, had often dreamed of seeing an opera, or a fine play, but had certainly never imagined a poor girl such as herself would someday attend one. And dressed in such finery, with a titled husband sitting across the coach from her.

A husband, she noticed by the lantern's glow inside the coach, who appeared to be brooding. Perhaps he regretted giving her the diamonds, or had thought to mentally question the price of her gown. More likely, he realized they would soon be among his fellow snobs, and she would be an embarrassment to him. A reminder of his father's supposed ill will toward him and worse, an unwanted revision to a life he quite preferred absent of her company.

"I don't believe I have ever seen Mr. Graves smile at anyone," he commented. "I had thought it an expression beyond him."

Christine laughed. "Surely having been long in your employment, you have seen him smile."

His frown deepened. "No, I'm sure I have not. Not until tonight," he added thoughtfully. "I believe he likes you."

She fiddled with the fur draped across her lap. "Do you find me so unlikable?"

His gaze shot across the coach to her face. "I did not mean to imply I think you unworthy of a smile from Mr. Graves, Christine. It has just occurred to me that during these past five years he's worked for me, he's never smiled at me. Or called me anything save my formal title."

Was her husband pouting due to his servant's formal treatment of him? She tried to keep her expression serious. "Have you given him grace to address you differently?"

He shrugged. "I suppose not."

"And have you ever smiled at him, prompting a similar display of goodwill?"

The amount of concentration he gave the matter almost made her laugh again.

He sighed. "No."

Christine chose her words carefully. "I believe there should be a certain amount of respect displayed between an employee and an employer, but that friendship should know no class."

His brow lifted. "Are you suggesting that I befriend my own servants?"

"I am suggesting you see them as people first," she quipped. "All God's creatures, whatever their stations in life, feel pain no less than any other, need food no less or—"

"Or costly gowns to wear to the theater, or sparkling diamonds dripping from their ears," he interrupted dryly. "Greed, dear wife, knows no class either. Wouldn't you agree?"

Settled in her fine gown inside his fine coach, a fortune adorning her throat and ears, Christine had to admit that at times she liked the life he offered well enough. Long ago, in her youngest childhood memories, she had known hunger. Before the old marquis had found her there among the parish poor, and taken pity upon her small soul. And she supposed her greed was no weaker than Gavin's, if it was somewhat nobler.

She pulled the curtain back on the coach window, refusing to answer. They were stopped in the traffic, and on a street corner stood three children huddled together against the chilly night. The youngest child wailed softly, the sound pulling at Christine's heartstrings.

They were dressed in rags, with only dirty cloths tied around their feet in place of shoes. Christine pulled the curtain back further. The hopeless stare of the oldest child found her, and in a single glance his miserable life flashed before her eyes.

"It will be a short life, I think," she whispered softly to herself. Her gaze strayed across the coach at the man watching her. Christine moistened her lips and drew the curtain completely aside.

"Child! You, the oldest, come here!" she called out.

"What are you doing, Christine?" Gavin asked quietly, but she paid him no heed.

"Hurry and come!" she ordered.

The tallest lad, probably little more than ten, shoved the smaller children behind him and approached the coach.

"Where is your mother?" Christine asked.

"Sick," the boy answered. "Too sick to find us food for three days now."

"And what of your father?"

"Drunk," the boy spat. "What sorry wages he makes is all spent at the gin houses."

With trembling fingers, Christine reached up and pulled the diamonds from her ears. "Hold out your hand, child."

"Christine," came Gavin's warning, louder this time.

Again, she ignored her husband, and placed the diamonds in the child's hand. "These should feed you well and fetch a doctor for your mother. Now hurry home to her."

"Christine!"

Gavin's voice made her jump, made the child outside the coach jump as well. "Go!" she shouted at the boy, because already her husband had reached for the door. As he grabbed for the handle, she clutched his arm.

"Did you not tell me the gifts were mine to do with as I wished?"

"Are you mad?" he bit out. "You'll have that boy's throat slit before he makes it home!"

Gavin broke from her hold and bounded from the coach. The children were already running. "Wait for me here!" he shouted up at the coachman. "And guard my lady well."

He took off, his leather boots clicking loudly against the cobblestones as he raced after the children. Shoes or no, the little beggars were fleet of foot. Ahead, they ducked into an alleyway. Gavin rounded the corner in time to see them turn left at the alley's end. He picked up his speed, afraid once he reached the point where they'd turned, he'd see no further sign of them.

Slightly winded from his run, he reached the end of the alley and just as he suspected, didn't see a sign of the fleeing children. A door squeaked closed across the street. It was pitiful place that looked as if the whole sorry flat would come tumbling down at any moment. Being who he was, Gavin thought nothing of crossing the street and barging into the flat.

The door nearly came off its broken hinges as he entered. He glanced across the dim interior of the room, a pitiful excuse for a fire barely ablaze in the grate, and spotted a woman lying on a dirty mattress on the floor. Her eyes were wide and full of fear.

"We've nothing to steal," she croaked. "Please go and leave me and my babes alone."

His gaze swept the small room and found the children huddled together in one corner. "I haven't come to steal from you, but to retrieve something taken from me."

The woman tried to sit, but in the end only managed to turn her head toward the children. "I'll raise no thieves, I've told ye that often enough," she scolded them. "It be no great sin to beg when there's no food in yer belly, but—"

"We didn't steal," the oldest boy interrupted. He rose

from his crouched position and moved toward his mother. Opening a dirty hand, he displayed the ear bobs. "A fine lady gave them to me," he said. "An angel, I thought she was."

His mother gasped upon seeing the diamonds, then narrowed her gaze on the boy. "Ain't no lady going to give the likes of us her jewels. Ye stole them, didn't ye, boy?"

"He did not steal them," Gavin interrupted, because ill as she appeared, the woman looked as if she might box the boy's ears. "My wife did in fact hand them over to him, but against her better judgment. I'd like them back."

The woman stared at him as if either he was daft, or most certainly the woman in question belonged in Bedlam. "Give them back to him, son," the woman instructed.

"But she gave them to me," the boy insisted. "I could fetch you a doctor, we could buy food and real shoes!"

A frail hand reached up and cupped the boy's face. "Ye're a good lad, Daniel, but to keep the jewels now, when the owner has asked for them back, would be the same as stealing. Do as you've been told."

Angrily, the boy broke from her. He rose and approached Gavin. Although obviously reluctant, he held out his hand, palm up. "Take them then," he snapped, his gaze running over Gavin's clothes. "Me younger brother and sister may well starve tonight, and me mom might pass on from being sick and weak, but that's none of your matter, is it?"

Gavin's gaze strayed past the lad, to the sight of the boy's mother resting on the dirty mattress, the smaller children now huddled around her. The youngest child, a small girl, wore the eyes of an old woman. Something inside Gavin twisted, like a knife being thrust into his gut. How easily he could have lived this life, been thrown out into the streets to fend for himself after his mother's death.

Instead, he'd continued to live a life of luxury, if one of pain. And only because the old marquis would not have further scandal brought down upon his name. The reason, Gavin supposed, the old man had been so hell-bent on seeing him shamed once he became a man of his own means. Gavin reached out and snatched the diamonds from the boy's palm, sliding them inside his coat pocket. Before the boy could withdraw his hand, Gavin grabbed it.

"Jewels must be turned into pounds, and I fear you would not live long enough to make such an exchange." He reached into his coat and withdrew a small velvet pouch, placing it into the boy's hand. "There are enough pounds here to fetch a doctor for your mother, and to buy food. Do not carry all of it at once, as you stand to lose all you have to some ruffian trained to hear the jingle of coins."

The boy's mouth fell open, but Gavin continued. "Did you say your father had a weakness for the gin houses?"

"It's a sorry day I met up with that one," the woman supplied. "He'd rather see his head filled with gin than to see to us. 'E don't come home much, and when he does, it's just to sleep off a drunk and bat me and the children about."

Gavin had seen the fading bruises on the woman's pale face, and he now also saw one along the jaw of the boy standing before him. He had no tolerance for men who beat women and children.

"In one week's time, I will send a coach to this sorry address to collect you and your children. I have a country estate where you will work in my employment, and your children will never know another night of cold or hunger."

Shock claimed the woman's features; then tears filled her eyes. "I must have already died and gone to heaven," she whispered. "Why would the likes of you care what becomes of the likes of us?"

A blush crept into Gavin's face. He'd chosen to ignore the plight of those less fortunate because they were constant reminders of the lie he lived. He'd consoled himself with the fact there were too many to save. But these four, he could rescue.

"It's because of the angel," the boy whispered. "If she hadn't given me the jewels, he'd have never chased us here and saw our sorry lives. She's the one what saved us."

"Christine," Gavin said softly, recalling he'd left her in a coach with only a coachman for protection and the night crawling with more than beggars. Yes, he supposed she was responsible for saving these poor souls. A matter he would give some thought to at a later time.

"Come, lad, and fetch a doctor for your mother. I'll walk with you."

"God bless you, sir," the woman called. "And here I don't even know the name of my employer."

He tipped his hat. "Gavin Norfork, the Marquis of Greenhaven."

Her eyes widened again. "But they say he's the very devil," she whispered.

"Devil or saint, it matters not which one will see your children away from this hovel, does it?"

She shook her head. "No, sir."

"If you are not well enough to yet travel in one week, send me word at my dockside offices," he instructed. He steered the boy toward the rickety door, then turned back. "I do not give you leave to bring your husband to Greenhaven. I have no employment for drunkards and wife-beaters."

"The man's been no good husband to me," she said. "I will not shed one tear to leave his mean fists behind us."

Gavin nodded. "And I do not wish to purchase his gin, either, so hide the money well, and use it sparingly so as to not arouse his suspicions."

"That we will," she promised. "Thank you, kind sir. And thank your dear lady for us," she added.

He hoped his "dear lady" had not been set upon by thieves, or worse. Embarrassed by the raw gratitude shining in the woman's eyes, he nodded smartly and ushered the boy outside. What had Christine been thinking to give the boy her jewelry? Had she done so to show him how little a gift from him mattered to her? Somehow, he didn't think so.

Good Lord, he thought, only her heart had ruled her in that insane moment. Her heart, and an overwhelming compassion for three poor children standing on a street corner. He wondered if she'd perhaps seen herself as a child reflected in the small girl with dirty blond hair and eyes too wise. He shuddered at the thought, and could not in all honesty fault her for greedily desiring his inheritance for her own gain.

And yet, if greed truly drove her, why would she part with the jewelry? Why wouldn't she instead jealously guard the diamonds? The boy walking beside him thought her an angel. When she'd floated down the stairs earlier in her wispy white gown, for a moment, he'd thought her one, too.

But angels did not admit to having lovers. Angels did not demand annulments from their husbands. Christine remained a mystery, a feat no other woman had managed to maintain in his eyes for any extended period of time. Soon, he assured himself, he would discover all of her secrets.

Chapter Thirteen

Her Majesty's Theater burst at the seams with London's elite. Christine tried to refrain from becoming caught up in the excitement, as she was still angry at Gavin. He'd finally returned to the coach, and without a word, slipped the diamond ear bobs back onto her ears. But how could she in good conscience enjoy herself when all she could think of was the poor children who would spend another night cold and hungry? Simple. She would not enjoy the evening.

"I know you're angry with me," Gavin leaned close to whisper. "But for appearances sake, you might smile. As it stands, you look nervous, unsure of yourself."

Well, she supposed, she appeared that way because she felt very nervous and unsure of herself. Christine forced a fake smile to her lips. As of yet, no one had approached them as her husband steered her through the crowd. Only polite nods of acknowledgment were extended to His Lordship, but none, she noted, had included her.

Of course she would be shunned. Her background alone

demanded that much. And she'd made a bad start into society the night she attended the duke and duchess's gala. That she'd done so on purpose, and still intended to behave badly, made her hold her head high.

It was all a game, she told herself—the stakes too important to allow intimidation by the snobbish set. Boldly, Christine met the stare of every gentleman she passed, wearing what she hoped was a confident expression. They proceeded up a stairway, and were ushered from that point to Gavin's box seats.

She couldn't have been more pleased to find William waiting for them. He wore formal attire, acceptable but not necessarily grand. The man was handsome, she supposed, but not overly noticeable.

"What a wonderful surprise," she said, taking his hand. "His Lordship"—she purposely stressed Gavin's formal title—"didn't tell me you would be joining us."

He flashed Gavin a weak smile. "I'm afraid I came on a whim. I do hope I'm welcome."

Her husband lifted a dark brow. "Of course you're welcome, cousin." Gavin turned to her. "In the past I've offered him my seats many times, and he has always refused. It's nice to see him take a sudden interest in the arts. He should get out more."

Christine squeezed William's hand. "Yes, William, you should mix with polite society. How ever will you meet eligible young women if you don't?"

William lifted her hand to his lips. "I fear the only young women I find enticing are, unfortunately, ineligible."

It was Christine's turn to blush. William's warm hazel eyes were fastened upon her too intently to misinterpret his statement.

"Are you flirting with my wife?" Gavin drawled dryly.

The man gave him no response for a moment, then

released Christine's hand. "There's no harm in that, is there, cousin?"

Gavin smiled, but it wasn't all that pleasant. "I don't know, is there?"

With a sigh, Christine glanced between the two men. "Please put an end to your manly rivalries this instant." She took William's arm. "Of course William may flirt with me. As your cousin, it is his duty. And as his, it is your duty to allow him the liberty."

Both men continued to stare at each other. Then Gavin suddenly laughed. He slapped William on the shoulder. "She's not shy to call things as she sees them, is she, cousin?"

A smile found its way to William's mouth as well. "No, she is not, and in that regard, I do not envy you."

Gavin seated her in front, taking the chair beside her, which left his cousin to sit behind them. Christine would have much preferred William next to her. But then, she reminded herself, she was not there to enjoy herself.

Her gaze scanned the crowd below, marveling at the richness of the costumes, the feathered plumes the women wore in their hair, and the glitter of the jewels. As grand as she'd thought her gown earlier, she now felt rather unadorned.

Although lovely, the diamonds around her throat and on her ears were unobtrusive compared to some of the gaudy displays twinkling around her. Having the sensation of someone staring at her, Christine let her gaze stray to the left.

Her husband's beautiful mistress was seated in the next box. Christine hoped she did not visibly react, though she knew she had stiffened. The woman didn't glance away, but ran a cool appraising glance over her, then seemed to dismiss her.

The lady did not seem to find Gavin so dull. Her gaze caressed him in a manner Christine found vulgar. Vulgar and insulting. But her husband seemed not to notice the lady's attention, as his gaze was still riveted upon Christine.

"You have a lovely profile," he said. "I should like a silhouette done of you."

She fought down any pleasure she felt over his compliment, and reminded herself how angry she remained with him. "Whatever wasteful indulgence you choose to spend your money on is none of my concern," she said.

"I believe the opposite," he drawled. "I thought I might make a gift of it to you so you may show me how little my indulgences mean to you and throw it out in the streets."

Her gaze snapped to his handsome face. "Is that what you thought I meant to do with the ear bobs?"

He lifted a brow. "What else can I believe? That you are an angel of mercy? That you are that rarest of jewels who possesses that rarest of qualities—a truly selfless heart?"

No, she couldn't have him believing that of her. He'd said if she were that, he would give her his heart. "I care not what you believe of me," she said, then glanced away as if bored by the conversation.

"I won't deny that as truth," he countered. "But if you did feel a moment of compassion for those poor children, know that I gave them coin for food and to fetch a doctor for their mother. They will not go hungry this night."

Christine's heartbeat quickened. She turned toward him again, placing a hand on his arm without thinking. "You came to their aid?"

He smiled. "No, my lady. You came to their aid. I simply exchanged the gifts so you would not appear tonight without your jewelry."

"Oh," she whispered, her disappointment in him surprising even herself. "They were fed so I would not be an embarrassment to you."

166

His gaze drifted away from her. "I will not have society thinking I'm a pauper who cannot turn my wife out properly."

"I was under the impression you care little what society thinks of you," she countered. "Yet you go to extremes to make certain I do not shame you in their eyes."

He made a pretense of picking imaginary lint from his coat. "Before the marquis—my father's death," he amended, "there was only my soul at stake. Now I have more pressing issues to consider."

"Your inheritance," she identified.

"The title," he corrected. "Marquis sounds so much better than . . ."

She waited for him to finish the sentence, but he did not, and the orchestra began tuning up. A hush fell over the noisy crowd. With some embarrassment, Christine realized she'd completely forgotten William's presence. She turned and offered him a small smile of apology.

William wasn't looking at her, but seemed to be studying his cousin thoughtfully. No doubt he'd been privy to their conversation. His expression took her aback, as she swore it reflected hatred, or at best, a deep resentment. His gaze strayed to her and the expression quickly fled, replaced by a smile.

Slightly shaken, Christine faced forward again. The stage curtains were drawn. The audience clapped. A moment later, the players appeared and everything else faded from her thoughts. The music, the strong, skilled voices of the opera singers, totally captivated her.

"Do you understand Italian?" her husband bent close to ask.

"Not as well as I should," Christine admitted. "It seemed a useless pursuit in my schooling. I never thought I would travel abroad or attend an opera."

"Then I shall explain what is happening," Gavin offered.

She felt a rush of genuine gratitude. "Yes, please."

Gavin whispered the plot twists in her ear, moved by her responses, certain he could spend a lifetime watching her and never once become bored by a single expression that crossed her delicate features.

Admitting as much startled him. He'd been caught up in the moment. As had she, for Christine slipped her hand into his, and Gavin suspected she did so without a single thought to her actions. He marveled at the soft feel of her skin, the small perfect hand resting in his. So fragile for a woman of such spirit.

The thought of raising her fingers to his lips and kissing each one surfaced. Gavin quickly stifled the urge. Doing so would alert Christine to her innocent action and she would snatch her hand away, denying him the pleasure of further contact. Strange that he could draw such pleasure from an innocent act.

Before, only naked flesh and the hot, sweaty promise of passion to come could stir his senses. Automatically, his gaze strayed to the next box, where he'd felt Adrianna's eyes focused on him throughout the night.

Adrianna, whose hand he had never once wanted to hold, whose face, although beautiful, had never made him want to capture it on paper so that he might cherish it for all eternity. Adrianna, who stared at him still, her face pale in the dim lighting, her eyes round with shock. Her expression caused him to glance around, believing whatever she found shocking might be found elsewhere. Then Gavin realized it was he who astounded her, or rather, the attention he paid to Christine.

"What is happening?" Christine whispered urgently.

His attention shifted back to the stage. "Their love is doomed," he explained softly. "She is promised to another and cannot break her pledge."

Her fuller bottom lip trembled slightly, and Gavin wanted to soothe it with a kiss.

"B-but she loves him," Christine argued passionately. "Why can't she break her pledge?"

The curtains closed, the lamps were turned up. Gavin smiled at Christine and gave into the battle he'd been fighting. He lifted her hand to his lips and gently kissed her fingers. "Because then, my lady, there would be no further acts to follow intermission."

She snatched her hand from his. The tears in her eyes were blinked back. "I fear I've become quite caught up in a fairy tale," she explained. "Please forgive my . . ."

"Passion?" he finished. "But I like your passion, Christine. I like the way it slips past you, unheeded by your mind. It is truly genuine, and should not cause you embarrassment."

But she was embarrassed. Horrified that she'd allowed herself to become so moved by actors merely playing parts. And when had Gavin taken her hand in his? And why in creation were they sitting so close to one another? Because he'd been telling her the story unfolding on stage, she remembered. His low husky voice had been teasing the tendrils of loose curls around her ears.

"Shall I fetch you a glass of champagne, Christine?" William inquired, moving his head forward.

Her embarrassment deepened as she realized he'd been sitting behind them, probably distracted by Gavin's explanations of the play and having trouble seeing over the both of them in the bargain.

"That would be lovely, William," she responded.

He stood and left the box, which left Christine alone with her husband. She fingered the silk skirt of her dress nervously.

"Would you like to stand for a while?" Gavin asked. "Or we could mingle with the others who gather downstairs during intermission."

Although she didn't care to mix with the crowd, Christine reminded herself of her mission. She couldn't very well flirt and cause speculation with other men with only her husband for company.

"I would like to go downstairs," she said. "But what of William?"

Gavin rose and offered her a hand up. "We shall look for him."

She took his hand and together they made their way downstairs. The buzzing of voices was so loud Christine wondered how people could converse with one another at all. Of course, after standing beside Gavin for a few moments, she realized it would not affect them. No one approached them, or more to the point, her. She felt no shame for herself, but for Gavin, she supposed, having his precious society shun him would be difficult.

"Perhaps we should return to the box," she said.

He lifted a brow. "I would have never thought you a coward."

Her back straightened. "I am not a coward."

"Neither am I," he said. "We will stand our ground, if we must stand it alone."

How proud a bearing he possessed, she realized in that instant. As if he dared any and all to question his presence among the elite or his right to be there. The rest of the crowd seemed to pale beside Gavin. Was that the reason she had difficulty taking her eyes off him? Rescue came a moment before her husband took note of her disability.

"Gavin, old boy," Chester Thorton called in his usual jolly manner. "And the lovely Christine."

James Dumont hurried toward them alongside Chester, and their haste reminded Christine of a horse race. She knew they both had a fondness for betting, and had to question whether or not it was a race with a wager attached.

The two men reached them in the same instant, and a moment later, both reached for her hands, each bringing one to his mouth to plant a quick kiss.

"I believe James was first," Christine said with a laugh.

"Blast," Chester muttered. "He always wins my money."

"It is not proper etiquette for a gentleman to kiss a lady's hand unless she first gives him permission," Gavin pointed out dryly.

"I don't believe you asked for permission earlier, Your Lordship," Christine countered just as dryly.

He smiled, the crooked smile she found irresistible. "But unlike my friends, I have never claimed to be a gentleman, as you well know, wife."

The added endearment brought a lift of Chester's brows and a smug smile to James Dumont's lips. Christine found herself quite flustered by so short a word. She immediately sought distraction.

"Are you enjoying the production?" she asked the young gentlemen.

"Not nearly so much as we are enjoying watching His Lordship's box," James answered. "You are a blessed balm to the eyes, Christine."

She lowered her lashes demurely over the compliment, using the guise to glance at Gavin. He didn't appear angered by his friend's bold compliment, but merely seemed to accept that it had been given.

An older gentleman joined the group. Christine recognized him from Gavin's office. Mr. Collins, she believed. He bowed politely to her, then turned to her husband.

"Might I have a moment of your time, Your Lordship?" he asked. "I fear there will be a small delay in the business we discussed."

"Can it not wait?" Gavin countered, his gaze lingering over Christine. "I'm sure my wife would be bored by such matters."

"We will entertain Christine," Chester piped up. "And look, here comes your cousin to make our group respectable."

171

Christine glanced in the direction of Chester's nod and saw William making his way toward them, a glass of champagne in hand. "I'm positive I will be perfectly fine without your company, husband," she said.

He frowned at her use of the endearment, she supposed because she had spoken it too sickly sweet to be counted as anything but sarcastic. With a curt nod to all, he allowed himself to be led away by Mr. Collins.

William reached them, handing her the glass. "Thank you, cousin," Christine replied.

A moment of awkward silence settled among the group. She suspected William didn't feel comfortable in the company of two dandies such as Chester and James. She decided the only things they all had in common were their ties to her husband and the first part of the opera.

"Did you enjoy the performance thus far?" she asked William.

"Yes," he answered. "I found the 'performance' quite fascinating. A superior job of acting."

The stress he'd placed on the word performance did not go unnoticed by her. Nor his reference to superior acting. Christine had the distinct impression the performance to which he referred was not the one that took place on stage, but rather in the seats directly in front of him. Was Gavin the actor he had complimented? She couldn't fault his attentiveness throughout the evening. Was his interest in her and her pleasure a deception?

"I thought the sopranos a little flat," Chester commented.

"Oh, no," Christine argued. "I have never heard such beautiful voices."

"But you are a babe when it comes to the opera," James said. "This is not the best opera I have seen."

A discussion broke out between James and Chester as to which opera they had both seen should be considered the best. Of course neither could agree, but Christine found their arguments a pleasant diversion. She sipped her champagne and listened, surprised not much later to find other voices involved in the dispute. Male voices.

She glanced about and found herself completely surrounded. Her gaze snagged on one man who stared at her beseechingly. It was the young man who'd danced with her at Adrianna Shipley's gala. Thomas Wentworth. He was also the fop who'd bravely brushed the side of her breast with his hand.

"Christine, ah, Your Ladyship," he stepped forward to whisper. "I must have a word with you."

Nervously, her gaze flitted over the gentlemen surrounding her. James and Chester had gone from arguing to wagering over how many would agree with each man's choice for best performance so far seen this season. William eyed her curiously, then excused himself from the group.

"You have my permission to speak to me," she said to Wentworth. "But here, not in private."

He moved closer. "I must beg your forgiveness for my behavior when last we met."

"I would think so," she agreed.

"To have deserted you on the dance floor must make me the worst coward in your eyes."

Deserted? She thought he'd been apologizing for fondling her indecently. "I don't think you a coward, Mr. Wentworth, but merely a wise man looking after his best interests."

A stain of red crept into his cheeks. "Your husband is not a man to anger. He is quite accomplished with both a pistol and a sword."

She searched for Gavin in the crowd, but couldn't locate him. "Has he ever killed anyone?"

Wentworth laughed. "Well, no, probably not outside of his duties in the war. But I have seen his skills displayed," he assured her. "In fencing jousts, and on hunts. I have never seen him beaten at any contest."

"I don't suppose you have," she said, mostly to herself. She batted her lashes in what she hoped was a flirtatious manner. "If my husband is so feared, why are you speaking to me, Mr. Wentworth?"

The red stain in his cheeks deepened. "Because, dearest Christine, your husband is otherwise occupied."

She followed his gaze, expecting to see Gavin conversing with Mr. Collins. It was not the older man who stood so close to her husband, staring seductively up at him. It was his mistress, Adrianna Shipley.

Chapter Fourteen

Persistence, Gavin had once believed, was an admirable trait in any person. He now had reason to change his mind. Adrianna had stepped into his path on his way to rejoin Christine. His wife, meanwhile, was surrounded by admirers, including that idiot Thomas Wentworth.

"Let her enjoy herself," Adrianna crooned. "I would hate for you to make a fool of yourself over her yet again."

"I mean only to see that tongues do not wag," he said, trying to relax his features.

"If you storm to her side, pretending to be the jealous husband, it is your behavior that will have them wagging," Adrianna countered. "Why not let the orphan bride have her fun, and us ours?"

He sighed. "I thought I made myself understood in the park," he said.

Adrianna smiled, then reached forward and placed her hand on him. A very private part of him, to be exact. "And I thought I made myself understood as well."

His gaze darted around the room. "I believe your hand is resting on a place where it does not belong."

Her smiled widened. "It has rested there before."

"But not in public," he ground out.

She suddenly frowned. "You've become a bore, Gavin. There are too many bodies crushed together for anyone to notice where my hand is resting, and I think not long ago, you wouldn't have minded. In fact, I'm sure you would have found us a dark corner, lifted my skirts, and had me then and there."

"Regardless of my reputation, I would have never compromised you in that fashion." He tried to step away from her, but without luck. She was right. There were too many bodies crowded together, leaving him little room to maneuver.

"Do not play the gallant with me," she snapped, then schooled her features back into a pleasant mask. Her hand strayed bravely toward the top of his trousers. "It is your recklessness that excites me. And, I suppose, your coldness that heats my blood. Not to mention one other impressive asset you possess."

Gavin's fingers closed around hers. "Adrianna," he warned, but was interrupted before he could say more.

"My lady, if you would kindly remove your hand from my husband's trousers, I would have him escort me back to our seats," Christine said, her voice pleasant. "I believe the curtain is about to go up again."

Adrianna jerked her hand away. Gavin watched the two women take each other's measure. Christine emptied her glass and handed it to the duchess.

"Since you have the manners of a tavern whore, perhaps you will return my glass for me."

Stunned, Adrianna accepted the empty glass without thought. A titter of laughter followed from Christine's entourage of admirers. Then she walked away without so much as a backward glance. Gavin pushed his way through the crowd, finally managing to reach her side. He took her arm, surprised she did not snatch it away from him.

"Let me explain," he said.

"I saw enough not to need an explanation, Your Lordship. I may be, in your opinion, an uneducated country lass, and to make matters worse, an orphan, but I am smart enough to understand what a woman is looking for when she goes fishing inside a man's trousers."

"I didn't encourage her," he said quietly.

A sarcastic smile shaped Christine's lips. "You have let her fish there before, Your Lordship. I would say that is encouragement enough."

He had no rejoinder. To deny her words would be foolish, and insulting to his wife, since he'd admitted as much to her the first night they met.

"I'm sorry," he said, and sincerely meant it. "I have ruined your evening."

"Your conceit is the only thing about you that never ceases to amaze me," she ground through her teeth. "A ruined evening is little compared to a ruined life. And the duchess may fish in your pond all she chooses as far as I'm concerned. If you'll recall, I have cast my line elsewhere."

God, what a sharp tongue she had. And here he'd spent most of the night thinking her an angel. Gavin bit back a response and ushered her into their box. William jumped to his feet.

"There you both are," he said cheerfully. "They're about to raise the curtain."

"William, will you sit up front with me?" Christine asked.

His gaze moved to Gavin. "I think not, Christine, although the offer is kind. I do not speak Italian as well as my cousin, and could not explain the unfolding developments."

Gavin almost demanded he take his seat, but then people would be watching them, curious if the exchange downstairs had caused a rift between husband and wife. Gavin meant to have society believe they were well matched in temperament, if not in social status—less cause for an annulment.

"Take my seat, Christine," Gavin suggested. "I have just noticed you had to look around me to see the stage."

Better, also, that he placed himself between the duchess and his wife. Adrianna had probably recovered from Christine's insult and was enraged. Surprisingly, the sharp-tongued angel offered no argument, but the box was cramped and they had to brush up against one another in order to exchange places. She stiffened and pushed back against the balcony banister.

What happened next moved slower than time. He heard the wood give, saw surprise register on Christine's features, and then she was falling backward. He grabbed for her, but too late.

"Christine!" Her name left his throat in a strangled shout.

Loud gasps and screams from below propelled him to the edge of the balcony. He scanned the crowd below, his heart pounding, afraid he might find Christine's broken body among them. All faces were still turned up toward the balcony.

"Gavin!"

Her scream cut into him, made his heart pound louder in his ears. He bent and looked directly below. He saw Christine dangling above the crowd, holding onto a thin drape that ran the length of the theater as decoration.

"William!" he called. "Grab my legs and steady me!"

Gavin quickly scrambled to his belly, edging forward to dangle his arms over the balcony. "William!" he shouted again when he didn't feel the man grab hold of him. Gavin turned to find the box empty.

"Dammit," he swore, searching for something to steady himself. He knew Christine's weight would be little burden. But from this position, it was easier to pull one down than to pull one up. Two gentlemen appeared at the box door.

"Hold my legs!" he shouted at them.

Both hurried forward to do as he instructed, and with a sigh of relief, he eased his body further over the balcony.

"Christine, reach for my hands!" he shouted.

She glanced up, her face pale and her eyes round. "I'm afraid to let go! The drape, I fear it's about to tear!"

"Lower me more!" he instructed the two men behind him.

They pushed him forward until he dangled halfway over the balcony. He reached toward his wife, but could not snatch her wrists.

"Christine, you must let go and grab for my hands!"

Although he knew she must be terrified, his heart swelled with pride over her bravery when she nodded.

"I'll count to three!" he shouted. "Then let go and grab for my hands!"

Gavin looked past her to the floor below. Several men were gathered directly beneath Christine, waiting to either catch her or break her fall. She might survive if she were to miss his hands, but he wouldn't take that chance.

"Push me forward!" he instructed the men holding him.

"But Your Lordship, we may not be able to hold your weight!" a voice argued. "Would you see us all go tumbling over the edge?"

Yes, he wanted to shout, but knew he was being unreasonable. "Then hold me steady and be prepared for the a jolt when my wife grabs onto me!"

He felt them secure his legs tighter. Then he counted, "One! Two! Three!"

Christine wanted to squeeze her eyes shut when she let

go of the drape, but she needed to see Gavin's hands. She grabbed for them, missed, and dropped, then jerked when his fingers, like steel bands, encircled her wrists. Her arms felt as if they were being pulled from the sockets, but she hadn't fallen.

"Pull us back!" he shouted.

She stared up at him, and he tried to give her assurance with a strained smile, even if he could not hide the worry in his dark eyes. It seemed to take an eternity. Gavin's arms shook, but the steely feel of his fingers never surrendered their hold upon her wrists.

Gradually, he began to disappear until only his arms appeared, his hands still holding her securely. Other arms reached for her, but Gavin never released her, not even when she'd been pulled to safety. She sat on the balcony floor, him in front of her.

"Are you all right?" he asked, panting from his exertions.

"I-I think so," she answered weakly. "Except that you are holding my wrists too tightly," she pointed out.

He glanced down and released her, but then he touched her cheek gently. "Can you stand?" His hand trembled—his whole body, for that matter.

"Can *you?*" she asked with a smile.

"That's a good question. Shall we see?"

Gavin gained his feet first, helping her up. Her knees felt wobbly, but managed to support her weight. As soon as they were both standing, a loud cheer went up from below.

"I believe they are waiting for us to take our bow," Gavin said dryly.

"Then by all means, we must not disappoint them." Christine knew shock still claimed her, or she wouldn't be as collected as she portrayed. While she still maintained some dignity, she swept into a graceful curtsy. Her husband bowed gallantly. The crowd went wild.

"Do you wish to stay for the next act?" her husband asked.

Christine felt her composure slipping, felt her legs start to tremble. "I believe I have had enough drama for one evening. Could you please take me home?"

His gaze softened upon her. "Yes, my lady."

Rather than allow her to walk, Gavin swept her up in his arms, which caused another cheer to rise from the crowd below. Before he carried her through the box door and into the hallway, Christine thought to thank all of the gentlemen who'd come to their aid, as her husband seemed more intent upon getting her away from the theater.

His manners were horrid, his behavior with his mistress earlier, unforgivable . . . but he had probably saved her life tonight—had risked his own to do so.

The man was a constant contradiction. How could she continue to despise him when some saintly act followed upon the heels of every devilish one he committed? She had a mental picture of an angel and a demon each having a hold on one of his arms, tugging back and forth in a fight for his soul.

Gavin had managed to sweep her downstairs and out the door, finding his waiting coach and coachman, who snapped to attention because he'd been dozing. The man jumped down and hurried to get the door. Christine had almost made it inside when William's shout drew her up.

"Gavin! Christine!" He raced up to them, puffing for breath. "Thank God you are both safe."

"No thanks to you," Gavin remarked unkindly. "Why the devil did you take off?"

Still breathing hard, William answered, "I panicked. My first thought was to race downstairs and catch Christine if she fell. I couldn't get through the crowd."

"Poor William," Christine said. "We are perfectly fine, as you can see, and it was very brave of you to race

181

downstairs with the intention of catching me, wasn't it, Gavin?"

Her husband's frown slowly melted away. He nodded. "Yes, it was very noble. If you'll excuse us, William, I should take Christine home. The evening's turned into somewhat of a strain."

At his dry wit, William laughed, the tension draining from him. "If you can jest about the incident, I know you are in fact all right. The evening could have ended much worse than it has. Well," he said with a sigh. "Good night, then."

"Oh," Christine suddenly said. "Do you need a ride home, William?"

He shook his head. "Thank you, but no. I'll walk. My apartments aren't far from here."

"It's no trouble," Gavin put in, but William waved away the offer, tipping his hat as he set off.

The trembling in Christine's legs had spread up her body. She tried not to shake, but when Gavin turned back to her, his expression turning quickly to one of concern, she knew she had failed.

"Let me help you," he insisted, but she avoided his aid and hurried into the coach.

Gavin jumped inside and pulled the fur up around her. "Home, Franklin!" he shouted out the window. "And hurry!"

The coach lurched forward. His wife's pale complexion and her violent trembling had Gavin worried. When her teeth clicked together, he climbed beneath the fur with her and held her close. She protested for the briefest moment, but he shushed her, smoothing the stray curls from her face.

"It's a delayed reaction to your ordeal," he told her. "The trembling will subside once we get you home and snugly tucked into bed."

Or he hoped it would. If it did not, he would have a

doctor fetched. Which might be a wise decision regardless, Gavin decided. She continued to tremble for the remainder of the ride home. Once the coach pulled to a stop in front of his town home, Gavin jumped out and gathered Christine up, furs and all, hurrying to the house.

The coachman bounded up the steps and opened the door for him. Then, it seemed as if his household turned into bedlam. Graves appeared, rushing forward to snatch his hat from his head and the cape from around his neck.

"What has happened, Your Lordship?"

"Oh, my," Tillie gasped before Gavin could answer the man's inquiry. "My poor chick. What's wrong with her?"

"She's had a fright," Gavin answered, headed for the stairs with both servants fast on his heels. He climbed them, allowing Tillie to rush ahead and open Christine's door.

"Help me get her undressed and into bed," he instructed the maid.

"Tillie alone can help me," Christine said, although her voice came out shaky due to her trembling.

Settling his wife upon the bed, he said, "But the both of us will make faster work of it." Gavin bent and removed her shoes. He almost received a foot to the face.

"And I insist Tillie alone will help me undress," Christine barked, her voice stronger. "And the quicker you leave, the quicker we can see the task done!"

Frustrated, Gavin rose. He met his wife's steely stare for a moment, cursed, and left the room. Graves followed.

"What should I fetch the lady, Your Lordship?"

Gavin didn't know. He began pacing. "Maybe tea to calm her," he suggested.

"I've just put a kettle on," Graves said. "I'll bring her a cup immediately."

Following him down the hall, Gavin ducked into his own bedchamber. He stripped away his necktie and coat, then unbuttoned the high neck of his shirt. Grabbing up his brandy decanter, he quit the room. He walked to Christine's door and knocked.

"Are you decent?" he called.

"No, Your Lordship, she is not!" came Tillie's raised voice. "I've but barely got her unlaced!"

Gavin flexed the fingers on one hand, annoyed. If Christine would have simply allowed him, he could have had her stripped and into bed by now. Of course, his wife would not appreciate his talents in that area. Gavin raised the brandy decanter to his lips and took a swig.

He was no drunkard, but by God, he could use a drink. A thought popped into his head. A disturbing one. How had the banister broken with only Christine's slight weight pressing against the wood?

The appearance of Mr. Graves, teacup and saucer in hand, interrupted his thoughts. When he reached Gavin's side, a good splash of brandy was added to the steaming tea. The door opened a moment later.

"She's decent now," Tillie said stiffly. "But I be thinkin' she needs her rest."

"I want to make certain she doesn't need a doctor," Gavin countered. "Step aside, girl. Ah, Tillie," he corrected. "Please," he added as an afterthought.

Her brows raised, and Tillie's pursed lips softened into a smile before she stepped aside and bade him enter. Gavin handed the brandy decanter to Mr. Graves, then hurried inside. Although Christine was beautiful with her hair wild around her shoulders, and tempting to distraction as she relaxed against her pillows, her pale complexion still worried him. Gavin sat beside her on the bed.

"Has the trembling stopped?"

She pulled the covers higher. "Mostly," she answered.

He stuck his hand toward Graves for the saucer and teacup. "Drink this. It will calm you."

The trembling had not ceased, he noted when she took

184

the cup from him. Gavin steadied her hand with his and moved closer.

"Graves, have a doctor fetched," he instructed.

"No, that isn't necessary," Christine argued. "I'm sure I'll be fine shortly."

"I want to be positive," he countered. "Graves."

That one word sent the servant to a nearby table, where he set the brandy down before stepping smartly from the room. Now Gavin had to rid himself of the other shadow looming over him.

"Tillie, go downstairs and rouse the cook. Have her prepare your mistress a bowl of broth. It will give her strength."

"Right away, Your Lordship," Tillie said, for once doing as she'd been bidden.

Gavin steered the cup to Christine's lips and urged her to sip. She immediately coughed. "Good Lord, what is that?" she fussed.

"Tea," Gavin answered innocently. "Laced with brandy."

"It's horrible."

"I think you could do without the tea and just have a straight shot," he decided. "It will warm you."

He retrieved the decanter, at a loss what to do without a glass. "Just tip it up and take a swig."

She eyed him and the decanter with the same amount of disgust. "I will not."

He sighed. "Please, Christine. Don't be difficult."

After a moment, she relented, snatching the bottle from him. Her hand still trembled slightly when she tipped the bottle up and took a drink. She coughed again and shoved the decanter at him.

"Good God," she choked. "That is . . . wonderful. Why, it burns all the way down and settles warmly in the belly."

He cocked a brow. "Would you like another sip?"

Christine moistened her lips. "Maybe just one."

Again, he handed her the decanter. She took a sip, rather a gulp, and managed to swallow without coughing. When she handed the brandy back to him, Gavin took a swig as well.

"Brandy really is quite nice," Christine informed him. She held out her hand. "Look, it's already calming me." Her hand trembled and she frowned. "Maybe one more sip."

With a smile, he indulged her. Several sips later, the doctor arrived. Gavin left the room while the man examined his wife. He thought he heard her giggle a couple of times through the closed door. The doctor emerged shortly thereafter.

"How is she?" Gavin asked.

"Nearly drunk," the man muttered, frowning at the decanter Gavin held in his hand. "I imagine besides a pounding head, she'll be fine come morning."

Gavin started to enter the room, but the good doctor stepped in front of him. "She's sleeping peacefully now. It would be best not to disturb her further."

"I'll have her maid sleep in the same room," he said. "In case she wakes during the night."

"Very well." The doctor nodded. "But mark my words, she is gone for the night. Have someone fetch me come morning if she isn't feeling fully herself."

He walked the man to the stairs. Graves waited below. "Graves, send Tillie to tend her mistress once you've seen the doctor out. She's to sleep in the same room in case Christine awakens and is need of anything."

When Graves nodded, Gavin returned to his room. He paced for a while. The evening had been too eventful to allow him to relax, and despite the doctor's instructions, he went to Christine's room. She rested peacefully against the pillows. Gavin turned down the lamps and bent over his wife. He touched her cheek, assured by the warmth of her skin and the even sound of her breathing that she was well. Tillie entered and he brought a finger to his lips.

"Should I light the fire, Your Lordship?" she asked.

"Yes, but be quiet so as not to disturb her." He crept to the doorway. "And come for me if she wakes during the night and is not well."

"I never did hear what happened to put her in such a state," the maid whispered.

"That is a tale better left for tomorrow," he said. "And one your mistress will probably want to relay herself."

Although clearly disappointed she would have to wait, the maid went about her duties. Gavin left. Graves was in the process of stoking Gavin's own night fire when he entered his room.

"Is Her Ladyship all right?" Graves asked.

"Drunk as a sailor," Gavin drawled dryly. He smiled at the servant's startled expression. "A bit too much brandy to steady her nerves," he explained. "But the doctor said she should be fine by morning."

"Oh," the man sighed with relief. "Will that be all?"

Gavin walked to his comfortable chair before the fire and sat. "Aren't you curious as to what happened, Graves?"

The servant lifted a brow. "It is not my place to ask, Your Lordship."

"You asked downstairs," Gavin reminded him.

"Purely a reflex, and an improper one, Your Lordship."

Annoyed with his stuffiness, Gavin motioned him toward the chair next to him. "Come and sit, Graves. Have a brandy with me and I'll tell you a tale of an angel who gave her diamonds to three starving children, of a vixen who took on a duchess, and of a woman who showed courage as great as any soldier I have fought beside."

The man's brow lifted higher. "Is that an order, Your Lordship?"

"Yes, dammit," Gavin snapped. "And while we are

only men, sharing a glass and telling a tale, I give you permission to call me Gavin."

His servant stepped forward and poured the glasses. "As you wish."

"And you, Graves." Gavin accepted the drink he handed him. "What shall I call you?"

Seating himself with dignity, the man answered, "You may call me Graves. Or Mr. Graves, whichever you prefer." Then a smile, be it ever so slight, was awarded to his employer.

Chapter Fifteen

Other than a slight headache, Christine felt fine the next morning. Of course the moment Tillie had been assured of her well-being, the maid demanded to know what had happened the previous evening. There was too much to tell, so Christine only offered the high points while the maid helped her dress and brushed her long hair until it hung silky down her back.

They were discussing the style Christine's long hair should be arranged in when a soft knock sounded on the door. Thinking it would be Mr. Graves with her morning chocolate, Christine bade him enter. It was not Mr. Graves, but her husband, who entered with her breakfast tray.

"Good morning, Christine," he said pleasantly, setting her tray on a table. "Are you well?"

"Yes, Your Lordship," she answered, slightly breathless from the handsome sight of him. "I-I thought you would be Mr. Graves," she added lamely.

Gavin smiled. "Mr. Graves is not himself this morning, so I brought your breakfast in his place."

" 'E's ailing?" Tillie blurted out. "What's wrong with him?"

The master of the house gave her a dark look for her lack of manners, but answered, "Only a glass or two more of brandy than he is used to last night. His head is pounding. Do you by chance know a remedy that might help him, Tillie?"

"Me father was an awful drunkard," Tillie announced, as if she might have informed them her father was a tailor, or a butcher. "I know a little concoction me mam used to make for him so he could cart his lazy arse off to work."

"Could you make it for Mr. Graves?"

"Oh, aye," Tillie blustered, her cheeks flushing a pretty pink. "I'll have him right as rain in no time."

She flounced from the room without asking her leave of either her master or her mistress, Christine noticed. She was left standing alone with Gavin.

"Well, thank you for breakfast," Christine said, hoping he took it as a dismissal. He, of course, did not. Gavin walked over and removed the heating lid from her plate. She noticed a newspaper lying on her tray. He took note of her interest.

"There's mention of us made in the *Times* this morning."

"No doubt praises were sung to your heroism."

He smiled. "More were sung to yours."

She approached the tray. "You jest."

Lifting the paper, he handed it to her. "See for yourself."

Christine settled on the bed and scanned the paper. She came upon the article, very pleased that true to his word, there were comments about her courage under the circumstances. Her smile stretched when it was said that her curtsy to the crowd after her daring rescue made her instantly a success among the ton.

Reading further, however, caused her smile to fade. Her eyes widened and her mouth went dry. "This . . . this is horrible," she declared, slamming the paper down.

Looking very much the innocent, Gavin lifted a brow. "What is horrible, my lady?"

She jumped up, her hands balled at her sides. "You know good and well what is horrible! This unfavorable light they have cast upon us! They speak of us as if we are . . . are smitten with one another!"

His innocent look remained, even if the slight smile that appeared on his mouth spoiled the effect. "It must have seemed that we are to everyone."

"But it's a lie!" she insisted.

"But in print, nonetheless," he countered, sighing as if he, too, were upset such a seed had been planted.

This was a dreadful development. Christine couldn't have everyone believing she and her husband were in love with one another. Such a belief would ruin her plans. She paced back and forth.

"You shouldn't have been so heroic," she fussed.

Gavin fell into step beside her. "Forgive me for not allowing you to fall to your death."

She stopped. "I'm sorry," she muttered, then looked up at him. "I suppose I should thank you for saving my life."

His gaze rolled upward. "Not if you must force yourself to do so."

Placing her hands on her hips, she said, "Well, it does seem rather out of character for you. I thought you were only concerned for your own well-being."

The hurt that crossed his features had her regretting saying such to him. It was out of anger she'd attacked him. His vulnerability didn't remain exposed for long. He schooled his face into a sarcastic mask.

"Then you may go on believing so," he said. "In truth,

it was the fact that most of London's society gentlemen stood below staring up your dress that spurred me into action."

She countered before thinking her words through. "Why shouldn't they get a glance up my dress? Most of their wives have had their hands down your trousers!"

His face darkened a shade. "But that matters not to you, does it, Christine? You've cast your line elsewhere, and where the bloody hell is your little fish?"

Her emotions were getting the best of her, and the one that plagued her currently had green eyes, and was said to be a monster. The thought of other women touching Gavin, kissing him, loving him, suddenly infuriated her.

"My fish is not so little," she snapped. "And he is none of your business."

Gavin's hands shot out to capture her shoulders. "He is my business. He's trying to take something that belongs to me."

For a moment, the way his eyes softened upon her, she thought he might actually be referring to her. But that was ridiculous, Christine assured herself. All he truly cared about was the inheritance, and keeping his silly title.

"It is something you neither need, nor most probably want," she challenged.

"But there you are wrong," he said softly. "I do want it. Very badly."

Their eyes locked. And then, quite suddenly, they were in each other's arms. They were simply staring at each other one moment, and kissing the next. The heat that sprang to life between them, whether born of anger or passion, flared high and engulfed her, chasing all else from her thoughts but being in his arms.

She kissed him back, shyly touching her tongue to his, then more bravely delving into his mouth. He slanted his mouth over hers to deepen his claim on her lips.

A hot, delicious sense of urgency stole over Christine.

One that made her heartbeat quicken, and her fingers twist into his hair when he pulled her closer. She pressed against him, further impassioned by the hard, solid feel of him . . . and the heat that spread from his body to hers.

It was too much heat, because she couldn't breathe, felt as if she were suffocating, drowning in a raging pool of fire. When his hands slid from around her back and past her ribs to cup her breasts, she swelled into his palms, aching from somewhere deep within. She wanted to touch him, too.

Her fingers fumbled with the buttons of his high collar, clumsy until his took over the task, quickly loosening the buttons before they moved, she realized, with purpose to the tiny buttons at the neck of her own morning gown.

"Good Lord," she whispered, shoving him away. "What are we doing?"

He stood there as if momentarily stunned. "We're doing what we both want to do. What we have wanted to do since the night I carried you from a crowded ball to my bed."

She shook her head. "No. I never wanted this—cannot want this. This was never part of my plan. Never—"

He ended her protests with his lips. Christine melted against him, cursing her weak will, her hot blood, the damnable end to her sainthood. Difficult as it was, she managed the strength to rescue her mouth from his.

"If you truly have a heart, you will release me. Can you become the gentleman you have presented to me of late? Or are you still only a wolf in sheep's clothing?"

His eyes could burn with such fire, such passion. Or perhaps there was anger in them to add to their spark. He stared down at her, and for a moment, she thought he would kiss her again, but instead, he released her and stepped back.

"What I am, Christine, is only a man," he answered. "One you are slowly, but most assuredly, making insane."

Without another word, he walked to the door, opened it, and left. He did not close her door angrily, but she heard his own slam shut with enough force to rattle the house. Her gaze still trained on the door, she saw it open again. Tillie poked her head inside, looking like a frightened mouse.

"What's put the devil back into him?" she asked, easing into the room.

Christine burst into tears. Perhaps last night's events still affected her more than she realized. Maybe she was still shaken by her brush with death—that and her brush with Gavin. She walked to the bed and collapsed, burying her face in her hands.

A moment later she felt Tillie's weight settle beside her. The maid's soft touch only increased the flow of Christine's tears.

"There now," Tillie soothed. "What's 'appened to make my poor lady cry?"

Christine sniffed loudly. "It seems so hopeless, Tillie. This burden I've been given. This cause entrusted to me. I am only a woman, and not a strong one, or a brave one. I am but a poor orphan without knowledge from whence I came, and no skills to do battle with."

Tillie patted her shoulder. "I think you be very brave, m'lady. And your strength is one of character. Don't ye believe who a person becomes is more important than how they began?"

She blinked back tears. "You provide a good argument, Tillie." She gently took the maid's hand. "And your belief in me touches me deeply, but I have accomplished nothing since my journey to London. Instead, Gavin makes a mockery of my plans. He performs acts of heroism and sways all to believe that he and I are . . ."

"Are what?"

"In love," she nearly sobbed. When her maid lifted a brow, Christine said, "Which is a lie. A lie that strengthens his cause and weakens mine. I am not properly prepared to fight him."

Tillie sighed. "He has an unfair advantage," she agreed. "As I said in the beginning, it's a shame ye haven't someone to teach you, to help you win this battle ye've been given. A grand lady to guide you."

"Yes," Christine agreed despondently. "Only, I think a grand lady would not suffice in my situation. Better one who knows the cunning ways to down a man. One who creates scandal herself. A woman . . ."

"A woman?" Tillie prompted.

"A woman such as the Duchess, Adrianna Shipley."

Tillie said, "She's nothing but a coldhearted witch who cares for nothing but her own pleasures and her own wants. I seen that in her easy enough the day she came visiting us at the hotel."

Christine rose from the bed and began to pace. "She is certainly not anyone I would wish to befriend. But my gain might be her own, and she might help me because of it."

"You'd throw in your lot with yer husband's mistress?" Tillie squeaked.

The mere thought sickened Christine. But what was she to do? What choice did she have? Gavin threatened not only to thwart her plans, but to steal her soul. What had happened between them only a moment past proved his power over her. And it was a dark power—one that robbed her of reason and good sense. One that might compromise not only her quest, but her heart in the bargain.

"I will pay the duchess a visit," Christine decided. "I fear the only way to beat my husband at his own game is to meet him on his own ground."

Gavin left the house a short time later, his destination his dockside offices. But first, he had something of importance to investigate. Something that had kept him awake long after he and Mr. Graves had parted drunken company the night before. A dark suspicion had crept into him at the blackest hour of the night.

Her Majesty's Theater this time of morning was empty of all save those who labored to clean up the mess made by patrons the prior evening. He went upstairs to his box, not surprised to find two men replacing the banister that had broken beneath Christine's slight weight last night.

"Can I take a look before you secure it back in place?" he asked the men.

They glanced up from their task, both appearing startled to see him.

"Sorry, sir, but we've already put it back on," one man said.

"And anchored it tight this time, we did," the other added.

Gavin ran a hand over his cheeks, disappointed. A sudden thought occurred to him. "Did you replace the banister with a new one?"

One man shook his head. "Didn't have to, sir. As far as we could see, there was nothing wrong with the other one. Oh, it's a bit beat up from falling to the floor below, but a fresh coat of varnish will see it looking good as new."

"It wasn't broken?" Gavin further questioned. "And where you replaced it, the wood wasn't splintered?"

"No, sir," one of the men answered. "It just appears as if the thing came loose."

Gavin walked to where the men squatted and bent. He ran a hand along the wood brace where the banister had been secured. The wood was smooth save for a few slight dents.

"What are these indentions?"

Both men shrugged. "Don't know, sir," one man answered. "But there's some along the other side as well."

"Do they coincide with where the pegs were driven back in?"

"Now that you mention it, that they do," the worker agreed. He frowned. "Didn't think nothing of it, sir. But it seems as if—"

"The pegs were purposely loosened with an object of some sort," Gavin finished, his blood turning cold in his veins. "Did you see anyone up here this past week?"

The workers shook their heads before one said, "No, sir, but the players and people come and go as they choose. No one pays anyone any mind."

"Have you thought to check the other boxes for loose banisters?"

"We was ordered to do that first thing this morning. Don't want no more accidents happening."

"And did you find anything amiss?"

"Nothing," a worker answered. "Everything else is just as it should be."

"Thank you," Gavin said, then turned on his heel and started from the box.

"Don't look like no accident," he heard one man mutter.

"I'd say someone wanted a body to tumble from this box last night," the other agreed. "But was it the lady they wanted to fall, or the gentleman, or maybe the both of them?"

Those very questions plagued Gavin as he walked back downstairs and out of the theater. He intended to find the answers.

Chapter Sixteen

Christine knew it wasn't proper to pay a visit without first sending a note around asking for permission to call. She feared, however, that doing so in this case would simply see her request denied. She sat in a beautifully decorated parlor waiting to see if the duchess would receive her, and questioning her sanity at confronting her husband's mistress. Her escapade was daring, to say the least.

Requesting a meeting with a woman she'd insulted the prior evening, not to mention sneaking from the house and walking the distance unescorted, was not the action of a sane woman. A servant entered, adding to her nervousness.

"The duchess will meet with you shortly," he informed her. "Would you care for refreshments while you wait?"

"Thank you, but no," Christine answered. She couldn't eat anything with her stomach twisted into knots.

"Tea, perhaps?"

"Yes, please." Something to drink might pry her tongue from the roof of her mouth.

The servant left, and Christine fidgeted with her clothing. She wore the gray visiting gown Gavin said did not suit her coloring. It was a choice she wished she'd rethought a few minutes later when the duchess swept into the room, resplendent in a dark mauve creation that brought out the color in her cheeks and accented the paleness of her skin.

"To what do I owe this displeasure?" she asked snootily.

Christine saw no point in side stepping the matter. "I have to come to enlist your aid, m'lady."

"The proper form of address is Your Grace," she quipped, taking a seat across from Christine. "And what have you come to beg of me? That I leave your husband alone? Have you come to tell me that you have fallen madly in love with him and fear you cannot win his affections if I remain a temptation to him?"

A hand automatically flew to Christine's throat. "I have come to confess no such thing. I don't wish to win my husband's affections. In truth, all I want is to see our marriage dissolved. Gavin does not wish to bring further scandal down upon his father's good name by granting my request."

Adrianna's gaze widened. She leaned forward in her chair, but the soft rap before the servant reentered had her quickly regaining her composure. The man entered and presented tea service for two. His mistress waved him away when he started to pour. As soon as he departed and closed the doors, she leaned forward again.

"Are you mad?" she asked. "Why would you possibly want to see the marriage dissolved?"

The thought of telling the woman the truth surfaced, but Christine quickly dismissed it. Adrianna Shipley, although titled and set to inherit a fortune of her own once her elderly husband expired, might not wish to continue a liaison with a man who'd lost his title and possibly his social standing in the community.

"My reasons are of no concern to you, are they?" she said. "If the marriage is dissolved, Gavin will be free to marry again at a later time. Perhaps a time more convenient to you."

Adrianna cocked her lovely head to one side. "Marriage," she said thoughtfully. "To Gavin?" She shrugged. "When my husband dies, I will have no need to remarry, but I suppose if I did fancy a husband, yours would suffice. At least I know for certain he would never bore me in bed."

Jealousy reared its ugly head again, forcing Christine to be more snide than she intended. "In that particular area, I have no doubt at all," she agreed, watching the woman's smug smile fade. She could have pinched herself for saying as much, as if she had personal knowledge of the talents his mistress claimed he possessed. "But despite his . . ."

"Stamina?" the duchess provided. "Or perhaps you were going to say his—"

"His title and his holdings," Christine quickly declared, "I have no wish to be his wife. My heart and my destiny lie elsewhere."

The duchess sat back, studying her. "Oh, yes, the lover he claims you have." Her brows lifted. "If you prefer him over Gavin, perhaps I should meet him."

With assurance, Christine said, "I think you will never meet him, Your Grace."

Adrianna frowned. "A commoner, is he? Well, his brain might be small, but if he can tempt you from Gavin's arms, he must have an enormous—"

"He is not what I have come to discuss," Christine interrupted, fighting down a blush. The woman was vulgar for all her fancy trappings. "As I have told you, I wish to see my marriage ended, and I ask for your help."

Adrianna leaned forward and poured tea. "What do you ask of me?"

Christine picked up her cup and took a swallow. "To help me shame Gavin to the point he must look the fool if he will not order the marriage annulled. That is, to guide—"

"An actual annulment is out of the question," Adrianna informed her. "Not possible if the marriage has been consummated."

Suddenly taking to Tillie's habit of hand-wringing, Christine admitted, "It has not."

A flush, probably one of pleasure, spread over Adrianna's face. "You naughty girl," she scolded, although there wasn't much displeasure in her voice. "You have purposely led me to believe otherwise."

"I merely spoke upon assumption rather than experience," Christine countered.

Looking much like the cat who has fallen into a vat of cream, Adrianna purred, "Well, of course I'll help you, dear." She drummed her long fingernails on the arms of her chair. "You must take another lover. One who is included in our circle. Otherwise, who will know of your indiscretions?"

Christine rose from her chair, unconsciously taking up another's habit as well. Pacing. Her husband's answer for impatience. Christine did so out of nervousness.

"I thought only to pretend, that is, to appear as if I have taken other lovers."

"That won't do," Adrianna argued. "Men love to brag about their conquests. You must give some fortunate gentleman something to talk about."

Short of blurting out her state of innocence, and her wish to remain pure, Christine wasn't sure how to continue. "But are there not those who will also brag even if a conquest has not been made?"

Adrianna nodded. "To be sure. But there must be a

circumstance in which such a boast can appear genuine. A meeting where others bear witness that an opportunity for such an occurrence arose."

"A gathering? A ball?"

A sly smile stole over Adrianna's lips. "Not a decent ball. I happen to know of a masquerade ball that is to take place tomorrow night. I shall take you as my guest, and we shall see that your reputation is greatly compromised before the evening's end."

Christine's stomach twisted again. A cold feeling settled over her. Perhaps a forewarning that she should not have involved herself with Adrianna Shipley. But at least a plan had been set in motion. One that would further her own goal.

"Very well," she found herself agreeing. "But my husband mustn't know I plan an outing with you or he will become suspicious. And he certainly cannot attend the same function."

"No need to worry there. Gavin finds these balls . . . distasteful . . . and would not attend one. I trust you will find an inventive way of getting out of the house. I shall be waiting in my coach for you down the street."

Having made her bargain, Christine started for the door. She stopped. "How shall I dress?"

"I will find something appropriate for you," Adrianna offered politely. "You may change in my coach."

Christine nodded and showed herself out. Another chill raced up her spine. She didn't feel proud of herself for instigating trouble. In fact, she felt very much as if she'd just signed her soul over to the devil.

Gavin couldn't keep his mind on business. He'd tried to concentrate on his current problems with Mr. Collins's expedition, but his thoughts kept returning to events that had occurred the previous evening. The loose banister and the suspicion that someone meant either him, or Christine, ill will. More likely himself, Gavin reasoned.

He supposed he had enemies. Men he'd made jealous over either his thriving business, or a woman. Although in truth, besides Adrianna, he wasn't one to purposely pursue married women. And as he recalled, Adrianna had done the pursuing as far as *their* relationship went.

He'd merely accepted her blunt invitations to bed her, it being no secret that her husband turned a blind eye to her affairs or that she'd had many of them throughout her marriage.

Glancing across the room at William, he asked, "Do you know anyone who wishes me dead?"

His cousin's gaze shot up. "Beg your pardon?"

Gavin rose and stretched. "I asked if you know anyone in particular who'd like to see me dead."

"What an odd question," William blustered. "And why would you ask me such?"

After walking from behind his desk, Gavin went to the door and bade a clerk bring him tea. He turned back to his cousin. "I stopped by the theater on my way here. It seems as if the banister had been purposely loosened."

William's face paled. "The devil you say?" He rose as well, walking from behind his desk. "But who would do something like that? And for what reason?"

"The reason," Gavin said with a laugh, "is rather obvious. I feel certain I was the one intended to tumble from the box, not Christine."

The recipient of the news slumped to the edge of his desk. "I cannot believe what you are saying. If you are envied for your keen sense of business, and for your luck with the ladies, I believe you are also well respected by other men, cousin."

A clerk entered with Gavin's tea. Gavin waited until the man disappeared before speaking. "Thank you, William, but I have evidently earned some man's hatred rather than his respect."

"The duke?" William suggested.

Giving the suspect only a moment's deliberation, Gavin waved away William's suspicions. "If he wanted to kill off all of Adrianna's previous lovers, he'd have to hire a bloody army to see the job done."

"This is true," William agreed. "But I can think of no one else you've slighted. Your business dealings have always been on the up and up, your affairs with women, although common knowledge, certainly not a blatant slap in the face to anyone, except perhaps your wife."

"Christine would not purposely have the banister loosened, then lean against it," Gavin pointed out.

"Oh, I never meant to implicate Christine," William assured him. "But what of her lover? Maybe he's grown impatient with waiting for your wife to sway you to an annulment."

Gavin took a sip of tea and returned to his desk. He sat in his chair, considering the possibility. "But he would have surely warned Christine to avoid the danger."

"Not necessarily," William argued. "Do you really think Christine would involve herself in murder?"

Her beautiful face surfaced in his mind. The soft feel of her pressed against him and the sweet response of her kisses. "No," he answered honestly.

"Well, then, chances are, he doesn't either," said William. "He wouldn't tell her of his plan to rid them of you, or she would protest such a low-handed way to see herself free of the marriage, and with your fortune in her pocket, without having gone against the terms of your late father's will."

"Yes," Gavin said thoughtfully. "My death would insure that Christine inherits everything."

William shrugged away from his leaning stance against his desk and approached Gavin. "Of course I could be wrong. There is the possibility it was Christine who was meant to fall from the box."

"And what man, besides me, would stand to gain from her death?" When William remained quiet, thoughtful, he added, "Or are you suggesting that I am the guilty party?"

His cousin straightened indignantly. "Of course not. Why would you go to the bother of loosening the banister, then gallantly save her life?"

"You mean besides the obvious fact that I am not a murderer?"

"That fact aside, I suppose one could argue you saved her to appear gallant and caring about her, only to cast off suspicion when you make the next attempt—the successful attempt—upon her life," William said.

Having just taken another sip of tea, Gavin nearly choked. "That's preposterous!" he bellowed. "I would never do Christine harm and you know it!"

"Of course I know it," William soothed him. "But does anyone else?"

"We are not discussing my motives, William. We are trying to discern what motives another man might have for doing away with my wife."

William tapped his chin and sighed. "I can think of no reason another man . . . but wait, cousin. Who said it would have to be a man at all?"

Gavin frowned. "Are you suggesting a woman?"

"Your mistress."

"Past mistress," Gavin corrected. "I have broken off the affair."

His cousin's brow lifted. "Your discarded mistress. The plot thickens."

"That's ridiculous," Gavin argued. "Adrianna wouldn't have the strength required to loosen the banister, nor would she dirty her hands to do so."

"She could have hired it done easy enough," William said. "And the way she kept eating you up with her eyes last evening, I think the affair is perhaps only over for you."

True, Adrianna had failed to understand he wanted nothing further to do with her—had said she would be the one to decide when anything was over between them. And her bold actions last night had been dangerous. Dangerous to her more so than to him. She'd always managed to remain somewhat discreet in the past, not only with him, but with other men as well.

Men were expected to allow their sexual appetites to get the best of them. It was understood, if unfair that women were not given the same leeway. A man could rid himself of an unfaithful wife, but a woman could not do the same. Again, perhaps unfair, but the way of things.

Adrianna could be cunning, cold, and determined if she wanted something badly enough. But would she go to such lengths to keep a lover, when she could easily choose another? Gavin wasn't conceited enough to believe he'd driven her to such desperate measures, but for Christine's safety, he supposed it wouldn't hurt to question Adrianna.

He wouldn't do so privately, as someone might see them and misinterpret the meeting as a lovers' tryst. He rather liked the thought of society believing that he and his wife were smitten with one another. In love. It weakened any grounds Christine might claim for an annulment. And it hurt the chances anyone would believe their marriage had not been consummated. No, he would seek Adrianna out at some social function, one where being seen together would cause the least amount of gossip.

A gathering not held to regular standards. Maybe one of those perverse masquerade balls Adrianna had a taste for—a fleshpot of sin if ever one had been created. Orgies were all they were. Men and women coming together with no thought save to rut like beasts with one another, and with little care for whom they chose as a partner. Most who attended were not deeply entrenched in polite society.

They were women too good to marry a commoner, but

not good enough to marry a noble. Men who had made their fortunes with their hands, or by less respectable tactics. Riffraff they were called, and yet among them, a few blue bloods could be found. Young aristocrats with a taste for debauchery, and young women bored by their old husbands.

"I will speak to Adrianna," he said to William. "But I'm sure she is not capable of murder."

Even as he said the words, Gavin realized he didn't know her well enough to claim her innocent with assurance. He would seek his past mistress out at the next masquerade ball given. It would take some doing to discover the time and location, as those who attended liked to believe themselves a secret society of sorts, but for Christine's safety, find out he would.

Chapter Seventeen

Christine hoped the inner turmoil she felt the next evening did not make itself evident upon her features. She and Gavin were dining together, she at one end of the long formal table, he at the other. She could scarcely eat due to her nervousness, but made an effort as she would need her strength, and her wits, to later sneak from the house undetected.

Her gaze strayed to Gavin often. She was almost sorry about her intention to shame him. She tried to harden her heart against him, to reason she had no choice but to attend the ball tonight. Chances to see her plans through were few and far between. The sooner she forced him into an annulment, the better off they would both be.

"Do you have something on your mind?" he asked.

Deception, she suddenly thought. She glanced away from him, realizing he'd caught her staring. "No," she answered, returning her attention to her plate.

"Nothing?" he persisted. "I find that difficult to believe."

"Nothing in particular," she clarified. "I'm tired and think I will retire early this evening."

He lifted his napkin, wiped his mouth, and rose. "Are you feeling ill, Christine?"

She wanted to ward him off when he approached her. It was harder to fool a person at close range. "I feel fine," she assured him. "I am quite recovered from our unfortunate incident."

Gavin tilted her face up to him. "Which incident are you referring to?"

Her cheeks filled with heat. Making mistakes with a man one had to live under the same roof with, see on a daily basis, could take its toll upon a woman. She pulled free and stared down at her plate.

"Both of them," she answered.

He sighed. "I wish I had your ability. Forgetting either incident has been difficult for me."

As, in truth, it had been for her. She had relived falling in a nightmare last night, only to have the dream shift to the feel of Gavin's arms around her, the sensuous brush of his lips against her skin.

"I am certain in time you'll manage," she said. "If you will excuse me." She pushed her chair back and rose.

"I'm going out tonight," he said suddenly.

Christine tried to keep her features blank. "Have a pleasant evening," she commented, thinking to step around him. He blocked her exit.

"I plan to play cards with Chester and James. I've neglected our friendship of late."

He sounded guilty to Christine. Too eager to make his outing sound innocent, which naturally stirred her suspicions. She hoped he had no plans to pay the duchess a visit. Not that she cared with whom he spent time, or what he chose to do during that time, but Adrianna had already promised the evening to her—and the furtherance of her plans.

"Will you be late?" she asked casually.

His brow lifted. "Is there a reason I should come home early?"

"No," she quickly answered. "Stay out as late as you please."

"I had every intention of doing just that."

Realizing her jaw was clenched, Christine tried to relax. "Good night, then."

Gavin stepped aside and bowed. "Sleep well, Christine."

She refrained from muttering she would wish him the same, but suspected sleep was not how he intended to occupy his night. Instead, she swept past him without a word, out of the dining room and up the stairs.

When she reached the safety of her room, she leaned against the door, taking in calming gulps of air. She should be glad her husband would spend the night otherwise occupied. It made her own plans much simpler. And she wouldn't think about where he really might be going, or if just because he wouldn't be in Adrianna's bed, he wouldn't land himself in another's.

In fact, imagining him doing so helped her feel less guilt over her own deceptions. Christine walked to the adjoining servant's door and knocked softly. Tillie joined her, already wringing her hands.

"I'm not sure this is a good notion you've taken into yer head," the maid fretted. "If something bad was to happen to you, His Lordship would be very angry. He might blame me and—"

"I've told you," Christine interrupted. "If my absence is discovered, you know nothing about where I've gone, or with whom. Please, Tillie, learn to play your role as a servant convincingly. A titled lady does not tell her maid her every move."

"But I'm worried about ye, m'lady. I don't like ye going off with that woman. I don't trust her. Not as far as I can—"

"Tillie," Christine warned. "You and I both know I have had few opportunities to set my plans into motion. The duchess has agreed to help me, and my personal dislike of her has no room in the greater scheme of things. Wouldn't you agree?"

The plump maid sighed. "I've been thinking, m'lady. Is it so bad to be married to a rich man? A handsome man? Wouldn't it be simpler to remain his wife and do what you can for as many poor souls as possible?"

Christine supposed her mouth dropped open. "How can you even suggest I remain married to Gavin? You consider him the devil's own—are scared to death of him. You—"

"Are not the one already married to him," Tillie pointed out. "And I'm not so certain you feel about him as I do. You're not scared of him, or you wouldn't risk sneaking out tonight. And I've seen the way you look at him at times, and I can tell you like what you see. A better plan may be to make him fall in love with ye, and then he might become more generous to those ye wish to help."

"I will not hear another word of this nonsense," Christine pronounced. Make Gavin fall in love with her? Remain his wife? Bear his children? Ridiculous! Any other woman might have the luxury of doing so, but not her. She'd been given a quest, a mission in life. A far grander calling than simply being adored and well loved by a handsome mortal.

"Arrange my hair," she instructed Tillie. "Then it's downstairs with you to keep Mr. Graves distracted."

Tillie's face brightened. "Oh, aye, I'll keep the stuffy man out of your way for the evening. Don't you worry about that, m'lady."

Christine suppressed a smile. She had a feeling that if her plans didn't give Tillie a reason to pester and flirt with the head servant, she would have protested far more. Christine seated herself before her dressing table and let Tillie arrange her hair. The process took some time, but not nearly enough in Christine's opinion.

She had more than an hour before she was to sneak from the house and meet Adrianna's coach. Christine spent the time carefully choosing a gown, although she knew she would change into whatever the duchess thought appropriate before she reached the ball. She would arrive in disguise, but after flirting and dancing with every man present, she would accidentally lose her mask so that she might be recognized.

After that, Christine had no idea what she should do. Adrianna would advise her, she felt certain. After all, the woman wanted her husband. Judging by her vulgar behavior at the theater, she wanted him badly. Christine tamped down the sudden stab of jealousy she felt. It wasn't jealousy at all, she told herself. Annoyance. Yes, irritation that the woman couldn't keep her hands off another woman's husband.

Not that Christine actually considered Gavin her husband. If she considered Gavin her mate in truth, actually loved him, well, she supposed she would tear the woman's hair out strand by strand. Maybe snatch that fake beauty mark from her cheek, and hope it was, in fact, real.

"But I don't love him," Christine said aloud, feeling better at hearing verbal confirmation of her feelings. She relaxed and set to work. Changing her gown several times helped to pass the time, and before Christine knew it, the appointed hour had arrived. She snatched her cape from the bed, threw it around her shoulders, and stole from her room.

Gavin had visited more than one gentlemen's club before he finally caught up with Chester and James. The two pounced upon him the moment they spotted him, demanding details about his mishap at the theater. Gavin played down the incident, and didn't mention the probability that foul play had been involved. His two friends were worse than old spinsters when it came to spreading gossip.

If someone did mean him or Christine harm, better the party involved believed him ignorant of the threat. Gavin stood a better chance at catching the culprit should he or, as William had suggested, she try anything underhanded again. With that in mind, Gavin chose a seat at the gambling table with his back facing the wall. At least he knew Christine was at home, safe.

Perhaps he should have told Mr. Graves about his worries. Maybe hired someone to guard the house in his absence. Still, it was more likely that he had been the target rather than Christine. Besides Adrianna, no one would see his wife as a threat. And it made more sense that his wife's elusive lover would plot against him. The spineless cad stood to gain the most by his death.

"Are you going to bet, my friend, or simply stare a hole through your cards?" Chester asked.

Glancing up, he realized both Chester and James were gazing at him impatiently. Gavin threw a few coins on the table.

"Have either of you ever attended one of the secret balls that take place under the cover of darkness in our fair city?" he asked, hoping to sound casual.

James lowered his cards. "Are you referring to the masquerade balls?" he whispered. "Those disreputable gatherings where it is said men and women who aren't even acquainted dance nearly naked together and think nothing of slipping off to do more?"

"Yes," he answered. "Those balls."

James glanced around and said quietly, "You aren't

thinking of attending one? Not even you would stoop to such disgraceful practices."

The last statement caused the lift of one brow. "Your faith in me is comforting, James," Gavin said dryly. "But I have a reason to attend. I need to meet in secret with someone who is known to attend these affairs."

Both men frowned at him. Chester was the first to voice his displeasure.

"The duchess, I have heard, is not above attending these affairs. At least, that is how she once amused herself before you stumbled into her bed to take over the task."

Guilt surfaced. Gavin tugged at his tight collar. "I do not recall either of you being so judgmental concerning my activities before."

"We did not know Christine before," James said, providing the reason for their disapproval. "Why stoop to scraps when there is far better fare waiting at home for you?"

But his wife was not waiting for him, eagerly anticipating his return. Christine couldn't care less where he went, or with whom he spent time. She hadn't even acted suspicious that he might be doing something other than playing cards with his friends. In fact, she'd seemed rather anxious to see him gone.

He'd hoped, because of what had happened between them in her room, that impassioned embrace that had resulted from an argument concerning other lovers, that she might care. But he was a fool to believe so, and more of one to hope so.

"It seems as if you have both placed Christine upon a pedestal that is shaky at best," he said.

Gavin didn't particularly want to tell his friends about Christine's lover. They were both too loose-lipped to be trusted with the information. Yet he wanted it understood he wasn't to be run through by them while she escaped persecution and remained the innocent in their eyes.

"Christine has a lover," Gavin said. "She's admitted as much to me."

Chester's mouth dropped open. "I don't believe you."

"It is not a thing a man brags about," he countered.

"I do not believe it either," James cut in. "She is too . . . well, she seems innocent. An innocence that cannot be feigned."

"No, it radiates from her like the sun shines through a sky of wispy clouds," Chester said. "She is good and kind."

"And the same woman you were both wagering about the night she intruded upon London society," Gavin reminded. "I believe you were discussing her lack of polite manners and considering taking her as your mistress, Chester."

The man's face turned red. "But I did not know her then. Certainly did not know that she was your wife. Looking back upon that evening, I can only believe that Christine's brazen behavior was simply a bad act."

"A brave attempt to cause her husband embarrassment over the many embarrassments you have caused her," James added.

"Good, kind, brave," Gavin muttered. "You're both too smitten with her to see her for who she really is."

"And I think, my friend, you are too afraid of the consequences of seeing her as she truly is," Chester said.

"What consequences?" Gavin growled.

Both men exchanged a smug glance.

James spoke first. "If you see her as she truly is, rather than what you wish to believe of her, you are in danger of losing your heart."

Disgusted with the conversation, Gavin threw his cards on the table. "Romantic fools, the both of you."

Truth be known, he did want to see her as his friends saw her. Innocent? God, yes, she seemed so. Her kisses were passionate, but inexperienced. Even her fingers at the buttons of his shirt had seemed an innocent action, one without conscious thought of what she did, or implied, with so bold a gesture.

Who was she really? Besides a woman who had taken over his thoughts, his life. A woman who drove him to distraction with his desire for her, but who had somehow managed to make him want more than her body.

She made him long for something he could put no name to. Something he had yet to experience in his lifetime. Love? Hell, he hoped not.

"You have folded with four queens, my friend," Chester said quietly. "I believe your thoughts are elsewhere."

He glanced down at the table and winced. He still needed information concerning the masquerade ball. The next one scheduled and the location.

"I'll wager neither of you can find out the information I need concerning the ball," he said.

Although a gleam of addiction entered both men's gazes, neither took up the challenge.

"I will have no part in helping you shame Christine further," Chester said.

"Nor I," James agreed.

Gavin sighed. "I have no intention of shaming my wife, but only wish to protect her. I need a word with the duchess concerning her continued belief that the affair between us has not ended. And I need to meet with her in a place where I can disguise myself so that word we have been seen together is not spread all over London."

"Then, the affair is over?" Chester asked, wanting confirmation.

"For me it is over," Gavin answered. "And has been since the night Christine intruded upon her ball."

"Do you swear?" James eyed him mistrustfully.

"Yes, dammit," Gavin bit out. "I cannot inquire after the information myself or it will cause speculation. Especially since Adrianna's partiality for such social inter-action is not a well-guarded secret."

"He presents a valid argument," Chester offered.

James nodded. "I'll wager I can get the information before you can, my friend."

"How much?" Chester asked.

Gavin blocked out their ceaseless battle to win wagers from one another, secure in the knowledge that the information would soon be given to him. What he was not prepared to hear from Chester, who had finally managed to win a wager over James, was that a ball was scheduled that very evening, and at the home of a disreputable chap who had made his fortune dealing in human suffering. The sale of slaves.

Chapter Eighteen

The ball seemed hideous to her. Christine had scarcely arrived, and already she wanted nothing more than to leave. The costume she wore, fittingly, represented a sacrificial virgin. The tight gown of white gauze was too thin to be considered decent, not to mention that it draped only one shoulder, leaving the other bare.

Inside Adrianna's dim coach, Christine hadn't realized how easily her flesh could be seen beneath the material. Thank heaven she'd worn her cape inside, and after almost allowing it to be taken, had noticed her indecent state.

Now her fingers clutched the cape close around her. The delicate mask of white satin covering her eyes unfortunately did not hide her mouth, which she supposed might be hanging open. Everywhere she glanced, couples were groping and pawing one another. Harsh laughter and raised voices frayed her already threadbare nerves.

"You must relax." Adrianna steered her further into the ballroom. "Your expression alone bears witness to the fact you have never attended one of these socials before."

"And tell me again why I would wish anyone to believe I have," she said sarcastically.

Adrianna's fingers tightened around her arm. "Because tonight you are here to create a scandal, to cause tongues to wag and speculation about you to run rampant. Isn't that what you want, Christine?"

She tried to tell herself that she did—that being here wasn't as wrong as it felt. Her assurances were of little comfort. In a darkened corner to her left, a man boldly fondled a woman's bare breast. Christine quickly looked away, and choked down the panic threatening to consume her.

"I should like to leave," she said.

"In good time," Adrianna countered. "You wanted my help, and you shall have it. Now, show some spine. Here comes our host to greet us."

A short, round man wearing a bird mask came toward them. He staggered for a moment, righted himself, and continued.

"Your—" he began, only to stop himself and giggle like a woman. "I mean, madame."

He bowed, nearly toppling over in the process. His mask nearly came away, as well. He righted it and reached for Christine's hand.

"And who is this vision?"

Christine jerked her fingers away when he planted a slobbery kiss upon her hand.

"Now, sir, you know our identities must be kept a secret," Adrianna teased, playfully swatting him with her fan. "My friend is a member of high society and married as well. We must protect her reputation at all cost."

The bird man tried to present a sober face, as if it was possible with the big beak of his mask making him look ridiculous. "Of course, madame. At all cost." He spoiled any hint of gallantry by giggling again. "Too bad she's upper crust, or I could sell her for a pretty price. Perhaps the lady would like to steal upstairs with me? I am a man who can keep a secret."

Christine didn't want to accompany this man anywhere. She started to say so, but Adrianna spoke first.

"Oscar, my dear," she whispered. "I'm afraid this dove is not soiled enough for you. But could you point us in the direction of bluer blood?"

The idiot smile died on his lips. "Here, madame, we are all equals," he bit out.

"But she has come to meet one gentleman in particular," Adrianna said, trying to soothe him. "A Mr. Thomas Wentworth."

Christine's head jerked in Adrianna's direction. "What?"

"Excuse us," the duchess said to their host, guiding her away.

They didn't get far before Christine drew up, forcing her companion to do the same. "Did I hear you correctly? Is Mr. Wentworth the sort who would attend a ball such as this?"

Adrianna moistened her rouged lips. "Not under normal circumstances, but I sent him a note requesting he meet me here tonight. And I took the liberty of signing your name."

Rage engulfed Christine. "How dare you! I have no desire to meet Mr. Wentworth here, or anywhere else for that matter. I would not falsely give him the impression that I am interested in him."

"But you are," Adrianna insisted. She paused as a servant stopped with a tray of drinks, took a glass for herself, and shoved one into Christine's hand. "Only a man who moves in the same circles as the rest of us will suffice tonight. What good is compromising your reputation with lower-class men whose gossip will never reach Gavin's ears?"

She hadn't thought of that. And clearly, she hadn't given enough thought to accompanying Adrianna on this horrid venture. Coming here had been a mistake. She wanted to go home and rethink her decision to shame Gavin into an annulment. Perhaps now that he'd come to know her, she could be truthful with him.

But would the truth see her mission fulfilled? Gavin was not a bad man. There was good in him. Maybe if she told him the truth, he would see her quest as a noble one and find the compassion to sacrifice his own wants to do what he must for the sake of many.

Lying to herself. Christine knew that was what she was doing. Looking for an escape from her current predicament. She wondered if she could slip out the door and find her way home. Even as the thought surfaced, a rough hand closed around her arm.

"What do we have here?" a drunken voice slurred. A face loomed before her, wearing a devil's mask complete with horns. "Fresh meat?"

"Kindly remove your hand from the lady's arm," a distinguished voice warned. "She is with me."

Christine turned to see a tall man standing beside her. Although he wore a simple black mask, she recognized him as Thomas Wentworth. Under the current circumstances, she thought better of denying his claim. The drunk devil released her, muttered a few curse words, and stumbled off in search of easier prey.

"Thank you," she said softly.

He took her hand in his. "I could not believe my good fortune when I received your note."

She glanced around in hopes Adrianna would explain matters. The duchess had disappeared. "I'm afraid you have been misled, Mr. Wentworth. I did not send the note. Adrianna Shipley sent the invitation."

"The duchess?" He frowned. "But why would she do that?"

Christine's cheeks stung with embarrassment. The situation was awkward at best. "The matter is difficult to explain."

"I'm all ears," he countered.

And if she recalled correctly from the last ball she'd attended where Mr. Wentworth was present, all hands, as well. "Please forgive the misunderstanding, and I will not involve you in my . . . problems."

"But I wish very much to be involved," he declared passionately, bringing her hand to his lips. "I adore you."

"Please do not," Christine ground through her teeth, wresting her hand away. Heads were starting to turn in their direction. If once she had thought it a grand idea to be the center of attention, and of scandal, she could not in truth say she still felt the same.

"I'm only here to cause my husband shame. And I will not subject you to his wrath."

Thomas smiled. "For one kiss, I would face his temper and the devil himself."

She lifted a brow. "I don't believe any man would tempt the end of Gavin's sword for one kiss, sir. You have obviously had too much to drink."

He threw back his head and laughed. "It is your beauty and your wit that makes my head spin, dearest Christine. Come, dance with me. I promise not to abandon you on the floor this time."

A dance was not what she wanted, but escape seemed unlikely, as Adrianna had obviously deserted Christine to her own fate. She reasoned dancing might be better than standing alone, vulnerable to the attentions of another drunken man who had every right to assume the worst of her, given that she was attending such a ball.

"One dance," she agreed. Then she would leave with or without the duchess.

Wentworth took her drink, set it aside, and led her into the flow of dancers. Christine knew she looked ridiculous still wearing her cape, but refused to part with the wrap. She had to surrender her hold upon the outer garment in order to dance. It fell open, and she hoped no one would notice. Thomas did, his eyes widening at the sight of her gown before he politely focused them on her face.

"Are you really an orphan?" he asked.

"Yes. I grew up in a small parish not far from Gavin's country estate."

"I find your humble beginnings hard to believe. Your face is perfectly sculpted. Very fine bone structure. You must have blue blood somewhere in your background."

Which she did not believe for a moment. But Wentworth obviously felt it necessary to believe in order to justify an attraction to her. Good heavens, he was a worse snob than Gavin.

"My mother was probably a whore and my father a drunken sailor who took comfort in her arms for one night," she said. "I have no false illusions concerning my bloodline."

The man holding her, and somewhat closer than was decent, frowned. "There are rumors floating about that you had a dalliance with the old marquis, and that is why he felt honor-bound to see you properly set up."

Christine blinked. "The marquis was like a father to me," she whispered, outraged. "Who would spread such vicious gossip?"

He shrugged. "It is just a theory. And even you must admit that a titled gentleman being forced to wed a girl of your station would naturally seem curious to most."

"And an abomination," she added sarcastically. "I had no more desire to marry Gavin than he had to marry me."

"Then, you are not in love with him as the reports concerning the two of you suggest?"

For some unknown reason, the proper response would not bound from her lips. "No," she finally managed.

"Then you are free to pursue an affair of your own?"

Ronda Thompson

She was not free to do any such thing. Explaining such to Wentworth would only confuse the man. "I am free to behave as badly as my husband does," she finally said. "Or, at least, to appear as if I do."

"Trying to get back at him for his affair with the duchess, is that it?"

"Trying to force him into divorcing me," she snapped.

Thomas drew back. "Whatever for? You've been handed a life of luxury, and yet you wish to see the marriage dissolved? For what possible reason?"

Cursing her loose tongue, Christine quickly recovered her common sense. "I find marriage too stifling," she answered. "I wish to be free so that I may pursue—"

"Other options?" Thomas interrupted. A smile stole over his lips. "Perhaps being a man's mistress would suit you more?"

That would probably suit Wentworth more, Christine thought. He would count her unworthy of being his wife, even if he felt no qualms about desiring her. She was almost tempted to call his bluff. To see how eager he was to risk angering Gavin.

"He would have to be a wealthy man," she mused.

"My family is not poor," Thomas said. "And I am the oldest son, soon to inherit."

"How nice for you," she said dryly.

"And for you." He beamed with pride. His smile quickly faded. "But a divorce is not easily granted, and I frankly do not see why Norfork would fight you on the issue. As it stands, no one knows why he has not demanded one already given your . . ."

"Background," she finished for him. "Gavin can be quite stubborn. He . . ." She hesitated, searching for a reason without divulging the true one.

"He's in love with you," Thomas said with a sigh.

Her gaze snapped to the man's face. "He is not," she assured him.

224

Thomas twirled her from the floor and led her to a refreshment table. He took two fresh glasses of wine, handing one to her. "Come now, Christine, we all saw his daring rescue at the theater. And his face was pale as a ghost when you fell. And it did not go unnoticed by most that he sat very close to you during the performance, whispering in your ear and eating you alive with his eyes."

"My Italian is not good," she said. "He was simply explaining the play to me. And of course he rescued me. What man wouldn't?"

"Some wouldn't," Thomas argued. "They would be much more concerned about placing themselves at risk."

Christine took an unfashionably large drink of wine. Wentworth was starting to unnerve her. "I suppose most failed to notice that the duchess had her hand down my husband's trousers during intermission."

Wentworth laughed. "Her persistence is admirable, but everyone knows he broke off the affair the moment you arrived in London. He has not been with her since."

"Surely that is a lie," Christine persisted.

"Well, I cannot be certain. But that is the rumor. Along with gossip that he has not been with another woman since you moved into his town home."

Her hands started to shake. Christine took another sip of wine to steady them. She suddenly felt queasy. Her heart pounded so loudly she feared Wentworth would hear it. Had Gavin given up his wicked ways? Had he given them up for her?

Ridiculous, she told herself. If he played the besotted husband, it was to strengthen people's belief that they were a happily married couple and secure his hold upon the inheritance. She must remember that when these bouts of weakness for him overrode common sense. She had to undermine his efforts.

"Thomas," she said sweetly, fortifying herself with another sip of wine. "Are you the type to speak freely of your female conquests?"

His face displayed the proper amount of outrage. "Certainly not."

She frowned. "Then go away. I have no use for you."

The man nearly choked on his drink. "I beg your pardon?"

More casual than she felt, Christine shrugged. "A man who will not help me shame my husband by spreading rumors concerning my lack of virtue is of no use to me." She purposely allowed her gaze to scan the room. "Surely there is a man here somewhere who will kiss and tell."

"I will kiss and tell if that is your desire," Thomas assured her. "That is to say, I will let it be known you have been free with your charms without identifying the man involved as myself."

Her gaze cut sideways at him. "I'm sure you would."

His hand touched hers again. "And since I am in disguise, no one need know which man you slipped upstairs with, only that you did."

She tried not to jerk away. "I see no reason to stage such an elaborate hoax when you have already agreed to spread the rumor."

"One wagging tongue may not be enough," he pointed out. "But if several people saw you go upstairs with a man, the news will travel faster."

Although she supposed he had a point, Christine wasn't certain she could follow through with such a plan. She didn't feel comfortable enough in Wentworth's company to spend time alone with him.

"You do understand it is an act?" she questioned.

Wentworth smiled. "Of course."

"But no one will recognize me in the mask."

"Then you must accidentally lose it before we reach the stairs."

He took her arm and guided her back through the dancers, and toward the long staircase on the far side of the room.

Gavin adjusted his mask before entering the ball. He'd luckily encountered a drunk man leaving just as he arrived, and bribed him into parting with it. He wasn't inside for more than a minute when he wanted nothing more than to leave. The guests were loud and obnoxious, the wine thrust into his hand of poor quality. More wine was puddled in different areas of the floor. At least he hoped the wet spots were wine.

He dodged the puddles, his gaze searching the room for a sign of Adrianna. Recognizing her might have been more difficult had she not molded her lush body into a gaudy golden gown. It was not anything to be proud of, but he knew her curves well. She wore a spiked headdress of gold, and a golden mask. He assumed her costume depicted the sun.

He watched her for a moment, wondering why she stared into the distance, and what had placed such a smug look upon her partially exposed face. His gaze followed hers, but found nothing but a staircase. He waited until she turned away and walked back toward a table loaded with glasses of wine before he approached her.

"Adrianna," he said quietly. "A word with you if I may."

She jumped, spilling wine down the front of her gown. Adrianna cursed, then glared up at him. Her gaze widened.

"Gavin?" she whispered.

"I see my disguise is about as convincing as yours."

"What are you doing here?" she croaked.

"I wanted a meeting with you, and in a place where few people might see us together." He glanced around. "At least, few who matter."

Slowly, the shock receded from her frozen mouth, replaced by an expression of satisfaction. "I knew you would seek me out me again. And I am willing to forgive you for ignoring me of late. You will make it up to me, won't you?"

He cleared his throat and glanced away from her. "It is not that sort of meeting I wish to have with you."

Her seductive smile faded. "Besides our enjoyment of one another in bed, we have little in common. What could we possibly have to discuss?"

Gavin saw no reason to be less than blunt. "Christine."

For a moment, she looked startled again. "Why would I care to discuss her with you?"

Taking a sip of his wine, then wincing, he answered, "I know you don't care for her, but do you hate her enough to wish her harm?"

The duchess pulled at her earlobe, a nervous gesture he'd seen her make in the past. "Harm her in what way?"

"In any way."

Instead of speaking, she took a sip of wine. He waited patiently until after her third sip.

"You have not answered my question."

In a sudden fit of anger, she threw her drink to the floor, shattering the inexpensive glass and creating yet another puddle. "Do I want to see you rid of her? Yes," she hissed. "Do I want you back in my bed? Yes!"

He glanced around, silently cursing her for calling attention to them. "Adrianna, I will never return to your bed, whether I am married or not. I thought I'd made myself clear regarding that issue on more than one occasion."

Her eyes glittered dangerously, and for a moment, he thought she might unsheathe her claws and come at him. Then she threw him off guard with a dazzling smile.

"Poor fool. You will not come to my bed, but even as we speak, your wife is upstairs in the arms of another man."

Instantly, his gaze flew to the stairway on the far side of the room. Gavin forced his heart back down his throat, turning to regard her with calm assurance.

"You lie."

She smiled again, but in a cunning fashion. "I am not lying, Gavin. I brought her here, at her request, and I even arranged a meeting between your wife and a certain gentleman."

There went his heart up his throat again. "Her lover?" he asked, and hated the raw sound of his voice.

"Probably by now," she answered. "Although I don't believe he is the original lover. Not the first, and I seriously doubt the last."

"Which room is she in?" he demanded.

Adrianna almost purred. "Now, how would I know?"

"Because I saw you staring at the stairway when I entered," he ground through his teeth. "Tell me!"

She only smiled at him.

Cursing under his breath, he turned from her, making his way with purposeful strides toward the stairway. Adrianna's laughter followed him.

Chapter Nineteen

Thomas Wentworth was no gentleman. He played the part well if it suited him, but currently, he'd chosen to present Christine with his true side. An aspect of his character she did not care for at all. When he took a step closer, she raised the candlestick clutched in her hand.

"I've warned you to keep your distance," she said. "And I also told you downstairs this was to be a pretense."

"I have learned that what a woman says and what she means are usually two different matters," he countered, bravely taking another step toward her.

She backed from him. "It is not so in this case. Move from my path and let me leave."

"Not without something for my trouble tonight." He flashed her a lewd grin. "I cannot kiss and tell if there is nothing to tell, Christine. One kiss is not so much to ask, now is it?"

One kiss was more than she planned to give the cad. She wouldn't be bullied this way. "I would hate to smash your skull with this heavy candlestick, but if that is the only way to make you regain reason, I will."

Wentworth sighed. "You have too much spirit for a poor orphan girl who should still know her place, even though she has managed to rise above her sorry circumstances."

Christine's anger flared. "And what place is that?"

He glanced toward the bed. "Why, beneath your betters, of course."

Temper clouded common sense. Christine threw the candlestick at him. He ducked and the object whizzed past his head and hit the wall behind him. Only then did she realize he had used her anger against her. Unarmed her. Christine frantically searched for something else to wield as a weapon, but Wentworth was upon her in an instant.

His fingers dug painfully into her arms; then he shoved her backward onto the bed. Christine kicked out at him, but the delicate gold sandals on her feet caused no damage. She tried to roll to the side. The man quickly threw his weight on top of her. She clawed at his face. He grabbed her wrists and flung them above her head.

"I have no wish to hurt you, Christine," he said. "I'm asking you to be rational. For whatever reasons a woman chooses to attend these balls, she should come prepared to face the consequences."

She tried to bring her knee up between his legs. He simply pressed her down deeper into the soft mattress.

"You would have never made it out of this house tonight without falling victim to some man's lust," he continued. "Don't you prefer me over that riffraff downstairs?"

"You are no different," she bit out. "If you do not get off me this instant, I shall start screaming!"

His mouth became a tight line of frustration. "I will not force you, but a kiss is hardly worth all this outrage. Just submit and I will let you go."

Not for a moment did she trust his word. To kiss him

willingly would only lead him to believe she might allow him other intimacies as well. She struggled, trying to buck his body from hers. The effort proved futile.

"You feel good," he whispered, his lips brushing her ear. "Your body is meant to pleasure a man."

He transferred both her wrists into one large hand, the other sliding down her body toward her breasts. Christine opened her mouth to scream, but the loud crash of the door banging against the wall made her gasp instead. Wentworth's head jerked in the direction of the noise. Christine struggled to see beyond him. In the door frame stood the silhouette of a man. A very tall man.

"This room is occupied," Thomas sneered. "Be off! Find your own woman. I have no mind to share."

Rather than leave, the figure stepped into the room. He wore a black mask, but reached up and removed it.

"I believe that is my woman, Wentworth."

"Gavin," Christine gasped.

"Norfork," Thomas groaned, quickly rolling away from her. He jumped to his feet and took a defensive stance. "This is not what it appears," he rasped.

Gavin lifted a brow and moved further into the room. "If it is not what it appears, do tell me what it is."

Christine waited for Wentworth to admit he had attacked her. She called herself a fool for being surprised when he did the opposite.

"She invited me upstairs," he said. "Sent me a note inviting me to meet her here. I'm only a man," he added with a nervous laugh. "Too weak to resist her charms."

"That is a lie!" Christine shouted.

Gavin turned a cool glance upon her. "You did not invite him upstairs?"

She scrambled up from the bed. "Well, yes, but—"

"And do you have the note?" he said, turning to Wentworth.

The man fumbled in his pocket and withdrew a slip of

paper. He walked to Gavin, but only stood close enough to extend it to him. Christine watched Gavin snatch the note, scan it, and slip it inside his pocket.

"I didn't write the note," Christine said. "The—"

"Out," Gavin said again, the order directed at Wentworth. "And if even a breath of this reaches my ears, I will cut off your tongue so that you cannot brag again."

Wentworth swallowed loudly, nodded, and hurried from the room. Christine rushed to Gavin, clutching his arm.

"Let me explain," she whispered.

He glanced down at her hand upon his sleeve, and when he glanced back up at her, she released him. A shiver raced up her spine. His eyes were cold.

"I believe this situation is self-explanatory." He nodded toward the floor. "Put on your mask. I'm taking you home."

Perhaps now was not a good time to tell him what had really happened, Christine decided. She reached down, scooped up the mask she'd dropped when Wentworth tried to kiss her the first time, and fixed it back into place. Gavin replaced his mask as well.

Although he took her arm and escorted her from the room, Christine knew he did so more out of duty than gallantry. Together, they descended the long stairway, walked past guests still dancing and openly fondling one another, and then toward the door. A flash of gold drew her gaze.

Adrianna stood a few feet away, some man draped around her, and the gleam of satisfaction in her eyes said if Wentworth would have no part in spreading rumors, she had no such qualms. Well, Christine supposed she had achieved her objective tonight, even if she felt sickened by her chosen plan of action.

Sickened, and more. Why should the coldness in Gavin's eyes, the tenseness of his arm, cause tears to well

233

up in her eyes? She felt a deep ache inside her chest, as if her heart was breaking in half. Neither reaction made sense to her. She wanted to displease him. To make him deplore her. Didn't she?

For two days Gavin eluded all contact with his wife. He left early and arrived home late. Scandal. It was everywhere. The rumors. The snickering behind his back. He knew he played the hypocrite by being angry, for now he understood how Christine must have felt those two years he had chosen to ignore her. But dammit, neither of them had known one another then.

He had been charming, attentive, had given her gifts, and still, it appeared as if she preferred any man over him. What must he do to make her forget her silly quest to see their marriage ended? What must he do to win her fickle heart?

"What?"

He glanced across the office at William. "I said nothing."

"You were muttering," William told him. "You've been muttering for two days now. The rumors will die down. Once everyone has had time to reflect upon Christine's behavior, they will most likely come to the conclusion you deserved being duped. She will become London's darling all over again."

"She was scarcely London's darling for more than a night," he said dryly. "Mr. Graves told me the day after the incident at the theater, she received several invitations to various social functions. Then, the day after the masquerade ball, she received several apologies that each and every function had been canceled."

"Well, cousin, you can't really blame everyone. Your 'darling' entertained another man upstairs at that gutter snipe Oscar Fielding's horrid ball. Several people saw her accidentally drop her mask before she reached the stairs."

Gavin lifted a brow. "Several people? And what the bloody hell were they doing there?"

William rolled his gaze upward. "You know how rumors work, cousin. No one spreading them was actually present. They heard it from someone else, who heard it from someone else, and no one particular person is a valid witness."

Instead of commenting, Gavin returned to his work. He was in no mood to shuffle papers, nor did the thought of going home appeal to him.

"You're angry, aren't you?"

He glanced back up. "Yes, I'm angry. People should mind their own business instead of minding mine."

"No, I didn't mean at society. I meant at Christine."

Glancing away, Gavin answered, "Of course I'm angry. She's undone everything I've tried to accomplish. She's made me a laughingstock, and worse, a man to be pitied. A man, rumor has it, who cannot please his own wife in bed."

"I daresay only the men are spreading that one," William commented, using his driest tone. "Most of the women know better."

"Don't rub my nose in my own infidelities," Gavin growled. "Do you think I don't know I'm the worst hypocrite of them all?" He rose, walking from behind his desk to take up pacing. "I cannot even shout at her because my behavior in the past would make doing so ridiculous. Instead, I must swallow my anger, hide my hurt, avoid spending time in my own home for fear I will storm into her room and demand an explanation. For greater fear she will not have one."

He stopped, rubbing his forehead. William proved uncharacteristically quiet. Gavin glanced at his cousin, surprised by his stunned expression.

"My God," he whispered. "It's finally happened."

"What?" Gavin muttered darkly.

William did not readily answer. He shook his head and stared at Gavin as if shocked for a few more moments. "You have fallen in love."

"I have not," Gavin protested, perhaps too quickly and in a voice too loud, he realized a moment later. "How can I feel love when I've never been taught the emotion? How can I love a woman who continues to baffle me? An angel one minute and a harlot the next? How can I give my heart to a woman who is out to destroy me? To take away my title and my lands? My place among decent society?"

William shrugged. "You tell me."

Running an impatient hand through his hair, Gavin said, "I'll tell you this, cousin. I do not love Christine. I don't even like her. I will prove as much, too." He began his pacing again. "I will go home. I will eat at my table and allow her to share the same air. But I will not shout at her. I will not be angry with her. I will not even question her concerning the ball. And do you know why?" He didn't allow William a chance to answer. "Because I bloody damn well refuse to care!"

"Why do I even care?" Christine asked herself, pausing in the garden to admire a bush loaded with rosebuds. She glanced around, embarrassed that she'd posed the question aloud. But she was alone, as it seemed she had been all of her life.

"He's no saint," she continued, moving toward the honeysuckle vines that climbed a white terrace. She paused before the blooms. "I warned him I would shame him the first night we met," she explained. "All I have done is accomplish what I set out to do. Why should I feel so badly about it?"

The blooms had no answer for her. She sighed. Gavin hadn't spoken to her, hadn't been home most of the time these past two days. The night of the ball he'd said nothing in the coach. Had only bid her a strained good night once they reached home and the top of the stairs, then gone into his room without another word.

Let him brood, she told herself. Let him suffer the shame she had suffered. He deserved to be humiliated. She thought that assuring herself of these things would make her feel better, but it did not. And she had cried when the notes began arriving canceling all the social functions to which she and her husband had been invited. Cried at the sadness that she would never fit in among society, that she had never fit in with the poor people of the parish.

The old marquis, kind as he had been to her, had alienated her from those simple country folk by giving her an education, treating her as if she were special. And although all the families of the parish had in a sense adopted her, none had claimed her as their own. The closest thing she had to a family was the staff at Greenhaven. And even that, it seemed, was not right.

Her title placed her above them, and her background separated her from Gavin's class. She belonged nowhere, and she suddenly felt very lost. And very confused. Gavin had no qualities she admired in a man, and yet, she did admire him. She supposed if for nothing else, for his honesty in being who he was—what he'd been raised to be. He had not attacked her behavior over the ball, and she sensed he'd refrained from doing so due to his own past indiscretions.

He might be a man with little compassion, but he was not, at least, a hypocrite. But besides being handsome, and charming when the mood suited him, she found nothing in him that should cause her confusing emotions.

Her first reaction, when he'd barged into the room where Wentworth had tried to take liberties with her, was to explain the circumstances. To assure him what he saw was not as it appeared to be—to chase away the hurt she'd seen in his eyes. If it was indeed hurt, because he so quickly disguised his emotions.

More likely, it had only been anger she'd misinterpreted as hurt. Anger not that she might have a dalliance with another man, but that she'd managed to have one that people had witnessed and would gossip over. Gossip that would undo his efforts to have society believe they were a loving couple. Gossip that might perhaps force him into seeking an annulment or looking the fool.

But would one such incident be enough to make him part with his inheritance? Although the town home and all its wonderful furnishings, probably purchased with his own money, would not fall under the terms of the will, Greenhaven had to be worth a small fortune.

It would help many to have that fortune transferred to charities. And this was her quest. Not to find a home of her own or to have a family.

She started back toward the house, wishing she could return to Greenhaven, to the parish, in order to strengthen her convictions. She missed the staff, and the simple country life she lived there. Suddenly, a ruckus at the back of the house drew her attention from her nostalgic musings.

A coach was being hitched to a team of horses. Curious, she veered off toward the stables. The sight of a woman waiting near the coach increased her curiosity. Christine approached her. "Excuse me, ma'am," she called. "May I be of some help to you?"

The woman turned, and although she wasn't old, she looked pale and used up for her years. "I be Sarah Watts, and no, His Lordship has kindly seen to my needs."

"His Lordship?" Christine repeated, stopping beside the woman.

"Oh, aye, he's a saint, that one," she gushed. "It took me a bit longer to recover from my sickness, and I feared he'd forget his offer to me, but he didn't. He sent the coach after I had my boy tell him I was ready, but one of the horses went lame before we got out of the city and we had to come to his fine house to replace the animal."

Christine's confusion grew. She started to ask what offer His Lordship had made to the woman, but three rowdy children came darting from the stables, interrupting her intentions.

"Hey, now," the woman scolded them. "You three mind yer manners here."

The rowdy group ran up to them. The oldest boy glanced at Christine. His face suddenly filled with awe.

"That's her," he whispered. "That's the angel I told ye about. The one what gave me her jewels."

It took Christine a moment to recognize the boy. His clothes were clean and he had shoes on his feet. "I remember you," she whispered, her gaze roaming over the children she'd seen begging on the streets. "What are you doing here?"

"We're going to live in the country," the boy explained. "And me mam says we'll never be cold or hungry again. The gentleman, he promised."

Tears suddenly filled Christine's eyes. Still confused, she glanced at the woman, who nodded, confirming the boy's statement.

"But how, why?" Christine asked, puzzled.

"His Lordship took pity on us," the woman said. "He reclaimed those jewels for you, but he gave us money for food, clothes, and me a doctor. He seen the bruises on my face, given to me by my no-good husband. His Lordship offered me a position at his country estate. Only, he tells me he don't provide work for drunkards and wife-beaters, so he says to hide the money, then to send the boy to tell him when I'm well."

"Gavin did that?" she asked, shocked.

"He's a fine man," she said. "I can tell by the looks of ye he ain't never raised his fists to yer face. That he's one to put food on the table and this nice roof over yer head. Ye can count yer blessings. Yer a lucky lady to have a man such as His Lordship. I don't care what's been said about him."

Christine dutifully replied, "Yes, I am very fortunate." She glanced down at the boy, who still stared at her with an expression akin to awe, and smiled at him. "And you, young sir, will love the country."

To her surprise, he threw his arms around her. "If you hadn't given us your fine jewels, the gentleman would have never chased after us and seen how sorry we lived. Me mam could have died. Ye truly are an angel."

She smoothed his hair into place. "No, I'm only a woman. And a very happy one at the moment."

"All hitched and ready," the coachman called.

The woman took Christine's hand, squeezed it, and climbed into the coach. The smaller children scrambled inside after their mother. The boy stepped away, his cheeks flushed red.

"Will ye come to see us at this grand place we're going to live?"

"Yes, I will," she promised. "You'll take up right away with the others there. All of them are good people."

He grinned again and hopped into the coach. Christine watched as the coachman took his seat, flicked the reins, and the coach pulled away. The children all leaned out of the windows and waved to her. She waved back, smiling, her spirits soaring.

Then her smile faded. By seeing that Greenhaven was auctioned off to help the poor, she would be putting her friends, and this family moving down the road, out of work.

Chapter Twenty

Christine couldn't have been more surprised when Gavin joined her for dinner that evening. She knew he'd come home some time ago, but expected he'd leave again rather than spend time in her company. He looked very formal sitting at the end of the table. Distant in more ways than one.

She supposed she could treat him with the same chilly disdain he used toward her, but she couldn't help but be proud of him for what he'd done for Sarah Watts and her children. Her spirits recovered once she'd decided she would find everyone at Greenhaven gainful employment before the auction. Her husband's act of kindness and compassion told her that there might yet be hope for Gavin's soul.

So enthused by the prospect was Christine, she rose, walked the long distance to the end of the table, and bent with the intention of kissing him soundly upon the cheek. Gavin jerked back from her as if she meant to hit him, which left her with a pucker upon her lips and no place to put it.

"What are you doing?" he asked.

Embarrassed, she straightened. "I wanted to thank you for what you did today concerning Sarah Watts."

He glanced down at his plate. "I have no idea what you're talking about."

She wouldn't be put off. "Yes, you do. The coach returned to the house to replace a lame horse. Mrs. Watts told me about your offer for employment at Greenhaven. It was very kind of you to take pity upon her and the children."

Slowly, his gaze lifted. "And of what concern are the woman and her children to you? I thought you gave the boy your jewelry to spite me."

Christine pulled out a chair and took the seat next to his. "My motives don't change what you have done for the poor family. I find your actions very admirable."

He didn't return the smile she gave him. Instead, he turned his attention to his meal. "Is that all you have to say?"

She frowned. He wasn't making the least effort to converse pleasantly with her. Of course, he was still angry about the ball, or to be precise, her destruction of the facade he wanted the two of them to present to society.

"Would you have me say more?" she ventured.

Again, his gaze lifted. He appeared as if he meant to say something other than the short response he gave her. "No."

Christine drummed her fingernails on the table. "Then perhaps you have something you wish to say to me?"

In a deliberate tone, he answered, "No. I do not."

"Nothing at all?" she pressed.

"Nothing at all," he bit out.

With a sigh, she rose and walked back to her seat at the end of the table. When he failed to pay her the slightest attention, she moved her fork noisily around on her plate. She watched him eat, noting his perfect table manners and his ability to ignore her, then grabbed up her knife. She scraped the knife loudly against the fine china of her plate, causing the most annoying squeak.

It went on for a ridiculously long time before he pounded a fist upon the table. "Will you please stop that!"

She glanced up innocently. "Stop what, Your Lordship?"

He ran a hand through his hair. "You know what."

"I'm afraid I do not," she insisted, widening her eyes.

"That noise," he said, casting her a dark look before returning his attention to the meal.

"Oh," Christine sighed. "I thought you might be asking me to please stop having affairs with other men."

He swallowed the bite he'd just taken with difficulty. "Would asking do any good?"

She shrugged. "I suppose not."

Gavin snatched up his wine glass, took a long swallow, and eyed her over the rim. "Would it be out of the question to ask you to at least choose more carefully?" Wentworth is a boy, a fop, and an embarrassment to me."

"To your good reputation?" she asked sarcastically.

"To my reputation as a man," he specified. "At least respect me enough to choose someone as . . ."

"Accomplished with the ladies as you are?" she said, finishing the sentence he would not. She tapped her knife against her plate and pretended to be thinking. "But that leaves no one, does it, Your Lordship?"

Gavin tugged at his collar. "I'm sure there is someone," he muttered.

"Perhaps you could make me a list," she suggested. "Or better yet, perhaps the duchess could supply one for me."

"Do not bring her into this," he warned.

She let her knife fall to her plate. "It has just occurred to me to ask what you were doing at the ball."

"Obviously not the same thing you were doing."

Scraping her chair back, she stood. "Not so obviously," she argued. "Did you go there in hopes of meeting Adrianna?"

He threw his napkin in his plate and also rose. "I will not lie to you. I went there in hopes of having a word with her."

Christine laughed, and realized she'd learned to do so as humorlessly as Gavin. "I seem to recall a similar conversation one morning in my hotel room. A word? A chat? Is that what they are calling it these days?"

He stormed toward her. "I said I would not lie to you, and I have not. I thought speaking to her at such a gathering, and in disguise, would cause less gossip."

Almost tempted to believe him, she asked, "And what did you wish to speak to her about?"

His gaze would not meet hers. "That, I cannot tell you."

"Hhmnn," Christine responded, turning on her heel. She had every intention of retiring to her room, but Gavin's next question drew her up short.

"Why Wentworth? Why any man, for that matter? This cowardly lover you claim, I thought you might love him."

Her cheeks stung with shame. What a sad day. To be brought down by a man with Gavin's dark reputation. "I do love Him," she said, referring to a higher being and her long-felt desire to serve, to rise above her humble beginnings in a way she felt truly mattered. "At the ball, Wentworth. I meant merely to appear as if I were a willing partner. But then . . ."

The warmth of his hands settled upon her shoulders. He spun her around to face him. "What are you telling me, Christine? That Wentworth took liberties with you against your wishes?"

The humiliation of that night swept over her again. "I tried to tell you, but you wouldn't listen. Wentworth played the gentleman, offering to help me create a scandal with the understanding it would be a pretense, but once we reached the room . . . well, he is no gentleman."

Gavin's fingers tightened upon her shoulders. "I will call him out for this!"

"No," Christine pleaded. She placed her hands upon the front of his shirt. "I will have no man's death on my conscience. Besides, I should not have gone there. What happened is my own fault."

His hand reached out and traced the line of her jaw. "Your only sin was trusting in people who are not trustworthy." Suddenly he snatched his hand away and the softness faded from his eyes. "And going there with the intention of shaming me in the first place. You have made me a laughingstock."

Christine removed her hands from the front of his shirt and stepped back. "I told you sometime ago I had every intention of doing just that. And if you'll recall, you were the beast who had me pinned beneath him that night, taking liberties I did not willingly grant you!"

Gavin blinked. His face turned red. "But that was different," he blustered.

"How so?" Christine demanded.

"You are my wife."

"That makes no difference," she shot back. "I did not know you, or you me. Face the truth, Gavin Norfork, you are no different from Thomas Wentworth. No different from any of the predators at that horrid ball."

His face paled somewhat. He stared at her for a few minutes; then color returned to his face. Too much color. She thought he actually blushed.

"Good God. It seems I have no argument to present on my behalf. I'm sorry, Christine. Sorry for that first night when I took liberties with you, and sorry for all the times since when the thought that you might not want me, desire me, was beyond my selfish comprehension. I will not make that mistake again, or mistreat you in such fashion."

When he turned and left the dining room, all the righteous indignation building within her suddenly evaporated into thin air. What was this? An actual apology from Gavin? Good God, indeed. The man was actually turning into a human being.

"What a horrid development," she whispered.

No, she corrected herself. It was a grand one for her cause, but perhaps a dangerous one for her heart. She felt it softening toward him. Even felt tempted to go to his room and tell him there were times when he'd taken her in his arms when he had not mistaken her desire for him. But that would have been foolish. Why invite more trouble into her life, when she clearly had enough to deal with?

Tillie popped her head into the dining room. "Will you be needing me this evening, m'lady?"

She'd seen very little of the maid of late. Tillie had taken to doing more around the household. Christine suspected her energy resulted from her wish to pursue Mr. Graves.

"No, Tillie. Have you plans?"

"Just a bit of card playing with the staff," she said. "It was my idea, you see. To bring them all closer together."

Christine lifted a brow. "And will our Mr. Graves be included in the game?"

Tillie blushed. "I certainly hope so. He rarely rubs elbows with the rest of the staff. Thinks he's above us all, I suppose."

"But you've a mind to change his attitude?" Christine predicted, smiling at the pretty maid.

The woman returned her smile. "You have your mission and now I have mine, m'lady."

At the mention of Christine's mission, she felt the smile fade from her lips. "Run along, then," she said to Tillie. Christine left the room and went upstairs. She paused before Gavin's closed door. Perhaps it was time to be truthful with him. To dispel his ridiculous notion that she had ever entertained a flesh-and-blood lover. To beg him to have pity on more than the Watts family and have their marriage dissolved.

She raised her hand to rap on the door, then let it fall to her side. Gavin might have shown promise at becoming more compassionate to the feelings of others, but she sensed he was not ready to make such a sacrifice. Not yet, at least. More, she wasn't certain what it would take to turn him completely around. She supposed his behavior had resulted from something lacking in his past, or he wouldn't have wandered so far from decency to begin with. But what?

"Love," Gavin muttered irritably. He shrugged from his coat and threw it on the bed. "What a ridiculous notion. A silly emotion, for that matter," he continued to rant.

Mr. Graves stepped from the shadows and retrieved his coat, reminding Gavin of his presence. Unfamiliar heat rushed to Gavin's face when the servant lifted a curious brow.

"You could warn a person when you're hiding in the shadows, Graves," he muttered.

"I have been hiding in the shadows for years, Your Lordship. I believe it is expected of me."

"Well, now I expect you to clear your throat or some such indication that you are present," he snapped.

"As you wish, Your Lordship."

Gavin walked to the table where his brandy decanter sat. He started to pour himself a drink, then decided if he drank every time Christine managed to upset him, he would indeed become a drunkard.

"Graves, do you think me a beast?"

The man never missed a step on his way to hang Gavin's coat in the wardrobe. "Of course, Your Lordship. That is also expected of me, only in different circles. If

247

you were an easy master with no bad reputation to be bandied about, I'd have nothing to talk about when I meet with my fellow manservants over Sunday brunch."

Gavin blinked. "I never thought you the type to gossip, Graves."

"Everyone is the type to gossip, Your Lordship. But have no fear. We consider ourselves far too superior to let anything we speak of leave the company of our small group."

"Well, that is a relief," Gavin drawled dryly. "Tell me, why do you think me a beast?"

Graves shrugged. "I suppose because you are a titled nobleman. The two usually go hand in hand. Most are more secretive about their dark deeds. And most try to at least hide them from their wives."

"Oh, there was my mistake," Gavin said, his tone still dry as dust. "Being too honest can have its drawbacks."

"Flaunting one's bad attributes and being honest about them are two different things," Graves pointed out. "But, if it is any consolation, I believe you may be on the mend."

Gavin lifted a brow. "Pray continue."

"It was very nice, what you did for the poor woman and her children. And the fact you did not hit Her Ladyship for her bad behavior at the disgusting ball she attended speaks good of you."

"I would never hit a woman!" Gavin thundered.

"Well, you see, you are not as bad as some think."

"And how did you learn of Christine's recent indiscretion?" Gavin asked.

"I said I do not gossip outside my circle. I did not say I do not listen to gossip outside my circle."

Gavin plopped down into his comfortable chair. "I must ask you a favor, Graves. One of the utmost importance, and one you must keep from your mistress."

The man stepped closer. "What is it, Your Lordship?"

"I have learned that the banister falling from the box was no accident. The railing had been purposely loosened. Keep a close eye on Christine and the house in my absence."

"Do you think she is in danger?" Graves whispered.

"I'm not sure. I could be the target, and her lover the culprit."

"Her lover?" Graves asked, then snorted indignantly. "My mistress has no lover. I have been around enough society women to know when one is chaste and one is not. Her Ladyship has no lover, has never had a lover. I would stake my own reputation upon that."

Gavin sat up abruptly. His heart started to pound at an embarrassingly fast pace. "You are mistaken. She has admitted to having a lover."

Graves stared down his straight nose at him. "Then for whatever reason, she has lied to you."

Gavin sat back with the same abruptness. "Then she cannot be too virtuous, Graves. If in fact you are right, which I still greatly question."

"Think long and hard upon the issue, Your Lordship. You, with your reputation, should be equally skilled at judging a woman's character, or her virtue. When you've given the matter thought, you will see that I am right. Then, you must discover her motives for lying."

"I can think of none," he said.

"Perhaps the most obvious is the hardest to accept."

Gavin glanced up at the man. "Enlighten me, Graves."

The servant sighed, as if growing weary of always having to take on such a burden. "Perhaps to keep you at a distance. To make her less desirable in your eyes."

Without thought, he said, "Then she has failed."

A considerable amount of time passed before Graves cleared his throat. "Will that be all?"

Recovering, Gavin asked. "Are you in a hurry to quit my company?"

Ronda Thompson

Graves picked imaginary lint from his own immaculate coat. "There is to be a card game downstairs among the staff. I feel as if I should oversee the affair."

Gavin almost smiled. "And I suppose my wife's pretty maid will be in attendance?"

The man wiggled his nose as if he'd caught a whiff of something unpleasant. "It seems she is the instigator. And prone to gossip, I might add, which is why I feel I should be present to staunch such bad behavior."

"By all means. Keep an eye on her."

"That I will," Graves assured him, and even smiled, although just barely.

Wishing to be alone with his thoughts, Gavin dismissed the servant. "Good night, Graves."

The man walked to the door, then paused. "My Christian name is Henry, and I give you permission to use it on occasion, but only in private circumstances. Good night, Gavin."

Gavin's gaze strayed to the closing door. He laughed. "Good night, Henry." Upon Graves's departure, he immediately sobered. Had Christine lied to him about having a lover? And why? To make him think her unworthy of being a wife? Given his own past indiscretions, he could not judge her by such ridiculous standards.

But he could admit, with the same unwanted emotion that had plagued him of late, that he hoped she had lied to him. He had more than one reason to demand the truth. Not only to appease the silly hope in him that she was as unspoiled as she seemed at times, but because if she had no lover, then who the hell was trying to kill him?

Chapter Twenty-one

Or who might be trying to kill Christine? Gavin dwelled on his worries the next morning. He still thought it unlikely anyone would harm his wife, but he had to be certain. And he'd just been given word a coach had arrived outside his office, bearing the only suspect who came to mind.

"You will find something else to occupy yourself with?" he asked William.

His cousin shrugged. "I thought you might wish me to remain in case she tries to molest you again."

Gavin was not amused, either by the thought of his cousin having to protect him from a mere woman, or by the prospect that Adrianna might have a mind to repeat the same performance she'd enacted the night of the opera.

"I can handle the situation," he assured William.

William rose and walked to the door. "I'd be willing to wager she will end up handling you, cousin."

"Then you would lose," Gavin assured him. "You may return in one hour."

His cousin bowed, and Gavin couldn't swear to it, but he thought the gesture somewhat mocking. As soon as William had departed, Adrianna flounced into his office.

"Your Lordship," she gushed, hurrying to him before he barely managed to stand. She threw her arms around his neck. "I'm so happy you sent for me."

Gavin pried her arms loose and stepped back. "I would like to ask you a few questions, Adrianna."

Her red lips immediately turned into a pout. "Questions? But I thought you had decided to get back at your wife for that little impasse she committed the other night."

"You thought wrong." He walked around his desk to put more space between them. "I asked you at the ball if you would ever harm Christine. You did not answer."

"Christine!" she snarled. "Why must every conversation we have of late center around that homely orphan?"

He lifted a brow. "Christine may be an orphan, but she is far from homely. Which you are aware of."

Adrianna marched around the desk to join him. "So she is beautiful. Am I not beautiful as well? Why do you prefer her over me?"

"Christine is my wife."

"And another man's whore!"

His annoyance with her rose faster than he anticipated. "You, of all women, have no right to cast stones. And you placed her in danger by taking her to that disgusting ball. Wentworth didn't play the gentleman with her."

She smiled, more of a sneer. "Perhaps that was because she didn't play the innocent with him, as she obviously does with you. Why are you so blind to her faults?" She stepped forward and placed a hand upon his arm. "Why have you allowed someone so unworthy of you to come between us?"

Gavin gently removed her hand from his sleeve. "Christine did not come between us. There never was an us, Adrianna. Only a few stolen occasions when we took pleasure from one another, nothing more."

Adrianna stomped her foot childishly. "I wanted you to fall in love with me. All of my lovers do. And I have always been the one to weary of the relationship and put an end to it. You have insulted me."

"I didn't mean to. I have no deep feelings for you, and I never led you to believe otherwise. But I didn't ask you here to discuss a matter we have already discussed."

"Then what do you want?" she demanded.

He decided bluntness had always served him well in the past. "The night of the opera. The banister pulling free and Christine falling was no accident. The pegs had been purposely loosened. Did you have anything to do with it?"

Although he suspected Adrianna possessed great acting skills, the shock that registered on her face seemed genuine. "What are you implying? That I would murder your wife?"

"I can think of no one else who would wish her harm."

"Then you must think harder!" Adrianna yelled. "How dare you accuse me of attempted murder. You're good, Gavin, but you're not that good!"

A sense of relief washed over him. His ego aside, he hoped it unlikely a woman would murder another over a desire to have him in her bed again. "I had to ask, to make certain," he said. "For Christine's sake."

"For Christine's sake," she growled. Her eyes narrowed on him. "Has it occurred to you that you might have been the target, Gavin? That her lover, and your wife herself, might have been plotting against you?"

"Her lover perhaps," he admitted. "But Christine would have known about the banister and steered away from it had she been a party. And besides, she wouldn't be involved in such a scheme. She doesn't have the heart of a murderer."

Adrianna's narrowed eyes suddenly widened. "Not of a murderer, but she does, I believe, have the heart of a marquis. Your heart."

A denial was not quick to form upon his lips. "I have never given it to anyone before. What makes you believe so?"

She sighed, then fussed with her gown. "I saw the way you looked at her during the opera. The way you leaned close and whispered in her ear. The way you watched the emotions cross her features, unable to hide your own." She glanced up at him. "It is true, although I didn't want to believe it. For now, I can no longer desire you, but only pity you, as I do all men who are weak."

"And love is a weakness," he said, having believed that himself for most of his life.

"My fool husband worships me. He has given his heart to a woman he knows will slip off behind his back given the first chance and lie with another. He knows to try and stop me is to lose me, and he will play the fool rather than part with his precious ornament. I despise him for loving me too much to demand I honor him as a husband."

"But you wanted me to love you," he reminded.

"So that I could despise you as well," she admitted. "And perhaps because I thought you were incapable of that emotion. Now, I see that you are not, and I no longer desire you."

Gavin walked away from her. "I think, Adrianna, you are the one to be pitied. Good day."

"You are no different from my foolish husband," she said to his back. "You love a woman who does not love you in return, who does not even wish to be your wife. Oh, yes, she told me so. Save your pity for yourself."

The door closed, ending forever the affair between himself and Adrianna. Was he in love with Christine? Love was said to be a gentle emotion. But it could rip and tear and expose a man to the bone. He had thought it a weakness more than a feeling.

It was a weakness that had turned a once-loving, adoring man into bitter, hateful monster. A weakness that tore a mother from her child's arms and sent her off on her own selfish fancy, and to her death, with his common father. How badly he had wanted to erase that day, and truly be the doted-upon noble son of a titled gentleman. To have his father bounce him upon his knee, and look at him with pride, instead of hatred.

And damn if he hadn't tried to be that son. To shroud himself in snobbery. To shame the old marquis with the same enthusiasm all young nobles shamed their fathers. To fit into a world that had no rightful place for him. How the old man must have hated passing his title to him. But he had long since lost the chance to disinherit him. To deny him as his rightful heir. And all of his father's actions had been to protect his own shredded ego. Never to protect Gavin, or even his mother's reputation.

A knock at the door chased away his dark memories. He bade whoever stood on the other side to enter. It surprised him to see his coachman step into the room.

"What is it, Franklin?"

"Mr. Graves sent me," he said. "There's a problem at the house."

"Christine?" he whispered, fear clutching his gut. "Has she been injured?"

"No, Your Lordship," the man answered quickly. "But she's requested a coach to take her to Greenhaven. Mr. Graves said to tell you she received a note from one of your servants there, and then quickly requested escort to the country. We didn't know if we were to honor her wishes without your consent."

The fear did not subside, but rose to the vicinity of his heart. A note from Greenhaven? Perhaps her lover, if she did have one, had requested an audience with her there.

"Should I refuse her, Your Lordship?"

His first instinct was to answer yes. "No," he answered instead. "Take her where she wishes to go."

"Very well, Your Lordship."

The coachman left, and with his departure came a sudden thought. *Trust Christine.* For all he knew, there was a perfectly logical explanation for her being called to Greenhaven. Or he could follow her and see if he could catch her with this lover Graves claimed was nonexistent. And of course her safety was still an issue, if Adrianna could be dismissed as a threat.

"Was that your coachman?" William strode into the room.

"Yes, cousin, and I believe the hour you were to be gone is short by some time."

William waved away his reprimand. "I saw the duchess leave. Well, what did she have to say in her defense, and why was a member of your staff here?"

"You mind my business well," Gavin drawled.

His cousin lifted a brow. "I have minded it well for two years, have I not, Your Lordship?"

"Yes," Gavin said with a sigh. "You are an invaluable member of my staff, William."

The man's gaze narrowed upon him for the briefest second. "And what more can a man ask for than serving his wealthy cousin?"

"I pay you well," Gavin reminded him. "It is by your own choice that you choose to live modestly."

"Force of habit," he countered. "Now, pray tell me, did your past mistress confess to trying to do away with your pretty wife?"

"She said I was not worth murdering another woman over," he answered.

A clucking sound followed. "Slipping again, old boy. Well, for all we know, the banister that should have been loosened was hers. Now, what was your coachman doing here?"

"Christine has demanded to be taken to Greenhaven."

William's brows shot up. "So, you've finally managed to run her off as well."

"She received a note from a member of my staff there and asked to be conveyed to the country with all haste."

"Sounds suspicious," William remarked. "Do you think the note was from her lover?"

"I cannot know for certain," he answered, gathering up his coat and hat.

"But you intend to find out," William presumed.

"Yes."

"And as usual, I will manage your affairs in your absence."

"Thank you, William," Gavin said on his way out. "You are truly invaluable to me."

"As you are to me," William countered.

Gavin paused, turning back. "You did not sound sincere just then. Have I made you angry, cousin?"

"Forgive me," William said. "I am upset over the possibility of your wife duping you."

"But I thought you liked Christine. Championed her in just such a cause."

"That was before I saw her work her magic upon you, cousin. Beware, Gavin. People are not always what they appear to be. Be careful she doesn't stab you in the back, or more fittingly, in the heart."

Gavin nodded. "I will take care," he said, then left the office, very much hoping to prove his cousin wrong.

Christine packed only a few necessities. Tillie had been given the day off, and if the maid didn't return from her shopping soon, Christine would have to leave her behind. Not that she suspected Tillie would mind such an arrangement. With her mistress gone, she would have more time to flirt with Mr. Graves. Still, Christine could have used an extra pair of hands.

She had received a message from the vicar of the parish. Sickness had struck there, and his hands were not enough to tend all the poor souls in need. He could think of no one other than Christine who might come to their aid. And aid them she would.

She opened her jewelry case and removed the diamonds Gavin had given to her. They would serve to buy medical supplies and secure the services of a physician. The thought of simply asking Gavin to help had surfaced, but then, he might forbid her to go and do what she could. The poor souls were her family and she wouldn't be barred from tending them.

Mr. Graves tapped on her open door, then stuck his head inside. "Franklin has the coach hitched and ready, Your Ladyship. May I carry your luggage down?"

Christine slipped the long velvet box holding her jewelry into a small valise. "There is not much to carry, Mr. Graves. I can manage."

"And your maid, mistress. What shall I tell her?"

She cast him a guarded glance. Very clever, Mr. Graves. He wanted the information himself. "Just that I have gone back to Greenhaven for a while. You must see to it she doesn't spend her days with idle hands, Mr. Graves. I've noticed the silver could use a good polish. That should keep her occupied until my return."

He frowned over her sparse explanation. "Does the woman know how to polish silver correctly?"

"No, but I leave her instruction in your capable hands." She took her small valise from the bed and moved toward him. He moved aside and let her pass, his head bowed respectfully. Christine stopped and touched his cheek. "I shall miss you, Mr. Graves. Take care."

His gaze lifted. "And you will take the sunshine from

this house with your leaving. Hurry home, Your Lady-ship."

Home? Here? Yes, this did almost seem like home to her now. Christine had grown comfortable beneath Gavin's roof, after all. Which was a dreadful mistake. This could never be her home in truth, not unless she failed in her mission. Her quest must be temporarily put on hold until she saw to this new dilemma. Then she would have to decide on a new plan of action.

"Good-bye, Mr. Graves," she said, and hurried from the room and downstairs. The coach waited for her in front of the house. Franklin jumped from his perch atop the coach and assisted her inside.

"I must make a few stops before we take the road to Greenhaven," she told him. "Do you know a place where I might pawn my valuables at a fair price?"

He frowned. "If you need funds, Your Ladyship, I am certain His Lordship—"

"That is not the question I asked," she snapped, impatient to get under way. "Do you know a place?"

Franklin nodded. "Aye, I do, but it's not a place for the likes of you, fair lady. I'll do your business."

She nodded and settled back in the coach. "Let us be off, then. I'm in a hurry."

"Yes, Your Ladyship," he dutifully replied.

Christine breathed a sigh of relief when the coach lurched forward. The country estate was not more than a half a day's ride, but she wanted to reach the parish before nightfall. She'd changed into one of her sensible gowns and after wearing silks and satins, it seemed shabby to her indeed. How quickly she'd become spoiled by the finer things in life. Of course, she wasn't going to Greenhaven to socialize, she reminded herself. She had work to do.

The coach stopped a short time later, and judging from her surroundings, the driver was correct in assuming she would not want to conduct business there herself. She lowered the curtains to shield her from view after she'd given him the jewelry to pawn. Then she waited, and waited. Finally Franklin spoke softly from the other side of the curtain. She drew back the covering and took the pouch he quickly slipped to her. It was heavy with coin. The wait had proven productive.

"Where to now, Your Ladyship?"

"The nearest hospital," she instructed. "And, Franklin, please hurry."

Her stop at the hospital took longer than Christine had anticipated. She had trouble getting anyone's attention, as the place was obviously overcrowded and understaffed. The jingle of coins purchased the notice she needed. She secured the services of a doctor, who promised to bring supplies purchased with her coin, but the man could not reach the parish until morning. She would make do the best she could until then.

Franklin didn't hide his curiosity when she emerged, but Christine told him nothing. If he knew she intended to nurse a parish full of sick people, he might balk and demand she tell his employer the reason for her flight to Greenhaven. Christine would not risk being told her position forbade such sacrifice.

Finally, they were on their way again. Christine settled back and tried to relax. Not an easy task with her current worries. Still, she knew she must rest in order to preserve her strength. She closed her eyes. At some point, she must have dozed off. The rattle of the coach door opening roused her.

"Are we there already?" she asked, expecting to see the coachman stick his head inside. It was not Franklin.

"Gavin," she said, surprised.

"Hello, wife." He threw a valise inside the coach before climbing in, then rapped on the ceiling with his cane. The coach moved onward.

"What are you doing here?" she demanded.

He shrugged. "I haven't visited Greenhaven in years. Thought I might meet the staff, have a look around."

Christine narrowed her gaze on him. "You don't care a whit about Greenhaven except for the title and the lands that go with it. You're spying on me."

Gavin removed his hat and placed it on the seat beside him. "I call it looking out for my best interests."

"I call it underhanded," she shot back. "How did you get here?"

"My horse is tied to the back of the coach. I had to conclude some business, have my clothing packed, so it took me longer than I expected to catch up with you."

Christine felt her shock at seeing him turn to rage. "Could you not trust me? Not even this once?"

"You have given me few reasons to trust you, Christine. Nor, to my knowledge, have you ever asked me to do so."

"I am asking you now. Please tell Franklin to stop the coach so that you may return to London."

"Why?" he asked. "Why have you been called to Greenhaven, and who sent you the note?"

She was sorely tempted to throw the truth in his suspicious face, but fear that he would not allow her to continue the journey kept her silent.

"If you cannot tell me, then I cannot trust you," he said, and the lowness of his voice told her he, too, had become angry.

They sat in strained silence for a few moments. The next instant a shot rang out. The coach suddenly lurched forward and Gavin was thrown against her. "What the bloody hell," he bit out, righting himself. He scrambled to the window and shoved the drapes aside.

"Franklin!" he shouted.

There was no answer.

Chapter Twenty-two

"Get down on the floor," Gavin ordered.

Christine didn't move. Her eyes were wide with shock. The coach picked up speed, and Gavin strongly suspected no driver sat perched atop in control of the horses.

"Christine!" he shouted again, then shook her. "For heaven's sake, woman, get on the floor!"

The urgency in his voice roused her. She scrambled from the seat and crouched on the floor. Gavin opened his valise and withdrew a pistol. He shoved it in the front of his trousers and grabbed the coach door.

"What are you going to do?" Christine asked weakly.

"See what's happened to Franklin and try to stop the horses."

"But you might be killed!" she argued.

"If I don't stop the coach, we might both be killed."

He didn't hesitate long enough to hear further arguments from her, but swung the door wide, drew his pistol, and slid an arm through the window to help steady himself. He ducked his head outside the open door. A shot whizzed past, dangerously close. Christine screamed.

"Are you hit?" She shouted.

"No, you fool! But you will be if you don't get back inside and take cover this instant!"

Gavin fired a few shots at the trees lining the road behind him. He wanted whoever pursued them to know he was armed. Damn, but the trees were too thick for him to spot anyone. He slid his arm from the window, then reached for the railing atop the coach. He found it, held on, reluctantly tucked the pistol into his trousers, and managed a two-handed grip on the railing. The coach hit a rut, jarring his feet from beneath him.

Suddenly, his body swung from the coach, leaving him dangling. A shot slammed into the coach next to his head, splintering wood. He pulled himself up with all his strength, expecting the sting of a bullet to find his flesh at any moment. He managed to pull his upper body up over the top. Franklin still sat in the driver's seat. Gavin felt relieved to see the man struggling with the reins.

"Franklin!" he shouted.

The man jumped. He turned, a trickle of blood running from a small gash on the side of his head.

"Give me a hand!" Gavin ordered.

The driver transferred the reins to one hand and stretched out the other toward Gavin. With the man's help, Gavin scrambled over the top. He drew his pistol, aiming behind them.

"Are you hurt?" he shouted at Franklin.

"Just a nick, but it knocked me out for a moment!" the driver called. "Now I can bring these horses to a stop!"

"No!" Gavin warned him. "Let them have their heads until I see if we are still being pursued!"

The coachman nodded, and Gavin scrambled down beside him, aiming his pistol over the top of the coach. They thundered down the road at an alarming speed, hitting ruts in the road than nearly unseated them both. He worried about Christine.

Lord, he hoped she wasn't being knocked about as badly as he and the driver were. When a good while passed and no further shots were fired, he ordered Franklin to slow the horses. It took both of them to bring the frightened animals to a stop.

His pistol drawn, Gavin jumped down and wrenched open the coach door. Christine was still on the floor, her arms over her head.

"Are you all right?"

She glanced up. "Are you?"

"Yes. I'll ride with the coachman on top in case the danger hasn't passed."

"Franklin." Christine scrambled up. "Was he shot?"

The true concern on her face touched him, and the slight bruise he saw forming along her jawline pulled at his heart. He reached out and gently traced the bruise.

"The bullet only grazed his temple, but he briefly lost control of the horses. I believe he'll be fine."

"Thank God," she whispered.

Gavin helped her up. "We will not take a leisurely trip to Greenhaven with possible danger still stalking us. Hold tight and if more shots ring out, resume your position on the floor."

Christine nodded. "Who do you think it was? Highwaymen out to rob us?"

That was very possible, but given the other strange happenings of late, Gavin suspected they were not victims of chance. "Probably," he answered. "We must be off again."

She reached forward and touched him. "Do be careful."

He took her hand, turned it over, and placed a gentle kiss upon her palm. "Anything for you, my lady."

Something leapt into her eyes, a spark, a tiny reflection of an emotion he had not seen there before. It warmed him from the inside out.

"Stay alert to danger," he said, then closed the coach door and jumped up beside Franklin, strangely light-hearted considering their circumstances. He decided in that moment that he very much wanted to see that warm spark in her eyes again, wanted to claim it as his, and his alone.

Christine breathed a sigh of relief when Greenhaven came into view. Then her stomach knotted with worry. How would she slip away to the parish with Gavin dogging her heels? She supposed she could wait for the cover of darkness, but the thought of those in need had her quickly rejecting the idea. She had planned for Franklin to drive her straight to the parish once they reached Greenhaven. Now, with the coachman hurt and her husband along, she had to think of something else.

As the coach pulled to a stop in the circle drive before the massive estate, she realized her thinking time was over. Christine didn't wait for Gavin to get the door. She bounded from the coach and walked to the front, watching him help Franklin down. She made a quick diagnosis of the coachman and deemed him not seriously injured.

Nevertheless, she rushed forward.

"You must get him inside," she instructed her husband. "That cut needs to be cleaned and the damage surveyed."

He nodded, helping the coachman toward the front doors, which immediately swung open as the servants spilled out of the house.

"Christine!" the head servant, Martha, shouted. She ambled toward Christine with her heavy girth, smiling broadly.

"Oh, dear," Christine said under her breath. She couldn't be detained, as this might be her only chance to make a mad dash toward the parish. She couldn't risk Gavin refusing to allow her to help those in need of her services, and she dared not delay a moment longer in reaching the vicar.

No one paid her handsome husband or the coachman a hint of attention. Her friends all rushed forward to hug her and convey their happiness at seeing her again. Christine drew herself up indignantly, although she was bursting with happiness to see them all again.

"Is this the way you greet the master of the house?" she asked, nodding toward Gavin, who looked rather dumbfounded by the servants' disregard of him. "His Lordship is tired, thirsty, and the coachman needs to be tended. You will all show him the respect he deserves."

Smiles faded and expressions turned from joy to flustered confusion. Christine hated hurting these people, her family, but she needed attention diverted away from her at the moment. The staff members turned to Gavin, all sweeping into awkward bows and clumsy curtsies. She might have laughed had the situation not been a serious one.

Chaos ensued. Too many tried to help at once, and Sarah Watts and her round-faced children stood quietly at the back of the group, but were all smiling. Gavin was thankfully swept up in the whirlwind and pushed toward the house. Christine used his distraction to glance about.

His horse, Pegasus, still stood tied to the back of the coach. Did she dare steal her husband's mount and try to ride the animal? It made more sense to her than running all the way to the parish. She stepped toward the animal.

"Christine? Are you coming?"

She jumped, spinning about to see Gavin poised before the doors, servants still littered about him. "I want to fetch my valise and I'll be right in," she called.

He looked as if he might argue, perhaps insist one of the servants bring her bag, but the staff, accustomed to Christine doing for herself, pushed forward and Gavin disappeared into the house. Christine didn't hesitate now that her chance was at hand. She ran to the back of the coach, untied Pegasus, and used the rear step to mount.

The animal pranced nervously with an unfamiliar rider upon his back. She set her teeth, reined the horse toward the parish, and kicked with her heels. The stallion's speed almost unseated her, but she twisted one hand in the animal's silky mane and held on for dear life.

Having been relieved of the burden of Franklin, Gavin followed those ushering him into the kitchen. The coachman was settled into a chair while the large woman, obviously his head servant, had a look at the injured man. She issued orders to have the wound cleaned, then turned to Gavin.

"So sorry, Your Lordship. We expected Christine might come, but we weren't expecting *you*. What be your pleasure? Food? Drink? Or would you like to rest?"

He glanced around the once-familiar kitchen. Not much had changed, but of course he hadn't ordered any changes to Greenhaven. Had tried not to think too much about his childhood home.

"Your mistress needs attending first. As you can see." He nodded toward the coachman. "We met with trouble upon the road. She's been knocked about some in the coach."

"Oh, dear," the woman exclaimed. "Poor chick." She hurried from the kitchen, leaving Gavin no choice but to follow.

Except for servants rushing about, there was no sign of Christine inside the large foyer behind the massive front doors.

"Maybe she's already gone up to her room," the woman said, then hurried on.

Gavin found the prospect unlikely. Knowing Christine, he'd expected her to rush into the kitchen and fret over the injured coachman. Were she of true snobbish society, she might not give the servant's condition a thought, but Christine was different. And he admitted he found her differences endearing.

Although frightened by their brush with death on the road, she'd held up well under the strain. She hadn't gone into hysterics or suffered the vapors, as he supposed most women would have done. Her courage and spirit constantly surprised him. Gavin realized he'd never truly respected a woman until Christine had intruded upon his life.

While he waited for information regarding his wife's whereabouts, Gavin reluctantly strolled the downstairs portion of the house. It was still a cold, dreary place, he noted. One that dredged up old hurts and bitter memories of an unhappy childhood. He supposed he should have ordered the house redecorated after the marquis's death, but had thought it a waste of effort and money.

He'd had no desire to spend time here, in this house where his heritage lurked in every dark corner: the truth of his mother's betrayal and his common bastard status. The past mocked him here, made him feel undeserving of all that he had, all that was not his by right.

The head servant appeared again, out of breath from her climb up the stairs and back down again. "The mistress is not in her room," she informed him. "Or upstairs at all."

"She must be here somewhere," Gavin muttered, and traced his steps back to the kitchen. The coachman looked better with the blood cleaned from his face and a fresh bandage wrapped around his head. "Has Christine been here?" Gavin asked.

All occupants of the kitchen shook their heads. He walked out again and toward the massive front doors. After swinging them wide, he noted the coach had been moved. Gavin bounded down the steps and toward the stables. He heard the labored breath of the woman servant as she tried to keep up with him.

The coach horses were being unhitched. Gavin strolled up to a groom. "Have you seen Her Ladyship?"

"No, Your Lordship," the young groom replied. "But her valise, we noticed, is still inside the coach along with yours. We will fetch them to the house."

A knot began to form in Gavin's stomach, a suspicion to take shape in his mind. "Where is my horse?"

"Your horse?" the groom replied, confusion clouding his features.

"The stallion that was tied to the back of the coach," Gavin snapped.

The lad paled. "We saw no horse when he we went to fetch the coach, Your Lordship."

Fury the likes of which he'd never experienced engulfed Gavin. He'd hoped she had no lover, that she was as kind and pure as he swore she was. That she was that one selfless soul. That rarest of jewels. That one woman who could teach him all life had failed to teach him. He turned to the servant woman, noting her face had turned as pale as the young groom's.

"Where is she?" he demanded.

The woman bit her lower lip, but did not answer.

He wanted to shout at her, but instead, he asked, "What is your name?"

Her eyes widened. "Martha, Your Lordship."

"Martha," he said calmly, "as you know, your mistress is not an experienced rider. The stallion is headstrong and spirited. I fear she may injure herself."

"Oh, dear," the woman fretted. She raised a hand to her lips and unconsciously nibbled at one plump finger.

"You know where she has gone, don't you, Martha?" he asked softly, although he wanted to grab the woman and shake the information from her.

"I believe so, Your Lordship," she mumbled due to the

finger she failed to remove from her mouth. "But you should not go there. It would put you at risk."

Risk? From her lover? Was he the sort his servants knew to be dangerous? Of course he was dangerous, Gavin thought angrily. The man had been trying to kill him, and without regard to Christine's safety in the bargain!

"I must make certain Christine has arrived at her destination safely," he reminded the servant. "Please, Martha, tell me where she's gone."

She removed her finger from her mouth, but her bottom lip trembled. "You will not harm her?"

He wanted to shake the woman again. "I would never harm her."

"I saw the bruise along her jaw," she said, both lips now trembling.

Gavin ran a hand impatiently through his hair. "She received the injury during the ride. We were set upon by thieves," he said, although now he felt certain Christine's lover had followed her to London, had been in the process of following her back to Greenhaven, and had seen Gavin catch up to the coach. "I told you she had been jostled about."

"Oh, that you did," Martha said, her relief evident.

"Now," he said, fighting his impatience lest he frighten the woman. "Where has she gone?" When the woman still seemed hesitant to tell him, he added, "She could be hurt while we speak. Injured from a fall from the horse."

"The parish," the woman blurted out. "She's gone to the parish."

Of course. He wanted to smack himself on the forehead. That was where she had been raised. Where she'd surely met the man. They had probably been sweethearts since childhood. And Christine, innocent that she was, loved him blindly, unaware he was capable of murder.

Greedy to get his hands on not only her, but the inheritance.

"Groom, saddle me a horse," he instructed.

The lad ran to the stables. Martha, he noted, still stood there chewing on her bottom lip.

"Thank you, Martha. You may return to the house."

Her chewing ceased long enough for her to whisper, "Remember, Your Lordship. You promised you would not harm her."

"And I will keep my promise," he assured the woman. But her lover, Gavin thought, would not receive the same consideration. He felt the pistol resting against his side, still stuffed snugly in the top of his trousers. If the man thought he would take his title from him, or much worse, take his woman, Gavin would use the weapon to assure him otherwise.

When he reached the parish, Pegasus, his stallion, nickered a greeting to Gavin. He felt relieved to see the animal tied outside, confirming that Christine had made the trip safely. Then he took the well-deserved liberty of being furious with her. She had been a fool to risk her life by riding the horse, and a fool to run to her lover's arms the moment they reached Greenhaven. How could he be so wrong about her?

How could she seem to be one woman one moment, and another one entirely the next? It wasn't her fault, he told himself. Love could blind even the most innocent, he realized, further exonerating her. She simply did not know this man for what he was, and it was up to him to make certain she saw her lover's dark side. Gavin dismounted, tied his mount next to the stallion, and removed his pistol.

Without ceremony, he marched to the church doors and kicked them open. His pistol aimed, he was not prepared for the sight that greeted him. There were people lying about everywhere. Judging by the moans that greeted him, they were sick people. His gaze moved over them, some staring at him with eyes wide with shock, others too sick to even respond to his intrusion. A familiar face moved into his line of vision, a beautiful face whose tempting lips were parted in surprise.

"Gavin?" Christine said, then walked toward him. "What in God's name are you doing here?"

When her gaze settled upon the pistol in his hand, he lowered the weapon. "I might ask you the same thing."

Her hands went to her waist. "I would think it obvious, but since you burst in here waving a gun, you may be too addle-witted to draw the correct conclusion. I am helping these poor people."

"What's wrong with them?" he asked, his gaze scanning the room again.

"Cholera, I fear," she answered. "You shouldn't have come here."

Gavin's hot blood seemed to freeze inside his veins. "Neither should you have, my lady." He took her arm. "Come away this instant."

She tugged her arm from his hold. "I will not. I haven't traveled all this way to desert the vicar and these good people in their time of need. He could count on no one except me to help, and help them I will."

"Christine," Gavin ground out, angry and humbled by her in the same instant. "You place yourself at risk. I cannot allow you to stay."

"You cannot force me to leave," she countered. "You may drag me kicking and screaming back to Greenhaven, but I will return at the first opportunity given to me." Her gaze softened. "Understand, there are people in this parish I dearly love. People I consider my family, my friends—"

"Your lover?" Gavin interrupted. "Is he here?"

Her gaze widened for a moment, then just as quickly narrowed. "Is that what you thought? That I would steal your horse and risk my neck to meet with my lover? I suppose you also thought I pawned the jewelry you gave me in order to pamper him?"

"You pawned the jewelry?" he asked, surprised because he had no idea she had done so.

She nodded. "For a doctor and medicine. He's to arrive tomorrow morning."

Gavin felt like a fool. And he was damn mad at Christine for placing him in that position. "Why didn't you tell me?" he demanded. "Why didn't you ask for my help? Instead, you led me to believe the worst of you. To suspect the note you received was from your lover requesting a secret meeting."

A loud retching sound began somewhere in the back of the room, and Christine immediately started to turn away. Gavin stepped around her, blocking her escape. "You didn't answer me."

"I have no lover," she bit out. "I have never had a lover, and as for not asking for your help, what do you care about these people? You would have ignored their plight and forbidden me to come!"

Her accusations wounded him as deeply as her confession had momentarily elated him. Did she think so little of him? Did she believe him a monster who would have not lifted a hand to help these people had she but asked? Maybe that was exactly how he would have behaved at one time. Caught up in his snobbery, his desperate need to have society believe he was of noble blood, he had been the most un-noble of men.

"I am sorry you think so little of me," he said. "And sorrier still that I have given you cause. Regardless, I cannot allow you to risk becoming infected with the sickness."

"I am not leaving," she repeated.

"Neither am I," he countered.

She brushed past him. "Then roll up your sleeves and make yourself useful."

The thought of dragging Christine kicking and screaming from the parish surfaced, but then Gavin glanced around him again. He looked into the eyes of those staring at him with feeble hope. And then he saw the way that they looked at her. As if she were their salvation, their angel of mercy, the one true light in their dark world. And he realized that she was. In their world, and in his.

Chapter Twenty-three

By midnight, Christine felt as if she had nothing left to give, that her spirit as well as her strength had been drained. She'd done all she could to make the sick comfortable, but the doctor was sorely needed. And Gavin had been a godsend. He'd not shirked from any duty she'd given him, and his presence alone seemed to soothe these people.

It was as if a man of means among them, along with a man of God, could do battle on their behalf and they'd emerge victorious. And she prayed they would. Prayed with all her might. A gentle hand upon her shoulder had her glancing up from sponging the brow of an old man.

"I have not had time to thank you for coming, Christine," the weary vicar said. "But I knew I could depend upon you. You give these people hope."

"It is you who give them hope," she countered. "I only give them what little I can."

He knelt down beside her. "You give of yourself, which is the greatest gift. Through you, they see that anything is possible. A young orphan woman becomes a marchioness, and yet the change in her status does not alter her heart."

She glanced toward Gavin, who held a sleeping babe in his arms while he spoke softly to the child's mother. "My heart is torn," she confessed. "Split between what I feel is my true mission, and what I feel as a woman, plagued by human weakness."

His gaze followed hers. "None of us has been blessed with the assurance by God we follow the path He intends for us. We can only hope that what we perceive as our purpose is His purpose as well. We can merely trust that He has led us down the path for a reason, and hope our hearts can find the answers to the riddles He has given us."

"But there is no riddle," Christine insisted. "I have been chosen for a special purpose only revealed to me after I married Gavin Norfork." She took a deep breath and whispered, "I have been chosen to serve the poor."

A gray brow lifted. "You have always served them, child," he said gently. "And God is not often so clear in His instructions. It is a sin of pride to believe you have been martyred, Christine. Perhaps your mission is not to save many, but to merely save one." His gaze strayed again to her husband.

"But it cannot be," she persisted. "Where is the glory in that? When I have been given a chance to do so much more, why—"

"You will be given the answers in time," he interrupted, frowning his disapproval. "Place your faith in that, and not in your need to be more than who you are."

He left her confused. Both humbled by her conceit and indignant that he could not see her true mission, which had been clearly spelled out to her in the late marquis's will. She rose, stretching her aching back, her thoughts whirling.

Of course the kind vicar did not know all she knew. Surely if he did, he would see she had no choice but to continue in her quest for the annulment. What were her own selfish needs and wants when compared to the needs of so many others? And it was her own need that drew her to Gavin in that instant.

She walked to where he sat on the floor, the babe still nestled in his arms, the child asleep, and him as well. She had never really seen him sleeping. His features were relaxed and he looked almost innocent. Her stomach fluttered and her heart softened.

How sweet he looked with the babe in his arms, and how kind he'd been to stay and risk his own health. And brave. He had been courageous, with no fear for his safety, on the road earlier that day. Gavin was such a confusing man, to barge into the church waving his gun in search of her lover, then to worry for her well-being, and finally to resign himself to working right along beside her.

He was a mystery. A constant unraveling of traits, good and bad, that she had not known he possessed. A man quick to admit his own dark deeds, and quicker still to apologize for them. True, desire for him lurked beneath the surface of her carefully guarded humanity, but there was more she felt for him. Much more. A need to comfort him, protect him . . . love him.

She shook her head, as if by doing so she could cast the thought out, never to return. She could not have Gavin and help the poor. And she could not help the poor and have a life of her own. A life with a husband who held his own babes in his arms. She sighed, admitting in a moment of weakness that she wished there might be a way she could have both. The life she secretly longed for, and the destiny she felt had been given to her.

Gavin opened his eyes, as if he'd sensed her regard of him. He smiled, then closed them again, looking strangely content among the most common of souls. A nobleman who had come home, at long last.

Gavin rode to Greenhaven with an exhausted Christine before him in the saddle. She slept, her head nestled against his shoulder, her body snuggled close for warmth. The doctor, along with a few medical supplies, had arrived just before dawn, and never had Gavin spied a more welcome sight. Christine had nearly fainted with relief when the man had looked at several patients and dismissed cholera as the culprit.

More than likely, the man further concluded, spoiled food was responsible. The vicar admitted the parish had been given a dead cow, and the animal had been butchered and the meat divided among the families. He himself had not taken a share so that there would be more for the others. Gavin shivered slightly as the physician brought out his jars of leeches. Bleeding, he assured him, would draw the poison from their blood and help them to recover.

Gavin wasn't certain draining a person's blood was a healthy practice. Today, he would send a servant to London for another doctor, the man he'd called to the house for Christine the night she took her spill from the opera box. He was said to be the best, and certainly the pup who'd arrived this morning was still wet behind the ears.

These poor souls, after all, were the closest to family Christine could claim. It was his duty to see them professionally treated. And, he supposed, cringing at the thought of them converging upon an already dead animal for meat, properly fed as well.

Christine stirred in his arms, then settled back against him, sighing with what he thought a contented sound. He ran his fingers through her wild curls. She was an amazing woman. An inspiration to the parish folk, and the only person who had made him think seriously about his own selfishness over the years.

A night of being forced to stare into the hopeless eyes of a hopeful people had shown him the error of his ways. By chance, and not birthright, he could have lived a life similar to theirs. And by ignoring those less fortunate than himself all these years, he had ignored his own common blood. As if ignoring either could simply make the problem go away.

"Where are we going?" Christine mumbled against his shirt.

"To Greenhaven, my lady. And then to bed for you."

"But I must return," she argued, trying without much strength to struggle. "They need me."

He placed her head back against his shoulder, and within minutes, she was sound asleep again. He kissed the top of her head. "So do I," he admitted softly.

The stables were his first stop, where the young lad he'd met yesterday rushed forward to take his horse and the one he led. Gavin carried Christine to the house, impressed when Martha was quick to open the door, as if she'd been watching for their return.

"Oh, Lord," she fretted. "Has she taken ill?"

"Quiet," Gavin warned. "Your mistress is exhausted and needs her bed."

"Where is that lazy maid of hers?" Martha whispered.

"Back in London, probably trying to seduce my manservant."

Martha's eyebrows shot up. "Found her a fellow, has Tillie?"

Gavin said nothing further, imagining he'd given the household good gossip for the evening. "Sarah Watts. Send her upstairs to tend my lady."

"But she's no lady's maid," Martha blustered. "She's the newest employee, therefore the lowest on the ladder."

He gave the servant a glance to remind her who decided

matters concerning the status of employees, or more precisely, who paid their wages.

"Right away, Your Lordship," Martha quickly agreed. "Her Ladyship's room is the third one upstairs on the right. Across from the master bedchamber, which we've made up for you, Your Lordship."

Although he preferred a different room than where the late marquis had slept, he said nothing. He carried Christine upstairs, frowning upon entering her sparsely decorated room. Good Lord, he paid her a handsome allowance. He'd expected she'd redecorate at least the bedchamber she chose. He recalled her clothing when she'd first come to London.

Not much better than a servant's dress. As soon as she rested, he would ask her what she did with her allowance. And with a sudden warm rush in the vicinity of his heart, he would demand an explanation for lying to him that she had a lover, when, in fact, she did not. He settled her upon the bed, then straightened, a sudden thought dawning upon him.

If Christine had no greedy lover out to steal her love and his inheritance away from him, then who the bloody hell had been throwing rocks at his horse, loosening his box banister, and shooting at him on the road?

"Your Lordship?"

He turned to see Sarah Watts hovering just outside the door. "Come in, Sarah, and tend to my lady. She has exhausted herself."

The woman shyly entered. "I am glad to have this chance to thank you again for what you've done for me and my babes."

"Do you like it here, Sarah?"

Her face, the bruises now almost gone, shone brightly with a healthy glow. "The other servants, well, they've not accepted us totally as of yet, but they're good people. And my children, why, they already have roses in their cheeks and plump little bellies. They love it here. Although . . ."

"Yes?" he prompted.

"It's a bit dark and dreary, this place," she whispered. "Ye should spruce it up a bit."

He almost smiled. "I will consider the matter."

Her eyes suddenly widened. A hand flew to her mouth. "Oh, beg your pardon. It was not for me to be telling the likes of you what he should or should not do."

"It seems to have become a habit among my staff," he said with a sigh. "Take gentle care with my lady. And if she wakes and thinks to get up and return to the parish, come and fetch me immediately."

"Yes, Yer Lordship," Sarah replied.

Gavin had almost made it from the room when she stopped him. "Oh, sir, I nearly failed to tell you what Martha forgot to tell you downstairs, so worried was she about the lady."

"What?"

"There is a gentleman waiting for you. Your cousin, I believe he is. Arrived late last night, but of course you and the lady were not at home."

"William?"

"Yes, I believe that is his name."

What on earth was William doing at Greenhaven? Perhaps a problem with business. "Where is he?"

"The study, I believe, Yer Lordship."

After casting a lingering glance toward Christine, who still slept like the dead, he quit the room and went downstairs. William sat in the study, a dusty book in one hand and a cup of tea in the other.

"William? Why have you come? Is there a problem with a client?"

"Good to see you, too," William drawled, snapping the book closed. "I have come, dear cousin, in fear you might do something foolish like murder your wife's lover. I believe you are smitten enough with her to commit such a crime."

"You may be right," Gavin admitted, then smiled broadly. "But it seems that Christine has no lover, has never had one. She told me so yesterday."

William nearly upset his teacup in the process of placing it on a saucer. "And you believe her?"

His smile faded. "Why shouldn't I?"

Shrugging, William answered, "Why did she tell you she had a lover if she does not?"

Gavin walked further into the room. "That, I do not know, but I intend to ask her once she regains her strength."

"Is she ill?"

"Only tired from tending the sick at the parish. Christine and I were up nearly the whole night helping the vicar."

"You touched those filthy beggars?" William exclaimed, rising from his chair. "No telling what diseases they carry."

Gavin strolled to a table where the tea service sat. "I didn't know you were such a snob."

"No more one than you are," he countered, joining him. "Well, if she is telling the truth, you may discount her lover in any attempts upon your life, if indeed you are not mistaken in the matter."

After pouring himself a cup of tea, Gavin took a sip. "We were set upon on our journey to Greenhaven," he confessed. "The coachman lost control of the horses and I nearly took a bullet in the head. I don't believe I am mistaken."

"Good Lord," William breathed. "You and Christine might have both been killed. But you could have simply been the target of a robbery," he pointed out. "And the banister, as I said, could have been loosened by a less-than-skilled thug. Your box could have have been mistaken for another's."

"It would put my mind at ease to believe so," Gavin admitted. He slapped his cousin upon the shoulder. "And it would also put me more at ease if you will stay with us until Christine and I return to London. You may ride in the coach with us in case we are set upon again, and help me to fend off the brigand."

William smiled sarcastically. "Oh, goodie," he quipped, causing Gavin to laugh.

"I must beg your pardon for being a bad host, but I need rest, and I must send for a more qualified physician for the poor people at the parish." Gavin moved toward the door. "The one Christine secured is inexperienced, I believe."

"Gavin?"

He turned to find his cousin staring at him in the oddest fashion. "What care you about these people at the parish? They do not fall under your jurisdiction. You have no duty to them."

William's attitude had begun to wear on his nerves. Was he like him? Yes, Gavin admitted, he supposed at one time he had been very much like him.

"Those poor people are Christine's friends. She looks upon them as family, and if that were not cause enough, they need my help."

"Half the starving bloody country needs your help," William fussed. "Would you send us to the poorhouse ourselves in order to care for them?"

"Don't worry, cousin," he said softly. "I will not dip into your salary."

William appeared properly chastised. "Of course, what you do with your money is not my business."

"Exactly," Gavin said, then turned and left the study. As he searched for a servant to fetch the other doctor, he decided William would do well to spend more time with

Christine. He never realized his cousin thought so highly of himself, or so lowly of those below his station. William could use a lesson in humanity.

Christine wiggled her toes beneath the covers. She arched her back, stretching like a lazy cat, then opened her eyes. At first she felt confused about her surroundings. Where were the pretty wallpaper and the expensive furniture? Then she remembered. This wasn't the London town home, but Greenhaven. Although how she'd come to be in her bed, she couldn't recall.

The fact that she shouldn't be there at all, but at the parish helping the vicar, had her scrambling up. She started to throw the covers back, realized she wasn't alone, and instead jerked them up to her neck.

"What are you doing here?"

Her husband smiled. "Watching you sleep."

He sat on the edge of her bed, appearing to her as if he should have been sleeping himself rather than wasting his time watching her.

"I would think you could find a more productive way to occupy your morning," she said, smoothing her unruly curls.

"To be certain, my lady," he agreed. "Slipping beneath the covers with you proved the greatest temptation."

She felt a hot blush settle in her cheeks, noticed that it spread over her whole body, for that matter. "Thank you for refraining," she muttered. "Now, be off. I need to dress and return to the parish."

"No."

"No?" she echoed. "Are you forbidding me to dress, or forbidding me to return to the parish?"

"Both," he answered. "First, we will talk."

She'd dreaded this confrontation. Of course, as soon as she'd confessed the truth about her lover, or rather her lack of one, she'd known he would not simply let it go without a discussion.

"You have me at a disadvantage." She nodded to the bed, indicating her lack of decency. "Allow me to make myself presentable."

Gavin's gaze flitted over her. "I find you very presentable." He reached out and tucked a wild curl behind her ear. "And if you wish to dress, I will play your maid."

"You don't resemble a maid," she bit out. "And I'm certain your skills are better suited for undressing a woman."

He sighed. "For a woman who has lied to me from our first meeting, you are irritably judgmental, Christine. I have made no secret of my past indiscretions, nor has anyone else. But I won't have you throwing them up in my face given every opportunity. I have neither undressed, nor dressed, another woman since you came to London."

So Wentworth, worm that he was, had been correct concerning Gavin's lack of infidelity. Christine tamped down the tide of pleasure rising within her.

"Do you want a pat on the head?" she asked coldly. "Or perhaps you expect more?"

"I expect nothing," he answered, his expression open. "Except the truth. Why did you lie to me?"

Chapter Twenty-four

It was time to tell him. "Because the truth would not have swayed you to my cause," Christine answered. "You would have laughed at the truth, then promptly dismissed it as being unimportant."

"And the truth is?" he prompted.

She took a deep breath. "The truth is, I want the annulment for the poor. So that Greenhaven and its profits can be auctioned off to help feed and care for as many of them as possible."

His face didn't register the surprise she anticipated. But he said, "I find that hard to believe."

"It is the truth," she insisted.

The warmth that flooded his eyes took her by surprise. "What do you do with your allowance, Christine?"

She bowed her head. "I give it to the people of the parish."

He reached forward and lifted her chin. "I didn't mean I find it hard to believe you want the inheritance for the poor. I meant, I have trouble believing there could be

286

anyone as good as you are. A person so selfless, compassionate, and unconcerned with her own plight in life. You are truly that rarest of gems, Christine."

Oh, no. He mustn't look at her that way. As if he were doing just what he promised he would if he ever found such a woman. As if he were giving her his heart then and there, never mind that she could not accept his offer. Never mind that she found herself desperately wanting to do just that. He leaned toward her, and she knew he meant to kiss her. And that she wanted him to.

It was a kiss unlike any he'd given, or taken, from her before. A tender brush of lips, sweet, as she imagined a kiss would be between two innocents. A kiss that spoke of uncertainty, either about his own feelings, or about how she would respond. She let his mouth rest against hers, touching, but just barely, and his gentleness, his shyness, stirred her more deeply than passion ever could.

She pressed her mouth more firmly to his, grazing his bottom lip with her teeth, then softly sucking it into her mouth. She tasted him, taunted him, and reveled in her own sensuality. For the first time she felt what it was like to be the seductress, instead of the seduced.

He bent easily to her will, returning her kiss, delving into her mouth to explore her, but with an aching tenderness that ignited her desire more quickly than if he'd stormed her senses. He didn't touch her, did not pull her into his arms or try to take more than she wanted to give, and by not doing so, he made her want to give more than she should dare surrender.

Her hands twisted in his hair, pulling him close to feel the heat from his body. To let it warm her—chase the morning chill from her skin. He did touch her then, his hands moving to her shoulders, not to pull her closer, but to gently push her away.

"You fire my blood, Christine," he said, his voice low and husky. "And we both know I am no saint. I want to love you completely, but I also need you to commit to me in the same way."

The hot passion unfolding inside her suddenly cooled. And so quickly it made her shiver. "I cannot," she whispered. "I am torn. Confused by my own weaknesses and my duty."

Gavin rose, torn also by taking what she might give, and demanding what he truly desired. He'd known little of love before he met her. Before she came into his life intrusively, and made herself the one woman he could not resist. The one woman who could teach him about love, and yes, about sacrifice. Now he understood the two went hand in hand.

His mother had sacrificed her life for love. He had thought her weak and selfish for doing so. But now he understood the emotion's power, and its pain. Christine's reasons for lying to him, for shaming him, were just and good. She would martyr herself for a worthy cause, and for God, but she could not commit herself totally to him. And because of his own past, his own lies, he could not truthfully ask her to give so a noble a heart.

"I want to be more than only a weakness to you, Christine," he said. "And I will leave you now to run to those who are worthy of your affections."

She scrambled from the bed, unmindful that she wore her underclothes. "You mustn't think yourself unworthy," she said. "I sense in you a goodness you have long denied. Perhaps a denial that was not your fault, but only a result of your station."

"No," he said, staring down into her lovely eyes. "It was a purposeful denial. One that only served me. Don't confuse yourself upon that issue."

"But you can change," she insisted. "You have changed already."

"Yes," he admitted. "But have I changed for the sake of goodness, or for the sake of pleasing you? And do I want to please you for my heart's sake? Or for the sake of my title and my lands?" A title and lands, he mentally added, that did not rightfully belong to him.

Her gaze lowered. "That is something only you can answer. Can you give up your father's inheritance for the poor, Gavin? Can you give up your title and your lands? For them?"

She deserved an honest answer, and the first response that sprang to his lips was: "No, I cannot." He walked to the door and opened it, pausing with his back to her. He thought suddenly about those of the parish, the poor who roamed the streets of London. The children who slept in filthy flats with empty bellies. She was their champion, and if he could not love them as selflessly as she did, he could love her unselfishly. "But I can give it up for you, Christine," he said. "You will have your annulment."

The sound of the door closing held a hollow tone. Christine stood there, shivering in her underclothes, hardly believing his parting words. She had beaten him. Had bent him to her will. Had battled for her cause and emerged victorious. Then why did her heart not sing with joy? Why did it feel so heavy inside her chest?

Tears sprang to her eyes, not of happiness, but of sorrow. Sorrow for what she felt she had lost, rather than elation over what she knew she had won. She wanted to run after him, but for what purpose? Certainly not to ask him to reconsider. To cling to his precious inheritance so that the battle between them would rage on. So that she would remain his wife, like it or not.

Perhaps being his wife was not unpleasant to her at all. It might be that she enjoyed her fancy clothes, his luxurious town home, and the thought of never being hungry or poor again. With no title, only a first name, had she secretly desired the one that came with his?

And what of her worthiness? Was her quest one of heartfelt concern for those less fortunate, or one that the vicar had warned her about last night? The sin of pride. The need to be more than who she was. Had her mission been a chance to serve God, or an opportunity to serve her own selfish needs? Having everyone believe her a saint, instead of only a simple orphan girl, might have influenced her decisions.

The questions whirled inside Christine's head. At her journey's beginning, she had felt strong in her convictions, sure of herself and of her intentions. But now, nothing seemed clear to her. Not even her feelings for Gavin. She loved him, but felt guilty for doing so. As if she'd let not only the poor down, but herself as well.

Rubbing her temples, she knew she needed sanctuary. A place to sort through her emotions. She would seek solace where she'd always gone to think, and to pray. The parish church, where heart and duty called her to return.

Gavin had watched Christine leave for the parish some time ago. He'd sent her in the coach with two armed coachmen, one riding up front, the other on the back, and he'd told the men to say they were along to assist in whatever way they could. All that had happened to him and Christine might have been coincidence, but he would take no chances with her life.

To keep his cousin from becoming bored, he suggested they ride around the estate and look over the fields, which William gladly accepted. Gavin felt a smidgen of pride, riding these lands, but soon they would no longer be his. It was news he was not yet ready to relay to his cousin.

He glanced at William, noting the man's odd expression. His cousin's gaze roamed the fertile fields and lush countryside with . . . what exactly?

"Do you envy me all of this, cousin?" Gavin asked.

William's head turned in his direction, a somewhat startled expression on his face. "Don't be ridiculous."

Gavin lifted a brow. "I would not be ridiculous. Most

men would covet this land, the estate, a title to go along with it."

"I am not most men," William countered. "I am happy for your good fortune, cousin."

"And you don't resent that I have allowed you to run the estate these past two years since the marquis's death, and although I have paid you a fair allowance, I have kept the profits of your labors?"

His cousin shifted in the saddle. "What are you getting at, Gavin?"

He shrugged. "I'm just curious. Are you satisfied with your life?"

William snorted softly. "Is anyone? Are you?"

He'd thought he was at one time. Now, he knew for certain he was not. The lies had begun to wear on him; his battle to ignore them had made him unfeeling and unkind. He had shunned love as a weakness for fools, for poets, for the poor because they had nothing else. He hadn't realized that it was the greatest gift, and one within the reach of all mankind. Pauper or king.

"No," he finally answered. "In the past I have been greedy and selfish. Bitter over circumstances I could not change. In the future, I wish to change that about myself."

William's mouth dropped open. He quickly closed it, his face turning red. "What nonsense are you spouting?" he demanded. "Good Lord, you seem less and less like yourself every day. It's that woman. Christine. She has turned you into a . . . a . . ."

"Human being?" he supplied.

"A softhearted fool," William shot back. "Everyone, your sweet Christine included, is greedy for something, dear cousin. Make no mistake about that."

"And what do you covet, William?"

Again, his cousin seemed startled by the question. "Being your relation is gift enough," he then blurted. "The cousin of a titled nobleman. It adds color to my drab little world."

"And so would inheriting everything were something to happen to me," Gavin added thoughtfully.

William's face turned a darker shade of red. "Good Lord, Gavin, are you accusing me of something?"

Gavin sighed, then rubbed his forehead. "Of course not, William." He didn't know why he'd even asked the question. "You are my only relation since your mother's passing. The only one of true blood. It's a bond I take most seriously. Forgive me for putting you ill at ease."

His companion visibly relaxed, then gazed over at Gavin. "Has Christine said something to you about me to raise questions? Suspicions?"

"No," Gavin quickly assured him. "From what I gather, Christine is fond of you. I thought at one time you admired her, as well."

"Oh, I did," William said. "I do. That is, I could still, if I weren't worried you might do something foolish on her behalf."

Such as give her the annulment she wanted, along with Greenhaven and its lands, Gavin thought. "She has no lover for me to murder," he reminded his cousin.

"Perhaps not," William agreed. "But she has her fingers upon your heartstrings. And I fear soon she will have them upon your purse strings as well."

"Your worry over me, and my fortune, has been noted," Gavin said dryly. "And I appreciate your concern, but whatever mistakes I make with Christine affect only me."

"How can you say that?" William demanded. "You are my only means of support. Do you think I could work for anyone else who would pay me as handsome a salary as you do?"

Gavin lifted a brow. "I do well enough without the income from the estate. And as for the salary I pay you to run Greenhaven, I could supplement you for it by making you a partner, which I should have done by now," he admitted.

"A partner?" William snorted disdainfully. "In a shipping firm? Do you believe that is all I aspire to be?"

His reaction startled Gavin. "What exactly are your aspirations, cousin?"

William seemed to get control of his emotions. He took a deep breath and let it out slowly. "Be rational for a moment, Gavin. Has it not once occurred to you that I am younger than you, and not nearly so inclined to die by either the sword or the pistol of a jealous man? That you may never produce an heir, and that I, being your only living relative, stand to inherit for myself, and my own family someday, were something to happen to you?"

Of course he understood William's position to inherit. "It is only land, William," he said. "Only a title. You can make your fortune with me, and never have to worry over such matters."

His cousin's face reddened again. "The title is everything," he ground out. "It is what kept you from being tossed out of polite society years ago. It is what keeps you securely snuggled inside the fold now. It is what keeps you from being labeled as merely rich riffraff. Being wealthy by more than your own hard work. The title is the prize. It is your future security among a society that would never let you in otherwise."

"Or you," Gavin said, understanding.

"Or me," William admitted. "Your mother made my family name a curse. I have had to live in the shadow of her shameful behavior, live off the scraps you would throw me, and forever be the pitied poorer relation."

Gavin had never thought to see William in that light. Had never thought that his mother's actions had destroyed his life as well. His heart went out to him.

"I am sorry, cousin," he said. "But a title cannot make you any different than who you are. Not on the inside. I know, I have told myself the opposite for some time now. Better to turn your aspirations elsewhere. I have agreed to give Christine the annulment. Greenhaven and its lands will be auctioned off for various causes. The title is lost."

William's gaze widened. He paled. "Are you insane?"

Gavin came close to telling him the truth. To confessing that the title and the estate were never really his to begin with, and that they would not really belong to William were he to inherit. Gavin's mother, William's aunt, had not brought anything but her beauty into the marriage. Her father had been an impoverished earl. A man who'd fallen on hard times and auctioned her off like so much property to a titled man smitten with her beauty.

"No, not insane," Gavin said. "Relieved to be rid of it if you must know the truth."

"I beg of you to reconsider," William pleaded. "Your feelings for Christine have clouded your good judgment. You don't really believe she wants to see the inheritance given to the poor, do you? I say she has some scheme—"

"I do believe it," he interrupted, casting William a warning glance. "I believe it because it is true. You were right about her in the beginning. She wants the annulment because love is enough for her. Her love and compassion for the poor souls who are not as fortunate as you and I."

William opened his mouth, Gavin suspected to argue, but he cut him off. "The parish is not far. I intended to check on Christine, make sure all is going well there. Will you join me?"

"Heavens, no," William answered.

Gavin smiled, although not much. "They have ruled out cholera. I don't believe food poisoning is contagious."

"Mark my words, if they don't carry cholera, they carry something else as foul." William reined his horse toward Greenhaven. "No, cousin, I'll go back to the estate and think of a way to make you reconsider this ridiculous decision you have made for the sake of love."

"I wouldn't waste time with it," Gavin called. "I gave Christine my word. I won't take it back. And it is for my own sake as well as hers that I have made the decision."

Words floated back to him. Muttered phrases as William rode off. Surely William would come to accept his decision, and in time realize that a fortune made by one's own hands held more merit, title or no title.

Besides, there wasn't anything William could do about the matter. He had no choice but to accept the loss of Greenhaven, and the title that went with the estate.

Gavin reined his stallion toward the parish. Seeing Christine, having his senses knocked about and feeling as if his heart were hanging upon his sleeve, held little appeal to him. The sooner they parted company forever, the better. For he couldn't trust himself not to do something foolish with her. He couldn't trust himself not to beg her to stay.

Nor was he certain he wasn't above seducing her, getting her with child in order to make her stay. But he couldn't ask her to stay, to be his wife in truth and the woman he would love and honor until all time. Not without telling her the truth about himself.

Of course there was one positive aspect to telling her the truth.

Christine could hardly reject him for having common blood. At least he didn't think she could. She was of common blood herself. He hoped she would not reject him, because despite his resolve, he felt certain he would give into his feelings for her and do exactly all he feared he would do. He only prayed he would not do so in vain.

Chapter Twenty-five

Having bathed and changed into her nightclothes, Christine sat by the fire brushing her long hair. She'd argued about being sent home from the parish, but the good doctors, the kind vicar, and her overprotective husband had all insisted she get a good night's rest. She admitted the situation there seemed well under control, and with a lighter heart felt certain everyone would soon recover. But Greenhaven held too many temptations for her—the one across the hall being the greatest.

She still had an absurd desire to argue with Gavin over his decision. To ask him if he realized all he would forfeit to her. His family home. His title. She didn't know that much about polite society, but she knew they set store by such things. Without them, would he be turned out of their circles?

Could he find himself a decent wife? His own wealth would buy him a decent wife, she consoled herself. Not a consoling thought at all, she decided a moment later.

Would some greedy woman chase him for his money alone?

There was the fact that he was sinfully handsome, she admitted. She supposed women would be willing to marry him for his surface attributes alone. And he was quite charming, she added. And certainly he was not stingy with his wealth. Given time, and the right woman to guide him, to remind him when his snobbery made him unbearable, to nurture his budding compassion, well, he'd be perfect.

"What woman in her right mind wouldn't want him?" she asked aloud. "But will any love him? Will any love him the way I do?"

There, she had said it. And said it aloud. She could not take the words back any more than she could deny the truth . . . the truth of her heart. She supposed she had loved him from the moment she'd first seen him. Loved him before she knew his name, or that he was her husband.

She'd loved him even when she thought the worst of him, and now loved him more because she had seen his goodness. Perhaps she had known from the beginning that he desperately needed someone to love him. That the vicar's words that morning on the hill held meaning for her. That kindness could overcome bitterness, and love could thaw the coldest heart.

But did she belong with Gavin? Could she ever fit into his life, or become accepted by his peers? Christine didn't • know. She was confused. Torn between what she thought to be her mission in life, and how she felt about her husband. Without his title, she felt certain Gavin would be shunned with her as his wife. To make matters worse, there was the gossip about her they had left behind in London—gossip of her own making.

She wouldn't have Gavin resenting her someday because he should have married a woman more suitable.

Perhaps a woman with a fortune and a title of her own. A woman such as Adrianna Shipley.

"I'll kill him first," she vowed, suddenly furious at a prospect she had herself suggested to the duchess. She wouldn't see Gavin married to a harlot such as that woman. Christine rose from her position before the fire, walked to her bureau, and replaced her brush.

"She can never love him," she told her reflection. "Not with her selfish heart. He deserves more. He deserves to be loved by a woman who can love him unconditionally. Love him with all her heart has to give."

Her gaze strayed to the door. She stared at the wood as if she could see through it and into his bedchamber. She'd fought a battle for many, but it had not made her a saint, or even a martyr. She was still just a woman, with a woman's weakness and a woman's heart.

Tonight, she would give in to her weaknesses. She would love Gavin with all her heart. And tomorrow . . . well, she would see what tomorrow brought, and if she felt any less confused about her place in the world.

If she and Gavin parted ways, if she never loved again, Christine would have this one night with him. One night when she took selfishly, without regard to consequences, or future worries of hunger and poverty. She had spent her life in service of the poor. Now, she would do this one thing for herself.

Her calmness over her decision surprised her. She knew what she intended to do. What she intended to give. And yet the knowledge did not shock her into changing her mind. Instead, she felt anxious to go to him. Hungry for his lips, and the feel of his arms around her. Excited by the thought of his warm, smooth skin pressed against hers.

With purpose, she moved toward the door. Christine placed her hand on the knob. Not yet, she told herself. It was still early. Gavin was probably not yet abed. She would wait until the darkest time of night, when sleep held him firmly and she could slip into his arms and seduce him. She moved to the bed and sat, folding her hands in her lap. And she waited.

Gavin tossed restlessly in his bed. He was neither fully asleep nor totally awake. He would dream, only to realize he was dreaming and rouse himself, only to dream again. Thoughts of Christine plagued his waking moments. He should have gone to her earlier and admitted his love for her. He should have asked her to remain his wife. He hadn't because he was a coward. He'd been afraid to confront her. Afraid of what she would say, or worse, what she wouldn't say. He couldn't remember a single thing he'd gone after in his life that he hadn't gotten. Nor could he remember wanting any of those things as much as he wanted Christine. And he didn't feel as if he deserved her.

His feelings had nothing to do with blood or position. Christine was pure, and kind. Truly a rare jewel. What right did he have to want her love? He, the worst of sinners, the darkest of souls? He was not worthy enough to touch the hem of her gown, much less anything beneath it. And how did a mere mortal go about loving an angel? With his heart mostly, he decided. And gently with the rest of himself, he thought. Very gently.

A moment later he was dreaming again. A dark figure on a horse chased him. He ran, his body moving with sluggish strides, his feet sinking into mud as he struggled to escape. The man appeared beside his bed, no, not a man. A woman. An angel silhouetted by the glow from the fire behind her. He blinked, and wondered if he could do so if he were truly asleep. He blinked again because the angel appeared to be naked.

"Christine?"

She sat beside him on the bed, placing a finger to his mouth. A moment later she removed her hand, only to lean forward and press her lips against his. Her long, silky hair spread around him, brushed his shoulders and chest. If he were dreaming, he hoped he didn't wake. Not yet.

He opened his mouth, allowed her inside to taste him, tasted her as well. While their lips were joined, she slid beneath the covers, and the womanly feel of her soft, ripe curves dispelled the notion he might be dreaming.

Gavin jerked away as if he'd been singed by the heat of her flesh. "What are you doing, Christine?"

Her lips returned to his, nibbling, teasing. "Isn't it obvious?" she whispered. "I am seducing you."

If he wasn't dreaming, he'd surely died and gone to heaven. Never in his wildest imagination had he thought she would come to him this way, or any way for that matter. But here she was, in his bed. And here he was, ironically willing to question her presence there.

"Do you know what happens when a woman slips naked into a man's bed?"

She kissed his neck. "He will ask her foolish questions, so it would seem."

Her hand slid over his chest, across one nipple causing it to harden . . . along with the rest of him. Gavin snatched her wrist. "Do you have any idea what you are doing?"

His wife pulled back to look at him. "I'm afraid I do not, but hoped you would instruct me," she said, then ran her teasing tongue across his lips.

He gasped, deciding to shock her into sanity. Taking her hand, he slid her fingers down his body and settled them over his hardened manhood. In the firelight, her eyes widened. She swallowed loudly. He expected her to wrest her hand away and scramble from the bed. What she said next was not at all what he'd imagined.

"Do you mean to make love to me with that, or merely impress me?"

He supposed his mouth dropped open; her tongue was inside it the next moment. Her fingers wrapped around his sex, and he nearly jumped out of his skin. He removed her hand and brought it to his pounding heart, then broke from her lips to whisper, "I don't think you know what you're doing at all, Christine."

She frowned. He suddenly found his wrists captured by her hands. She brought them up over his head, then she slid on top of him, her full breasts pressed firmly against his chest, her long legs resting against his.

"I rather think I do," she countered.

Gavin bit back a groan. She was killing him. He'd thought her an angel of mercy. But she had no mercy.

"If you don't stop, I am going to make love to you," he warned her.

She lifted a brow. "Are you? Or are you just going to talk about it?"

He set his jaw and reversed their positions, encircling her wrists above her head. The feel of her beneath him stole his ability to resist. For whatever reasons, she had crept into his bed, and though they might have seemed important a moment ago, they no longer mattered. He kissed her, explored her mouth, and he tried to be tender, but the kisses she returned were neither shy nor gentle.

Trailing a path of kisses down her neck, he cupped her breasts, his thumbs brushing her nipples erect before he bent to taste her. He traced the small rose-colored circles surrounding her hardened buds, then took a nipple inside his mouth to suck gently. She arched beneath him, gasped, and entwined her fingers in his hair.

Although her soft moans slammed into him like a battering ram, weakening his control, he continued to worship her. And it was not with the mere intention of exciting her that he did so, but because her perfection awed him, gave him such intense pleasure he couldn't help but touch her, marvel over how anything so perfect had been created by two mortals.

And he felt humbled as well. Mindful for the first time

of what a special gift it was for a woman to give herself to a man. And fully understanding that this woman, and only this one, already had more of him than his desire, the pleasure she gave him, or the pleasure he could give to her. She had his heart. And suddenly he knew that she loved him as well. If she didn't, she would not be in his arms.

It was an unfamiliar feeling to him. To have his heart ache with love, even as his body ached with need. To have so many emotions running rampant through him at one time. But then the strongest emotion, his need for her took over, compelled him to simply feel, to seek, to pleasure her and find pleasure with her.

Sliding his hand over the flat indention of her stomach, he touched the soft curls that crowned her womanhood. She tensed when his fingers found her, warm and moist, but he kissed her to soothe her inhibitions, kissed her until she opened to him.

He stroked the place where her sensation centered, gently at first. Slowly, steadily while he kissed her. The heat built between them, hotter, higher until he felt her moving against his fingers. She gasped, her nails biting into his shoulders. Her body tensed beneath him, and he knew she was reaching, striving to obtain what in her innocence she could not grasp. Not yet did she understand. But soon.

What was this torture? Christine's body felt on fire, her insides clenched. Her thighs trembled, and it seemed as if her heart pounded not in her chest, but between her legs. It was agony, and yet ecstasy, and if it did not stop soon, resolve itself in some manner, she thought she might die. She didn't understand what she sought, what she hoped to gain by moving against him, harder, faster, but neither could she control her actions.

His skillful fingers increased the pressure against her throbbing flesh. She heard his breath, ragged in her ears, or was that hers? She heard him moan, a deep tortured sound, or maybe it had risen from her own throat, risen with the tide that crested, rose higher and higher, then broke over her.

Her insides clenched, convulsed and forced the most intense pleasure she had ever experienced to claw a path up her body, to crash like a violent wave against her. She held on to him for fear of drowning, fear of being swept away to a place of no return, calling out his name as if that alone could anchor her in his world.

Then the storm calmed, cast her from its fury into the solid strength of his arms, his kisses on her face. She returned to him on slow ripples of sensation and floated in a limpid pool of warm contentment. With a sigh, she opened her eyes to look at him. If his expression was tender, in his eyes, the storm still raged.

He bent and kissed her tenderly before moving on top of her. His arms trembled in his efforts to keep his body from crushing hers beneath him, then he settled between her legs. She felt him. The sheer size of him shocked her very much back into his world.

She tried to control her fear. She had known full well this was where her journey would end when she'd crept across the hall to his room. In spite of her assurances, she squeezed her eyes shut and tensed.

"Christine," he whispered huskily. "Look at me."

Looking at him was no hard task, she admitted, and opened her eyes again. He was beautiful. The firelight danced upon his tawny skin, and his dark eyes were alive with passion, desire, and something more. An emotion so raw there was no way she could not identify it. Love.

She lifted her arms and placed them around his neck, drawing his lips to hers. He kissed her, not as gently as before, but his passion fired her own, and for him, this one man, this one night, she could suffer whatever she must. Or so she thought.

The pain came so swiftly it tore a gasp of surprise from her lips. Instinct made her struggle, try to push him away, but he would not go. Instead, he pinned her with his body, not at all making efforts to retreat, but pushing on, claiming her while she could only lie beneath him and gasp over her discomfort. He filled her completely, filled her to the point she felt certain she could take no more of him. Then he stopped. He bent his forehead to hers.

"Am I hurting you, Christine?"

So kind of him to ask. After the fact. "Yes, you hurt me."

"I know." He pulled back to look at her, his gaze warm and caring. "And I'm sorry. But am I hurting you now?"

She took a moment to decide. There wasn't pain anymore. Only a strange unfamiliarity that his body now possessed hers. "No," she answered.

A sigh of relief left him and he pressed his forehead to hers again. She couldn't see what he had to be relieved about. He wasn't the one who'd felt the sharp stabbing pain. Or perhaps he had, for all she knew of lovemaking.

"Did I hurt *you?*" she asked.

"No," he answered, his lips lowering to hers.

"Am I hurting you now?"

His mouth paused inches away. "Yes. Your questions are straining my control."

Christine had no idea what he meant, but then, maybe she did. "You mean you'd like to get on with it?"

He thrust suddenly inside of her, causing her to gasp. "Yes," he answered, sounding for all the world as if he were in agony.

Since she no longer felt pain herself, she said, "All right then. Go ahead."

Gavin pulled back to look at her. "And what do you plan to do, my lady, while I'm getting on with it?"

She wasn't at all certain what she should do. "Lie here quietly?" she ventured.

He smiled, the slow sensuous expression that made her pulse leap. His lips brushed hers, then he said, "I think not, wife."

Chapter Twenty-six

Her gasp of pain when he'd taken her virginity had cut into Gavin. He would have gladly suffered in her stead, but since that wasn't possible, he could only make amends by loving her gently. He kissed her sweet mouth with tenderness, allowing her time to realize he wouldn't hurt her again.

As much as it strained his control not to move inside of her, he held back, waiting for her. Gradually, she returned his kisses. Her tongue probed into his mouth and her body, innocent no longer, acted on instinct alone when she pressed her hips against him. He bit back a groan. Again, her tongue slipped into his mouth and her hips arched, and control became another discarded thing of the past.

He let go—gave himself completely to her, and if when he began moving inside her, he sensed a hesitation on her part to finish what she had started, the pause was a short one. He thought he'd known passion before, but whatever he had known paled beside what exploded between them.

The heat consumed him. Her heat. The tight feel of her wrapped around him, the heady nectar of her lips, her fiery passion and her bravery at giving herself completely to him, all combined to make loving her the sweetest torture. He could have easily spent himself then, but Gavin struggled for the control he'd already lost. He fought for her, for her pleasure, knowing his own would not be as great without hers to make it complete. And for that purpose alone, he settled the beast within him.

He cupped her breasts, teasing her nipples before he slid his fingers between them, touching her again where he knew her pleasure awaited him. He stroked her gently, continuing to move within her. Slowly, steadily, until she matched his rhythm. Higher and higher the flame grew between them, making their bodies slick against one another.

The fire leapt to life in her eyes. The sounds of her soft moans and gasps teased him, but still he fought for control, waited for her. Her back arched. She tightened around him. Then her body found release, forcing his own surrender. The explosion rocked him, propelled him to the deepest core of her to thrust again and again, gasping her name.

His life seed poured into her, unraveling whatever bonds remained that held his heart from hers. He died a slow death and died it gladly in her arms. Would die it again and again until the end of eternity, if she would but allow him. He trembled from keeping his weight from crushing her beneath him. Gavin rolled to the side and pulled her into his embrace. He thought his heart might pound out of his chest, but gradually, it slowed and he could breathe again.

He smoothed Christine's unruly curls from her forehead as the fading tremors of his climax rippled over him. A moment later, she lifted a hand and ran her fingers down the side of his face. His sweet angel, innocent wife, and as close to a saint as he would ever know, asked very clearly, "May we repeat that again, Your Lordship?"

Gavin struggled up on one elbow. "This minute?"

She smiled. "After a short rest."

Bending down to nuzzle her ear, he answered. "I am your most humble servant, my lady."

Words came to him. Things he wanted to say to her. Confessions, declarations. But the soft steady feel of her breath against his neck told him she had already drifted away from him. He closed his eyes and allowed himself the pleasure of holding her. Of knowing she would be there when he woke. Of hoping she would be there always.

It was she who woke first a while later, stirring him with kisses on his neck, nibbling at his ear. He'd planned to speak with her about their future, but every time he tried, she kissed him into silence. In the end, he always surrendered, rolling her on her back to love her again.

Christine woke in yet another unfamiliar bed, and unfamiliar room for that matter. She sat up. The sheet slithered down her naked flesh. If last night's events had not immediately come rushing back to her, the soreness of her body would have reminded her quickly enough of all that had transpired. She glanced at the empty place beside her. And where, pray tell, was her most humble servant this morning? The door opened and she snatched the sheet up to her neck. It was her humble servant with a breakfast tray.

"Good morning, my lady," Gavin said, his voice a low husky caress.

He looked remarkably well, for a man who'd gotten little sleep. "I do hope you've brought me something to eat," she said. "I'm famished."

Gavin sat the tray and himself beside her on the bed.

"I have brought you ample nourishment. You'll need your strength."

Yes, Christine thought, she would. But not for the reasons his naughty smile suggested. She felt no less confused this morning concerning her place in life. If anything, only more puzzled.

"I should return to my own room," she said.

His smile faltered. "I had hoped you would think of this as your room while we are here."

"Gavin," she began. Christine took a deep breath and plunged ahead. "I think I should return to the parish."

"The parish?" He frowned. "We will go later to check on everyone."

"You don't understand," she said. "I-I mean, I think *I* should return there, stay there. It is where I belong."

Most uncharacteristically of him, he didn't bother to hide his surprise, or his hurt. "What are you saying?"

Looking away from him, she answered. "I'm saying the marriage is over. You are free now to either return to your former lifestyle, or choose another wife."

"I see."

It wasn't necessary to see him for her to recognize his flat tone. "I do wish to thank you for your hospitality to me during our marriage, and for your sacrifice," she said.

"Last night you thanked me well enough."

Her gaze shot up. "How dare you say that to me!"

His eyes softened. "And how dare you suggest I would want to return to my former lifestyle, or assume I would want another wife." He reached across and took her hand. "I love you, Christine."

Thank goodness she wasn't standing or her knees would have buckled. She knew he loved her last night, but knowing and hearing the words from his lips were two different things.

"You mustn't," she whispered.

"I do," he insisted. "And you love me."

Snatching her hand from his, she said, "I never told you I loved you."

"Yes, you did," he argued. "You told me last night. And you said it more than once."

She wanted to run from the room, from the truth of his words, but she couldn't do so naked. "I don't recall saying any such thing to you."

He rose, moving to his valise to dig out a shirt. A moment later he handed it to her. "Your blood stains my sheets, Christine. You told me you loved me the moment you crept into this room, into my bed."

Lifting her chin defiantly, she said, "Perhaps I was merely curious. I wanted to see for myself what all the fuss was about concerning your reputation with women."

After removing the warming cover from the plate of her breakfast, he lifted a brow. "And did you?"

She feared he was no longer taking her one bit seriously. "Your reputation has not been exaggerated," she admitted. "I'm sure you will be welcomed back with open . . . arms among the single set. I would hate to deny so many of your talents."

His mouth formed a straight line. "But denied they will be. When I give my heart, I pledge the rest of me along with it."

The man knew what to say, she'd give him that. She turned her back and tried to wiggle into his shirt. No easy task to perform while sitting down.

"Then I'm happy for your future wife. A faithful husband is a blessing."

"You are my future wife!"

She scrambled from the bed. "I became your wife once against my own wishes, I will not be forced again."

The anger drained from his face. "I would never force you. Why are you doing this? Denying me my greatest desire? To be your husband in truth. To love you for all time."

The answer didn't come quickly to her. For a moment, she couldn't recall why she couldn't be his wife, love him for more than one night. He lost his patience with her.

"If you fear remaining my wife will jeopardize the promise I made to you, you're wrong. I will still give up my title and estates to help the poor. I'll give aid to those at the parish. I'll—"

"Stop," she interrupted, feeling tears burn the backs of her eyes. "I know you'll do all of those things, and not only for me, but because you have learned compassion. Why I cannot be your wife has nothing to do with money."

He placed himself before her. "Do you not love me?"

Her heart felt as if it would split open. "It has nothing to do with love, either."

Lifting her chin, he asked, "What does it have to do with, Christine?"

She blinked back the tears burning her eyes. With love came sacrifice, and it was time to make hers. "I will not shame you further. You deserve a wife more suited to your station. One who will be an asset and not an embarrassment. I'm not—"

"Do not dare say you are not worthy," he interrupted, anger in his voice again. "It is I who am not worthy of you. You are the bravest, the kindest, the most selfless woman I have known. You are a light that came into my dark world and showed me the way."

"I am an orphan," she bit out. "I am a woman gossiped about and shunned by your society. You will resent me in time."

"I will only love you more in time," he argued, pulling her into his arms. "And I don't care what is said about you, or about me for that matter. I'm not who you think I am, Christine."

His words were starting to sway her. To give her hope. Today he loved her, wanted her, but a year from now

311

when they were outcasts, when they were still gossiped about and snickered at on the streets, he would not feel the same. She must spare him that, and spare herself the day when he would regret this moment and love her no longer.

"I cannot think," she said, pushing him away. She brought a hand to her forehead. "I need a bath, to dress and reflect upon this for a while."

"But then we'll talk," he insisted. "There are things about myself I must tell you. Things I should have told you already."

"Yes," she promised, if for no other reason than to get away from him. To put space between them before she threw herself into his arms and agreed to stay with him.

"Finish your breakfast," he instructed, moving toward the door. "I'll order a bath brought up to your room."

He left and Christine walked back to the bed and collapsed. Her mind whirled. Could her and Gavin truly find happiness together in spite of their different backgrounds? She wanted very badly to believe they could, to believe she had misjudged his need to be included among the aristocracy.

They would all think him mad when they learned he had given up his title and auctioned his family estate for the poor. Believe him madder yet if they learned he could have dissolved his marriage, but chose to honor his vows instead. But none of that mattered to her, as long as it did not matter to him. Hope struggled to life inside of her. Might the path she had walked not led purposely to Gavin?

Could she really have both? Him and the bequest to the poor souls in need? The possibility was heady. The possibility was wonderful. The possibility was heaven itself. She nibbled at her breakfast, glanced around the room, and saw Gavin's valise sitting on a chair, clothes draped half-in, half out of it. She supposed that without

Mr. Graves, he didn't know how to put away his things.

Putting them away for him would be a wifely chore, she supposed. For just a moment, she wanted to pretend she was his wife, would remain his wife. She rose from the bed, removed several shirts from his valise and moved to the massive bureau. She thought the drawers might still hold the late marquis's clothes and tugged hard, surprised when she nearly pulled the empty compartment clear away from the dresser.

Curious, she opened all of the drawers. They were empty. Well, almost. She saw what appeared to be an envelope stuck at the back of one drawer. After trying to snatch it, she realized it was lodged beneath the loose back section. She tugged and it came free. Only it wasn't one envelope, but two tied together. Gavin's name stood out clearly upon the first envelope. But that was odd. Only Gavin, no last name or title attached. She glanced at the second envelope and blinked. Her name was scrawled across the parchment.

"What on earth?" she whispered. Christine walked back to the bed and sat again. She wouldn't open Gavin's envelope, as it was addressed to him and therefore private. But her own? If it was in fact hers. But she couldn't be sure it wasn't unless she opened the letter and scanned the contents.

She tore it open. A moment later she realized the letter was from the late marquis. She smiled, then frowned over his first words to her. They cut into her as swiftly as a knife. Gavin, he stated, was not his son. Not of his blood, and undeserving of his title or his estate.

"Oh, my God," she whispered. The news would devastate her husband. But why would the old marquis, who'd been so kind to her, tell her such a horrible thing? Christine read further, feeling her eyes grow wider. She read until they filled with tears, until her hand fell limply to the bed, the letter still clutched in her white-knuckled grasp.

"Oh, Lord," she whispered. "How can I tell him he isn't who he thinks he is?" She drew a shaky breath. "Or that I am not who he thinks *I* am?"

Chapter Twenty-seven

"Playing lady's maid, are we now, cousin?"

Gavin turned from Martha, who hurried away to order a bath drawn for Christine. William looked as if he'd gotten even less sleep than him the previous night, though he'd warrant not for the same reasons.

"You're up early," Gavin said to his cousin. "Have you had breakfast?"

"As a matter of fact, no. Maybe you'll join me and we can talk."

He hated to be rude, but wanted to speak to Christine as soon as possible. What he had to say to her would not wait. And he suspected the longer he gave her to reflect upon remaining his wife, the more excuses she would present to him. He had to dispel her notions that class separated them, when in fact, it did not. He also had to convince her that a title and a position among society was no longer important to him.

"We'll talk later," he said, moving away. "I must see to something."

"Or someone," William drawled dryly. "Have you managed to get her into your bed yet, cousin?"

Gavin stopped and turned around, peeved. "It isn't like you to ask such indelicate questions, William. Nor are my private affairs any of your business."

William smiled. "That is answer enough." He sighed then walked toward him. "I'm glad. Maybe now that you've finally satisfied your curiosity about her, you'll realize she is only another woman. Certainly not worth giving up your inheritance for."

"Christine is my wife, William, and you will refer to her with respect."

He lifted a brow. "Oh. That good, was she?"

Anger quickly overtook him. "I will refrain from punching you in the face, cousin, only because in the past your sarcastic remarks concerning women did not bother me. But take warning, they bother me now."

"Have you changed your mind about giving her an annulment, then?"

Gavin's impatience with his cousin grew with each question William posed. He wanted to see Christine, to speak with her. "I'm in the process of trying to convince her to remain my wife."

William let out a heavy sigh. "You have finally come to your senses."

"I still plan to honor my promise to see the estate auctioned," he said.

As quickly as William had relaxed, he stiffened again. "There is no reason to auction the estate if she agrees to remain your wife. Why not keep them both?"

"Because I promised her!" he snapped. Gavin immediately regretted losing his temper. "You are my only relative—my friend. Can you not wish me happiness with Christine?"

"Can she make you happy, cousin?" William asked.

The answer came easily to his lips. "Yes." He felt like

a schoolboy when he added, "I'm in love with her. And for once in my life, nothing else seems to matter."

"So it would appear," William muttered. He sighed again, then smiled. "But of course your happiness is important to me. If having a woman whose station is clearly beneath you for a wife, and if the gossip won't strain the relationship, I am happy for you."

He considered telling William about his own hidden secret, but then there would have to be explanations and the time taken to make William understand Greenhaven was not, nor would ever, rightfully belong to either of them. First, he would tell Christine, then he would tell his cousin. He did something next he had never done. Gavin walked over and hugged William.

"Thank you. You have been a good friend to me over the years. Stood beside me. Together we will make our shipping company the largest in the world. And if I can convince Christine to remain my wife, it may not be long before you're bouncing our babies upon your knee. It will no longer be just the two of us."

His cousin's face paled a shade. Gavin laughed and slapped him on the back. "You don't have to bounce my children on your knee if you don't want to, William. Now, wish me luck."

"You have always had the devil's own luck," his cousin muttered.

Supposing William meant his words as a compliment, Gavin set off for the stairs. He bounded up them, nearly running over a child in the process. He steadied the girl. A boy came bounding down behind her, laughing, then another yelling, "I'll get you two!"

Both boys came to an immediate stop when they spotted Gavin. "You shouldn't run on the stairs," he told them.

The youngest of the Watts children, the girl on the step above him, glanced up. "You were running," she said.

"I was walking fast," he corrected, then smiled at her.

317

"Very fast," she added.

"How are you, Daniel?" he asked the oldest boy.

"Too loud," came his mother's voice at the top of the stairs. "Sorry, Yer Lordship. These three couldn't be quiet or still if I gagged 'em and tied 'em up."

Gavin included Sarah in his smile. "This house is too quiet," he decided. "It needs the sound of children's laughter."

She smiled in return. "I hope you'll be telling that to the rest of the staff. These three give them fits."

"I'll mention it," he promised. He turned the little girl toward the bottom of the stairs. "Run outside, but not on the stairs. One of you could take a tumble and get hurt."

The little girl walked slowly the rest of the way, then the boys followed her, but, before they reached the bottom, the two were walking very fast, and giggling again, too.

"You have fine children, Sarah," Gavin said, moving a few more steps toward the landing.

"That I do," she agreed. "I'd have me a whole house full if I'd have had a man who'd help me care for them. Oh," she suddenly exclaimed. "I was just to the lady's room to see if I could be of assistance to her, but she's not there. I heard noises coming from across the hall. Yer room, Yer Lordship. I didn't know if I should peek me head in. I assume it be the lady in there, and she's crying. I heard her with me own ears, and I should know well enough the sound of despair."

Christine crying? His Christine in despair? Gavin didn't take his own advice to the children. He ran the rest of the way up the stairs, then burst into the room. His wife sat on the bed with her back to him, wearing his large shirt, her shoulders shaking. "Christine?" he called softly.

She turned to look at him, tears streaming down her face. Instead of finding comfort for whatever grieved her in his presence, a sob escaped her lips.

Gavin rushed to her side. "What's wrong?"

When she wouldn't look up at him, he went down on one knee. "Christine," he said her name again, confused.

"Oh, Gavin," she breathed. "I have the most awful news." She lifted a letter. "I-I don't know how to tell you."

"Tell me what?"

Her beautiful tear-filled eyes slashed into him. "The letter. It's from the marquis. He, he told me that . . ."

"I'm a bastard," Gavin finished for her.

Christine's gaze widened. "You know?"

"Heartless old man," he muttered, rising. He ran a hand through his hair. "Yes, I know. I've known since he told me at the tender age of five. My mother had an affair with one of the help. I supposed she loved the man, or she wouldn't have tried to escape with him, leaving me behind. They were both killed in a carriage accident."

Rising, Christine asked, "You knew and you didn't tell me?"

A stab of guilt shot through him. "I planned to tell you. In fact, this very morning."

"How convenient," she said softly.

His gaze searched her face. "You understand I could not give you that ammunition before . . . I mean, before I fell in love with you. Before you made me see the error of my ways and I realized the title and the estate were no longer important to me."

Gavin went to her, placing his hands upon her shoulders. "I have lived my life trying to be the son I could never be to that man. A servant told him my mother had confessed to her that I was not her husband's son, but the son of her lover. I should have known that selfish bastard would make certain you found out about me, if he would not tell the rest of the world. He was bitter and cruel. He—"

"Was *my* father."

He thought his heart might have stopped. "What?"

"The marquis. He was my father. I am a bastard, as well."

Gavin stumbled away from her as if he'd been hit. "What cruel joke is he trying to play?"

"Not a trick," she insisted, taking a step toward him. "Don't you see? Now it makes sense. He didn't make you marry me to humiliate you. He made you marry me so that I could lay claim to something he could never give me."

"The inheritance," he said. "Greenhaven really belongs to you."

His wife shook her head. "No. I cannot lay legal claim to it because not only am I a woman, I am illegitimate. The same as you."

"Who are you?" Gavin demanded.

She was not who she thought she was—not the daughter of some whore and possibly a drunken sailor or other lowly man. "My mother was French. The daughter of a royal line. The marquis, although wealthy and titled, was still not good enough for her family. They fell in love, and when he realized she would be disowned by her family were she to marry him, he left her and returned to England."

"But he left her with child," Gavin said.

"Obviously," Christine agreed. "He didn't know about me until he spotted me at the parish one day. He wrote that I am the spitting image of my mother. Once he learned the strange circumstances surrounding my birth, he knew that she had disguised herself and tried to reach Greenhaven, but of course she never did."

"And he could not publicly acknowledge you without bringing the cursed scandal down upon his name he so detested," he bit out angrily.

"He could not acknowledge me without putting my life

in danger," Christine defended her deceased father. "My blood is tied to the throne of France. Even bastards have been know to claim a country—and known to be murdered in their sleep to assure they never do."

His face suddenly paled. To Christine's surprise, Gavin laughed. He continued to laugh until she became concerned.

"Do you find my background humorous?"

He quickly sobered. "I find it ironic. Only a short while ago, you worried you were not worthy of me. I told you then, that I was not worthy of you, and now there is even greater truth to my words."

Christine rushed to him. "No, Gavin. You must never think you are unworthy of me. You were right. I do love you."

"You mustn't," he repeated her earlier words.

She threw her arms around his neck. "But I do."

"How sweet."

Both she and Gavin jumped, turning to see William standing at the open door. She supposed seeing him there, obviously listening to their conversation might be counted as disturbing enough, but the fact he held a pistol upon them made it even more so.

Chapter Twenty-eight

"Cousin?" Gavin asked. "What are you doing?"

"Listening," William answered, then he walked inside and closed the door behind him. "Gavin," he said, shaking his head sadly. "You should have told me you were a bastard. And you." His gaze swung toward Christine. "Should not have let me overhear that you are the true heir to Greenhaven."

"Our bloodlines are of no concern to you, William," Gavin said. "And drop that bloody pistol. You might shoot one of us."

William smiled, but it did not reach his eyes. "That is the purpose of the weapon, cousin. I had hoped you wouldn't force me into doing this here at Greenhaven, where I fall under suspicion by being your only guest. But after our conversation downstairs, I realized I have no other choice."

Gavin nearly charged the man, but Christine held tight to him. She couldn't believe William had just threatened them. She'd thought she knew him—had considered him her friend, but now she saw something in his eyes Gavin had obviously failed to see until this moment. Hatred, and an honest threat to them both.

"Have you gone mad?" Gavin demanded.

"I have simply grown weary of waiting for someone else to see to your death, cousin. I was content to bide my time, sure you would meet your demise at the end of some jealous husband's hand, but then *she* came along." His cold eyes settled upon Christine. "At first, I didn't worry over her. And I did find her quite fetching, which I didn't hide."

He stared at Christine for a moment, his gaze softening, but only for a moment. "But all along I figured if you didn't dissolve the marriage, I would find a way to rid myself of her later."

Gavin stepped in front of her. "You will never harm Christine! You'll have to kill me first."

William brought the pistol up, aiming at his chest. "If you insist," he sneered.

"Gavin," Christine whispered, placing a hand upon his shoulder. "Don't provoke him."

"Move to the bed and sit," William ordered.

"You won't shoot me," Gavin said. "We are cousins. I'm your business partner. Your—"

"A thorn in my side," William snapped. "An obstacle who stands between me and a fortune that could be mine. That is all you are to me. All you have ever been. Shall I prove it?" He cocked the pistol.

Christine gasped. She grabbed Gavin's hand and led him toward the bed. "We must do what he asks," she pleaded.

Her husband obeyed, but Christine knew he did so only to appease her. And she wondered how long he could continue to hold his anger at bay.

"You are frightening Christine," Gavin said calmly, despite the fact that she felt the cousins' tension thick in the air. "Let her leave, and we will continue this discussion."

William snorted over the request. "I cannot let her leave, cousin. Not now. And she should be frightened. My aim is quite good. I have practiced. Did I not hit your horse square on the rump with a rock?"

"You threw that rock?" Gavin's jaw muscle clenched; she heard his teeth grind together. "And at the opera, it was you who loosened the banister, and—"

"And, yes, it was me on the road shooting at your thick head," William finished, flashing him a smug smile.

Christine's stomach lurched. She felt sick—scared to death over what might transpire in this room. Gavin had reached the breaking point. He nearly trembled with suppressed violence. She held his hand tighter, afraid his emotion would get him shot.

"Gavin trusted you," she said, hoping to appeal to William's humanity, or if she failed, to at least stall for more time.

The man's gaze swung to her. "Yes, he did, poor sap. You are to be commended, Christine. If you had to win a man's love, you couldn't have picked a better one. Gavin is so blind when he loves someone. So devoted, so trusting. Even though he knew all along I stood to gain the most by both of your deaths, he could not accuse me. Could not believe me capable of murder. He cannot believe it now."

"I did love you," Gavin said, despite his stony countenance. "You are the only true family I have left."

"Yes," William hissed. "But I have never loved you. My mother died in shame over her sister's foolish actions. The marquis cut off our funds and we were barely more than paupers until you reached manhood and took me under your wing. But then I had to become your servant."

"I never thought of you as a servant." Gavin stood. "I thought of you as my friend. Almost a brother."

The pistol steadied on him again. "Sit down, *friend*. I

want to tell you why you must die before I end your life."

Reaching forward, Christine took Gavin's hand again. "Don't be foolish. We must listen to what William has to say."

When the madman cocked the pistol, her husband reseated himself. Gavin positioned himself, however, to where his body would take any bullet aimed in their direction.

"You never treated me the way you treated your snobbish friends," William whined. "You thought of me as the pitied poorer relation. You ordered me about just as you ordered everyone about. And my hate for you grew. Even as I smiled and pretended to care for you, helped you run your business, I hated you more every day."

Stealing a glance at her husband, Christine saw the sudden appearance of tears soften Gavin's steely expression.

"Forgive me, William. I battled my own ghosts, and didn't care who I trampled in order to fight them. Our relationship can change. I do care about you, regardless that my actions have not always shown my feelings."

"Too late," William growled. "And now you've turned into a gushing idiot. Talking of children and what a happy family we will all become. I cannot risk you producing an heir, cousin. And now I cannot risk your wife challenging me for the inheritance. I might have let her live until this new development. No one would challenge my claim against that of an orphan who had no right to marry above herself in the first place. I might have even tried to make her mine. But now . . ."

Christine shivered at the thought and Gavin tensed beside her. Her husband would lunge for his cousin, she felt him gathering himself and knew she must distract the man.

"I didn't see through you right away," she said to William. "But in time, I would have. I had already begun to suspect your feelings for Gavin were not genuine."

"Good for you," he snarled, but he lowered the weapon for a moment. "Beautiful and smart. Of course I saw that about you from the beginning. And I also saw the threat you posed to poor Gavin's heart. I think he loved you from that first night, by the way. He just didn't realize. . . . Just a little gift I give you before I kill you both."

"You won't get away with this." Gavin's fist curled into a ball inside her hand. "I may not have seen you for who and what you truly are, but someone will put it together."

William walked a few feet away, but didn't lower the weapon. "Not so, cousin. Christine has just supplied me with wonderful evidence as to why you would take her life. You killed her because she found out your secret. She wanted the marriage dissolved and found a way to see herself free. Free to marry her lover, which is another reason you killed her. Out of jealousy because you loved her so. Once you realized what you had done, you took your own life. I will play the part of the shocked cousin, paralyzed with grief and confused about these awful events. Then I'll take all that I have deserved for so long. I will be the poor cousin no longer."

"You're insane," Gavin bit out. "Did I not tell you a title cannot make you more or less than you already are? It is not worth selling your soul to the Devil. Greenhaven doesn't belong to me or you!"

"We shall see," William countered. He steadied the pistol on Gavin. "If it makes you feel better, this is harder than I imagined. Face to face this way. I fear I'm experiencing a moment of sentiment." He sighed. "Oh well, it's gone now."

He cocked the pistol and Christine knew she must do something. She jumped up from the bed, causing William's attention to momentarily shift to her. In that brief instant, Gavin made his move. Before William could turn the pistol back toward him, he was upon the man.

In horror, Christine watched them struggle.

Briefly, William managed to aim the pistol at Gavin's head, and she screamed. But the elder cousin was also the strongest of the two. Gavin forced William's hand down.

She started to rush into the hall and shout for help, but a shot fired. Christine froze, as did Gavin and William, both staring into each other's eyes. William was the first to stumble back. He glanced down at the bright red stain seeping through the front of his shirt. When his gaze lifted, his expression was one of surprise.

"You always have to win, don't you, cousin?" A weak smile punctuated his defeat. William crumpled.

Gavin caught him, easing him to the floor. "William," he whispered, his voice cracking. He glanced up at Christine. "Hurry, tell someone to fetch a doctor!"

There was no need, she realized. William was dead. His eyes stared, sightless at the ceiling above. Still, her husband tried to rouse him.

"Hold on, William!" he ordered.

When Gavin shook him slightly and received no response, Christine walked over and knelt beside her husband. She placed a gentle hand upon his arm. "He is gone, Gavin."

The pain in his eyes when he looked at her slashed long, bloody streaks into her soul. Gavin did in fact love deeply, unconditionally.

"Why?" he whispered.

She shook her head sadly and wrapped her arms around him. Christine didn't know if he asked why his cousin had to die, or why William had become so consumed with envy and greed he'd murder his own blood relation. There seemed no acceptable answer to either.

They buried William two days later in the family cemetery—the place where Gavin's mother, and Christine's father had also been laid to rest. It was a beautiful spot atop a hill overlooking Greenhaven.

327

Christine had given Gavin the envelope her father addressed to him, but she didn't believe he'd read the letter, and wondered if he ever would. She supposed she couldn't blame him if he did not. Probably the marquis had made a last effort to appease his own conscience concerning his cold treatment of a man he'd claimed as a son for all the world, but never in his heart.

Gavin had told everyone at Greenhaven that William died when the pistol he was showing him accidently misfired. She admired him for that, for loving and protecting William even though he had betrayed him. Of their future, nothing else had been decided. She'd given Gavin the past two days to think, and took time to contemplate herself.

Heart and head had finally come together upon a decision for her, now she must find out what Gavin had decided. Christine ushered the old vicar to the door and outside. He'd presided over William's funeral earlier that morning.

"Are those at the parish faring well?" she asked.

"Very well," he answered. "Thanks be to your help, and to the help of your husband. The wagon of fresh food he sent the parish people was very kind. He's done much to compete with your sainthood in their eyes."

"I'm not a saint." She recalled the night of passion she spent with her husband. "And neither is he," she added dryly.

"But together, you can accomplish more than if you are apart. And if you both find happiness while you serve a greater master, it is no sin."

Her spirits lifted despite the solemn occasion and the damp weather outside. She couldn't say that Gavin was in truth her destiny, but she could say with assurance he was part of it. She gave the vicar a chaste kiss on the cheek, which caused the man to blush with pleasure.

"Your past," he said. "Have you come to accept who you are, Christine?"

She gave it only a moment's thought. Learning that she was the daughter of a woman in line for a throne, and a titled man of wealth had not changed who she was, or what she believed. It had changed nothing.

"I am an orphan," she answered, which was still true. "And a very fortunate woman to be have been raised by a community of many who love me, and the kind heart of an old bachelor."

Tears filled his eyes. "I am so proud of you. We all are."

She smiled warmly at him and squeezed his hand in parting. Then she went in search of her husband. He stood a short distance from the house, staring out over the lands.

"Gavin?" she asked softly.

He didn't turn to face her. "If your father would have disowned me as he should have, William would still be alive. He would have had no reason to allow greed to turn him into a monster."

"Some men will find a reason when there is none," she said, joining him. "You cannot blame yourself."

"I can blame the bloody title," he argued. "The title and my own selfish ways. I'm well rid of Greenhaven. I only wish I had realized how unimportant it was earlier in life."

Glancing at his somber countenance, she said, "Had it been unimportant long ago, you and I would have gone our separate ways from the beginning. You would not have challenged me for the inheritance or wed me because of it for that matter."

His gaze met hers. "Then there is another reason to curse it, and me. You thought you married a nobleman, instead you now find yourself strapped to a bastard whose bloodline cannot come close to your own."

Anger sprang to life inside of her. "Do you think your bloodline matters to me? If you do, you don't know me at all."

He glanced away from her. "I can't ask you to stay with me. Not now."

"I am your wife," she bit out. "Your wife in all ways. Were you lying when you said you loved me?"

Gavin turned and pulled her into his arms. "Those are the truest words I have ever spoken. I love you so much it hurts inside. But I have lied to you, Christine. Not telling you the truth about myself from the beginning was the same as a lie. I am a sinner, a bastard, a—"

She placed her fingers against his lips. "You are the noblest of men, Gavin. I wanted to be a saint, martyred so that I could feel good about who I am. So that I might feel as if I had a purpose much grander than the simple life given to me. What I have learned is that it is no small thing to be woman, loved by a man, joined in spirit and purged by the goodness that flows in both of us. Alone, we can each only do a little for those in need, but together, the possibilities are endless."

Gavin took her fingers from his lips and gently kissed them. "I have spent my whole life trying to be of noble birth, only to find one woman's love has turned me from a pauper into a king. Stay with me. We will forget titles and estates, and simply love one another. We'll build our own world, far from the wagging tongues of the ton. We will sell the estate and help the poor. We—"

"No," she said softly.

The excitement dancing in Gavin's eyes faded. "No?"

"We will not sell the estate," she clarified. "It occurred to me yesterday, while the Watts' children were running around the house making racket and their mother tried to quiet them; Greenhaven needs the sounds of children's laughter. Greenhaven will become a refuge for the poor orphans who have nowhere else to go."

Gavin snatched her arms and pulled her close. "That is an excellent idea, wife, but if ever you plunge a knife into my heart like that again, I'll have to punish you. I'll take you to sea aboard one of my ships, keep you locked in my cabin and in my bed for months on end."

Christine smiled. "Then I must think of another way to wound you, Your Lordship."

His suggestive smile waned. "I am no longer your lordship, Christine. I am only Gavin Norfork, a wealthy businessman."

"You must keep the title, Gavin," Christine said. "Not because it is important to either of us, but because we must set an example for those with wealth to follow. As Marquis and Marchioness of Greenhaven, our deeds will be held in far greater esteem by those who can also help, than if we are simply Gavin and Christine Norfork."

He frowned. "But neither of us can lay legal claim to the title or the estate. We would be duping everyone."

A perfectly wicked smile broke out upon her lips. "But only for the good of all mankind," she said innocently.

Gavin laughed. "You are scandalous, Christine." He pulled her close and kissed her.

There was on thing more Christine felt needed to be addressed between them. She ended the kiss and stared up into his dark eyes. "The letter from my father. Did you read it?"

"No."

She knew he had every right to hate the marquis. But the man she knew, had been changed by love. He had been kind to her, had looked after her. "I know you can never forgive him, Gavin, but for me—"

"I have forgiven him," he shocked her by saying. "I know he had regrets in the end. I also know he did love me. He proved it in a way words never could."

"How?"

He kissed her forehead. "He gave me his greatest treasure. Not his title or his estate. He gave me you."

Tears filled her eyes. "Oh, Gavin, I do love you so. And Greenhaven, with it's ghost, will live again with the joyous sounds of children's laughter. If it holds no happy memories for you, it can for others."

"There is one fond memory I have of Greenhaven," he corrected. "The night an angel slipped into my bed, and together, we shared a small piece of heaven."

The passion in his eyes warmed her if the dreary day could not. "I suppose we should try to remember the good, and forget the bad."

His brow lifted. "I rather hoped to repeat the good, rather than recall it."

She smiled. "Let's go home, Gavin. Back to London."

Gavin wrapped his arms around her, resting his head on top of hers. "We should probably rescue Mr. Graves from Tillie."

"Perhaps he does not wish to be rescued," she countered.

"I think you may be right, my lady."

The sun suddenly broke out above them, as if God decided to smile upon them in that instant. Christine pressed her lips to Gavin's in a kiss as full of promise as the sunlight pouring down upon them, a promise to love and laugh and do all they could for those in need. A promise to be ungoverned by rules or class. A promise to count themselves the most fortunate of people, because they have found life's true treasure. The gift of love.

Enter a tumultuous world of thrilling sensuality and chilling terror, where nothing is as it seems, and where dreams and nightmares blend into heart-pounding encounters too enticing to be denied, too frightening to be forgotten. In our new line of gothics the most exciting writers of romance fiction explore dark secrets, forbidden desires, the hidden part of the psyche that is revealed only at the midnight hour and by . . .

Candleglow

Available January 2001   0-505-52412-0

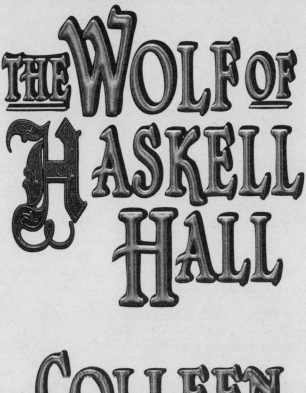

THE WOLF OF HASKELL HALL

COLLEEN SHANNON

Chapter One

Cornwall, England, 1878

Pain. Thirst. Hunger. The three demons ran alongside him in the gloom, dark harbingers leading him to a future more terribly beguiling with every step he took deeper into the moor.

Once, he had struggled against this fate. He'd traveled to the ends of the earth to avoid it. But neither the burning sands of the Sahara nor the bone chilling cold of an Andean hut had quieted the call of blood to blood.

Such was the fate of his father.

And his father's father, back into the mists of time when Druids chanted and danced naked in the . . .

Moonlight.

He lifted his face to the siren call. Now that he accepted his family's curse as a blessing, the wanton moon no longer terrified him. Power surged through him with every alluring ray, making his senses acute to things no mere mortal could understand.

The taste of home upon his tongue with the salt damp of the marsh.

The feel of moss-covered ground beneath his bare feet, springy yet firm.

The touch of mist writhing like a woman's silken skin against his bare torso.

The sight of wild things darting about in the cover of darkness, secure that his flawed human eyes could not see the red glow of their heat. And sounds . . .

The laughter floated toward him, both a taunt and a temptation, drifting on the wind. He lifted his nose and sniffed. Through all the other smells of the fecund Cornish night, he caught the most seductive scent of all: woman. For an instant, he stood where he was, both grounded on the soil of home, yet lost in the dilemma of his kind. The remnants of humanity whispered in one ear—

—and demons howled in the other.

Louder, and far more seductive.

Pain . . . a stab so acute that it felt as if his rib cage must expand to hold the muscle and bone his frail human frame could not contain.

Thirst . . . His tongue, unbearably sensitive now, lapped out to taste a pond, but the thin water didn't have the texture and taste he craved.

Hunger . . . It twisted his guts into knots. He bent double, fighting the dark urges, but then the laughter came again. With it, the last of his humanity faded away, a pinprick disappearing into the dark maw of the night.

In one agile bound, he whirled and scaled the tall hedge separating him from his prey. Down, down the slope into the clearing, where the latest Haskell heiress galloped her horse in the moonlight. Her long silvery hair was a banner waving behind her in the stiff breeze, taunting him with the need to catch it and pull her out of the saddle. Unaware of him, she urged the white mare on to faster strides.

Not fast enough.

How easily he kept pace, power surging through him from the tips of his curving fingers to toes growing into claws.

Feet silent on the damp earth, he gained on her with every step.

And then, as he got close enough to leap, all his senses narrowed down to one driving urge.

The need to feed.

He was tensing to spring when he felt the Other bound into step beside him. They bared their fangs at one another, stiff neck hairs bristling as they growled. For an instant, they matched each other step for step, jostling for position as they battled over who would have first taste.

And then, as even her dull human senses came alive to the danger, the woman looked over her shoulder. She screamed, trying to wheel her mount away from them.

But it was too late.

For her.

And for him . . .

Three Months Later

Delilah Hortense Haskell Trent drew the light curricle to a halt just inside the wrought-iron gates of Haskell Hall. Delilah and her two servants stared up at the odd mansion.

The Hall glowed like a sanctuary in the gloom illuminated by a half moon. Lights spilled from every window, as if the servants were determined to do their part to welcome the new mistress. But the bright displays only accentuated the building's sad state of decay.

It was a hodgepodge of architectural styles, from the simple Georgian pilasters and flat front of the central portion to the fussy Victorian wings on both sides, each capped with octagonal towers. Still, the overall effect might have been charmingly eccentric but for the sagging shutters, peeling double front doors, and moldering, ivy-covered stone that needed a good regrouting.

The gravel drive in front, however, was cleanly swept, and the grounds were immaculate.

"Blimey, she's a frowsy bitch, drawers a-droppin' round her knees at the first sign o' interest," came the ribald appraisal from Jeremy, Lil's groom, bodyguard, and favorite general nuisance.

Lil didn't even glance at him, for she'd long since given up trying to make him keep a civil tongue in his head. But he had other qualities she valued more than politesse.

As usual, Safira gave him a censorious look out of slanted, exotic eyes luminous against her burnished Jamaican skin. "Mon, ye have no need to stir up trouble before we even set foot inside the place."

"Trouble don't need stirrin' up here, me dusky beauty," Jeremy retorted. "It follows, bold like, right through the door with us. I can feel it in me bones."

This time, Safira didn't argue. Her lovely dark eyes got huge as she fingered the talisman at her throat and stared up at the Hall. "Mistress, the little bandy cock could be right, for once. Maybe we should turn around and catch the first boat back to America."

Lil spared them each an amused glance before she clicked her tongue to the horse. "Sometimes I'm not sure which of you is more superstitious, the voodoo priestess or the Cockney sailor who quit the sea because his captain had the temerity to bring his wife aboard."

Neither of them retorted with their usual spunk, so she left off her teasing. It was too late to turn back now. She was in England, the land of her mother's birth, for the first time, and she intended to enjoy every moment.

She had, after all, crossed an ocean to get here, drawn as much by curiosity as by duty.

Without her presence, the tiny village of Haskell would fail, or so she was assured by Mr. Randall Cottoway, Esq., of Jasper, Diebold and Cottoway, London solicitors. The estate would be parceled off among various male relatives, the villagers and miners likely put out of work, if she did not stake her rightful claim to the inheritance. She, he'd informed her with typical lofty British superiority, was needed back in Cornwall. Surely—he'd made plain with a scornful glance around her mother's overly-lavish drawing room—she could afford a few months and a few pounds to save the estate for future Haskell heirs.

"Such a bequest, coming down through the distaff side of the Haskell family, is highly unusual in English law," the solicitor had stated. "Because you are the last known female heir with Haskell blood, if you do not satisfy the terms of the inheritance by living on the property for six months, then everything will finally pass, after three centuries, into the male hands of several distant cousins related only to the patriarchal side of the family." He'd tipped his ridiculous bowler hat, left a packet of papers, and exited, obviously relieved that his duty was done and he could return to civilization.

Like her stoic Scottish father, Lil could be coaxed, she could be cajoled, she could be reasoned with. But she could never be bullied.

Challenged, however, was another matter.

So here she sat in her curricle under the hulking building that seemed to brood down at them. For a craven instant, she felt a quiver of unease shiver down her sword-straight spine. She had much of the sheer practicality of her stalwart father, and little of the flighty moodiness of her mother. However, as she stared up at the Hall, a strange foreboding niggled its way through her usual calm, as insidious as the gathering fog.

Had she done the right thing in coming here?

The doors burst open. Light flooded the darkness as smiling servants filed out. She had no time for regrets, or foolish fancies.

The next day, Lil sat in the salon partaking of that peculiar English ritual that had been the one legacy her mother seemed to cherish: high tea. Lil had never told her mother, since they always seemed to have plenty to argue about, but, like her father, Lil despised the taste of tea. However, since she had no wish to be considered more of a heathen American than she obviously already was to these people, she forced herself to drink it.

As she bit into a cucumber sandwich, Lil had to admit that no one knew better how to make gossip a high art than the English. Even the snooty Denver socialites who'd never accepted the Trents—their scandalous riches actually made, they'd whispered, by Mr. Trent's own hands—could take lessons in hypocrisy from these country ladies.

Mrs. Farquar of Farquar Hill, gushed, "*So* brave of you to venture here across the sea, all the way to *Cornwall* from America. Of course, I make no doubt that even *our* desolate moors are positively *teeming* with social occasions compared to what you probably knew in . . . now, *what* was the name of that town you're from, my dear?"

Biting back the urge to tell the plump little busybody that Denver even had gas lights and paved streets, *really* it did, unlike the parts hereabout, Lil politely wiped the corners of her mouth with her linen napkin and responded, "Denver. Colorado."

"Oh yes," piped up Mrs. Farquar's horse-faced daughter, "you remember, Maman. That's where all the gold and silver miners moved after they made their fortunes."

Both ladies darted complacent looks at Lil out of the corners of their eyes.

It hadn't taken them long to investigate her background. How had they managed it so quickly in this backwater? Lil's teeth snapped down on a scone this time, but she managed to hold her tongue.

However, Jeremy, who'd been setting a new fire for them in the grate, had no such qualms. Dusting his hands off on his breeches, he said out of the corner of his mouth, "Aye, same place as many a pretty English rose went a-scoutin' fer a rich husband if she could get it, and a rich protector if she couldn't." Jeremy raked Miss Farquar with his wintry blue eyes. "Ye could try your luck, gel, but a man'd as lief mount a thoroughbred as a nag, and back ye'd be quick-like, puttin' down yer betters."

Both women goggled at him in shock.

Hiding a smile behind her napkin, Lil gave him a severe look over the linen. When her mouth was straight, she lowered the cloth, hoping her voice was sterner than her merry green eyes. "Jeremy, leave the room at once, and never speak to my guests so again!"

As usual, he read her like a book. He gave his cocky little half salute and strolled out with his peculiar rolling gait, not in the least abashed.

"Well, *really!* How do you bear such a . . ." Mrs. Farquar's outrage stopped mid-spate as she stared at the door. Her daughter did likewise, and the looks on their faces made Lil swivel in her chair in alarm to see what horror stood there.

At first she could make out nothing in the dark hall way, but then the shadow moved into the room and resolved itself into a man.

A very tall, powerful man.

He wore work breeches and calf-high boots that molded his long legs, giving them an obscene clarity and beauty of power and form that would have made a lesser woman than Lil blush. His white lawn shirt was so thin that she could see the shadow of his chest hair, so she knew he must be dark. His face and hair were shaded under a broad-brimmed work hat. And his hands . . . she shivered as she stared at his hands.

The nails were blunt and clean, but his long fingers had a tensile strength and . . . readiness expressed in every flagrantly male sinew of his indomitable frame. And when he walked into the room, he was silent despite his size. He flicked a short quirt against his leg, broadcasting dislike as if he had no more patience for the two gossips than Lil did. His rudeness in not removing his hat spoke loudly of his opinion of them.

Mother and daughter muttered excuses and fled, snapping the drawing room door closed behind them.

Only the sound of the fire crackled, but Lil refused to be intimidated by her own estate manager. For this man could be none other than Ian Griffith. "Why did you not knock, Mr. Griffith?" She glanced at the mantel clock. "You are early for our appointment."

"If you wish, I'll go back out and return in five minutes—mistress." The deep, soft voice put a slight emphasis on the last word, and the intonation gave erotic meaning to the polite usage. Still, he did not remove his hat, and she had the peculiar feeling the omission was as much for his own protection as for hers.

Why would he be afraid of her gaze?

The urge to move her chair away from him almost overcame her, but instead, Lil tilted back her silvery head of fashionably coiffed hair and stared boldly up into the shadow of the hat, her own green gaze steady. She caught the glitter of eyes as he let them wander from her small, slipper-shod feet, up her green taffeta gown, past her full hips and small waist, to her generous bosom, pausing on the vee between her breasts before traveling on to her white throat. The glitter grew brighter as he watched the pulse pound there, but then he whacked the quirt hard against his leg as if to punish his own thoughts, and the glitter snuffed out like a light.

That was why he seemed so threatening, Lil instinctively realized. This man had the measured control of a leashed tiger. It would suffer you to feed it and train it and play with it, only so long as it pleased. But once that power was unleashed, and the wildness broke through. . . .

Nonsense. "Remove your hat, if you please." He was just a man, and she was no ninny to be so intimidated.

A sharp intake of breath betrayed his shock at the curt command, but he raised that large, capable hand and pulled off the hat.

It was her turn to gasp. His face was not conventionally handsome. His cheekbones were too high and exotically slanted, his blade of a nose too long, his lips too full and wide. And his eyes . . . she tried to delve into them and take the true measure of this man as she'd had to do so often since her father died, but the amber depths were too opaque and secretive to allow her in. They were fringed with long, dark lashes that would have looked feminine on a less primal face.

Curly midnight hair cascaded over his tanned brow, and long sideburns pointed like accusatory fingers down the sides of his strong, square jaw. As if to emphasize the obvious: *I grant favors if I will it, but I never ask for them. Cross me at your peril.*

Every hackle on her body stood on end, and it was all she could do not to leap up and fire him on the spot just to avoid feeling so intimidated. Instead, she managed coolly, "Do you have the books ready for me to examine?"

"Yes, I do." He stalked to a cabinet against the wall and took out two black ledgers.

Lil rose and walked over to the Louis XV desk in pride of place in the middle of the room. The furnishings in the house were as eclectic as the facade, but there were a few priceless pieces, of which this was one. She sat down, expecting him to deposit the ledgers and move away.

Instead, he pulled up a chair. His nostrils flared as he obviously caught the subtle whiff of her perfume, and her own senses went on full alert. He didn't touch her anywhere as he leaned over her shoulder, but she felt his body heat and smelled a faint scent of something indefinable emanating from him, something earthy and primitive that raised her hackles again . . .

. . . and made her long for his touch to soothe them.

The neat columns, written in a bold dark hand, wavered before her gaze. She took a deep breath and tried to concentrate. But she felt the expanse of his shoulders so close that all she would have had to do was turn and she could investigate their width with her own tingling hands.

She leaped up, knocking over the gilded, spindle-legged chair. "Leave them with me. I will study them later, at my leisure."

An insolent smile tugged at the corners of those full lips as she fled back to her safe seat. She was too off balance to get up and slap it away, as her instincts urged.

"And the rest—mistress?" asked that deep, soft voice. "What of the new pump for the mine? The schoolroom in the village that needs a new roof, and—"

"Not today. I am . . . fatigued." Oh no. Next she'd make the age-old lady's excuse of the headache. Warily, she watched him rise, pick up the books, and come toward her. She almost leaped up to run, but he only veered around her to put the ledgers back.

To her intense relief, he put his hat back on and shielded her from those steady, unnerving amber eyes. "A true Haskell," he said with mild contempt. "I had hoped that somehow, you might be different. Good afternoon." Turning on his heel, he stalked out, steps soundless even on the wood floor. The soles of his boots must be as soft as the shank.

Still . . . She had never met such an unsettling man. She pressed her hand to her hammering heart, vaguely aware that this strange pounding was not just arousal, or fear, or even excitement.

It was a combination of all three. She stood to pour herself a brandy with a shaking hand, thinking the spirits would soothe her agitated nerves. But the smooth burn of the liquor warmed her in unexpected places instead, reminding her of the way Ian Griffith walked, and talked.

And stared at her with secretive, burning eyes.

She tossed her glass into the fire, furious at her own weakness. She strode out of the room, vowing not to think of him again.

She broke her vow before she crossed the floor.

In the ensuing days, to Lil's relief, she didn't have to see Ian Griffith again. For over a week, she had her hands full with the household itself. The former owners had lavished money on the outbuildings, the stables, the greenhouse, even the old chapel on the grounds, but they'd been parsimonious with the interior. Every piece of furniture needed a good stripping and repolishing, every brass fixture needed shining, and the rugs and draperies . . . Lil sneezed just looking at them.

Lil had been unofficial chatelaine of her father's three Colorado homes since she was in her teens, and she knew much of running a household, even one almost as complicated as this. But here, a mine, the enormous stables that held everything from broodmares to carriage horses to thoroughbreds, the village school, and even some of the shops, were also Haskell-owned. For these, she needed her estate manager. But she refused to fetch him, and he seemed equally content not to come calling.

She wondered where he lived. She wondered if he was married. She wondered why he seemed to dislike the Haskells. And then she wondered, to her own fury, why she bothered wondering.

When the house is ready, she told herself staunchly. *It's only that I'm busy. He doesn't intimidate me at all.* But she wasn't facing a mirror when she thought it.

Finally, almost two weeks after her arrival, she pulled off her apron and crossed the last item off her list. "Downstairs finished," she said with a weary sigh of satisfaction, blowing a curl off her forehead as she smiled at Mrs. McCavity, the housekeeper. "Now the upstairs. We'll start with the towers. . . ." She broke off at the look on Mrs. McCavity's face. "Yes?"

"Well, milady, that is—"

"I bear no title, Mrs. McCavity. You may call me Delilah."

A horrified look crossed the woman's face. "Sure and the saints themselves strike me down afore I so disrespect me betters. What was your Da a-thinkin' to name ye after a heathen woman?" She blushed as her Irish brogue got the best of her.

Lil laughed. She was always tickled to find the clue to a person's humanity. In her servants. In her friends. Even, on occasion, in her enemies. Everyone had some mannerism or way of speaking that betrayed his strengths and weaknesses. The more emotional Jeremy was, the more colorfully he cursed. The more frightened Safira became, the more she retreated into her magic. When Mrs. McCavity was shocked or moved, she reverted to the brogue of her childhood.

And Ian Griffith? How vividly she could visualize that dark, enigmatic face. But she saw no weakness there. And little humanity.

Lil collected her scattered thoughts. The housekeeper looked puzzled, and she'd been so hardworking and kind that Lil felt she had to give the poor woman some explanation as to why her new mistress was so different from the former ladies of the Hall. "If you'd known my Pa, you'd understand that he challenged me from the time I was born to be better than a name, a title, an

346

inheritance. 'Delilah,' he would say, 'a name has no more bearing on who we are than money defines what we are. Ye have three scourges to overcome—me trade, your name, and the filthy lucre that will be either the bane o' yer existence or yer deliverance. Take yer weaknesses and make them strengths.' " Lil's smile grew misty as she stared at Mrs. McCavity's attentive face. "I've always done my best to follow his advice. With the result that I fear I am not much welcomed in Denver drawing rooms, and doubtless will not be here, either."

"There you are wrong, mil—ma'am. Money in these parts hides an enormous quantity of sins." Mrs. McCavity ducked her head as if she was sorry she'd spoken so frankly, and she reached for the huge ring of keys at her waist. "Now, where do you want to start upstairs?"

"The towers." Lil led the way, but she turned back when she realized the housekeeper had not followed.

"We . . . are not supposed to go into the north tower. The south tower was set up as a governess's suite, but since we currently have no children in the house, it is vacant."

Frowning, Lil scarcely listened to the second half of the explanation. "You are telling me I own this estate and am not allowed to enter parts of my own ancestral home?"

" 'Tis an agreement made many years ago with the Griffith family by the first mistress. So long as a Griffith runs this estate, he may live where he pleases in the house, as he pleases, with no interference from the owners. The Griffiths have lived unmolested in that tower for almost a hundred years."

Lil was appalled. "Such an agreement could not possibly be legally binding. Why, if the house were sold—"

"And morally?"

Lil clamped her mouth shut. No wonder Ian Griffith strode around like he owned the place! In a way, he did.

Without another word, she turned on her heel and led

the way upstairs—to the south tower. But as they traversed the connecting hallway, she couldn't help looking in the opposite direction and wondering. Her steps slowed.

Each tower had its own entrance and exit. What guests did Ian Griffith invite inside? How many women had succumbed to his animal magnetism? What did his bed look like? Were his arms and long legs as muscular as they looked? She didn't have to close her eyes to visualize him sprawled on white sheets, all wild dark power and wild dark urges that made a woman—

She caught Mrs. McCavity's gaze. Blushing, she turned sharply in the opposite direction. Would she could turn her thoughts so easily.

That night, even after a soothing soak in the hip-deep copper tub, Lil was still restless. She tossed aside the weighty tome she was trying to read on the biology of Bodmin moor, which lapped at the very foundation of this house. But improving her mind would have to wait for a less stressful day.

She'd worked herself to the point of exhaustion, and had two glasses of sherry that night instead of one, but still she couldn't quiet her overactive imagination. She simply would not be able to sleep until she saw the north tower for herself. Ian Griffith had left word with the butler that he had gone into Bodmin for supplies and would not return until the next day, so she was safe invading his abode.

Wrapping the tie of her sweeping cashmere negligee tightly about her trim waist, shaking back the deep ruffles at her sleeves, she collected the enormous ring of keys the housekeeper had given her. Most were marked, but two, larger and more ornate than the others, were not. One of them had to open the north tower.

She had the right, she told herself, to be sure that illegal activities were not being conducted in her home.

If she found an opium pipe, or smuggled goods, or . . . or scandalous pictures or novels . . . well, she'd have every reason to fire the arrogant blackguard.

On the long trek to the opposite wing of the house, her slippers made little sound in the thick carpets, but the lantern she carried threw her shadow upon the wall. Strange the way she danced, in a joyous way quite opposite to the sick, anticipatory queasiness in her stomach.

She looked down. Her hand was shaking.

She stopped. What was wrong with her? She was a woman grown, an experienced woman in every way since she'd made the mistake of letting her former fiancé talk her into his bed. She'd broken off the engagement when she found out that he, despite his greater guile than the others, also only wanted her money. He had not been a kind lover, and she'd had no interest in the act, illicit or sanctified, since.

Which was why her current obsession troubled her so. She took a deep breath, closed her eyes, and visualized her father's bright green eyes smiling at her. "Face yer fears, me darlin', and ye'll be the stronger for it."

"Yes, Pa." Hitching her skirts above her ankles so she could walk faster, she quelled her own foolish fears and hurried into the north wing. Sure enough, the stout oak door that met her, banded with steel like a Norman baron's of old, yielded to one of the ornate keys. She shoved the door inward and listened.

The round stairwell was pitch-black, and she heard no sounds above. The entire household was asleep, as she should be at this ungodly hour, so she entered the gloom and shut the door quietly behind her, but left it unlocked.

In the feeble lantern light, the curving stairs and stone tower seemed to stretch to infinity. Finally she reached another door, this one glossy black and even heavier than the other. She tried the door handle, but it didn't open. She fumbled with the key chain again, and to her relief, the same key that opened the lower door also unlocked this one.

Taking a deep breath, she shoved the heavy portal open. The octagonal space inside was very dark. She quickly lit the gas sconces beside the door, and then the lamp next to the sofa before the fireplace.

She looked around, and some of her suspicions about her manager began to fade. No den of iniquity here. Only a tiny kitchen and dining area in one corner, and a living area across, plus a long table set up before shelves packed with books to make a rudimentary library.

A small but comfortable suite of rooms, a gentleman's retreat, all dark paneling and lush green velvet. Tasteful but spare. None of the heavy Empire and rococo styles so in vogue in this era when Queen Victoria ruled with a small but indomitable hand. Simple Sheraton writing armoire, marble-topped tables, monkish straight-backed chairs. The only nod to decadence was a plush emerald green silk divan that looked as if it should have a Turkish pasha reclining upon it.

Or an houri.

Wishing she could rid her head of such sensual images, Lil carried the lantern to illuminate the painting above the fireplace mantel. It was a picture of the moors. Because the walls of the tower curved slightly as the angles of the octagon met, it did not rest flat. Perhaps that accounted for the picture's odd depth and radiance.

The moors she'd seen on the train coming here had never looked like this. Yes, they stretched beyond sight as this one did, and yes, they were filled with intriguing patches of green, where moss or plants relieved the unrelenting brown. And yes, when the sun went down and night ruled, she'd even seen the same luminous, low-lying mist. But that moor had been intimidating, bleak, offering more peril than pleasure.

The same moor depicted in this painting was sensual, glowing with jewel tones of green and sapphire, where lichen-covered rocks dotted the muddy wastes, and pools of blue water reflected back the cloudless sky above. Even the mountains, hazy in the distance, had been added with bold, loving strokes. Here, they were not jagged teeth consuming the sky as they'd seemed to Lil, but hands offering a bounty of life and joy found nowhere else on earth.

Lil stumbled back a step. She wasn't sure why the image was so disquieting and riveting at the same time. Whoever had painted this loved the moors. Loved them as a man loved a woman, or a mother a son.

But there was something else . . . something troubling. She couldn't quite put her finger upon it, but the brushstrokes were deep, the dollops of paint standing up from the canvas in a style she'd never seen before. As if the painter used violent, passionate strokes to exorcise demons along with his emotions.

Had *he* painted it?

She visualized that primal male face, tried to picture him wearing a beret, daubing paint upon this canvas. . . . Her mind balked. No, a man who looked as he did doubtless sported with guns, or horses, or women. He had the soul of a conqueror, not an artist.

Rubbing at her tingling nape, Lil forced herself to turn away. She looked at the armoire. She should search it, set her mind at ease once and for all that her manager had none of the strange tastes or motivations she suspected. But she couldn't. She already felt interloper enough.

Blowing out the lamps she'd lit, she walked toward the door. But something drew her gaze upward. A small circular stair led to another level of the tower, and she knew that must be the bedroom. She blew out the last lantern, but even when the lamp she held was all the light remaining and the spiral stairs were but an impression upon her unconscious, she still found herself walking toward them.

She had to see where he slept. Only then could she get these visions out of her head. She had set one foot upon the first rung when the voice came, rough and low, right over her shoulder.

"If you wanted a tour, all you had to do was ask. And by all means, I agree with your priorities—bedroom first."

Gasping with fright at the sound of that deep, melodious voice, Lil whirled. Her slipper caught, and she would have fallen if Ian hadn't reached out and grabbed her. For an instant, every nerve in her body came alive to the touch of his hard warmth pressed so scandalously close. Through the thin layers of her lawn nightgown and fine cashmere robe, she could feel every expansion and contraction of that powerful rib cage.

His breathing had quickened, too. Despite the hard, even stare of those impenetrable amber eyes, he was affected by her as well.

Lil stumbled back and fell to her rump upon the third step. The lantern slipped in her nerveless hand, and she would have dropped it if he hadn't taken it and set it on an adjacent table.

The light from below threw his strong face into sharp relief as he drawled, "Would you care to bounce on my bed?"

Cursing her fair skin, hoping he couldn't see her blush in the half-light, Lil retorted, "You mean my bed?"

"Oh, you may own the mortar and stone, mistress, but I own the furnishings." His gaze raked over her, lighting upon her bosom like a touch. He might as well have said it: *With time, I will own you, too.*

Hoping her throbbing pulse wasn't visible beneath her thin robe, Lil stood and waved him back so she could exit the narrow spiral stair that had her imprisoned. He

352

stood so close that his long legs almost brushed her feet, and . . .

. . . he didn't move. "I am not a dog to obey hand signals. I suggest you put your tongue to good use, or I will give it a better one." And for the first time, a smile stretched that dark face. His white teeth gleamed and he actually leaned closer, running his own tongue against the edge of his teeth in a way that made her mouth tingle.

Strange, how his canines were slightly more prominent than his incisors. . . .

And then she was dumbfounded at his insolence, torn equally between outrage and temptation. She turned away in the only direction open to her—up. If, deep inside, she wasn't quite sure whether she wished to escape him or herself, well, of that, no one had to know. Least of all Ian Griffith.

Her former manager. She'd give him his walking papers first thing in the morning.

When she was halfway up the stairs, she stopped and scowled down at him, feeling secure in the distance between them. "I will examine your room for myself. And if I find nothing untoward, I may reconsider my decision to discharge you." She expected him to explode in wrath, or maybe even show a bit of remorse.

His smile only deepened as he nodded that arrogant dark head. "Be my guest. I guarantee you'll be surprised at what you find. But we might as well have truth between us, even from the beginning."

Lil almost ran up the rest of the stairs, holding her skirts high enough so that she didn't trip, but still careful to leave her ankles covered.

The room that came to life in the flare of the gas lamps she lit was unlike any she'd ever seen. Round, simple, whitewashed stone. Again, spare, but the velvet bed hangings on the vast four-poster were burgundy, tied back with gold ropes. At the foot of the bed was a bench, and upon the bench was a man's silk dressing gown. It was fiery red, and it had something embroidered on the back, something she couldn't quite make out. Her hands itched with the need to pick it up, but instinctively she knew not to.

Touching his things would lead to touching his person.

So she turned away, and it was then she noticed the easel and canvas set up beneath the enormous curving window. Next to it was a table and a sketchpad. Feeling as if she was finally finding some clue to his secretive personality, she walked toward the table. She was reaching out to pick up the pad when that voice spoke again, right over her shoulder this time.

"Go ahead. Discharge me if you wish."

She started and whirled. How did he walk so silently?

No smile upon that enigmatic face now as he said softly, "But you will still not be rid of me. Any more than I will be rid of you. The Haskell women and the Griffith men have been linked for centuries, Delilah. Your blood is as hot with the bond between us as my own."

Still holding her gaze, he reached around her for the sketchbook. He flipped it open and showed her the top picture, the next, and the next.

Heat started at the top of her head and ran like magma to her toes. The images got progressively more sensual.

And progressively more shocking.

They were all of her. Face only, then bust, then from the waist up. Dressed lightly at first, then only in chemise and stockings. Finally . . . as he flipped through the sketchbook, he ended on a full-length nude.

Of herself. Her arms lifted wantonly toward her lover, her lips ripe with a sensual smile as she lay upon the very bed in this room. Wanting him.

For she knew now, beyond doubt, that he had

sketched them. And he had painted the landscape over the mantel. This driven, powerful man was an equally driven, powerful artist, able to appease his own hunger with these wanton images. How had he been able to draw her so accurately? Even the shape of her breasts, the size of her nipples, the triangle between her legs.

All the conflicting feelings troubling her for the past two weeks seemed to coalesce in her mind. Her senses narrowed to a minute speck, and then exploded outward in one glorious emotion.

Fury. Before she put thought to action, her hand lashed out and slapped that arrogant face hard enough to jerk his head to the side.

"You bounder! You have no right to even think of me so, much less . . ." She broke off with a gasp as he caught the back of her skull in both his powerful hands and tipped her head back. His touch swept through her like a tidal wave.

For a moment she was pristine, like a beach never stepped upon by human foot. And then he shoved her against the wall, pressing into her with his masculine frame that so strangely seemed to fit her own.

And she was marked.

Marked forever after, no matter what came of this night when it seemed only the two of them were awake in all the world. She felt the imprint of him, indelibly stamped through the shivering sands of pride and propriety straight to the bedrock of her soul.

When he kissed her, she tipped her head back to meet him.

And finally, she saw emotion in those strange amber eyes. . . .

Chapter Two

Lil had been kissed before, many times. Awkward kisses, earnest kisses, even a few experienced kisses. But this dark invader of her home, her mind, and ultimately, she knew, of her body created his own lexicon. One her body interpreted even as her mind resisted.

Those lips were as warm and unyielding as the rest of him. But the way they moved—his exploration was unhurried, as if he'd always known her.

Kiss? How banal.

Invasion. Intimacy. Consummation. He'd barely touched her, yet already he'd filled her with his wild strength as surely as if he held her spread-eagled to the bed.

And Lil, stubborn as only one of Scots ancestry can be, tilted her head back to welcome the thrust of his tongue. He dipped, and danced, and tasted the rim of her teeth, lips suckling gently all the while. And she didn't just allow him intimacies she'd allowed no other.

She welcomed them.

She curled her tongue shyly around his, wondering why the moist heat didn't disgust her as it had with the others. When she answered the sexual foreplay so explicitly, the tenor of his embrace changed. During that first kiss, his hands had touched only the back of her skull, cradling it not with tenderness but with surety. As if he knew she knew he had strength enough to crush it—but no need.

He was already in her head.

But when she kissed him back, inexperience made eloquent by passion as great as his own, a shudder ran through that strong frame.

And Lil rejoiced. With a fierceness that almost frightened her. He was not so indomitable after all. He, too, had weaknesses. And he could not exploit hers without exposing his own.

The primitive symmetry was so seductive that Lil pulled her hands free from the heated trap between their bodies. He broke the kiss, looking down at her curiously. He was so much taller that her hands had to trail up from his waist, past his strong chest, over his sturdy collarbone before she could finally clasp the back of his neck.

His hands went slack upon her head and his eyes went strangely unfocused. As if he needed the touch of her hands upon his flesh like he needed breath and water. And when she tugged his head down, tilting it to the side so *she* could kiss *him*, a stronger shudder wracked him.

The next thing she knew, her robe and nightgown were open and his rough palm was learning the generous heft of her breast. Lil gasped into his consuming lips, but then his tongue thrust again, and the dark urges went wild within her. She thrust her breast into his hand. He sensed her need and circled her nipple gently with

357

his thumb. She was already hard, and the grazing of that callused thumb made her long for the feel of his mouth there.

He took her in, suckling her nipple with nothing of the infant about him. He was all primitive male, tasting her, knowing her, completely.

Almost. . . . as if he took his birthright from the tip of her most vulnerable femininity.

Reject him? Slap him? The thought never crossed what little mind she had left. She could only slump, weak over the strong support of his arm at her back, and feel her heart fly to meet the gentle suction.

And then something curious happened. He rested his cheek against her left breast, eyes closed, long dark lashes like shadows upon his face. As if he didn't just listen to her heartbeat.

He felt it.

He hungered for it.

He wanted to hold it in his hands and feel its vibrant life.

His mouth opened. His tongue circled the rim of his teeth. Lil stared down at him, her own eyes dark with a desperate passion she could not control. For an instant, it seemed his canines grew to fangs. Still she could not move. She could only wait, helpless in his grip.

But if she was a victim, so was he.

A moan escaped him, high-pitched, eerie, the sound of a wolf in pain. But when he turned his head to nuzzle between her clothes, the wool and silk dropped to her waist. Both her breasts were bare to him, high, round, firm, and white. Capped by thrusting, blushing nipples pouting for his kiss.

They were so much the essence of woman vulnerable to him that he drew a deep, shuddering breath. The wildness that had almost overtaken him was buried under the needs of a man for a woman. His expression grew tender. Gently kneading her flesh, he buried his

358

face in her, drawing life, and strength and purity. And Lil was fed, too, from the bounty of the exchange.

Unbearable hunger in one breath, satiated in the next. The need only became more acute when she lost the feel of his mouth upon her flesh as he switched from one breast to the other.

The burning ache didn't stop at her breast. It went from her torso, down her legs, to her very toes. And it was so shocking, so atavistically beyond her control, that sanity returned for a split second as that mesmerizing mouth drew away.

For one sobering instant, Delilah, miner's daughter, doughty Scots heiress, looked down upon that wild black head so intimately placed at her bosom.

With a cry of despair, she caught his thick hair in her hands and pulled his head away, squirming free. Pulling her clothes over her shamed flesh, she ran.

Ran as she should have the minute he appeared.

Down the spiral stairs, through the tower, all the long way from one wing to the next. Faster, faster—but far too slowly. No matter how fleet her feet, her heart almost burst with the knowledge her mind refused to heed.

Too late.

He had possessed her this night, in every way a man could. The intimate thrust of his manhood into her would be no more invasive or consuming than the feelings rioting through her from the wild tangle of blond hair to the tips of her tingling toes.

The second she reached her room, Lil threw every bolt and lock on the door. A long cheval mirror mocked her, but she turned away, stripped off her clothing, and threw the garments in the fire. Never again could she look at them.

For thirty minutes she scrubbed her torso, using strong lye soap, not the gentle French perfumed bar, until her skin was red and almost raw. If a hair shirt had been at hand, she would have slept in it.

Finally, the sky pink with dawn's first blush, she pulled on her primmest night rail and climbed into her bed. Even then, she tossed and turned, chaotic images whirling through her confused mind.

Ian painting upon the moors.

Ian, his lips curled back in a snarl as he listened to her beating heart.

Ian holding her with a tenderness no man had ever shown her, not even her own father.

And it was that last image that brought tears to her eyes and made the burning ache he'd left in his wake all the more difficult to quell. He gave tenderness so awkwardly, so shyly.

Like a man who'd known little of it in his own life.

Lil had been attracted to men before—heavens, she'd even slept with one she'd thought herself in love with. But nothing—no sane counsel her father had ever given her, none of the manners that snooty Eastern finishing school had taught her, not even Jeremy's salty oaths or Safira's mysterious philosophies—could quiet the torment in her mind and body.

Ian Griffith frightened her.

He thrilled her.

He mystified her.

And as certainly as she breathed, the next time he crooked a finger at her, she'd come running.

With a frustrated groan, she pulled the feather pillow over her foolish head.

But still he lurked there, even at the edge of sleep.

And doom. . . .

Cougar's Woman
Ronda Thompson

On the journey to meet her fiancé in Santa Fe, Melissa Sheffield is captured by Apaches and given to a man known as Cougar. At first, she is relieved to learn that she's been given to a white man, but with one kiss he proves himself more dangerous than the whole tribe. Terrified of her savage captor, she pledges to escape at any price. But while there might be an escape from the Apaches, is there any escape from her heart? Clay Brodie—known as Cougar to the Apaches—is given the fiery Melissa by his chief. He is then ordered to turn the beauty into an obedient slave—or destroy her. But how can he slay a woman who evokes an emotion deeper than he's ever known? And when the time comes to fight, will it be for his tribe or for his woman?

___4524-9 $4.99 US/$5.99 CAN

Dorchester Publishing Co., Inc.
P.O. Box 6640
Wayne, PA 19087-8640

Please add $1.75 for shipping and handling for the first book and $.50 for each book thereafter. NY, NYC, and PA residents, please add appropriate sales tax. No cash, stamps, or C.O.D.s. All orders shipped within 6 weeks via postal service book rate. Canadian orders require $2.00 extra postage and must be paid in U.S. dollars through a U.S. banking facility.

Name_____
Address_____
City_____ State_____ Zip_____
I have enclosed $_____ in payment for the checked book(s).
Payment <u>must</u> accompany all orders. ❑ Please send a free catalog.
        CHECK OUT OUR WEBSITE! www.dorchesterpub.com

PRICKLY PEAR

RONDA THOMPSON

Daddy's little girl is no angel. Heck, she hasn't earned the nickname Prickly Pear by being a wallflower. Everyone on the Circle C knows that Camile Cordell can rope her way out of Hell itself—and most of the town thinks the willful beauty will end up there sooner or later. Now, Cam knows that her father is looking for a new foreman for their ranch—and the blond firebrand is pretty sure she knows where to find one. Wade Langtry has just arrived in Texas, but he seems darn sure of himself in trying to take a job that is hers. Cam has to admit, though, that he has what it takes to break stallions. In her braver moments, she even imagines what it might feel like to have the roughrider break her to the saddle—or she him. And she fears that in the days to follow, it won't much matter if she looses her father's ranch—she's already lost her heart.

___4624-5 $4.99 US/$5.99 CAN

Dorchester Publishing Co., Inc.
P.O. Box 6640
Wayne, PA 19087-8640

Please add $1.75 for shipping and handling for the first book and $.50 for each book thereafter. NY, NYC, and PA residents, please add appropriate sales tax. No cash, stamps, or C.O.D.s. All orders shipped within 6 weeks via postal service book rate. Canadian orders require $2.00 extra postage and must be paid in U.S. dollars through a U.S. banking facility.

Name_____

Address_____

City_____State_____Zip_____

I have enclosed $_____ in payment for the checked book(s).

Payment <u>must</u> accompany all orders. ❑ Please send a free catalog.

CHECK OUT OUR WEBSITE! www.dorchesterpub.com

In Trouble's Arms Ronda Thompson

Loreen Matland is very clear. If the man who answers her ad for a husband is ugly as a mud fence, she'll keep him. If not, she'll fill his hide full of buckshot. Unfortunately, Jake Winslow is handsome. Lori knows that good-looking men are trouble, and Jake proves no exception. Of course, she hasn't been entirely honest with him, either. She has difficulties enough to make his flight from the law seem like a ride through the prairie. But the Texas Matlands don't give up, even to dangerous men with whiskey-smooth voices. And yet, in Jake's warm strong arms, Lori knows he is just what she needs—for her farm, her family, and her heart.

Lair of the Wolf

Also includes the sixth installment of *Lair of the Wolf*, a serialized romance set in medieval Wales. Be sure to look for future chapters of this exciting story featured in Leisure books and written by the industry's top authors.

____4716-0 $5.99 US/$6.99 CAN

SAINT'S Temptation

DEBRA DIER

Seven years after breaking off her engagement to Clayton
Trevelyan, Marisa Grantham overhears two men plotting to
murder her still-beloved Earl of Huntingdon. No longer the
naive young woman who had allowed her one and only love
to walk away, Marisa will do anything to keep from losing
him a second time.

___4459-5 $5.99 US/$6.99 CAN

Dorchester Publishing Co., Inc.
P.O. Box 6640
Wayne, PA 19087-8640

Please add $1.75 for shipping and handling for the first book and
$.50 for each book thereafter. NY, NYC, and PA residents,
please add appropriate sales tax. No cash, stamps, or C.O.D.s. All
orders shipped within 6 weeks via postal service book rate.
Canadian orders require $2.00 extra postage and must be paid in
U.S. dollars through a U.S. banking facility.

Name_____
Address_____
City_____ State_____ Zip_____
I have enclosed $_____ in payment for the checked book(s).
Payment <u>must</u> accompany all orders. ☐ Please send a free catalog.

DEBRA DIER
DEVIL'S HONOR

Known as the Devil of Dartmoor—the most dangerous man in London—Justin Trevelyan prefers the company of widows and prostitutes to the charms of innocents. The last thing he needs is an impertinent maiden and her two young sisters under his wardship. Yet from the moment he lays eyes on Isabel, he is captivated by her sweet beauty and somehow needs to protect her as well as possess her. But before he can gain an angel's trust, he has to prove his devil's honor.

___4362-9 $5.99 US/$6.99 CAN

Dorchester Publishing Co., Inc.
P.O. Box 6640
Wayne, PA 19087-8640

THE IMPOSTOR
ELAINE FOX

Melisande St. Clair knows who she is and what she wants, and when Flynn Patrick steps out of the water and into her life, she knows that his is the face of which she's dreamt. But when she is forced to travel with the handsome stranger, he claims he is from another time and makes suggestions that are hardly proper for a nineteenth-century lady. Although she believes no one could mistake him for an English gentleman, the Duke of Merestun swears that Flynn is his long-lost son. Suddenly, Flynn seems a prince, and all Melisande's desires lie within reach. But what is the truth? All Melisande knows is that she senses no artifice in his touch—and as she fights to remain aloof to the passion that burns in his fiery kiss, she wonders which of them is truly . . . the impostor.

___4523-0 $5.50 US/$6.50 CAN

Masquerade

Katherine Deauxpille, Elaine Fox, Linda Jones, & Sharon Pisacreta

In the whirling decadence of Carnival, all forms of desire are unveiled. Amidst the crush of those attending the balls, filling the waterways, and traveling in the gondolas of post-Napoleonic Venice, nothing is unavailable—should one know where to look. Amongst the throngs are artists and seducers, nobles and thieves, and not all of them are what they appear. But in that frantic congress of people lurks something more than animal passion, something more than a paradise of the flesh. Love, should one seek it out, can be found within this shadowy communion of people—and as four beauties learn, all one need do is unmask it.

___4577-X $5.99 US/$6.99 CAN